WHAT THE HELL DID I JUST READ

A NOVEL OF COSMIC HORROR

DAVID WONG

TITAN BOOKS

What the Hell Did I Just Read
Print edition ISBN: 9781785651656
E-book edition ISBN: 9781785651663

Published by Titan Books
A division of Titan Publishing Group Ltd
144 Southwark Street, London SE1 0UP

First Titan edition: October 2017
10 9 8 7 6 5 4 3 2 1

This edition published by arrangement with St. Martin's Press.

Design by Rob Grom and Titan Books.

A CIP catalogue record for this title is available from the British Library.

Printed and bound in Great Britain by CPI Group Ltd.

What did you think of this book?
We love to hear from our readers. Please email us at:
readerfeedback@titanemail.com, or write to us at the above address.

To receive advance information, news, competitions, and exclusive
offers online, please sign up for the Titan newsletter on our website:
www.titanbooks.com

For all of the old gang back home:
Big Joe, Fat Steve, Hoss, Chunk, Moose, and Tank.
May they all rest in peace.

WHAT THE
HELL DID I
JUST READ

"You want to hear a story? Well, buckle the fuck up."

PROLOGUE

It rained like we were a splatter of bird shit God was trying to hose off his deck. The three of us ripped through the downpour in a beige 1996 Saturn Coupe, me at the wheel.

I squinted drunkenly into the rearview mirror and tried in vain to find the headlights of the black truck that was chasing us, but I actually wasn't sure if its drivers needed headlights to see or if they even had eyes. I also wasn't sure it was a truck, or if it was black, or if we were being pursued at all. It was definitely raining, though.

My friend, John, was in the passenger seat and the only reason he wasn't driving was because, in addition to also being drunk, he was wounded—both of his hands were wrapped in the T-shirt he'd torn off to use as gauze. His wounds had not been inflicted by our pursuers, at least not directly—he had burned himself grabbing a fondue pot full of melted chocolate that we had been dipping fried chicken strips into (try it sometime, seriously). My girlfriend, Amy, was in the back seat. She

11

wasn't driving because she didn't know how, but she apparently did have enough expertise to judge *my* performance, screaming warnings at me to keep my eyes on the road and to watch out for that curve and *oh god we're all gonna die.*

In Amy's right hand—her only hand—was a little gray metal container about the size of a shot glass. That container was what the occupants of the truck were after, and I had known this the moment they had burst into John's living room ten minutes ago.

We had just been minding our own business, eating our chocolate chicken and making our way through a theme movie night (we'd picked out four films in which the ending is probably the main character's dying hallucination: *Taxi Driver, Minority Report, The Shawshank Redemption,* and *Mrs. Doubtfire*). In through the front door came this whirlwind of a half-dozen men(?) in black cloaks, all wearing what looked like rubber Halloween masks—drooping, expressionless faces with lifeless, skewed eyeballs. The lead cloak was wearing the mask of a puffy-cheeked infant and brandished a weapon that looked like a huge, electrified Toblerone bar—a series of black pyramids in a row, fed by cables that ran inside his robe. John's little Yorkshire terrier was yapping its head off, probably asking the intruders to take him away to a better home.

The "man" with the Toblerone gun had screamed, "WHERE IS IT?" in a voice like a spider that had learned to imitate human speech via some online courses it had taken. We hadn't had to ask what "it" was. John's house is my favorite place in the world, but there's nothing else in there you couldn't replace with a trip to Target or a garage sale held at a meth dealer's house. No, they had come for that little brushed steel vial Amy now held in her hand.

They weren't getting it.

So, John had grabbed the fondue pot and slung the molten contents at the thing with the spidery voice, inflicting hot brown splash damage on everyone in the room. Amy grabbed the vial from its hiding place (sitting in plain view on John's kitchen counter, next to a novelty bong shaped like a triathlon trophy) and we sprinted out the back door into a raging thunderstorm. We piled into my car, I floored it, and that's where we are now.

The rain was blasting directly into the windshield, the drops whipping toward me like hyperdrive stars. Visibility was slightly worse than what you get inside a car wash after they spray on that multicolored foam. Amy was yelling turn-by-turn directions at me and I was obeying, even though none of us had discussed where we were going. She ordered me to stop just as we arrived at a rusty bridge suspended over a roiling, swollen river. She threw open the rear door, sprinted out into the storm, and chucked the vial downstream as hard as she could. The angry, rumbling current swallowed it without so much as a *plop*.

John and I ran up to the rail and exchanged frantic "Did that really just happen?" glances. None of us spoke. A decision had been made and could not be taken back.

Amy had been right, of course, to do what she did. Goal Number 1 was to keep the vial out of the hands of the cloaked *things* that were chasing us and Goal Number 2 was to make sure they knew we no longer had it, otherwise they'd just strap us to chairs and try to torture its location out of us using some unspeakable method involving black magic and power tools.

John said, "When they get here, let me do all the talking."

I said, "Amy, when they get here, I want *you* to do all of the talking. I'll be busy restraining John."

Our pursuers, however, never arrived. I don't know how long we waited, leaning on the railing, watching the frothing current twisting and breaking below. Cold rain howled into our ears. John absently licked chocolate off his fingers. Amy shivered, her red hair matted against her skull so that it looked like she was bleeding profusely from the scalp. Maybe they knew we had chucked the vial, maybe they had never followed us at all. You're probably wondering who "they" are and who they work for and those are both great questions. We climbed back into the car.

John tied his wet hair into a ponytail, lit a cigarette, and said, "I fucking knew something like this was about to happen."

Amy tried in vain to dry her glasses with her wet shirt and said, "Well, thanks for letting us know."

I said, "If they dredge the river, they can find it."

"It floats," replied Amy. "Did you see that current? River flows into the Ohio, that flows into the Mississippi, that drains into the Gulf of Mexico. They'll never find it, unless . . ."

She trailed off but we all knew what she had left unsaid: they would never find the vial, unless the contents wanted to be found.

No ambush was waiting for us back at John's place.

The strange men-like shapes in their dark robes and Halloween masks were nowhere to be found, on that or any of the following nights. We had spent the rest of the evening dealing with the dog, as we had come back and found it lapping up the chocolate on the carpet. It turns out chocolate is toxic to dogs; it started puking everywhere and we had to rush it to the vet.

Or, that's how I remember it, anyway.

1. A CHILD GOT KIDNAPPED BY A DEMON OR SOMETHING

Me

I woke up on the floor of my junk room, a tiny second bedroom in my apartment that's piled high with the weird bullshit I collect. Though I guess that wording would imply that I seek this stuff out; I actually meant "collect" in the way that dead bugs "collect" on your windshield. The first thing I saw when I opened my eyes was four ventriloquist dummies, where they had been propped up around my face so that I'd find them staring down at me when I woke. I thought the things were creepy as hell, and Amy knew that, which is why she had put them there. She is a monster.

I sat up on my elbows, feeling like a rat had chewed its way into one of my eye sockets and then clawed its way out the other. I squinted and saw that stuck to one of the dummies was a Post-it Note that read:

You were sleepwalking again!

I went back to work
Muffin on the table
Love you
—Amy

At the bottom she had drawn a picture of a muffin, little scribbled dots to indicate blueberries. The dots were actually blue—she had gone and found a different pen to do that part.

It was still dark out, I could sense it even though the one window in the room was mostly obscured by a large painting that was leaning against it. It was a painting of a clown that the previous owner had insisted was cursed (that is, the painting was cursed, not the clown, unless he was, which is entirely possible). "Cursed" turned out to be a ridiculous exaggeration, though. What was happening was the painted clown's mouth was slowly changing shape with time, as if it was silently mouthing words. I don't doubt that if you set the painting in front of a time-lapse camera for a few months and hired a lip reader to examine the results, it would turn out the clown was saying something very creepy or even profound. Maybe it's a prophecy. And, if you want to pay to do all that shit, be my guest. But as far as I'm concerned, if the object isn't killing anybody, it isn't "cursed." I've had it in the junk room for four months and it hasn't inconvenienced me once.

My cell phone was ringing from somewhere nearby, which I assumed was what had woken me. I knew that at this hour, it wasn't somebody calling to tell me they'd accepted my job application, so it was either:

A) a drunken misdial from somebody, in which case I would dedicate my life to finding that person and murdering them;

B) an emergency;

C) an "emergency," and those right there are sarcasm quotes.

If it was Amy, then it was a good chance it was "B"— an actual emergency. If it was John, well, it could be any of the three.

A psychic once told John that his last words would be, "Hold my beer." When he was eleven years old, he had disappeared for two weeks, creating a minor media frenzy in the area. When he turned up again at home, unharmed, he told reporters and police that he had gotten lost in the woods and survived by killing and eating a Sasquatch. His sophomore year of high school, John was suspended multiple times because for every single creative writing assignment, he had turned in a different version of a story about a teenager (named "Jon") who was sneaking into the cafeteria and jerking off in the food. His senior year, he started a garage band that was quickly banned from every club, bar, park, and concert hall in the region due to his insistence on playing a song called, "This Venue Is a Front for Human Trafficking, Someone Call the FBI, this Is Not Just a Joke Song Title." When John's first girlfriend asked him what his ideal threesome would be, he had answered, "Me, Hitler, and Prince. I just watch."

In the fifteen years I've known him, I'd say 70 percent of the overnight calls I've received from John were drunken misdials, 5 percent were genuine emergencies (like the time he called to let me know he was about to be compacted inside a garbage truck), and 25 percent were "emergencies" and really I can't make those sarcasm quotes there large enough. Just in the past twelve months, the situations that John felt warranted a call in the wee hours of the morning included:

A) a dream/vision he had of me dying violently in Bangkok, with a warning to stay far way (note: we live in the American Midwest and I couldn't afford a plane ticket to Bangkok even if I sold myself into the Thai sex trade upon arrival);

B) urgently notifying me of a "cryptid" he had snapped a photo of in his back yard, which turned out to be a passed-out drunk in the back half of a horse costume;

C) the results of a blindfolded experiment he and his friends had performed that confirmed that all Froot Loops are the same flavor, just different colors ("we're doing Skittles next, get your ass over here");

D) his million-dollar idea for a "Punch Zoo," which is like a petting zoo where you get to punch the animals.

The last such call I had gotten from him was two weeks ago. It was just a few seconds of ambient party noise, before I heard John's voice say, "What's that sound? Everybody quiet, I—Ha! Hey Munch, check it out! I farted so hard it dialed my phone!"

But, of course, I couldn't just ignore his calls because

there was always the chance it was something apocalyptic. That was the hell of knowing John.

The phone sounded close, probably in the room with me. I knocked the dummies aside and pawed around the junk in my immediate vicinity. Behind the dummies was a piñata that the previous owner claimed was indestructible. So far, we'd tried shooting it with a shotgun and running it over with John's Jeep and, sure enough, the candy was still safely rattling around inside. Again, that's pretty weird, but what possible use is that to anybody? It's just a waste of perfectly good candy. If you're saying we should give it to the government so they can mimic its witchcraft or whatever to make better body armor for the military, I'm thinking you trust the government way more than I do. If it's a bona fide Object Cursed with Black Magic, handing it over to the feds would be like giving a toddler a chainsaw to cut his birthday cake with. "Oh," you're probably saying, "so it's better off in your apartment?" I don't know, dude. Do you want it? Send me your address. You pay for shipping.

I finally found the phone sitting atop a bookcase, next to a VHS box set of a series of 90s action movies starring Bruce Willis (*The Ticking Man, The Ticking Man 2, The Ticking Man: The Final Chapter, Ticking Man Resurrection*) that as far as I could tell, did not exist in this universe. We never watched them, nobody has a VCR, and they looked kind of shitty.

The phone's display said it was John calling.

I groaned and stumbled out into the living room to find that no one had broken in and renovated the place while I was out. There are reality shows where they do that, right? I heard the *plink-plink-plink* of the roof leaking in the bathroom, which the landlords wouldn't fix because my apartment is on the floor above theirs and the leak wasn't making it down to their level because, by pure coincidence, the drip was positioned to fall directly into my toilet. That was good for them, because it limited the damage the leak could do to my floor and their ceiling, but bad for us because it meant Amy had to hold a bowl in her lap when she peed (whereas I just let it drip on me).

The phone rang again. I went to the kitchenette and poured a mug of cold coffee from a pot that had been brewed yesterday, or maybe last month. It was five in the morning, according to the grease-clouded clock on the microwave. I found the muffin—blueberry, just as it had been depicted in Amy's illustration—sitting on the folding card table we eat dinner off of. It was next to a pile of random junk that had been mailed to me in the last few weeks but had not yet been filed away (and here "filed" means angrily flung into the junk room while muttering fuck words). Most of the stuff in there arrives like this, just strangers sending it through the mail. Sometimes you can get a sad glimpse into their lives via the packing material—one artifact came packed in wadded-up pages from that Jehovah's Witness magazine, *The Watchtower,* another was ensconced in shredded hospital bills, another in scraps of cardboard torn from three dozen boxes of the exact same Lean Cuisine frozen dinner.

Why do they send me this stuff? Well, you know how occasionally you get stuck with something purely because you don't know how to throw it away? Either because it seems too sacred to get smooshed in with moldy coffee grounds (an old Bible, an American flag, a birthday card from your grandma) or because it seems vaguely dangerous (old shotgun shells, a broken dagger)? All of the shit I've collected is kind of a combination of the two—sacred, lethal, or both. So, they dig up my address and stick it in the mail. "David Wong will know what to do with it!" No, I absolutely will not. It just piles up and the stuff that doesn't seem too dangerous gets sold on eBay (there's a whole "Metaphysical" category on the site now, it's great).

Among this week's junk had been a water-damaged "haunted" paperback copy of *Bad as I Wanna Be,* the autobiography of Chicago Bulls power forward Dennis Rodman. "Haunted" because this copy, and only this copy, had multiple chapters describing how Rodman conspired with several teammates to ritualistically murder over fifty prostitutes in the years they traveled with the team. It doesn't appear the book was doctored in any way, the pages have the same typeset as the rest, and they're exactly as aged. I did some Googling, could find no other reference to the existence of this edition of the book, or to the killings. As usual, I have no idea what it means.

Next to the book was a small piano-black twelve-sided box, each side etched with a different rune in emerald green. I waved my hand over the box and exclaimed, "*ODO DAXIL!*" The box unfolded and I felt radiant heat waft across my face. Inside was a glowing orange sphere the size of a marble. We got this one a couple of weeks ago. At first it didn't seem to do much other than emit quite a bit of heat but then, while John was over for

Pancake and Video Game Night, he thought he heard a tortured wailing from within the sphere. I initially dismissed the idea, as he was pretty drunk and I think he always hears tortured wailing when he drinks. Still, the next day we took it to the middle school where a friend and former bandmate of John's named Mitch Lombard (nickname, "Munch") had gotten a job as a substitute science teacher despite his neck tattoos. He studied the glowing sphere under one of their microscopes for a silent moment, then looked up from the viewfinder to whisper, "His suffering is unimaginable, but the heat of his rage could incinerate the universe a million times over. All is lost. All is lost." Munch had then passed out, blood running freely from his nose. That was the last time we'd discussed it.

I grabbed a pair of tongs from a kitchen drawer, picked up the glowing sphere, and dropped it into my mug of cold coffee as the phone rang for what I knew would be the last time before it would get dumped to voice mail.

I cleaved off a ragged chunk of muffin with my fingers and answered, "Fuck you and all of the ancestors who led up to you."

"Dave? We got a missing little girl. You got a pen?"

"If it's a missing child, call the cops."

"The cops called *me*."

I closed my eyes and let out a breath that smelled like I'd eaten an entire wet dog and washed it down with sweat wrung from a hobo's undershirt. Let me give you a tip: if you're ever the victim of a terrible crime—like, say, your kid goes missing—and you see the cops consulting with a couple of white trash–looking dipshits in their late twenties, it's time to worry. It's not because John and I are incompetent at what we do—and I assure you, we are—but because you need to start asking yourself a very hard question. Not "Will I get my child back?" but "Do I *want* to get my child back?"

I dipped my finger into the coffee, which already felt near boiling. I fished out the burning orb and placed it back into its container, which automatically closed around it. I took a sip, winced, and decided that the first person to ever drink coffee was probably trying to commit suicide.

I asked, "What makes it a, you know, a Dave and John case?"

"It's another locked room situation, it looks like. There's more, I'll explain when you get here. But it looks pretty John and Dave to me. Do you have a pen? I have the address here."

"Just give it to me."

"One-oh-six Arlington Street. Next to the vape store?"

"You thought I needed pen and paper to remember that?"

"And hurry. I've heard you've only got forty-eight hours before the trail goes cold."

"You heard that in a movie. Last week. We watched it together."

He had hung up.

I sighed and ate another hunk of muffin. I glanced out the window, the bottom half glowing pink from the neon sign of the business downstairs. They left that sign on day and night; the constant hum made me want to blow my brains out.

Oh, well. It's not like I have anything else to do.
Still, I was going to finish my muffin first.

Let me tell you what's bullshit about every supernatural horror movie. Whenever the monster or angry ghost lady turns up, everyone is skeptical for at least the first third of the running time. It's usually between forty and fifty minutes in that the protagonists begrudgingly admit that the ominous Latin chants emanating from the walls aren't a plumbing issue. In real life, the very second Mom sees something red oozing from the ceiling, she thinks "blood" not "water from a rusty old pipe." I *wish* people were as skeptical as they are in the movies.

This town, the name of which will remain undisclosed for privacy reasons, has been called the Bermuda Triangle of the Midwest. Or at least, I think I heard somebody call it that. I actually wish that was true, too, because there's nothing to the Bermuda Triangle—just a bunch of routine maritime disasters that grew in the telling. A cargo ship never arrives at port and the headlines coyly say it "disappeared." It didn't "disappear," guys—it sank. It's a boat, in the ocean. Shit happens. What goes on in [undisclosed] is . . . different.

My point is, it's hard to sort out the real stuff from the superstition. So, because I'm sick of getting your e-mails asking for advice, let me just quickly run through it:

1. If Your Home Has a Poltergeist

We got a ton of these calls after that movie *Paranormal Activity* came out, panicked people saying they had rocking chairs rocking by themselves, untouched drinking glasses scooting off a table, clocks running backward, etc. If you're in this situation, you can combat it using a technique known as "Getting the Fuck Over It." You're telling me you've got angry spirits of old murder victims or something floating around and they're causing less of a disruption to your life than an unruly house cat? Why not worry about your high blood pressure, or take a moment to see if your smoke detector batteries are up to date? Those things are way more likely to kill you than whatever is knocking over salt shakers in your kitchen at night.

2. If You Have Seen a Ghost

If you've seen, say, a translucent old woman in a long flowing gown drifting down your hall at night, that's almost definitely a hallucination or just a regular ol' dream. Think about it: why would a ghost be translucent? Smoke and fog look like they do because they're made of tiny particles suspended in the air. Are you suggesting the soul is made of tiny particles?

In reality, your whole idea of what a ghost looks like comes from Victorian era photos, when long-exposure cameras required the subject to sit still for several minutes due to the primitive technology. If the subject left halfway through, you'd get that ghostly image instead. Fun fact: this is also the reason nobody is smiling in those old pictures—try holding a smile for seven straight minutes. If you've *actually* seen a ghost—and I assure you that you probably have, within the last month—it would have just looked like any real, solid person. It's likely nobody saw that person but you and no, you can't photograph them. You're not seeing them with your eyes.

3. If an Evil Spirit or Demon Has Confronted You

If said entity appeared before you *and* started speaking, the good news is you're not losing your mind. Contrary to what TV and movies have told you, it's nearly impossible to have a hallucination that you can both see and hear—the mentally ill either just hear voices, or just see things, due to how the brain is wired. If you can both hear and see it, you're either just having a dream, or you have an actual demon in your home.

If it's the latter, you shouldn't bother listening too closely to what it has to say. It may sound really important—prophecies of future doom, that sort of thing—but I assure you, it's just toying with you. If you ignore it, it'll eventually get bored. The odds are it's not strong enough to possess you, kill you, or do serious damage to your property. If it tries, feel free to pray or put up lots of crosses in its field of vision; I've seen that work before. You don't have to go with Christian symbolism, but not all religions work (for reference, at the end of this book I have included an index of which religions are true and which are false—there are some real surprises). Also, try playing lots of 1980s era power ballads, they hate that. I think because it's the closest earthly approximation of the music they play in Heaven. I don't know, we're just guessing here. Conversely . . .

4. If an Angel Appears and Speaks to You

Here, the risks are different—if a messenger from the Almighty actually bothers to contact you, it's probably not the best idea to just ignore it. So, obviously, the first step is to make sure it's an actual entity and not a dream you're having, which is surprisingly simple: just ask the angel a question that you yourself don't know the answer to but that you can verify later (like, "What's the square root of 123,456,789?" or "What will be the final score of every football game this Sunday?"). If their information is good, well, then you know you weren't dreaming and whatever prophecies or advice they gave you could indeed be valid. Of course they, too, could be imposters, so if they ask you to do something morally questionable—like stab your own child or something—you'll need to use your own judgment. Let's face it: if there is a god and he's the type to think it's unreasonable to refuse such a request, we're all screwed anyway.

5. If You Have Been Abducted by an Alien

Cases like this are almost always simple sleep paralysis—a sort of wakeful dreaming during which it is common to see or sense strange visitors. Another fun fact: the typical "gray" aliens, with their bulbous heads and big almond-shaped eyes, didn't show up in abduction stories until 1964—about two weeks after similar aliens appeared in an episode of the sci-fi horror series *The Outer Limits*. The phenomenon of abductees claiming to have been probed anally didn't start until 1969, the year colonoscopies became common. What I'm saying is, the creatures that visit you in the night are either manifestations of your own anxiety or are making your anxieties manifest just to screw with you. Either way, the call is always coming from inside the house.

6. If You Have Seen a Monster

I've never understood the panic over monsters. I mean, which would bother you more, finding out your grandfather had died in a painful industrial accident, or that his head had been neatly snatched off his body by some giant, leathery winged horror? Dead is dead and in the latter case, he didn't feel a thing. So why should the monster be the one that gives you nightmares, aside from the miniscule chance that one day your grandad's chewed-up eyeballs might get shit onto your windshield on your way to work? Also, what if you kill your "monster" and it turns out it's like a werewolf situation, where the thing transforms back into a human as it dies? Your ass is going to jail.

If it's not threatening you, just let it be.

7. If You Have Seen a Man-Shaped Figure Made of Inky Blackness with a Pair of Eyes that Glow like the Embers of Two Smoldering Cigars

Congratulations! You're one of the few humans to have ever seen the universe as it truly is.

If it happens again, *run*.

2. A SCREAMING CLOWN DICK

I stepped out into the rain that had been hammering us relentlessly since Columbus Day. After a month of it, everything that wasn't pavement was a squishy muck that with every step squirted through the hole in my right shoe and soaked my sock. Drainage ditches were advancing menacingly across yards and parking lots, day by day. Over in what was left of the good part of town, they were putting down sandbags. No army of volunteers was coming to sandbag the dildo store.

Yeah, my apartment is above a sex toy shop, called the Venus Flytrap. Our neighbor on one side is the skanky Coral Rock Motel (which is convenient for the clientele there) and next to it is one of those tiny used car lots where the stock is surrounded by a high fence with barbed wire, bearing signs offering weekly payments and no credit checks (they don't mention the cars come with remote gadgets that can disable the engine if you miss a payment). On the other side of us is a tiny burned-out shop with a bashed-in front window exposing its charcoal guts to the world. I remember when that used to be a candy store, back when I was a kid. It always had this warm caramel smell, the scent of melted butter and sugar and holidays. No idea what happened to the kindly old couple who ran the place, all I know is that now raccoons nest in the blackened old display case and raindrops plink off the broken beer bottles that drunks have flipped through the window as they stumbled past.

I've always wondered what it would be like to live in a town that was actually growing, where vacant lots give birth to trendy restaurants and old warehouses are torn down to make room for brand new housing developments. A city like Seattle or Austin, where you can actually feel like human civilization is advancing forward, progressing toward some kind of goal. I bet it just changes your whole attitude.

My car, which I got for free because the previous owners thought it was possessed (the groans were actually from a defective power steering pump), carried me past a permanently closed Walmart—yes, even our Walmart went out of business—and into a neighborhood of large Victorian homes that had probably been the fancy part of Undisclosed back in the old days. Several of the houses had been turned into somewhat shady businesses—a consignment shop, a gun dealer, and the aforementioned vape store were all in a row, next to a blue Victorian home that was still a residence. At this hour, it was the only one with lights on inside. As I pulled over, my headlights flashed across a cop SUV parked out front, with John's Jeep right behind it. I sighed, checked my hair—it looked like a wig that had been flushed down a toilet and recovered in the sewer six months later—and dragged myself out into the rain.

When I got close to the SUV, I found there was an officer in the driver's seat, eating a McMuffin and playing a game on his phone. A kid with a square jaw and wavy movie-star hair. It wasn't somebody we'd dealt with before. He rolled down his window just a crack as I approached, enough to talk through it but not enough to let the rain splatter in.

I said, "Excuse me, is this where the missing girl is?"

"No, sir. If she was here she wouldn't be missing."

"Uh . . . okay, I got a call from John, I'm—"

"I know who you are. He's inside, with Herm."

I went up and found the front door was standing open. I didn't want to just let myself in, since people lived here and I wasn't police. I just sort of stood there awkwardly until the detective appeared a minute later. An older guy, face was mostly mustache—I felt like I'd dealt with him before but couldn't remember where. Clothes were more casual than what you see detectives wear in movies— khakis and a polo shirt under a windbreaker, looked more like a guy the landlord would send to repair your furnace, the type who'd bend your ear about filter maintenance on the way out. He let me inside just enough to get out of the rain, then put up a hand to stop me.

I said, "I'm David Wong—"

"I know. I remember you from your involvement in every single horrible thing that has happened in this town for the last several years."

"What about the mayor's bestiality scandal? I wasn't involved in that."

"That we know of."

John walked up from behind the detective, wearing a black overcoat and under it, a gray suit and tie. He yanked off his reading glasses and said, "Dave, this girl is just *missing as fuck*."

He handed me a photo. I asked, "Why are you wearing that?"

"Which thing?"

"All of it. I didn't even know you owned a suit."

"Oh, I have to be in court later. That public indecency charge. I'm going to fight it, lawyer dug up some good case law where they found that body paint counts as clothing."

I glanced at the picture. It was a little girl, all right. Elementary school age, long blond hair. The type of missing kid the news media actually notices.

John said, "I think this case is a screaming clown dick. The girl's name is Margaret Knoll, they call her Maggie. Parents are Ted and Loretta. She went missing a few hours ago."

I handed the photo back to John and said, "That's all the time it took the cops to decide it was Dave and John territory?"

The detective said, "How many bites do you have to take out of a shit sandwich before you figure out it's shit? Follow me. And wipe your shoes."

The house's interior was as depressing as the magazines at a Laundromat. It looked like maybe they'd just moved into it a couple of weeks ago, like they'd been there long enough to get the chairs and sofa in the right spots, but hadn't hung any pictures or otherwise decorated. The place just seemed lifeless.

The father of the missing girl was a tiny little guy with a mighty blond beard, kind of seemed like a character out of a fantasy novel to me. He had a tattoo on his right bicep that looked like it was from some military unit, a skull in front of an ace of spades. Probably no more than five years older than John and I but with a lot more miles on him. I figured there had been a tour in Iraq or Afghanistan or both, and it looked like he'd returned to a job of manual labor. He was on the sofa, rough hands clenched between his thighs, one knee bouncing. A caged animal. Seemed like the kind of guy who'd have a whole detailed routine for how to make up with his wife after he got rough with her.

Ted Knoll looked me over. What I was wearing could best be described as the opposite of a tuxedo.

He said, "You're the guy? You look like a bag of smashed asshole."

"Thank you for the feedback. So it's been explained to you? Who we are?"

"I asked for you. If it was up to me, cops wouldn't be here at all."

"Okay. Sure. So, what's going to happen is, I'm going to ask you a series of questions and it's not going to be at all clear why I'm asking them, some will seem random or even cruel. All I ask is that you simply answer those questions as best you can, and don't interrupt to ask me why I'm asking. If you don't know an answer, just say you don't know. Okay?"

He nodded.

"Is Maggie's mother here? I'd prefer to not have to go through this twice."

35

"She don't live here, we're separated. She don't know I'm talkin' to you and we're gonna keep it that way."

"Ah. All right, when did you notice your daughter was missing?"

"Got up in the middle of the night, don't know why, happened to walk past her room and saw there was no lump in the blankets. Went in to check, bed was empty, no sign of Maggie anywhere. Front and back doors of the house were both closed and locked. All the windows locked, too. We got an alarm system, either they figured out how to disarm it, or they managed to not trip it. Got security cameras front and back, looks like they went dark at around two in the morning, stayed off for an hour, just a black screen, like somebody knew exactly what they were doing. Like they'd planned it."

"All that aside, we're one hundred percent sure your daughter's not hiding in a closet, anything like that? We're not going to find her in the attic, or crawl space, or garage? Under a bed? In a kitchen cabinet?"

"I've torn this fuckin' place apart. She ain't here."

"In the days or nights leading up to this, did you have any strange dreams?"

"No."

"Did you see any shadowy figures, like maybe out of the corner of your eye, but when you turned to look, nobody was there?"

"No."

"Do you ever have memories of events that never happened? A presidential election that turned out differently than the newspapers say, a famous person you was sure was dead, turning out to be alive?"

"No. I'm not crazy, if that's what you're gettin' at."

"Did you see anything else unusual leading up to Maggie's disappearance?"

"Five days ago, a man named Nymph showed up and said he was going to abduct her soon."

John and I exchanged a look. John said, "I think that might be our first lead."

To Ted I said, "Did you call the cops after that?"

"I did not."

"Because you don't think this was just some local deviant. Or else you wouldn't have asked for us."

"Also, don't got much use for cops."

"Tell us about that encounter, from the start."

"It was last Sunday. After church. I was in the driveway putting an alternator on the Impala. Guy walks up, dainty little guy, looked like a fag, or a child molester. Got this lispy little voice, holding a cigarette between his thumb and index finger, like you'd hold a joint. Made this little duckface every time he took a puff, I wanted to punch him before he even said a word. Came mincing up the driveway, I didn't even see a car pull up or anything, he was just there. Maggie was in the yard with me, chasing the cat around. This guy comes up, says his name is Mister Nymph. Actually referred to himself as 'Mister.'"

"Wait, say the last name again?"

"Nymph, like short for 'nymphomaniac' or somethin'. That's how I heard it anyway."

It wasn't a name we'd run across before.

Ted continued, "So he looks over at Maggie, and he's got his leering look, you know, and says I have a beautiful daughter. Starts asking me a bunch of weird questions about her. Then he says—"

"What kind of questions?"

"Started out random things. How much does she weigh. Do we let her eat meat. I'm not answering any of these as he asks; I'm just asking him who he is, what does he want. But he just keeps up with the questions. And they just get creepier as they go. Does she shower or take baths. Do my wife and I allow her to see us naked. Do we let her shop for her own underwear."

"Like he was trying to get you agitated, then."

"Guess so, yeah. Told him to get off my property; he said he was just asking questions. I tell him he's got five seconds to get off my driveway, tell him that he's threatening my child, as far as I'm concerned. I say that in this state I have grounds to kill him where he stands, based on that alone. Finally he says, and he's saying it like he's shopping for a car, he says, 'I'll take her.' Says he'll be back in a few days to pick her up. I take a step toward the guy, big wrench in my hand. Then I turn to check on Maggie real quick, just a split second, then I turn back to Nymph and—"

"And he was gone," finished John.

Ted nodded. "I asked Maggie if she saw where the guy went, she said she didn't see nothin'. Said she saw me standing in the driveway alone, yelling at nobody. By the next day, I was doubtin' myself."

John said, "You thought it was a hallucination?"

Ted shrugged. "Came back from Iraq, had the PTSD, dreams mostly. Figured . . . I dunno. Also done some substances in my time, before Maggie was born, but I've heard about how that stuff stays in your system. I guess I wanted it to be that and not this other thing. The shit that they say goes on in this town. The reason everybody moved away, the reason I got this house for fifteen grand. I had always figured it was all panic and superstition. I've seen plenty of women and little kids torn to pieces, and the culprit wasn't no monster. Men do it just fine."

I said, "So, what exactly are you willing to believe?"

"I believe in results. I believe in technique. What you two do, either it works or it don't. If it don't, I'll find somebody else."

I said, "The way I try to explain it to people is this. You look outside in the daytime and there's the sun. It's there, everybody agrees it's there, everybody knows what it is. But what you don't realize is that the sun is also really *loud*. It's a giant ball of nuclear explosions. Have you ever been really close to a lightning strike? You know that clap of thunder that's so loud that it almost makes you piss your pants? Imagine hearing something that loud, nonstop, day and night—*that's* how loud the sun would be, even from a hundred million miles away. About a hundred and twenty decibels. The only reason you can't hear it, is because your ears aren't equipped to—there's no air in space to carry the sound waves. Do you understand? This universe is full of huge, powerful, noisy things that you just can't perceive the right way, due to how your sense organs are built. John and I, our senses are a little different than yours, that's all."

John said, "It's kind of like how you can't hear that your pet goldfish is just constantly screaming, but other fish can. Now this particular guy, Nymph or whatever his name is, he's not in our database—"

Note: We do not have a database.

"—but everything's a mystery until it's not. This looks

39

like what we call a 'locked room' abduction. Victim missing, but no sign of entry or exit. We've seen a few of them before."

Ted said, "If you don't mind me askin', how many of those times have you found the victim alive?"

"More than you'd think," answered John. The answer is one, by the way. "When they say the things that happen around here are beyond understanding, that's not always a bad thing. Sometimes weirdness occurs and everybody is perfectly fine afterward. Maggie could just turn up in her bedroom again, five minutes from now."

"Is that what you think will happen here?"

Before John could answer, I said, "We don't think anything right now. We've been at this for a while, and here's what we've learned—however you think it's gonna go, is not how it's gonna go. About here is where I usually tell people not to get their hopes up, but I don't think I need to say that—you know what the world is like. So, instead I'm just going to say that we'll do our best."

Ted nodded. "Part of the job is that guy, Nymph, whoever he is, we find him and destroy him. Alpha Mike Foxtrot."

John said, "You can take that to the fuckin' bank."

The detective held out his hands and said, "Guys, I'm *standing right here*."

Ted said, "So, if this is what we think it is, where do you start looking?"

I thought, *good question*.

John said, "The fact that he came to you in advance is important. He could have just snatched her in the night, presumably, but there's a game being played here. So that means there's a good chance we'll hear from

Nymph—or someone like him—very soon. At that point, we try to figure out exactly what 'game' he's playing. And then—"

I finished for him. "We don't fucking play it."

Ted nodded. He seemed to have gained some confidence from this conversation, which meant we had done a good job of concealing the fact that we had no idea what the hell we were doing.

The detective looked at his watch, nodded, and said, "Well, looks like you guys have it handled."

He turned and strode down the hall and out the front door. I hurried after him.

"Hey! You're not walking away from this—wait!" He stopped to open the door of the SUV. I put a hand on it to keep it closed and he gave me a look like I was a mosquito he was about to splatter. "Where are you going?"

"Oh, I have to call the feds, of course. We'll have a team from the FBI here in half an hour, they'll work with a local task force of a dozen of our finest men!"

He knocked my hand aside and ducked into the passenger seat. He slammed the door and the other cop started the engine. I knocked on the window and he rolled it down.

I asked, "Wait, was that sarcasm?"

"What do *you* think? I'll see you boys later. Or not. Who knows? I'm going back to the station."

"You can't just walk away from a missing child!"

"Watch us. You think this is my first day on the job? You think this is my first day in *this town*? You heard the story, even if we don't exactly know what's going on, we know enough. If *They* took her" (I could hear the capital

41

"T" in his voice), "then it's like trying to rescue an orange after it's been juiced. Not my monkeys, not my circus."

"It literally is! This is *your job*."

His shoulders slumped. He let out a tired sigh. "You're right, you're right. Here, let me give you something. It might help."

He stuck his right hand inside his jacket, then pulled it out to reveal he had his middle finger extended. He stuck his hand out of the window and sped off down the street singing, "FUUUUUUUUUUUUUUUUCK YOOOOOOOOOOOOUUUU!!!!"

I watched the SUV's taillights dissolve behind a gray curtain of rain. I would have called the guy's superiors to complain, but the chief would just say the same thing, only louder.

You might be wondering if the "They" he was just referring to is the same "they" who showed up at John's place a few weeks ago. The truth is that nobody knows. Lurking behind everything are these walking shadows who can manipulate a human soul as easily as a finger puppet is manipulated by a drunk mime's penis. Here in our world, there are people who do Their bidding willingly, others who do it unwillingly, and still others who serve Their purposes without even knowing They exist. So, yeah, I admit it probably does make it hard to fill out an arrest warrant.

I sighed and made my way back inside.

As soon as I arrived back in the living room, Ted said, "Thought he'd never leave. So if we're gonna hear from Nymph, when do you think—"

His cell phone rang.

3. JOY PARK

Ted's ringtone was "Flight of the Valkyries." He answered and immediately his expression made it clear who was on the other end. Not "Mister Nymph," but his little girl.

He squeezed his eyes shut and said, "Oh thank god. Shh . . . listen. Baby, where are you?" A pause. "What? Hey, tell me where you are . . ."

John muttered, "Put it on speaker." Ted tapped his phone and I heard the tinny voice of a little girl, in midsentence.

"We saw Prince Blacktail and we took a picture of him and Betty the Bear and I ate a chocolate pickle on a stick."

Ted said, "Maggie, where are you? Who are you with?"

"Do you want to talk to Daddy?"

"I'm here, this is me. We're at home. Where are you?"

"I can't hear, the people are really loud. It's really crowded. We're in line for the Night Wheel."

Ted looked at us. None of us had any idea what that meant.

John said, "Hi, I'm a friend of your dad's. Are you at a park? Like an amusement park? Tell us where you are and we'll come join you."

"We're at Joy Park! It was a surprise for my fly box!"

It was word salad. Ted closed his eyes, I imagined the rage and frustration turning his brain into a sputtering pot of chili. "Honey, can you hear me? Do you know what town you're in? Or, do you remember how long you drove to get there?"

"Do you want to talk to Daddy? Hold on."

"No, honey, I . . . are you still there?"

There was a pause, some faint voices on the other end. Finally, a male voice came on the line. It said, "This is Ted. Who's this?"

Ted, the one sitting in the room with us, looked at his phone, then looked up at us. We had no suggestions.

"Who are you, you son of a bitch? Bring back my daughter!"

From the phone, a man with a very similar voice said, "What? I ain't got your daughter, dude." A faint female voice could be heard asking a question, and the man on the phone replied to her, "No idea, somebody she dialed on accident."

The call disconnected.

Ted stood bolt upright off the sofa, looked at me, and said, "What *the fuck* was that?"

Another good question.

John said, "Try to call her back."

He did, and shook his head. "They turned it off."

John was quickly scrolling through something on his

phone. He said, "I tried doing a search for Joy Park. I don't find a *place* by that name. Not within driving distance. Lots of, uh, people."

I said, "Maybe we heard her wrong?"

"Even so, what place like that would be open before dawn?"

Ted said, "That sounded like *me*. On the phone. And in the background, that was Loretta. What *is* this?"

John said to Ted, "Keep in mind, again, that call was placed for a reason. What you heard, what you were allowed to hear, somebody did that to get you to react in a certain way. Regardless of who or what is behind this, never lose sight of what we said a minute ago—what's happening here is *a game*."

Ted's phone dinged—an incoming text. He showed it to us—a photo. A large, run-down building with a rounded, redbrick rooftop.

John said, "That's the ice factory."

I said, "The fact that he—or it—wants us to go there tells me that going there is a terrible idea."

"What's our alternative?"

I thought, *move to a different town?* but said nothing.

Ted said, "Let me get a weapon."

"A thing like this," I said, "probably cannot be killed with a gun."

"He's right," said John. "It will take several guns, at least. Can you dual wield?"

Ted nodded and jogged down the hall, a little too enthusiastically. I glared at John. "Any bystanders get shot, it's on you."

We were all in John's black Jeep Grand Cherokee, the hood of which was entirely covered by an airbrushed mural of Satan holding an ax, chopping the head off of a naked woman above the words EZEKIEL 23:20. The paint job wasn't John's work—the Jeep had come from the cops' impound lot and they wouldn't tell us anything about the previous owner, only that he was "Never, ever coming back." They had given it to John as under-the-table payment for some work we did for them, which I think was a good deal for the cops as I estimated the blue book value at about negative two hundred dollars. John and I were in front, Ted was in back. We rolled through the downpour, a sunrise having drowned somewhere behind it.

Ted had brought three guns with him and at the moment was loading bullets into a pistol magazine. He said, "All right, tell me exactly what I'm walkin' into here. In terms of their capabilities, strengths, vulnerabilities, anything you know."

I said, "You know how the earth is mostly run by assholes, who got their jobs either by accident, or by being the kids of other assholes, or via some other backroom assholery? Well, it turns out if you keep going up the ladder, past humans and into spirits and demigods and such, it's just more assholes for several more levels."

John said, "Most of the time you can't perceive them, the same as you can't detect bacteria in your taco meat until you're puking your guts out three hours later. But Dave and I are special. We were able to look behind the veil, thanks to some drugs we took, to see the debauchery these unholy bastards get up to behind the scenes, see how their fluids splatter into our reality. We've been face-to-face with beings that would give your nightmares nightmares. The first time, Dave didn't even flinch, he's like, 'You wanna see the real monster, it's standing right in front of you, bitch.' "

I said, "Also, don't believe anything John tells you. He tends to . . . embellish."

Ted, realizing that spiel had contained no useful tactical information said, "But these things, they can be killed, right?"

I said, "Sort of?"

John said, "You got a Facebook profile, right? You ever get like an annoying ex-girlfriend or something on there, and eventually you just block her? Well, killing the body of one of these things is usually like that. It gets them out of your hair but they're not really gone. Whether you see them again really depends on how persistent they are. Usually still worth it to try."

Ted nodded. No fear, no confusion—he was a soldier evaluating the situation and storing the data as it came, without judgment. He said, "Or, like when insurgents would shoot down one of our drones."

I said, "Yeah, that's actually a way better analogy."

We turned into the mostly abandoned industrial park and soon came upon an arched brick rooftop that appeared to be sitting in the middle of a lake—in reality, an old parking lot that was currently under about three inches of water, boiling with raindrops. Of all the creepy and abandoned places in Undisclosed, this one is probably the creepiest and most abandonedest. This is the infamous ice factory, a spot that many around here believe is a portal to Hell.

I guess that requires some explanation.

See, as recently as the 1940s, refrigerators were something only rich jerks owned. Everybody else had iceboxes—literal wooden boxes you had to cool with a big block of ice you bought. Those blocks were made in factories like the dilapidated one we were rolling up to right now. The place had been closed since the early 1960s, a brick building in the shape of a Quonset hut, with faint shadows above each window where flames had scorched the exterior.

Oh, yeah, that's the "portal to Hell" part. The factory was closed after a horrific fire in 1961, which no one ever isolated a cause for. The blaze supposedly burned so hot that it melted the bricks inside. I know that sounds like bullshit, but according to Munch (who worked as a volunteer firefighter and knows stuff like this), if you can get the temperature up to about four thousand degrees Fahrenheit, the clay in the bricks just liquefies like wax. They say the fire department didn't even throw water at it, they just kept their distance and watched it roar like a blast furnace, the sheer heat wilting trees for a hundred yards in every direction. And then, just minutes after the firefighters arrived, it went dark, like somebody just flipped a switch. Once it cooled down, city officials glanced inside, nodded, then boarded up the doors and agreed to never speak of it again. Nobody had ever bought the factory or the land, presumably because they were afraid the supposed portal would open again and that their insurance wouldn't cover the loss (and who wants to go to court over the issue of whether or not Hell itself counts as an "act of God"?).

The whole story was ridiculous, of course—even if a portal to Hell opened up, it isn't a physical, fiery place.

The ancient Hebrew word for Hell is "Gehenna," which was an actual location outside Jerusalem back in Bible days, a valley where people tossed their garbage to burn it. They used to roll the corpses of sinners down into that putrid burning trash pit as a final posthumous insult, and New Testament writers just took that idea and ran with it. The real "Hell," as far as John and I can surmise, is simply having to spend eternity with millions and millions of other terrible people with no laws, walls, or even physical bodies to separate them from you. An eternity spent swirling in a stew of ravenous, perverse appetites free of all restraints. Their torture is that they forever consume but are never satisfied, your torture is that you are forever consumed. Also, by the 1960s, consumer-grade refrigerators were common so the whole thing would have been a bad investment anyway.

The tires left twin overlapping wakes behind us as we rolled across the shallow pool of the parking lot. There were no visible vehicles or other signs of activity.

Ted said, "Do a slow lap around the exterior. See what we can see."

"Now," I said to Ted, "when we go in, I want you to keep one thing fixed in your mind. Whatever Nymph is, I can tell you what he almost certainly *isn't*, and that's a greasy pedophile in a suit with a smoking habit. What you saw in your driveway that day, that was just how this particular thing chose to present itself to you. It may look completely different now. Do you understand?"

"What, like a disguise?"

"Once," I said, "we had a dainty young woman come in asking us to investigate a haunting in her parents' house. We walk in, the door slams behind us, and the woman falls apart. All that's left is a pile of snakes where the girl had been standing, patches of their scales colored like the dress she'd been wearing."

Ted tried to picture it. "The whole time you talked to her, you didn't notice she was snakes?"

John said, "They have, uh, techniques, for that."

I said, "And then John started dating a girl named Nicky who I *assumed* was made out of snakes but it turned out that's just the way she is."

"She has been nothing but nice to you, Dave."

Ted said, "My voice, on the phone . . . you think these things took Maggie by pretending to be me? Is that what I'm gonna find in there, somethin' that looks and sounds just like I do?"

I shrugged. "Past experience has only taught us not to rely on past experience."

We completed our circuit and rolled to a stop, about thirty feet from the front door. John parked with the Jeep facing away from the building and left the engine running—in this line of work, you always assume that you're thirty seconds from needing to fly off into the horizon in a mad panic.

"Well," Ted said as he pulled the slide on his pistol and stuffed it down the back of his pants, "let's just assume ambush here." He nodded toward the building. "Only two doors. Those are choke points. I've got line and hooks. I say we get up on the roof, rappel down to the windows, come crashing in on the fuckers."

I said, "I'd break both of my ankles the moment I landed, before breaking my neck a half-second later. This is going to have to be a traditional 'walk in the front door' entry. At least for me and John."

Ted seemed pretty disappointed by that, but didn't argue. We circled around to the rear of the Jeep to retrieve our weapons. Ted brought out an M4 assault rifle (which I recognized from having used one in a video game recently) and a pump shotgun that he slung over his shoulder as a backup. John pulled out a gun with a six-inch-wide barrel, connected to a compressed-air tank he strapped to his back—one of those cannons they use to fire T-shirts at the crowd at basketball games. I would be carrying a small, faded wooden cross—supposedly carved from the very beams upon which the actual crucifixion was performed on Jim Caviezel in *The Passion of the Christ*. Taped to it was a pair of small Bose speakers, a battery pack, and an iPod shuffle loaded with 80s power ballads.

I explained our gear to Ted, who gave the weapons a skeptical look.

I said, "Trust me."

"What's the range?"

"For the music? Uh, I guess wherever it's audible."

"But it's not fatal to them? It's more of an area effect deterrent?"

"Yeah, they hate it a lot."

"How long do targets stay incapacitated?"

"I don't—"

"And the cross, do they have to see it to be affected, or is it enough to just be in proximity?"

"Uh, the second one I think—"

"All right, so what's the range?"

John said, "This is not an exact science, Ted."

Ted didn't reply, but his body language said it all. *I'm on my own here. Again.*

We sloshed through the standing water—I had never bought rain boots because I knew that it would immediately stop raining the moment I did—and arrived at the main entrance, an arched brick doorway partially boarded up by what looked like the original planks the crew had hastily nailed into place in 1961. Standing guard beside the door was a concrete snowman—about six feet tall, arms made of rusted rebar, the top half absolutely covered in bird shit. The eyes and mouth were three misshapen, eroded holes in the concrete, as if the thing was wailing in terror and dread. Rainwater puddled and splattered out of its ragged eye holes like flowing tears. The words MR FROSTEE were etched into his chest, like the epitaph on a particularly eccentric tombstone. The old ice factory mascot had seen better days.

A gap had been pried loose in the boarded-up doorway large enough for a person to slide through, but it looked like it had been that way since before I was born—there were still no obvious signs anyone had been here recently. John nodded to me and I hit the iPod, which started playing Bon Jovi's "Livin' on a Prayer." Ted clicked on a flashlight attached to the barrel of his rifle and aimed the light through the gap, sweeping it slowly across the interior. He slid inside, quickly whipping his head back and forth to check for anyone waiting to waylay us inside the door. John went next. I brought up the rear and clicked on my own flashlight.

The interior smelled like wet rust and a recently snuffed candle. A row of huge, charred machines loomed above us like the aftermath of a robot battle. There were tanks and pipes and gears and fifteen-foot-tall iron objects shaped like wagon wheels connected to chutes designed to deliver coffin-sized blocks of ice to ground level. All of it was warped and misshapen, metal parts caught in the process of drooping, dripping, or dissolving entirely according to their various melting points. I shined the light overhead. The brick had in fact liquefied and then cooled into thousands of tiny spikes that made the whole vast space look like a torture chamber. I imagined the curved ceiling snapping shut the moment some hooded inquisitor threw a switch.

We crept steadily forward, the music echoing around the dead space. A light flared up to my left—John lighting a cigarette. He said into the darkness, "All right, we're here, fartsong. What's your deal?"

No answer from inside the building, or at least none that could be heard over Mr. Bon Jovi insisting we have to hold on to what we've got and that it doesn't make a difference if we make it or not. We advanced, Ted swinging his gun lamp around in both directions to light up nooks in between scorched machinery in which enemies could be lying in wait. We passed through an open doorway into an emptier room that had probably been a loading area, a truck-sized door at the opposite end the only other exit. How numb would your fingers get, loading ice all day?

John said, "Come out where we can see you, you son of a bitch! I have to be in court at eight. So whatever you've got in mind, we need to wrap it up."

I said, "Yeah, and I have to pick Amy up from work soon, otherwise she has to get a ride home with this dudebro she works with and I think he's trying to get in her pants. It's a long story but the point is we don't have time to dick around."

Ted's phone rang.

Hey, that worked.

He motioned for me to cut the music, then put the call on speaker.

The little girl's voice said, "Hello?"

"Baby, we're here! Do you see us? I'm shining a flashlight."

"The Night Wheel was scary! I screamed when it started spinning and everybody's faces went away. We're going to watch the flying goats. They let me lick the luck lizard and we've been eating hot dogs that squirm in the bun."

"Maggie! Listen! I want you to yell for me. Yell anything, cry out real loud, so I can hear you."

She'd hung up. Ted cursed, tried to dial back again, and once again it rang, and rang . . .

John held up a hand and said, "Shh."

We all heard it.

A faint musical ringtone that I recognized as the theme song from a recent Disney movie. It was about a princess who has to learn to be independent or something.

The sound was coming from right below our feet.

Three flashlight beams swung down to illuminate the floor in front of us. There was a gap where the floorboards had been ripped aside. Below it was a patch of loose dirt, like a freshly dug shallow grave.

Ted dropped to his knees. He started digging away with his hands, flinging dirt behind him like a dog, crying out for his daughter.

But how would she have made the call from—

About a foot down, he found a phone.

Still on, smeared with mud. Ted tossed it aside and kept digging.

Something was moving in the dirt, in the shadows. Ripples in the clumps of muck, things squirming around his hands . . .

And then they were gone, as if having burrowed into the earth, hiding from the light. Or maybe it had been nothing.

Ted kept digging but there was no little girl down there, alive or dead. He sat back, chest heaving with the effort. He grabbed the muddy phone. He looked it over—it displayed only its lock screen.

He screamed, "Hey! Where is she? Nymph! You here, you son of a bitch?"

I shook my head. "She's not here, and neither is Nymph. It's a wild-goose ch—"

I had turned to walk away and immediately bumped into an inhuman figure that had been standing right behind me. I screamed and tumbled backward.

Ted jumped to his feet, whipped the shotgun off his back, and yelled for me to stay down. He fired and pumped and fired again, but John was yelling for him to stop.

"Hey! Hey! Cool it! It's just the snowman."

I looked up and the figure was of course just that stupid snowman mascot, now scarred across its chest from where the shotgun pellets had gouged the concrete and ricocheted away. Ted had succeeded in blowing one of its rebar arms off. In the panic and tension, we had forgotten that of course the MR FROSTEE mascot was there inside the factory, in the center of the storage room, where it had probably stood for eighty years. Where else would it be? I could now remember approaching it as we entered the room thirty seconds ago, plain as day.

Feeling ridiculous, I stood up and brushed myself off. I cursed when I saw that I had landed right on top of my iPod, smashing it. John was blinking at the snowman as if confused by it, then went to help Ted. He was sweeping his flashlight around each corner, determined to search every inch of the place before admitting defeat.

An hour of the three of us looking in and around the factory turned up no sign of either Nymph or Maggie. We rode back through town in silence, listening to the wipers squeak their complaints from the other side of the windshield.

Ted said, "What now?"

I said, "There are two threads to follow up on here. Who is Nymph, and where is Maggie? I'm guessing one will answer the other . . ."

John said to me, "You go to the library and see if you can find any reference to Joy Park, I'll take Nymph, see if I can find anybody else around town who's encountered him. If I track him down, I'll give you a call after I've killed him."

Ted said, "No. You get a bead on him, you call me. Not the cops, neither. I want to be the one to do it. I'm putting the word out for manhunt volunteers, get as many people lookin' as we can. Got a friend I served with, he can be in town by this afternoon."

"And I'm clearly not going to the library, John. I can search the Internet from my phone, from some place with free wifi, and pancakes. Speaking of which . . ." I was holding the muddy phone we'd found buried at the ice factory, turning it over in my hands. I turned it on, again just got the lock screen. "Anybody know how to hack a phone?"

"Amy probably does."

"Yeah, I'll ask. Wait, does that mean she can get into *my* phone any time she wants?"

"Only way to find out, put a bunch of pics of naked dudes on there and see if you can detect a change in mood afterward."

As we pulled up to the Knoll home, Ted said, "If what you're sayin' about imposters and such is true, we should have a system. In case that thing tries to imitate one of us."

I was taken aback. "Man, that's a good idea. You should do this for a living."

"You make a lot of money doin' this? The password is 'bushmaster.' Don't forget it, we encounter each other, we ask the password. Got it?"

John said, "Got it. Now, I figure we got forty hours before this goes from rescue to revenge, so there's no time to lose. I'll get on it right after I go to court on this public nudity thing."

4. A MONSTER'S PICTURES, A GRIEVING WIDOW, SEX

I felt water squish out of my pants when I settled into my Saturn. Through my weeping windshield I watched Ted trudge up to his front door, knowing that inside he was about to be ambushed by the accusatory silence of that empty house. I couldn't quite put my finger on it, but I just had a feeling this one wasn't going to end well. Maybe it's because they pretty much never do.

I pulled away and considered heading straight for Waffle House, since I'm usually much more effective with a big wad of cheap comfort food in me, but instead headed toward the used bookstore downtown. In the basement they had a collection of odd, out-of-print, and "banned" books. I would probably find nothing pertaining to this case, but Amy's birthday was next weekend and they had a signed copy of Douglas Adams's *The Hitchhiker's Guide to the Galaxy* that I'd noticed her gaze longingly at when we were there about six months ago. Look, I have a life outside of work, okay?

I dug out my phone and dialed as I turned down

Brown Street. The driver's side windshield wiper had a crack in the rubber blade that left behind an arc of rainwater right in the center of my field of vision—it had failed exactly in the way that would annoy me most.

Amy answered, "Hey! You're up early."

"Got a call from John, situation with a missing kid, thinks it might be a thing. Can you get a ride home?"

"A missing kid? Tell me everything."

"I just did, there's not much more to it. She just vanished, like she fell through a hole in reality. We followed up on one lead, turned out to be nothing. Not sure there's much to be done, and I'm *really* not sure how we're going to get paid."

"There's a missing child and you're talking to me about payment? I'm going to reach through this phone and slap you. And you know that's not easy for me. Did you find the muffin?"

"Already eaten. Did you say you could or couldn't get a ride home?"

"Shawn will do it. Hey, I was thinking about the argument we had yesterday, and having slept on it I've decided that you are even more wrong than I thought you were then."

"Looks like you need to sleep on it some more."

The argument had been over whether or not Neo should have just left everyone in the Matrix, since their quality of life was clearly better inside it than out. I say no, she says yes. I should note here that Amy has seen *The Matrix* at least thirty times. When I got her the Blu-ray for Christmas, she became visibly upset when she saw they had done this odd color correction thing that gave the whole movie a weird green tint. She downloaded editing software on her laptop and has been manually correcting it, shot by shot.

"Oh," I said, "and I just want to let you know that I've completely forgotten your birthday next week, because I'm a man and thus care nothing about your feelings."

"Oh, okay, thanks for letting me know ahead of time."

I pulled up to the bookstore, the interior still dark. I realized just now that it wouldn't open for another twenty minutes—I wasn't used to being up this early. I grabbed the muddy phone we'd picked up at the ice factory and turned it on, the lock screen asking for the four-digit passcode.

"Hey, do you know how to hack into a phone? Like to get past the lock screen? Did you ever have a class on that?"

"Whose phone is it? Do you know their social security number? Lots of times it's the last four digits."

"We found it looking for that little girl. I, uh, would be surprised if this guy has a social security card."

"Wait, does the phone belong to a guy or is this some kind of weird monster situation?"

"Don't know. It's an iPhone, if that helps. What code would an unholy predator of the night have on his phone?"

"I was sick the day they taught that."

I mindlessly punched in the code for my own phone—6669.

It unlocked.

Why did I know that would work?

I said, "Hey, I think I hacked it."

The home screen looked normal. I wasn't sure what I

was expecting. I tapped on the icon for any stored photos and video and braced myself for the worst.

The first photo was of a plate of breakfast food. Looked like eggs benedict.

I swiped it aside.

I sucked in a breath, and Amy heard it.

"What? What are you seeing?"

The second photo was of a little blond girl, bound and bleeding, her mouth gagged with duct tape. I was going to take a wild guess and say this was Margaret "Maggie" Knoll.

I said, "Not sure."

I swiped to the next photo. A picture of an orange tabby cat, licking the lens. I swiped again.

The little girl again.

Her limbs were a tangled, red mess.

She had been bound and gagged and then . . . *crushed* somehow. Like a giant had forgotten she was in his back pocket before sitting down.

I closed my eyes.

I wondered . . . at age eight, did she know? Was she aware of what kind of universe she had been born into? Did she have even the faintest hint that this was one of the possible outcomes of her life—that she wouldn't grow up to be a Disney princess, or marry a handsome man at a fancy wedding, or have kids of her own? That she would wind up terrified and alone, in the dark, as some monster's plaything? At the end, had she still held out hope that her daddy would come rescue her? Or that the crazy man would soften at the sound of her cries?

Or, in her final moment, had she gotten just a glimpse of just how little of a shit the universe gives about her? Did she have the realization that what she had always thought of as a normal human life was just a tightrope walk over an ocean of unfathomable suffering?

I hoped not.

I said, "Well, shit, Amy."

Amy said, "*What?*"

"I think we've got photos of the victim here. It's bad."

"What is it?"

"Bad. You don't want to know. We're too late, let's put it that way."

"Oh. Oh, god."

I swiped the picture. The next photo was of John, walking in the doorway of what looked like a church, holding the T-shirt cannon. I furrowed my brow. He was still in court, right?

Remember, Nymph wanted you to see what you're seeing. This, too, is part of the game.

I swiped.

John again.

Dead.

Eyes open. A cascade of dried vomit running down the side of his black faux-leather sofa. Drug paraphernalia on the glass coffee table in front of him.

"David?"

I thought, *no.*

This wasn't denial, this was math. Even if he'd skipped his court date, John hadn't had time to get home, change clothes (he wasn't in his suit, in the photo), get out his stash, and dose himself to death. This was bullshit. All of it. More games.

"Yeah, I . . . these are fake. There's pictures of us on here, but they're, uh, not real."

"Oh, that's creepy."

"Yeah, but that's good. Means the girl may still be okay. He's taunting us."

I swiped.

This one was of John and Amy. She was crying, John was comforting her. They were in my apartment.

Ignore it. It's nothing.

I swiped again.

Amy, crawling, screaming, a pale blurry shape descending on her from behind.

Seriously, why even bother looking at these?

She asked, "Are there any of me in there?"

"No. I've got to go. I'll see you in a bit."

"Come straight home! Don't leave me out of this!"

"You need to get some sleep, you've been working all night."

"There's a missing girl! *David!*"

"I love you."

I hung up and swiped to the next pic. Actually, this one was a video.

I braced myself, and hit play.

It was a shot from the passenger seat of the car I was sitting in, being filmed right now. The cameraman was watching me, watching the phone, in real time.

I turned and looked and—

Someone is there.

No one was there.

I looked back down at the phone and saw that I was holding a filthy, pink plastic toy that was only shaped like a phone, a faded and peeled sticker on the front bearing the likeness of a Disney princess. It had a single plastic button at the bottom, and when I pressed it, it played the theme from the movie. That's all it did.

I closed my eyes and groaned. It was going to be a long goddamned day.

NOTE ABOUT THE FOLLOWING
The accounts of events that occurred while I was not present—particularly those submitted by John— should not be accepted as wholly or even partially true. They are included here only to help fill in some gaps in the timeline of events, but in retrospect I now feel like they only add to the confusion. For this I apologize.

John

After they returned from the ice factory, John had stood in the Knolls' driveway, facing Dave and Ted. John's shirt was soaked through. He peeled it off and flexed, the rain splattering off his muscled chest.

"All right," growled Dave, rubbing a rough hand over his stubbled jaw. "Less than forty hours, that's what we've got to solve this. I'm gonna go search the archives for what I can find on Joy Park, you go see if you can track down this Nymph bastard. But John—you find him, remember *we need him alive.*"

John lit a cigarette. "I won't make any fuckin' promises."

Dave ran toward his Saturn, slid across the hood,

and landed in the driver's seat. He revved the engine and squealed out of the yard. John mounted the Jeep and unleashed the tiger under its hood, raindrops raking the windshield as he tore through the early morning gloom. He headed for the courthouse.

At least one piece of luck fell in their favor that morning, thought John: the judge in his public indecency case was Roy Heubbel. John and Dave had just six months prior freed his mansion from an entity that presented itself as a giant spider made of the bloody bones of his deceased wife. That meant he owed them one. Sure enough, the judge told the prosecutor to make a deal and John got off with probation and a promise to, in the judge's words, "Keep that anaconda caged. There are kids around, and you don't need to go setting them up with false expectations."

On the way out, John bumped into Herm Bowman, the detective who had bailed on the Maggie Knoll case earlier that morning. John grabbed the passing Bowman by the elbow and said, "Hey, we're still working this Knoll thing. We'd have already found the girl if I didn't have to come tend to this bullshit. But I knew if I didn't show, they'd put out a warrant for my arrest and I know how you guys hate having to get out in the rain. But now, I need your help."

Bowman shook off John's hand. "You want sympathy, you can find it in the dictionary between shit and syphilis."

"Ted didn't want me talking to the mother, Loretta, but I'm doin' it anyway. She live in town? What do you know about her?"

"Yeah, in that yellow house next to Taco Bill." He

didn't misspeak. That's the name of the restaurant. "But instead of wasting your time, why don't you just go back home and shoot up with whatever drugs you're on this week."

"I will," said John as he turned toward the door. "But first I have to go do your job."

Thunder clapped as John tore out of the courthouse parking lot. He flew past the closed drive-thru liquor store, past Curry's Tire and Body (with its terrifying mascot made of tires standing sentry out front) and Taco Bill—a Taco Bell that was given the order to close by corporate, only to be stubbornly kept open by the owner. He had altered the sign over the entrance (by sawing out an extra "L" from the sign in the parking lot, turning it into an "I" and attaching it with duct tape) and modified the menu to serve a combination of vaguely approximated Taco Bell dishes prepared by his wife, with a full range of hard liquor added to the beverage list. Smoking was allowed, and after 9 P.M. all of the TVs inside were switched to soft-core Cinemax porn. Everyone agreed it was not only an improvement, but was now the best restaurant in town.

Loretta's house was next door, a run-down 1970s era ranch house with filthy yellow siding that had probably been on there since the Carter administration. No distinct decorations on the outside, probably a rental. John knocked and a tired but handsome thirtysomething woman with mousy brown hair and sad eyes opened the door, clutching closed a bathrobe. She said nothing.

John said, "Ma'am, I'm not going to ask to come in because I've already intruded too much just by making you answer your door. But we're working with your husband on Maggie's disappearance, as consultants. I have a few questions but if you don't want to talk, I'll leave. Just say the word. I'm not the police, but I'm telling you now, they can't help you. And what's more, if we can't find the girl or the man who took her, then I think the cops will turn their eyes toward you and Ted as suspects. I don't want that to happen."

"Ted says Maggie was just . . . gone. Like she just turned into smoke and blew away. Was he telling the truth? He didn't . . . do something, to her, did he?"

"No. We have reason to believe it was, well, something else. I know you've been through an unthinkable ordeal this morning but I promise you I'm here to help. If you're worried that I'm armed, let me show you."

John peeled off his shirt, to show that he had no weapon stashed in his waistband. His naked torso glistened in the rain.

"All right, I'll give you a few minutes, then I have to get ready for work. Come in."

Loretta handed John a towel before retreating to the kitchen to make coffee. Hers was another barren home—a place quickly rented after the separation, maybe in hopes it wouldn't last long.

She came back with the coffee and John said, "Ted says he actually had warning this was about to happen. A strange man, named Nymph, came to the house a week ago, making weird threats. Did he tell you about that?"

"No. But we don't talk—"

"Did anything like that happen to you?"

"No, Ted asked me the same thing earlier, when he called. Did he tell you about the drawings?"

"The what?"

"He probably wasn't even listening. Here . . ."

Loretta shuffled into her bedroom and John followed. She handed him a stack of drawings on dog-eared construction paper. Magic Marker stick figures, flowers, houses, mountains. Fill colors spilling wildly over the lines. No matter who you are or where you're from, we can all look upon the raw, energetic creations of children and agree that they are very shitty artists.

Loretta said, "Those are all from the last week. We homeschool, I was doing an activity where she was to draw the future. Instead of spaceships and flying cars, she drew this."

The first drawing featured a crude house shape with a steeple. A cross on the front. So, a church. The next drawing was a crowd of stick figures, but in the background was that church again. The next was a drawing of the family—scribbled strands of yellow around the head of the smallest figure. And there was the church, up on a hill in the background. She'd even drawn a little angel floating in the sky above it, her haphazard scrawls making it look like it had about eight limbs.

John said, "This church? That's what we're looking at?"

"The church, and the man without a head."

John looked back down at the stick figure family portrait. Mommy, Daddy, Maggie with the hair . . . and next to her, another stick figure, with no circle where the head should be.

"The one with the crowd of people, you'll find him in there, too. He's in all of them."

"Did she ever talk about it? Like maybe it was a dream she had or something?"

"I asked her after the first one, the portrait of us at church. I said, 'Who's this guy here without a head?' and she said, 'That's not a guy, it's a drawing.'" Loretta laughed. "Maggie was like that. I thought she kept including him in the other drawings as a joke, because I had pointed him out. But now . . . I've spent all morning looking back on everything she said and did, picking it apart, trying to find clues. Like in a movie, you know, there'd always be some clue. In real life, nothing makes sense."

John said, "I'm going to ask you what is going to seem like a very strange question. Was there ever a situation where Maggie acted like she had spoken to you or her father, or otherwise interacted with you, only you have no memory of it? Like she had made up a memory of a conversation or maybe mistook someone else for you? Or Ted, either one?"

All of the color drained from Loretta's face.

Me

I walked among the shelves in the bookstore's basement, smelling that old-book scent that would probably mean nothing to future generations. Amy is all about that smell, of old paper and ink and time, pages touched by long-dead hands. I think she just likes that sense of being among ancient knowledge, feeling like the past is something sacred rather than the actions of a bunch of bucket shitters who were even more stupid and superstitious than we are now. To me, it just smells like old sweat and dirt, but it means something to Amy and that's what matters today. Even though the whole thing is completely pointless since she has access to every book ever written via a device that is never out of arm's reach.

That reminded me—I brought up my phone and did a quick search for "Joy Park."

Titties. My screen was full of them.

"Joy Park," as it turned out, was the name of a very famous, very big-breasted Korean porn star. After the pages (and pages, and pages) of Joy Park titty pics ran out, all I got was a couple of links to a place in Akron, Ohio—just a regular ol' park with basketball courts and such—and a few more non-porn girls with that name. Nothing related to anything weird, no news articles about missing kids, or occult rituals, or anything else remotely interesting. I tried searching for any mentions whatsoever of people with the last name Nymph and found that wasn't even a real surname, which I guess shouldn't have surprised me.

With that, I was out of ideas. Maybe John's thing would pan out. Or maybe he would destroy half the town again. I was cold and achy and wanted to go back to bed. My wet clothes were sticking to every part of my body. I sighed and made my way over to the shelf of signed editions, some of them in a scuffed Plexiglas case, some sitting out, depending on whether or not the author was still alive. I started to get a sinking feeling when I spotted a signed hardcover copy of *Fear Nothing* by Dean Koontz for $100. Next to it, a signed Neil Gaiman's *The Sandman* for $125.

I stared at the price tags and thought, *Why don't you fucking kill yourself?*

I have that thought a lot, actually. Hey, did you know that people making less than $34,000 a year are 50 percent more likely to commit suicide? I looked it up.

Did you know that number shoots up to 72 percent for the unemployed? I heard a guy on talk radio go on and on about how people on food stamps are living the good life off the government teat, and all I could think was, *Yes, it's such a party that sometimes we blow our fucking brains out rather than get humiliated by another government aid employee.*

A little while back, John and I had gotten drunk on the occasion of our ten-year high school reunion. Oh, we didn't attend the actual reunion—we had just started drinking after coming to the realization that it had been ten years and that we had made virtually no progress in our lives. "You know what it's like?" John had said. "The Rapture. Like from the book of Revelation, when all the souls of the righteous get sucked up into Heaven."

What he had meant was that there had been a point several years ago when everybody we graduated with were all equally poor. College kids, people working shitty customer service, the unemployed ones still living at home—all of us twentysomethings were all doing the same stuff for fun, going to the same parties. We had nothing, but we were young and thin (well, not me) and nobody expected anything from us. But then, one by one, the smart kids, the ambitious kids, the kids with rich parents—they all *ascended*. They got their degrees and careers and babies. Most moved away, and the ones who didn't, stopped hanging out. Until it was just us, the rejects. Left behind, the faithless and doomed, the broke and the broken. Ever since he'd said that, I couldn't stop thinking of it that way—that we had been cast out as heretics to the western world's one true religion.

My resume is worthless—it turns out that managing a now-defunct video store in your twenties while solving monster crimes qualifies you for absolutely nothing else. Society just doesn't need me—I'm that extra screw you have left over after you've put together an Ikea desk. Maybe you throw it in a drawer, thinking it'll eventually become obvious what it was for later on. Then, a few years down the road, you come across it while cleaning and just toss it out.

So, now I'm standing here birthday shopping for Amy, who at the moment, is the only one of us with any kind of a stable income. Using our joint account for this is basically taking money out of her purse to buy something for her that she may or may not even want. How do you set your price limit in that scenario? Spending too much isn't generosity, it's forcing her to work overtime next month to make up the difference. "Here, baby, for your birthday I stole another autumn Saturday from your life that you'll never get back!" Oh, and she's also having to pay for some of her prescriptions out of pocket, due to the cut-rate health insurance at the call center. She has back problems, and spaces out the pills so that a thirty-day prescription will last sixty. So, now I also have that cross to bear: my inability to learn a useful skill equals Amy's actual, physical agony.

Why don't you fucking kill yourself?

I mean, I *do* have a rare skill, but being able to piss a stream of turkey feathers is also a rare skill—"rare" does not equal "lucrative." Not that there aren't ways to cash in on being a freak show—we get offers. But charging a fee to do what we do—to free somebody's home from what they think is an evil spirit, or whatever—

automatically puts you in some very shady company and the scammers will always take most of the business. After all, they're just telling the customers what they want to hear. I'm, uh, not good at doing that.

I browsed the shelves, the titles seemingly arranged in random order. The copy of *Hitchhiker's* was still there, in the glass case.

It was $275.

Amy would not be getting this book for her birthday. And she would be fine with that. She knows the situation, she tells me not to worry about it every chance she gets. We have a roof over our heads, she says, we have food, we have electricity, we have each other. By medieval standards, she points out, we'd have been considered rich. Don't beat yourself up over an ideal dreamed up by a bunch of marketing jerks on the coasts whose BMWs trigger cocaine-sniffing dogs from six blocks away. It's fine, she says. You're doing important work. Remember that I love you.

Why don't you fucking kill yourself?

John

Loretta said, "About two weeks ago, Maggie spent hours running around the house with a flyswatter. I thought it was some game she had invented, stalking flies, swatting them. Then a few days later, she brings me this shoebox full of dead flies and says, 'Do I have to eat them all now?' I ask her what she's talking about, and she thinks I told her to do that. I thought it was a dream she'd had. I made her throw them away, and she didn't understand.

Is there . . . something wrong with her? Is that what happened? She became confused and wandered away?"

"I don't think so, but I don't want to eliminate any possibilities." John sipped the woman's surprisingly good coffee and studied the drawings. "This church she kept drawing, is this your church? Is church a big deal to you guys?"

"She'd never drawn it before. The one Ted took us to is that biker church, they hold services in that old motel. It doesn't look anything like a traditional church. In her drawings, it always has that steeple and that cross in the same spot."

"There is a church like this in town, do you know it? It's next to a pond? And a haunted coal mine?"

"No."

"Maybe she went there with friends?"

"It's possible. What do you think it means?"

"Maybe nothing. Maybe everything. I'll go check it out either way." John stood. "I'll leave you be, you've been a big help and I know this has been hard for you."

She stood, meeting his eyes.

"It *has* been hard. I've just been so lonely here, Ted coming back from the war and breaking things off like he did, now Maggie going missing . . . do you know what that's like? To have a hole in your life so big that your life is nothing but hole?"

"I think we all feel like that, at times. Those of us who are lucky, we have someone we can cling to in those times when life feels, as you said, like one big butthole."

"That's all I want, sometimes. Someone to cling to, if even just for a moment."

She dropped her robe. She was naked underneath.

John looked her up and down. "I'm in the middle of a case, miss. Time is of the essence. Your little girl's life could be at stake."

She stepped forward, running a finger down his chest. "I promise I won't be long."

"I can promise I *will* be long."

John let his pants fall. "I'm telling you right now, this won't cure your loneliness, or replace what your husband took from you when he fled. At best, all I can do is diminish his memory by giving you something far beyond what he ever could."

"That will have to do." She lay back on the bed. "But maybe even that is asking too much. You see, my husband was quite the—OH MY FUCKING GOD!"

"Do you want me to stop, Ms. Knoll?"

"IF YOU STOP I WILL KILL YOU."

And so he did not stop, until her orgasmic cries filled the lonely halls of her modest home. John thrusted his staff into the moist—

Me

"John," I said into my phone, "it is really, *really* important that you give me the actual story and not a bunch of bullshit. The truth is enough, you don't need to sex it up. So, please, back up and just boil it down to the parts that, you know, actually happened. The thing with the drawings of the church, that was real, right?"

"Yeah, a little traditional country style church, like you'd see on a postcard. White, steeple, probably some stained glass."

"Like the one at Mine's Eye?" That's a little wooded area with a pond around what had been a coal mine back in the olden days.

"Yeah."

"Okay, meet me there. The creepy kid drawing thing is a little cliché but it's literally the only lead we've got."

John said, "There's something else, though I don't know what to make of this, either. Ted's car got stolen. Old restored Impala. I found out just before I called you, it was missing from his garage when he got back from the ice factory."

"Huh. Maybe this whole thing was one big ploy to steal his car? Oh, I was able to get into the phone, the one we recovered from the ice factory."

John paused for a confused moment. "What phone? The pink toy one?"

"I don't . . . I mean, is that what it looked like to you the whole time?"

"Yeah, it had a Disney princess or something on it. When you asked about hacking it, I thought you were joking. Were you able to make it work, somehow?"

"Yeah. Maybe?"

"And?"

"It had photos and a video on it. Fake ones. There were pics of the little girl looking mangled and bloody, but I don't think it means she's actually been hurt."

"How do you know they were fake?"

"There were pics of us on there. We were dead in those, too."

"Hmm."

"Yeah. I have a question, John. Who's paying us for this?"

"What?"

"Amy doesn't get enough hours at the call center and I don't get any hours at the anything. Who's paying us?"

"It was never discussed. I don't think Ted has much money."

"The cops called us in, shouldn't they have like a consultant's fund in the budget?"

"I think that would require us having some kind of license or expertise or something. We've had this discussion before. Did you find anything on Joy Park?"

"Well, it's a porn star. Otherwise no."

"Yeah I saw that," said John. "You think those boobs are real?"

I consulted my notes. "I did some digging. If she got a boob job she got it early. She's about twenty-seven I think, her earliest shoots are from five or six years ago, and she had big boobs then. Looks pretty natural when she's on her back."

"You see that set where she's coming out of the pool? Jesus."

It felt like we'd gotten off the subject somewhat. Then I suddenly remembered what I should have done when the call started. "Hey, what's the code word?"

"The what?"

"The, uh, password Ted set up, to make sure you're you and I'm me."

John said, "Oh, right. It was . . . wait, why do I have to say it? If you're an imposter maybe this call is just a way to find out about the password."

"How would I have known we have a password at all?"

John considered for a moment. "It was 'bushmaster.'"

"Yeah."

"I remember because that was my nickname in high school."

"Though, if you—"

"Because I got so much bush."

"*Though, if you were an imposter,* I think I'd know within seconds. You think one of 'Them' could mimic the stupid shit that comes out of your mouth?"

There was a moment of silence before John said, "That's . . . actually a good question."

"What is?"

"If it tried to be one of us, would it know how to say everything we just said? About the boobs and such?"

"I wish *we* didn't know how to say it."

"Serious question."

"No. I mean . . . I don't think so. How could it?"

5. AMY'S BREAKFAST WITH EVIL

Amy

Amy Sullivan's cubicle neighbor, Shawn, was taking her home from work in his new Mustang. She was in the passenger seat eating a single-serving box of Cocoa Pebbles by shaking them into her mouth, then washing it down with a bottle of Orange Crush (the selection in the break room vending machine at the office actually matched her preferred diet really well).

Shawn asked, "Are you sure you don't want anything else to eat? You're just downing handfuls of sugar there."

"I'm fine."

"I don't know how you stay that size on your diet. I wouldn't be able to fit behind this steering wheel."

"I have a painting of myself in my closet, it gets fatter every time I eat."

"You have a what?"

She wondered if he was really just afraid she would spill something in his car, despite having told her it was fine every time she asked. Amy was trying to balance her meal with her one remaining hand and she knew it probably looked precarious. She had briefly experimented with a prosthetic left hand, to replace the one that had gotten lopped off in the car crash years ago. She and David had picked it out together from a catalog her doctor had given her—a metallic, Terminator-esque model that they both thought was hilarious. It kind of looked like she had gotten some of her fake human skin ripped off, revealing the robot underneath that had been there all along. Which, Amy had said, would actually make sense: if someone was going to create a cyborg intended to pass for human, it was more logical to disguise it as a hundred pounds of freckles and glasses than a muscular Austrian.

The hand had only lasted about a month, though, before she stopped strapping it on every morning. The reason, she told everyone, was that it just wasn't convenient to use—it looked like a robot hand from the future, but in reality was just operated by a cable that ran around her other shoulder, and she had to open and close it by shrugging. It didn't have little motors in it or anything, like Luke's hand in *Star Wars*—those were for people with Cadillac health insurance. It didn't have much in the way of grip strength, either, and she found herself just doing everything with her right hand anyway. It was just habit, she'd now lived without the other hand almost as long as she'd lived with it.

But the real problem was that, with the robot hand, it was like she suddenly had a PLEASE HIT ON ME sign draped over her neck written in a language that only the creepiest of guys could read. Those guys *loved* the robot hand, each and every one of them broaching the subject as if they were the first. She didn't know if it was a fetish thing or if they just thought they could get her cheaper because she was a damaged floor model. All she knew was that whenever she entered the one remaining video game store in town, all four male employees would follow her from shelf to shelf, desperately trying to make conversation ("Hey, do you have a *DotA* account?").

But the convention had been the final straw.

A group of former college friends had invited her to a gaming convention in Indianapolis and offered to pay her way (David would never have come within a five-mile radius of a gaming convention, even if he was bleeding profusely and just needed to pass it on the way to the emergency room). Everyone was going in costume, and Amy only needed a cheap pink wig and an afternoon modifying a white skirt and top to go as Ulala from *Space Channel 5*—a costume she had picked specifically because that character wore white elbow-length gloves. But she had accidentally left the gloves at home and everybody had thought the mecha hand was part of her costume, since to people unfamiliar with the game, the getup just registered as Generic Space Girl. Amy wondered if they thought she was so dedicated to the role that she had hacked off one of her limbs just to complete the ensemble.

Anyway, some pictures of her at the convention got posted on the Internet, and they went somewhat viral since Amy is kind of a minor celebrity in some circles. She had quickly gotten snowed under with messages from creepers, and at least three of them had dug up her phone number. Half the messages were asking why she didn't go for the more revealing version of the costume with the bare midriff; the other half were informing her that she was too ugly to wear such a thing in public. She was never in any actual danger, as far as she knew, but the sheer volume of it freaked her out and, well, brought back some bad memories. From that point on, she had this feeling like all eyes were on her the moment she stepped outside with the metal hand—she even had a panic attack, once.

So, she put it away. She never told David why.

The Mustang passed a flooded cornfield and Amy wondered if the road itself wouldn't be underwater a week from now. Or a day. She wondered if that would be a valid excuse to miss work, or if they'd just fire everybody who didn't own a canoe. At this rate, the office itself would be under before too long—she imagined everyone sitting at their desks, neck deep in flood water, taking calls while fish swam in front of their monitors.

She asked, "What happens to the rabbits when it's like this?"

"What rabbits?"

"Don't rabbits live in tunnels? And moles and mice and such? Do they drown, when it floods?"

Thinking quickly, Shawn said, "Rabbits are fast, they can outrun the water."

"But what if they've got babies? How would they get them out of there?"

"Baby rabbits are good swimmers. They're not like humans where they have to take classes, they can do it coming out of the womb. They're fine."

She wondered how long he would keep making stuff up if she kept asking. She had asked David that same question the day before and his answer had been, "It started raining weeks ago, those lazy bastards have had plenty of time to get to the high ground. What are they waiting for, FEMA?"

Most of the people Amy worked with were cool, which is one of the biggest factors in determining your quality of life, if you think about it. She had parlayed her five semesters of programming classes into a job that involved no coding at all—a call center for an alarm company, in which virtually all of the calls involved sensors getting tripped by dogs. Business had been booming for the home alarm sector in the area; everybody in Undisclosed wanted a system even though not one home in twenty had anything worth stealing. It was mostly scared people, hoping to fend off monsters. Whether or not the kind of creatures that turned up around town would even trip a sensor or show up on camera was a mystery to Amy, but of course she knew that what people were really buying was the ability to get a good night's sleep (which was ironic, considering Amy had applied for the eleven-to-eight shift specifically because she couldn't sleep herself). She liked it well enough, even at nine bucks an hour. She felt like a policeman, guarding people in their beds. Well, at least the ones who could afford a home security system.

Shawn said, "You guys have a plan if you get flooded out?"

"David says we can get a bunch of those inflatable sex dolls from the shop downstairs and strap them together as a raft."

Shawn laughed, but in a way that made it clear he didn't approve. David made constant jokes about how he thought Shawn was trying to "get into her pants," which meant that David did in fact think Shawn was trying to get into her pants. Amy had long ago learned the secret to reading people's minds, a mystical two-step process that involved 1) shutting her mouth and 2) listening to what they say. People will scream their secrets if you just give them a chance. Even the liars can't resist letting the truth ooze through the gaps.

So, David would make his snarky little remarks about Shawn and Amy would tell him that the guy was married. David would then say something to the effect of, "You have a lot to learn about guys, Amy." But he was wrong— she was pretty sure she understood the game better than he did. If she were to tell Shawn to pull over right now, then rip open her shirt and ask him to ravage her, he'd flee the car and stammer an apology, maybe politely ask her where her boobs had gone ("Oh, sorry, that was mostly bra"). He doesn't want to cheat on his wife; he wants girls to laugh at his jokes and be in awe of his car. He wants to feel the way he did back when he was a cool dude in high school and not a twenty-six-year-old slaving away in an office with a kid at home, watching his prime tick away one can of Red Bull at a time. It was all harmless.

They arrived at the apartment the sex shop wore as a hat and Amy saw David's car was gone. So, he was still out working his missing girl case—without her. She juggled her umbrella and headed around toward the side entrance, the pink VENUS FLYTRAP neon buzzing overhead. She passed the one-armed concrete snowman at the bottom of the stairs, headed up, shook off her umbrella, and pushed her way through the door to the apartment. She glimpsed the kitchenette . . .

And, just for a moment, thought she saw something strange.

It was David, standing there with a mixing bowl in one hand and a whisk in the other. Like he was in the middle of cooking something. But—and she wasn't even sure she really saw this—in that moment, he wasn't moving. Like, at all. He was standing perfectly frozen, facing the window to Amy's left. He wasn't mixing, he wasn't blinking, he wasn't breathing. He was just standing, for a solid two seconds. Then Amy came through the door and all at once he popped into action, like a video that had been unpaused.

Weird.

"Were you transfixed by something outside?"

David said, "What's that?"

"You were staring out the window."

"Was I? Just looking at the rain, I guess."

"Did you solve the thing with the little girl?"

"We did, she's back home safe and sound. Turned out there was nothing clown dick about it, it was just a local creep. We got the cops to track his phone and found his van. Whatever he was going to do, he never got a chance."

"Thanks to you!"

"Thanks to us."

"Holy crap, David. You guys are heroes! This is amazing!"

Amy thought she heard something unusual, but couldn't put her finger on it. Then she suddenly realized it was what she *wasn't* hearing. She poked her head into the bathroom and confirmed it: no *plink-plink-plink* of the roof leak.

"Hey! They fixed the leak! This is the best day ever."

"Actually, I did. Got tired of waiting on the landlord. I went up and it was pretty easy to see, there was just a gap in the flashing around an exhaust vent up there, all I had to do was squirt a bunch of silicone caulk in the crack. Took five bucks and fifteen minutes, should have done it months ago."

"Still, I'm impressed. Didn't know you even knew how to do that sort of thing."

"I didn't, I looked it up. It's not brain surgery. I'm making you waffles. You hungry?"

She wasn't, but said, "Starving!" David, it appeared, was having one of his Good Days.

He said, "Then have a seat. With what I've got planned, you'll need your energy."

She put on a devilish look. "Oh, *really?*"

John

John had been awake for twenty-two hours already and there was no sleep on the horizon, not when a girl could be getting molested/tortured/eaten or god knows what at the hands of god knows who. So, John swung by his house and changed out of his court appearance clothes, downed a mug of coffee, ate two Hostess CupCakes, and finished it off by smoking some crystal meth. Soon he was back behind the wheel of the Ezekiel Jeep and heading toward the church, feeling good as new.

Everybody likes to get preachy about drugs, John thought, because it's a handy way to deflect from their own even worse vices. Dave drank every night and rarely ate a meal that didn't leave a grease stain behind. Amy ran on sugar, caffeine, and pain pills, and would sacrifice an entire night of sleep to level up a character in one of her games. The people with health insurance get antidepressants and Adderall, the rich get cocaine, the clean-living Christians settle for mug after mug of coffee and all-you-can-eat buffets. The reality is that society had gotten too fast, noisy, and stressful for the human brain to process and everybody was ingesting something to either keep up or dull the shame of falling behind. For those few who truly live clean, well, it's the self-righteousness that gets them high.

John headed for Mine's Eye, a spot so scenic that couples actually hold their weddings there. Well, the ones who don't know the backstory, anyway. The little church and several rental cabins sat up on a hill that encircled a small weirdly colored pond. At the base of the hill opposite the church was the entrance to what had been a coal mine back in the 1800s, before it collapsed in a horrific disaster. Nobody ever attempted to reopen it because, you guessed it, the circumstances of the disaster were creepy as shit. The miners had collapsed the shaft in on themselves with dynamite, supposedly in order to stop what was in there from getting out. They had sent out one guy—the youngest—to tell everyone else not to attempt a rescue. The town dealt with it in the usual way, which was to simply put up a sign warning people away and otherwise never think about it again.

The whole area in front of the mine had filled with water over the decades, the mouth now appearing to be frozen in the act of puking loose rocks into the new pond. The minerals in the rock would turn the water emerald green, teal, or cobalt, depending on the color of the sky. So, on a clear day, there'd be this vivid shimmering pool that stood out sharply from the landscape around it, like a magical eye had opened. The church up on the hillside had been built after the collapse, as if someone had planted it there as a safeguard.

John followed a narrow road around the hilltops, passing the cabins and arriving at the church, which had a sign out front with whimsical slogans they swapped out every week (today's: CHOOSE YOUR AFTERLIFE: SMOKING OR NON-SMOKING). John thought the building itself did in fact look like someone had taken a "church" symbol on a map and blown it up to life size—tiny building, white painted wood, ornate doors on the front with a cross and steeple overhead. Two stained-glass windows on either side of the door. It also looked just like Maggie's drawing, though if you grabbed a hundred children and made them draw you a church, they'd all look like that. Again: shitty artists.

John reached the parking lot and found that Dave hadn't arrived yet, so he pulled up to wait for him, keeping an eye out for any horror that might be occurring. He tapped his fingers on the steering wheel. He realized he was clenching his jaw, and forced himself to stop. He grabbed the coins out of the center console. He polished them with his shirt, one by one, then placed them on the seat next to him in order of value and then date minted. He found he was clenching his jaw again—

There was a scream.

He was sure he had heard it. A little girl.

John jumped out of the Jeep. He reached into the

back seat and pulled out the T-shirt cannon. He ran up to the front doors, found them locked, then asked the Lord for forgiveness a split second before he kicked his way through.

Thunder clapped as John stepped through the entryway, shirt cannon at the ready. A half-dozen doves flew past him out the door.

Standing at the pulpit was a thin, shirtless man holding a cigarette.

Ted had described Nymph as a creepy sexual deviant type, but John didn't get that vibe from the guy at all. He had slicked-back hair and narrow, dismissive eyes—he struck John as a cutthroat stockbroker type, a guy who would sever a friendship over a lost game of racquetball. A small man, but wiry. Tight, compact muscles.

The wind picked up and the walls creaked under the strain. The rain went horizontal, spraying into the open door behind John. He slammed the door closed behind him with a backward kick.

John said, "Mister Nymph, I presume?"

The guy took a drag off his cigarette and said, "Congratulations on following a series of groaningly obvious clues. When you enter a room, do you see little equations flying around in front of your eyes?"

John brandished the gun. "WHERE IS SHE?!?"

"You tell me, John."

"You've heard of us."

"I have."

"Is that why you took the girl? To lure us in? Well, you've got us. Let her go. There's no reason to involve anyone else."

"Yes, we wouldn't want to traumatize poor Ted any

further, would we? Do you know why soldiers march in unison? Or why they are compelled to chant in groups? It's a form of hypnosis, it overrides the brain's critical thinking centers. It's the same reason we make schoolchildren shout the Pledge of Allegiance every morning. But, so difficult to adjust after the programming wears off. Tragic, really. And no, John, it turns out that in fact there exist things in this universe that are not about you."

Lightning flashed and brought a clap of thunder a half-second later. Close. The wind picked up again. Outside, a branch was wrenched off of a tree.

"What is it you want, then?"

"The same as all of us want. To feed and to breed. Do you wish to guess which I intend for little Margaret Knoll? Perhaps both."

"She's still alive."

Nymph took a drag off his cigarette. "Tell me, John. Do you believe in the existence of the human soul?"

"Oh, Jesus, I do not have time for this shit." Another blast of wind outside. Something heavy smacked into the wall. The ground shook with what John was certain was the impact of an entire tree collapsing nearby. The storm, bursting free of its restraints. "I don't think *you* have a soul, how about that?"

"Now we're getting somewhere! Why don't you think I have a soul?"

"Because you're a sick fuck who kills little girls."

"That tree that just fell—did it have a soul?"

"You're stalling. I'm not playing your game."

Nymph didn't answer, just stared and waited for John's reply. His silence, of course, made the statement for him: *You don't have any choice but to play.*

John growled, "No, a tree doesn't have a soul that I know of, but I also don't give a shit."

"Of course it doesn't. It's just a series of chemical reactions. Sun, water, air. It cannot refuse sunlight on moral grounds, or share water with a more deserving tree. It's just a machine that soaks up whatever sustenance it encounters."

The wind had become a steady howl, a sustained assault that whistled around the corners of the structure. There was a noise like something tearing loose from the roof.

"I get it," said John, now having to raise his voice to be heard over the maelstrom. "Trees are stupid. *Where is the girl?* Maggie, can you hear me?"

"Does a maggot have a soul?"

"Is this conversation going the way you planned it in your head? Do you sound clever, like an evil mastermind? Because if this was a video game cut scene I'd be skipping past all this shit."

"Of course, a maggot is no more ensouled than a tree; put it on a piece of rotting flesh, and it will eat. The concept of *not* eating what is in front of it is utterly alien. So what about you? Do you have a soul?"

"Dave is going to be here any second. If I were you, I'd start cooperating before he walks through that door. See, I don't think he cares about getting answers. I think he just wants to see you bleed. I think he gets off on it."

Undeterred, Nymph said, "Did you know that you can do a simple test to detect if a child has a soul? They did the experiment in the 1960s—you simply set an Oreo cookie on the table in front of them, tell them not to eat it, then leave the room. Some will resist until you return, the rest will reach out and eat it within minutes, or seconds. Follow up with that latter group decades later and you'll find they're all drug addicts, or in jail, or bankrupt. Because they are maggots, you see. Tell me, John, would you have passed this test?"

John could barely hear the man—the storm was now an enormous animal frantically gnawing away at the wooden shell of the church to get to the soft meat inside. John edged toward Nymph. He would only get one shot at this—meaning his weapon literally only had one shot.

Nymph said, "We know the answer to that, don't we? You undergo that test every single day. But I've wasted enough of your time. Why don't we go somewhere and talk this over like reasonable men? We're both reasonable men, aren't we?"

Nymph stepped out from behind the podium. He was wearing nothing except for a tiny pair of little girls' panties, which did nothing to conceal his massive erection.

The wind made the exact sound you hear when a freight train runs over your face.

John ran at Nymph.

With a hellish noise, the roof was ripped from the building.

Me

I wrestled with the decision for a few blocks but eventually decided to swing around and head for the apartment to get Amy. The wind was picking up and the storm was kind of getting scary—other cars had pulled off the road completely, the drivers such pussies that they refused to drive unless they could actually see the road. When I made it home and climbed to the top of the dildo store, I noticed that the neon sign had gone dark—the power must have gone out. I entered quietly and thought I'd find Amy asleep, but a quick search revealed she wasn't home.

This wasn't too alarming. She couldn't drive, but she still had lots of options. She could have hung back at work so as not to get out into the storm, or the dude giving her a ride may have had to run an errand on the way. She could have walked over to the convenience store across the street to get some junk food . . .

I noticed there were dishes in the sink. Used and then washed. A mixing bowl, a whisk, *two plates*. Had she invited that guy from work in for breakfast? If you don't know Amy, let me catch you up: that is absolutely not the kind of thing she does. Maybe the guy insisted? A box of Bisquick and a plastic bottle of pancake syrup were sitting on the counter. I tried to picture this dude insisting he come in—to *our* apartment—to make Amy pancakes, in *our* kitchen, and her agreeing to that . . .

My brain just froze up. I mean, if they had just succumbed to passion and banged in my bed, I could understand that. I wouldn't even be mad, as long as Amy was happy and they cleaned up afterward. But coming into another man's house and making breakfast for his girl in his own kitchen? That's some serial killer shit. Maybe somebody else stopped by? That's probably all it was. Hell, it's the sort of thing that on a different day, wouldn't have triggered a second thought.

I looked around for a note—Amy is big on leaving notes—and checked my phone to make sure I hadn't missed a message. Nothing.

I just stood in the middle of the kitchen for a moment, rain and wind crashing against the windows. I wasn't *worried,* necessarily. What, like the bad guys came for her and made her breakfast first?

I pulled out my phone and tried to call.

I got a voice telling me the network was down.

John

John flinched at the cacophony overhead, then looked up to see only sky. The entire roof of the church had been raggedly peeled off like the top on a box of macaroni and cheese mix. The storm washed in and it was like he'd stuck his head into the water going seventy miles an hour on a Jet Ski.

Half blind, John stumbled forward and reached the pulpit, trying to shield his eyes. Nymph wasn't there, but there was a door in the wall beyond. John reached it and found himself in a small break room. Another door to the outside was standing open. John pushed through, into the storm, in time to see taillights swimming into the distance.

John sprinted around to the Jeep and tore through the storm in pursuit. The visibility was so poor he had no idea if they were even on a road—all he could see were those blurry taillights on Nymph's car, a tiny black convertible. John didn't even consider backing off.

He didn't know who or what Nymph was and didn't

particularly care. What John had learned was that anything and everything in this universe feels pain. It's the universal constant, it's what keeps us in check. In his time doing this job, John had learned how to inflict all types of pain, on all types of creatures. For some it was a blade, for others sunlight, or the sound of a wind chime on a summer day.

John would catch Nymph, and he would find out what caused Nymph pain.

The taillights swerved and jerked in John's windshield and each time, John followed them. The car ran off the road and back on again, tires briefly spinning for traction on the muddy shoulder. Whatever Nymph was, John knew this: the guy had chosen the wrong vehicle for this pursuit. His little sports car lost speed in the muck and nearly hydroplaned when it hit standing water on the pavement, while John's Jeep plowed ever forward.

Finally, Nymph made the mistake John had been waiting for. On a long stretch of clear road, Nymph had floored it, racing off into the distance for a few seconds before he hit a large puddle and lost traction completely— John just saw a wild spray of white water, the taillights whipping left and then right—

The crash was over before John's brain could even register what was happening. First, the little black sports car swerved right into a utility pole head-on, the taillights bouncing on impact. A split second later, John smashed into the sports car, compressing it into the pole like a beer can. Between the two vehicles, it was no contest—the Jeep had crushed the fragile little convertible to half its size. It didn't even bend the Jeep's bumper guards.

For a moment, all was still. John's fingers were locked in a death grip around his steering wheel. Steam hissed from an exploded radiator—Nymph's, not his. The wind had calmed and once again it was just the steady rain, as if the gods' lust for violence had been appeased with a sacrifice. John gathered himself, yanked off his seat belt, and stumbled up to the driver's side door of the sports car. He reared back with an elbow and smashed the window.

Empty.

No Nymph in the driver's side, or passenger side, or the floorboard. No break in the windshield where he could have flown through on impact. Nothing.

John stomped back toward the Jeep—

Blood.

Dripping from the rear bumper.

No.

A little sports car like that wouldn't have much of a trunk in the best of times, but now it had been crumpled into a mangled space no more than a foot wide. The lid sat loosely on top, and under it John could see . . .

the little girl looking mangled and bloody

. . . something, but it was impossible to know, in the rain. If he never lifted the lid and got a closer look, maybe he could go the rest of his life never knowing what was in there. Like Schrödinger's cat, only by seeing what was in the trunk would it become real.

John slowly lifted the lid and he saw bloody little hands bound at the wrists by duct tape and a round little face with its mouth taped shut. A tangle of blond hair. Terrified eyes, wide open.

Dead eyes.

Margaret "Maggie" Knoll. Her fragile body obliterated on impact.

John's heart was hammering. He couldn't breathe.

He gently lowered the trunk lid, then growled and slammed his fist into the roof of the car, again and again. He was screaming now. Somewhere, he thought he could hear Nymph laughing.

John was making so much noise, in fact, that he almost didn't hear when a man said from behind him, "Did you get him? Did you get Nymph?"

John turned, and saw Ted Knoll.

6. THE RAIN CONTINUES, AND ALSO JOHN DIES

Ted was holding his shotgun, the barrel aimed down at the splattery pavement. John said nothing.

"I saw you tearing ass down the street, I was comin' the opposite way, recognized your crazy Jeep. I did a bootleg turn and followed as best I could . . ." Ted looked over the wreck. "Is this his? Is Nymph in there?"

John still couldn't speak.

"Hey, man, are you hurt? Talk to me."

Ted took a step forward.

He saw the blood.

He looked at the trunk, then he looked at John. Piecing it together.

John said, "Don't look in there, man. Don't."

"What? Is . . . is it . . ."

Ted edged up to the car, the gun still pointed at his feet.

"Don't, man."

Ted turned and met John's eyes. Just stared at him, his face a cracked dam holding back a flood of contempt. Making very deliberate movements, Ted slowly opened the trunk and took in what he saw inside.

John watched Ted's face. The whole mental process didn't take more than a minute. The man stared into the trunk, let the reality of it sink in, then squeezed his eyes shut and worked his jaw.

Then he calmly closed the trunk and, without turning around, said softly, "I thought I told you to call me. If you found Nymph. I said to call me, instead of trying to handle it yourself."

"There was no time, I—"

"Do you know why I asked you to do that? To call me?"

"If I'd had a chance—"

"Because," said Ted, sounding like he was using every ounce of his strength to contain himself, "this wasn't a matter of who gets credit for taking down the bad man. This was about getting my daughter back. *My* daughter. Not yours. And unlike you, *I have actual training.*"

"It wasn't my fault. Nymph, he took off, I followed, I thought I could tail him back to where he was keeping—"

"What training do *you* have? For anything? What have you worked hard for, your entire life? You sit at home and you play your games and you do your drugs and then when the shit goes down, you fall apart and people die. Because you don't have the necessary skills, because practice is boring."

"Listen, the guy who did this is still—"

"Shut the fuck up."

Ted raised the shotgun. Pointing it right at John's face. The father of the dead child bared his clenched teeth, rage and despair wearing the rest of him like a suit.

John put up his hands. "Whoa! Look, calm down. I'm not who you're angry at here—"

"We used to have this saying in the marines. 'Ten, ten, eighty.' Ten percent of people are heroes, ten percent are assholes, and eighty percent are nothing. Just blobs that go along. Leeches. Sheep. You understand? The world isn't in the shitty state it's in because of people like Nymph. It's *because of people like you*."

"You're not thinking straight! You're—hey! What's the password?"

"What do you think this is? It's 'bushmaster.' And this is for Maggie."

Ted fired. John ducked, not sure if the shot had missed or if he just hadn't felt himself die yet. Without pausing to find out which, John lunged for the gun. He didn't have a plan, he just wanted that barrel pointed in any other direction.

He got his hands around the shotgun and shoved the barrel up, aiming it at the sky. John's and Ted's limbs tangled and they went to the ground along the shoulder of the highway, splashing in the mud. Ted rolled over on top of John, rivulets cascading down around the man's face, his crazed eyes just inches away. The hot barrel of the gun was between them, touching John's chin.

John growled and gritted his teeth and tried to shove off his attacker—

BANG.

And then there was a spray of warm blood and Ted Knoll's face was gone.

Me

I waited for the storm to calm and then headed for the church at Mine's Eye, passing downed trees and severed limbs. When I got to the church, I found that their sign with the clever slogans had been crushed by a fallen tree. The roof of the church had also been damaged and rain was cascading in; I didn't know if that part was because of the storm or something John had done (his methods aren't subtle). Otherwise, there was no sign of John or his vehicle. Had he already come and gone? Maybe he went somewhere to ride out the storm? Then I noticed the tire tracks—deep ruts and sprays of mud dug by a vehicle peeling out across a wet lawn. I could see where the tracks joined the inlet road that curved around the mine. This looked a hell of a lot like a pursuit. I checked my phone and again got the "no network" message.

I followed the road for a stretch but found nothing and soon I was passing multiple points where a chase could have branched off in different directions. Eventually I just took two left turns and got pointed back toward town again.

Well, shit. I've lost Amy and I've lost John, within five minutes. By this afternoon I'll be the last non-missing person in Undisclosed.

Could they be together somewhere? Maybe he's the one who dropped by to have breakfast? I was lost, which as you're probably gathering, is something of a regular state of being for me.

My phone dinged the sound of an incoming text

message—the cell network back up, apparently—and I got a text from John that said, simply:

girls dead

And then it dinged again with a second message:

find nymph

And then, after some hesitation, a third:

im sorry

I called, he didn't answer. I texted back asking him to clarify:

fuck?

I slammed on the brakes and did a U-turn in front of a honking car. I headed to John's house, the only place I could think to find him.

What I fear most in this "job" (the sarcasm quotes are there to denote the absence of a paycheck) isn't some lumbering horror smashing its way through my windows. It's the groupies—obsessed fans who make the journey to Undisclosed based on the legends, like they expect to find a bus running monster tours around town. They come to try to get a glimpse of us, or to ask us to solve their problems and/or to tell them scary stories. This is why I never disclose the name of the town—the way I see it, the monsters might try to eat your soul, but at least they don't feel like they're owed anything.

That's why I like to move around. From one apartment to the next, places that don't require a lease, rarely leaving forwarding addresses (not that I don't still get my packages—the local postal workers know who I am, they make sure the bullshit arrives). John, on the other hand, bought a two-story house in town and proceeded to paint the entire thing flat black, from top to bottom, including the roof and the windows. He joked that he was turning it into a stealth house, but of course the intention was the opposite. Every weirdo who managed to reverse engineer our location could spot that place from a mile away.

I pulled up to that black house, John's Jeep in the driveway. I went around to the other parking spot at the rear and headed to the back door, hearing the dog yapping from inside. I wondered if I'd have to kick that door down, but it was unlocked. I turned the knob and prepared to be incinerated.

Oh, that's the other thing: John's entire house is now booby-trapped. The doors, for instance, are surrounded by four nozzles that *in theory* will fire four jets of propane-fueled flames, instantly turning any intruder into an intruder who is on fire. Won't this almost certainly catch the exterior of the house on fire, you ask? Yep. And, once the flaming intruder stumbles inside, the interior of the house will also be on fire. When I raised these concerns to John he simply said, "It'd be worth it."

I stepped inside, found that I was not ablaze, and

called out to John. No reply. His Yorkshire terrier—named Diogee—was at my ankles, barking his stupid head off. I told him to shut up. I started to reach down to him, then noticed I had the pink Disney phone in my hand. I'd grabbed it before I'd left the car, apparently, though I couldn't fathom why. I tossed it aside.

In the photo on Nymph's phone, John was sprawled on the sofa, a cascade of dried vomit from his body having desperately spasmed out its contents prior to death . . .

Entering from the back meant passing through the kitchen and into a partially open dining room/living room space that John had turned into what he called the "parlor." John had decorated his home—either by accident or on purpose—to look like a more affordable replica of a rich person's house in a 1980s action movie. Furniture of black "leather," chrome and glass end tables, massive sound system surrounding an even bigger TV, both purchased used. It was unspeakably awesome, in my opinion—cocaine decor on a crack budget.

John and I don't talk about finances, just like we don't talk about a lot of things. Each of us could see the argument lurking in the dark, so we just never flip on the light. I said earlier that there are reasons I don't try to cash in on the freak show aspect of our lives, but those are *my* reasons, not his. John was never much for the nine-to-five and I have caught wind of him doing everything from charging for e-mail "consultations" for haunting victims to selling T-shirts. Occasionally, he'll ask if I want in on it and I'll say no, and assume he knows I mean I don't want it to happen at all. He takes it to mean I just didn't want any of the money . . .

The living room area was just ahead, the sofa

obscured from view behind a section of wall to my right. I didn't move. I knew I was stalling. I didn't care.

In the photo there were drugs on the glass coffee table, a variety of them, an overdose buffet . . .

I called out for John a second time, and once again got no answer. I didn't expect one.

Where a lesser person would have had a dining room table, John had a pool table. On the green surface were painted the words: IN HERE? DOOM. I ran my hand along the felt as I glanced around the room. One end of the pool table was too close to the wall, and you couldn't extend your cue fully on the shots—it was a key part of the strategy to keep your balls away from that rail. The white wall bore scuff marks from the butts of cues striking it on the backswing, each mark representing a ruined shot. In the corner were stains on the carpet from where Crystal and Nicky had spent two hours on the body-paint job that would get John arrested (it was Halloween, all right?). On the ceiling was a faint chili stain from the rowdy aftermath of Guilty Pleasure Movie Night (Amy's had been *Twilight,* mine was *Weird Science,* John's was *Dude, Where's My Car?*). All these memories. Maybe I'll just stand here forever, thinking about them, instead of going into the living room and seeing what's in there. I thought, *If you never look, it's never real* and for some reason I heard it in John's voice.

Peering into the living room, I could see where above the mantel of the fireplace John had mounted two huge chainsaws, their thirty-six-inch blades forming an X. Diogee was still yapping away, bouncing on his little paws with each bark. It was driving me fucking crazy.

I forced my legs to move.

The sofa slowly came into view and I saw the bottom of one of John's Converse All Stars jutting out over the armrest. Lying at an unnatural angle, not moving. I could smell the gut-turning odor of a body that had purged itself at the moment of catastrophic failure.

I came around and there he was, and there was the stream of drying vomit, and there on the coffee table was a lightbulb with a plastic straw jutting out the back—a homemade pipe. One half of the bulb was charred from where he'd touched it with the lighter, again and again. And there was a bottle of pills and there was a syringe full of . . . whatever. This was not the aftermath of a quick midday pick-me-up. This was someone coming home and cooking up a combination intended specifically to stop his heart in a way that would be painless. I know, because I had spent some time researching the method myself.

I felt for a pulse. No need. He was cold.

Half of my universe went dark.

I collapsed into the black leatherish chair opposite the sofa. The dog, maybe sensing my mood, finally stopped barking.

im sorry

His last words had been a fucking text message.

I would have to tell Amy. I tried to imagine the conversation. I would have to track down John's father in whatever city his rockabilly band was playing. I would have to track down his brother, assuming he's still alive. I would have to help arrange for a funeral and go through John's stuff. Or maybe I wouldn't have to do any of those things. Maybe I didn't owe him any of that, because he had abandoned me. After he had talked me down half a dozen times, here he was taking the same easy way out he'd scolded me for. That was his final message. "It turns out, you were right. There is no other escape."

Why don't you just fucking—

There was a noise, from the direction of the bedrooms.

Footsteps.

7. THE BATTLE OF JOHN'S LIVING ROOM

John walked into the room carrying a package of cookies. He said, "Hey, do you like Oreos? There's something I want to try."

I jumped out of the chair and backed up, toward the kitchen. I looked back and forth from Dead John to Alive John.

I said, "Back the fuck up!"

John gestured toward the corpse with a cookie and said, "He's not real."

"What's the password?"

"It's 'bushmaster' but that doesn't matter. He knew it, too, and the real Ted is still alive. The password thing doesn't work, the clones or doppelgangers can imitate that, the same as everything else. I think they can dig into your brain or something."

I said, "Don't move."

I cautiously approached and poked the standing John with a finger, to see if he seemed solid. He did. To be sure, I wrapped my arms around his torso and squeezed, to detect any anomalous reaction. I found none.

"Okay. Yes, it is good that you are not dead. That is a positive. Wait, what's this about Ted?"

John glanced down at the sofa. "Wait, who do you see there?"

"I see *you*. Dead from a drug cocktail."

"Huh. I see Ted. Face blown off. From when I shot him."

"From when you *what*?"

John circled back and told me the entire story. I dropped back into the armchair, staring off into the middle distance, trying to make sense of it all.

"First of all, the entire roof of the church didn't blow off, I was there afterward. It was one corner, a few chunks of roofing and plywood. Second, did you say when you opened the door that *doves* flew out? Like in a John Woo film? Are you trying to parlay this series of events into a movie deal?"

"What matters is, I find out five minutes later that the real Ted is still alive. I talked to him. It was the exact kind of trick we were expecting. It's kind of encouraging, I feel like we were ahead of them this time."

"Wait, now how do you know the alive Ted is the real Ted? If the password thing doesn't work . . ."

"What you really mean is, how do you know I'm me and that's not really me there on the sofa, if the 'password thing' doesn't work."

"Oh. Shit. Wait, if you were the doppelganger, why would you tell me the password system doesn't work? You'd have kept that to yourself, to use against me."

"Maybe I'm stupid."

"The fucking conversations we have. Okay, how

109

about this—I ask you something that John would know, but that I or a replicant would have no way of knowing. Something we can verify, right now."

"Like what?"

"Where's your drug stash?"

"Why Dave, you know that I would never—"

"Goddamnit, John."

"Owl jar above the toilet. That way if I have to flush it, it's right there."

A trip to the bathroom confirmed this was true.

When I returned, John continued, "As for me and Ted, he just showed up out in the middle of nowhere. His car wasn't there, he just kind of materialized behind me. That's the thing—it used my state of mind against me. I was in such a panic, the whole flimsiness of the pretext was hidden from me until way later."

"And then you killed him. Or it. Whatever kind of shape-shifter this is, it can be killed, is my point. And it stays dead."

"Shot to the face. Pretty straightforward."

"Yeah, nobody likes that." I looked over at the corpse on the sofa. "So . . . what is it? Specifically? I mean, there's what each of us is seeing and then there's what it actually is."

"Something new, maybe? We'll need to come up with a name for it. It's my turn."

"Later." The naming of new creatures we encounter is something of a contentious issue. "For now, what do we do with it?"

He thought for a moment. "I wish we could get it to Marconi."

That's Dr. Albert Marconi. A famous expert in this

sort of thing. He rarely returns our calls.

I said, "Sure, let's just cram it into a box and mail it to him. Wait, how did you get it back here?"

"In the Jeep."

"Did you throw the corpse in your Jeep and drive it back here *after* you figured it out it wasn't Ted Knoll's body, or before?"

"What was I supposed to do? Leave him out in the rain?"

"But if you thought it was just a dead guy, a guy *you* shot, shouldn't you have called the . . . you know what, forget it."

John said, "We need Amy's brain on this. Is she still at work?"

"No, I don't know where she is."

"Wait, Amy's *missing*? Why are we dicking around here then?"

"She's not missing, she's out with somebody. They swung by and had breakfast, apparently. I don't know where they went. Phones were down."

"Who's she with?"

"I don't know. I thought maybe she was with you."

"You're not worried?"

"It's not like she was abducted, they ate a meal together."

"Like she left with somebody she knew, you mean. Or something she *thought was someone she knew*."

"Oh . . . fuck. FUCK!"

I dug out my phone and dialed. It rang through, but she wasn't answering.

"So help me, John, if all this shit was just a diversion so they could take Amy—"

Something grabbed my wrist.

It was John. The dead one, from the sofa.

Dead John's mouth opened so wide that his head was about to split in half. Then a second, vertical slit opened from his chin to forehead, his entire face opening like a blooming flower. His skull was hollow, the inside covered in tiny wiggling filaments.

The thing howled with its whole face. The floor shook.

I grabbed at the fingers clutching my arm. Some of the fingers came off, then grew tiny wings and flew away. I was only mildly surprised by that.

Dead John's body contorted as if it was a clay model that a giant pair of invisible hands had decided to give up on and start over. For the briefest moment, I saw what I thought was a pulsing swarm of small creatures, each about the size of my palm. But then they were gone and so was John. A new figure replaced him.

John screamed, "Nymph!"

Ted had described Nymph as a foppish sexual deviant; John had described him as a sleazy stockbroker type. To me, he looked . . . like me.

Not exactly me—a fit, tan, healthy version of me, with an expensive haircut. A version of me that hadn't gone off the rails. Wearing a nice shirt and pants instead of a stained T-shirt and cargo shorts. Yet, I saw my own eyes, and the scar on my cheek.

He said, "Greetings, knucklefuckers!"

John said, "Where's the little girl? And where's Amy?"

Nymph smirked and said, "The Master must feed."

"I don't care what you named your dick, this shit ends now."

"Indeed it does!" said Nymph. "Granted, the mere chewing of their flesh takes only sixty-six days. But once consumed, their souls live conscious in the belly forever, for it is their anguish that nourishes the Master. But don't worry, I will release one of the two, of your choosing. At this moment, I am posing this same dilemma to the mother and father of little Margaret. The four of you are voting. The girl with three votes will be released, the other's screams will echo through eternity. If no one receives a majority vote, both will be consumed. Someone must vote against their own, to save another. So what will it be? You have one minute to decide."

I said, "Wait! What if we refuse to vote? What if everyone refuses—"

"Then the Master will gorge on a double portion. Is your vote for your Amy? That is a vote to sentence a child to an eternity of torment. How will your Amy live with that choice, I wonder?"

I said, "Take me instead. Let both of them go, and take me."

He did that smirking head-tilt thing douchebags do. "Come on, even you must know that your meat is tainted."

John said, "I vote for both of them to go free!"

I said, "Yeah, me, too!"

"That is not one of the options." Nymph looked at his wrist. He was not wearing a watch. "Forty-five seconds! Of course, the confounding factor is how little Maggie's parents will vote. Perhaps, anticipating that you, as selfish assholes, will vote for your Amy, they will as well, knowing that then at least one can be saved."

John said, "Wait! I vote that the monster eats you."

I said, "I vote that the monster eats itself!"

"THOSE ARE NOT THE FUCKING CHOICES. Thirty seconds."

I said, "All right, I'm voting Amy goes free."

John said, "No, the monster is right, even if Maggie's parents vote the same, there's no way Amy can live with herself knowing she's alive because some other little girl is getting chewed up forever."

"There's no way she can live with herself if she's dead. And you'd be surprised what a person can get over if given enough time to think up rationalizations."

"No, I wouldn't."

"Ten! Nine! Eight!"

I said, "John, you have to vote! Wait, does Diogee get a vote?"

John said, "I vote for—"

My phone rang.

The screen said it was Amy. I answered.

"Amy! Is that you!?!"

Nymph's mouth snapped shut in mid countdown. He had not been anticipating this.

Amy said, "Hey, I've got a little girl here. She's fine, but I need you to come and get us."

"Amy! Listen to me! There's something after you! You and the little girl both! You need to—"

"I've taken care of it, we're fine, we're at that church by the old coal mine. Oh, and I need you to stop by Walgreens and pick up my prescription, they said it's ready. And can you get me a bag of those chocolate-covered pretzels while you're there?"

John

John heard Dave say, "Amy, is that you?" and felt the world shift on its axis. Nymph, standing there with his Gordon Gekko suit and slicked-back hair, sneered and turned in Dave's direction. The call had clearly not been part of his plan. John saw his opportunity.

John lunged for one of the chainsaws above the mantel. They were very much not just there for decoration (even if, as decoration, John thought they kicked serious ass)—they were always oiled and gassed up, ready to go. See, one thing John had learned about the various creatures they'd faced over the years was that almost none of them liked being sawed in half by motorized metal teeth. Simple biology, really.

John grabbed the chainsaw and performed a move he had spent hours practicing. In one continuous motion, he started the motor, spun, and swept it through Nymph's midsection.

He met very little resistance. The whirring blade buzzed horizontally through the man's belly . . . and then the top half of him was nowhere to be found. Everything above Nymph's navel just *dispersed*. What had been his torso was now a swarm of fist-sized buzzing creatures, whizzing frantically around the room.

John looked back at where Nymph was standing and saw that half of him was still there—everything from the waist down remained where it had been, including the man's expensive slacks and patent leather shoes. The legs started walking toward John on their own, then one of them whipped upward and kicked the chainsaw from John's hand.

Disarmed, John lunged forward and grabbed Nymph's lower body by its belt loops, intending to lift up the legs and chuck them across the room. Then they, too, began to dissolve, from the bottom up—Nymph's feet dispersed into those flying insects, which still appeared to be made of black polished leather. The ankles were next.

John followed the flight paths and saw that the shape-shifter swarm was swirling toward the far corner of the room. There, they were quickly re-forming into something new.

Something made for fighting.

John saw teeth and claws and spiked armor.

John screamed, "DAVE! GET THE—"

But as usual, Dave was already five seconds ahead of the situation. He had the T-shirt cannon in his hands and was already aiming it at the rapidly assembling creature in the corner. Dave aimed carefully.

One shot, Dave.

The cannon's payload was not, in fact, a T-shirt. It contained the Shroud of Turin—the legendary piece of cloth that the body of Christ was wrapped in after crucifixion. Experts were divided as to whether or not the shroud was real or a fake produced during the Middle Ages, an era when selling "holy" relics was all the rage. That was probably why John had managed to buy it for just $150 off eBay, which he thought was a good price either way (listing: $$$ ACTUAL SHROUD OF TAURINE—STAINED WITH SWEAT OF JESUZ—GOOD CONDITION—FREE SHIPPING—WOW!! $$$).

John was still uselessly clutching the hips of the rapidly disintegrating Nymph—his legs almost entirely gone now—and watched as Dave fired the shroud. It worked perfectly—the projectile unfurled itself in midair, the white cloth stained with the image of a knife-wielding Christ enveloping the creature.

The monster howled, the contact with the holy artifact burning it and binding it. John, still holding his remaining hunk of Nymph, ran over to it and with a scream of rage, mercilessly beat Nymph with his own ass.

The insect creatures dispersed. The swarm fled toward the open back door.

John dove toward a brass switch on the wall. He flipped it—

Flames roared from the four corners of the door frame. The bugs flew through the blaze and tumbled burning onto the lawn, shriveling up like lit tissues.

John watched them burn, and yelled . . .

Me

"And don't make me *ass* you again!"

Amy made a skeptical noise and I said, "Just . . . go with it. That's mostly what happened. It was really confusing."

Amy said, "I can't breathe, you're squeezing me." I released about 20 percent of the hug but kept my arms around her.

We had rolled up to the church at Mine's Eye to find Amy sitting under the portico of the front entrance with Maggie Knoll, both of them looking like they'd just swam up out of the ocean. Maggie seemed sluggish, like she'd been drugged, staring off into space. She was shivering and seemed to know only that she was wet and cold and wanted to go home.

Amy pulled away and said, "She was down there, around the mouth of the mine. Hidden under the water."

I said, "Really? How did she, you know, breathe?"

"They had an apparatus hooked up."

John said, "I can see it now—she wasn't drawing a picture of where she was going to be held. She was drawing a picture of what she would see—the view of the church, as seen from down there, under the water. Maybe she had dreams of it happening in advance or something."

We were talking about Maggie as if she wasn't sitting right there, but she made no effort to shed light on the situation. She had this blank look and I had the alarming thought that maybe she had suffered brain damage, from lack of oxygen or god knows what he (or it, or they) had done to her.

John said, "I was so close. Right here where we're standing."

I said, "To be fair, when searching for the lair of an unholy creature of the night, who would have ever thought to look around the haunted old coal mine?"

"I would have figured it out! The thing with Nymph got in the way. That's probably what he was doing, leading me away from her."

Amy was already walking away with Maggie. "Let's get her home, her parents are probably worried sick. David, can you drive the Impala?"

"The what?"

I saw she was walking toward Ted Knoll's cherry-red muscle car, which was parked behind the church—the car he had reported stolen earlier today. Amy climbed into the back seat so she could be there with Maggie for the trip, putting her arm around her and trying to keep her warm. Maggie laid her head on Amy's chest and closed her eyes.

I slid into the Impala, John went to the Jeep. In the back seat, Amy closed her eyes, like she was just going to doze off back there. As if I didn't still have a thousand lingering questions about all this.

I said, "So, you figured this out all on your own? How'd you even get out here? Who drove the car?"

She heard me, I know she did, but there was this long moment before she answered. Almost as if, say, she was quickly trying to come up with a cover story on the fly.

She said, "I came home from work, and there was a . . . thing there. Pretending to be you."

"Wait, what? Holy *shit,* Amy."

"I saw through it right away, it was all wrong. I tried to get away, but it put me in the car and took me out here. Probably was going to stuff me under the water with her and whoever else he collected."

"*Jesus.* I . . . Amy, I should have come right back home, I should have known they would come after you."

She closed her eyes again and said, "So, I got away and I was able to get her up out of the water and up the hill. Then I called you. That was it. I thought it would come after me but maybe it couldn't. Maybe the church repels it or something."

"You 'got away'?"

She didn't respond, even though it was clear I was asking for her to complete the story.

I said, "Amy? That's really all there was to it?"

"Yeah that's . . . mostly what happened."

We rode in silence the rest of the way to the Knoll house, shockingly only about five hours after I had been awakened by the call from John. Now, if John was telling this story, he'd probably say that the moment we arrived, the rain stopped and the clouds parted, as if the weather changed for everyone else just to reflect our personal triumphs and failures. But it didn't, it was that same drumming rain that had been slowly turning the town into brown gravy for the last month. I wondered if Maggie and her parents were going to have to celebrate her rescue by evacuating to higher ground.

Amy took Maggie by the hand and led her up to the front door. John and I followed. Ted and Loretta both came to the door, for one morning the couple having reconciled in the face of the outside threat. Loretta threw her arms around her daughter and Ted threw his arms around them both.

I said, "Did Nymph appear here? Demanding you and Loretta pick which girl gets saved?"

Ted said, "No," and Loretta shook her head.

Huh. So that had all been bullshit.

He said, "You get the son of a bitch?"

John said, "Let's just say he won't be coming back around. Not after he *made such an ass of himself.*"

"He what? Is he dead or not?"

"Yeah."

Ted said to his daughter, "You hear that, honey? He's all gone. The bad man is gone. You're safe."

She pulled away from her father. "No, he's not! He's right there!"

Maggie turned and pointed directly at me.

BOOK II

An Excerpt from *Fear: Hell's Parasite*
by Dr. Albert Marconi

To understand what occurred, we must ask ourselves a simple question, one which is surprisingly difficult to answer:

Why do we, as humans, have eyes?

Your natural response would be, "To see things, you doddering old fool," but as an answer, that is incomplete to the point of being incorrect. Your eyes fool you on a daily basis because they, quite simply, were designed for a very specific (and for the most part, obsolete) purpose. Remember, the vast majority of species on this planet do not have sight and get along just fine without it; you have no evolutionary need to become aware of the world's general appearance. You, as Homo sapiens, *have eyes primarily so that you can find and kill other living beings.*

The prey we hunted—gazelles and the like—have eyes mounted on the sides of their heads, so that they can see predators coming from all directions. Ours face forward and grant us depth perception, to measure the distance between ourselves and our fleeing dinner. The true, deadly purpose of human sight is also the reason the color red attracts our attention; it is the color of blood, the sight of which would have instantly sent up an internal thrill of alarm or elation, depending on the circumstance. Thus, today you see that hue screaming for your attention from stoplights, fire trucks, and fast-food logos—a calculated appeal to your hardwired bloodlust.

All of this is to say that our sight is very limited, precisely because it is skewed to serve a few specific functions, all of which are geared toward one singular goal:

Survival.

Thus, data that is not immediately relevant to that mission is filtered and discarded—you may have "seen" a thousand automobiles on your commute to work this morning but you will be unable to bring a single one of them to mind—unless, of course, a particular vehicle had swerved into your lane and caused a near-death experience. It is literally a form of tunnel vision, the limits of which you are largely unaware of moment to moment. It is therefore not difficult to circumvent this sense we call vision; even the common flea can effectively vanish before our eyes merely by jumping. It does not take any special intelligence or talent to deceive us. We would do well to remember this.

Now, extend this concept to the way in which you "see" the world in a metaphorical sense; the internal idea you have of the universe as you would describe it to an inquisitive alien. Remember, the brain and consciousness also evolved with survival in mind, to the exclusion of all else. Thus, your mental perception of the universe suffers from this same tunnel vision—it is in no way geared toward producing an objective view of reality; it only produces a view of reality that will help you survive. You will "see" the universe that you need to see. This is not a metaphor; it is an indisputable, biological fact born out of necessity.

Whether you "see" the universe as pure or corrupt, peaceful or violent, just or unjust, is largely determined by what you need to believe in order to motivate yourself to continue living for another day. Your perception of reality is therefore also very easy for other beings to hijack for their purposes. Think of the relationship between a cult leader and his followers. He will isolate them and make them believe they are an island in a sea of depravity, that signs of an eminent apocalypse are all around them. If he is adept at his task, members of the flock will readily lay down their lives in defense against this phantom threat. Ask them why, and they will state that their fatalistic beliefs are merely the result of unbiased, objective observation of the world around them. They are telling the truth! They just do not grasp the fact that they do not believe based on what they observe; they observe based on what they have been tricked into believing.

And so it goes for all of us.

8. ATTACK OF THE FUCKROACHES

Me

John took a bite of a walnut and chocolate-chip pancake and said, "Assuming the little girl wasn't just confused, what does Nymph gain by imitating you when he goes to kidnap her?"

I said, "Trying to find logic in anything They do is like asking what motivates glass to cut your mouth when you try to eat it."

We were at Waffle House, which I felt was a big step down from Denny's, which had been our comfort food refuge for years going back to high school. Our Denny's had never reopened after it burned to the ground a few years ago during an event we refer to only as "The Incident." Losing Denny's was one of those things that I wouldn't have thought would create a hole in my life, but it did (though still not as much as when all the stores in the area stopped carrying Mountain Dew Code Red last year). We'd worried that the Waffle

House had gotten flooded out already, but not only was it open, but the waitress claimed the chain is so famous for staying open during disasters that FEMA has a "Waffle House Index." They can actually judge the scale of a natural disaster by how many Waffle House locations have closed in the area.

Amy was nursing a cup of hot tea, and had made the comment that she was never going to eat waffles again.

I said, "Would you have preferred Taco Bill? I think they're still open."

"Can't stand the smoke. And the only thing I like there is those frozen things. The Choco Taco."

John said, "I wonder if there's a porno by that name."

Amy said, "And I disagree. About there being no logic. We need to find out exactly how and why it does what it does. Everything operates by rules. Everything has limits, everything has a weakness. You just have to understand them."

I noticed that the three of us had in turn referred to Nymph as "he," "they," and "it." I said, "Just to reduce confusion, let's all agree to refer to Nymph as a person, even though we all know he was not actually a person and was some kind of, uh, swarm of bugs that serve something else. The 'Master.' For now, we're going to refer to him as a man, just for simplicity's sake."

John said, "Well, he's not even the problem at the moment, right? The more immediate issue is if Ted goes looking for more evidence and every sign points to you having kidnapped his child."

I shushed John and gave a nervous look around. "Dude, we are in public right now."

"We're in Waffle House. Half the people here are

probably murderers. So, if he can imitate anybody, why not turn himself into her mom, or dad? Wouldn't that make the abduction easier? Going as you is no different from going as himself, you're a stranger to her. Plus, look at you. No little girl is going to follow you anywhere. It's a horrible disguise."

"So, maybe he did it to frame me? Just to be a dick? Look around—cruelty doesn't need a reason." I looked at Amy. "It's like those whales."

Once, Amy and I watched a BBC documentary series about sea life called *The Blue Planet*, because sometimes you just run out of stuff to watch. There was one scene where the crew tracked a gray whale and its newborn calf up the Pacific Ocean. These whales carry their babies for thirteen months, then after giving birth, they have to laboriously migrate thousands of miles north to find food. So, they're slowly swimming up the California coast to Alaska, mother and baby side by side the whole way, like characters in a Pixar movie. But then, a pod of fifteen killer whales comes along—a pack of hunters, silently coordinating as they stealthily surrounded the doting mother and her baby. They swam in and started pushing themselves in between the mother and the child, separating them, and then jumping on top of the calf to try to drown it (remember, whales are mammals that breathe air—they're not just spitting up at the surface for fun). The mother frantically tried to push the baby back up, so it could get a breath. But the killer whales just kept at it, for *six hours,* pushing the sputtering calf down and down again, while its mother watched. Relentless. Finally, they started biting at the infant, the churning water around them blooming bright red.

Then came the twist ending: as soon as the baby was dead, the killer whales just . . . swam away. They took a couple of bites out of it and just let its dead, broken body sink to the bottom. It turned out they weren't hungry; they had just killed a child in front of its mother, purely for fun. The final shot was of this mother whale, drifting aimlessly in the middle of the ocean, utterly alone. The killer whales swam off to live the rest of their lives healthy and happy and completely free of any consequence. There would be no justice for what happened, or even revenge. No one would console the mother. She was now completely devoid of purpose, in an endless, cold, uncaring ocean.

Amy had nightmares about it for six weeks after.

She sipped her tea and said, "Fine, but let's assume for the moment there's more to it. What's his goal?"

I shrugged. "Maybe just what he said. To feed or breed. Or both."

John said, "And he kept taking the Master's 'food' to the pond, which happens to be at the mouth of the old mine. So, being a highly trained expert in this subject, I'm going to go way out on a limb and say that the thing he's trying to feed is in that mine."

I asked Amy, "And you're sure you didn't see anything while you were there?"

"Well, there was this gigantic serpent with a million eyes and a thousand butts but I didn't think it was important so I didn't mention it."

"That'll be enough sarcasm, young lady. That's not helpful."

John said, "How did you get away, again?"

"I had my stun gun, the one you gave me. I waited

until David, or the thing that was pretending to be David, wasn't paying attention and then I zapped him. Right in the crotch. Over and over again. Then I grabbed the girl and we ran up the hill. It didn't follow, like I said."

Why is she lying?

John said, "Is there any chance it let you get away on purpose?"

"You guys seem to find it impossible to comprehend that I could have managed an escape without your help."

I said, "Come on, you know what we're saying here. I can't shake the feeling that everything we've done has been in service to what he wants. That this is all part of his plan."

"Either way," said John, "you know at some point we're going to have to go back to that mine."

"Unless," I said, "*that's* what it wants, and we'd just be opening Pandora's box."

John said, "Now I'm *sure* there's a porno called that."

"Okay, so how long until Ted goes to the cops with his story?"

"If we're lucky, he waits and gathers more information first. If we're unlucky, he's talking to them right now. If we're *really* unlucky, he doesn't go to them at all."

"Why would that be unl—oh, right. It means he intends to come gunning for me in a rampage of cold-blooded vengeance. So, uh, we've got to figure all this out before that happens."

"Okay, I'll get this next cup of coffee to go."

John wanted to stop by his house to "let his dog out" and neither Amy nor I pointed out that the unspoken second half of that sentence was, "And also do some of the drugs that let me stay awake for fifty hours at a time."

Amy and I waited in the Jeep. Once we were alone, I said, "When you were talking to my doppelganger or whatever—how long did it take you to figure out it wasn't me? I mean, you had breakfast with it, right?"

For the second time, Amy looked briefly like she'd been caught. She tried to play it off and said, "Not long. We ate and made small talk for a bit, but I was uneasy the whole time. You had a third arm but I figured maybe I'd just never noticed it before."

"I'm serious, Amy. You and I know each other better than we know anyone else in the world. It's creepy to think you could talk to a fake me through a whole meal before figuring out what was happening."

"You were acting weird, but how weird would somebody have to act before you started thinking 'supernatural imposter' instead of 'oh, they're being a little weird today'? You just seemed like . . ."

She stared at the rain for a moment.

"Like what?"

"Like you were in a really good mood."

"Okay."

"You said you had fixed the leak in the roof."

"Well, that should have tipped you off right there."

I expected her to laugh at this, but she didn't.

John reappeared at his door and, looking frantic, yelled that we had to come in and see something. As always, I felt that emotion for which there is no word in English—a momentary anticipation of something either incredibly dangerous or incredibly stupid. Whether he had found in his home a dozen mutilated corpses or a tomato that was sort of shaped like a dick, John would announce it in the exact same way.

We entered to find Diogee in the corner playing with something—snapping at it and batting it around with his paws. I thought at first it was a little wounded sparrow or hummingbird, but it was, in fact, one of the insect-like flying creatures that had previously been part of Nymph's human "body." It was wounded.

Amy said, "Don't let him eat it!"

I said, "Yeah, it'd probably make him sick, who knows what that thing's guts are made of. Don't touch it with your hands, either—find something sharp you can use to stab it from afar. John, which spears do you still have?"

Amy said, "Wait." She ran into the kitchen and came back with a clear plastic pitcher. "Grab the dog."

John was able to pull the thrashing dog away from its prize and Amy coaxed the little insect creature into the pitcher. She replaced the lid and John ran duct tape around the lip.

Amy said, "I need a knife or something, so we can cut air holes for it."

I said, "Who even says it breathes air?"

John said, "More important, who's to say it can't squeeze out of a hole, even a tiny one? Or that it can't spit venom or something? No, until we figure out what we're dealing with, let's err on the side of keeping it sealed."

John sat the pitcher on his coffee table and we all gathered around. It was hard to get a look at the creature, in the way that it's hard to look at the little bits of lint floating around in front of your eyes—it could almost perfectly blend with the background when it wanted to. Occasionally, it would drop its cover and for just a few seconds we'd glimpse its true body.

It appeared to be a pink, greasy, segmented thing, about the size of a child's hand, its body polka-dotted with shiny black spots (or eyes?) from one end to the other. The spots were hexagonal and, as we watched, they would expand until they covered the creature's body. Then, they would change color and project its camouflage, somehow. Along the bottom were two rows of thin little legs that ended in flexing, hooked feet. It had a large pair of translucent wings like a housefly, one of which had been damaged.

Amy said, "I assume we've never run into one of these before?"

John said, "It's my turn to name it."

I said, "No, John. Not unless you give it a name that actually makes sense."

John is very big on having us name every species and phenomena we come across, insisting that we should take a scientific approach and create a Charles Darwin-esque catalogue of our discoveries. We have to rotate this task because, despite claiming that it's all for science, John also insists on coming up with just horrendously unhelpful names. He was the one who classified a supernatural abduction as a "screaming clown dick," for instance. An insect-like parasite we observed inhabiting a person's mouth and speaking in their voice was dubbed the "flip whippleblip," and the inky black entities with the incomprehensible power to shape reality according to their whims are now known as "night sharts." You might have noticed that his names are too busy being whimsical or profane to actually be descriptive at all, rendering them impossible to remember and thus utterly defeating the purpose.

John thought carefully, then said, "It's limp and pink like a dick, and has wings like an insect. I hereby christen this organism 'the fuckroach.'"

Amy sighed.

The fuckroach buzzed clumsily around inside the pitcher, its gimpy wing having been damaged during our encounter and/or while being chewed on by Diogee. Convinced it couldn't escape its prison, it settled to the bottom and folded its wings over its body.

I said, "Well, Dr. Marconi *definitely* needs to see this."

John said, "I'll try his number." Then he pulled out his knife and started cutting open the pitcher. He was doing it because he needed his phone, and his phone was currently sitting at the bottom of said pitcher, which was otherwise empty.

Amy and I actually watched John slice around the tape and start prying off the lid. Then Amy shook her head like she was waking up from a trance and quickly reached out to snatch John's wrist.

"Wait. *What are we doing?*"

John stopped and all of us stared for a moment. I blinked, and the cell phone became that bug thing again, the image of the phone vanishing into its cluster of black, shimmering eyes. It tried to fly again, bouncing off the lid.

John said, "Okay, that was weird."

I said, "It didn't just make itself look like a phone. It convinced me it *was* a phone. Like, against all other evidence to the contrary."

John said, "It's like it can reach in and just turn off all the logic circuits in your brain. All of your critical thought goes out the window, like in a dream. Suddenly you're back in high school and a parrot with the voice of your gym coach is pulling all of your teeth out with its beak, but the whole time your only thought is: *How am I going to explain this to the dentist?*"

Amy said, "It happened when it put its wings down. I think its body can make it *look* like something else, but when it layers the wings it becomes . . . hypnotic. Or something. I think we need to cover it up. So we can't see it."

John grabbed the American flag blanket from the back of a nearby armchair and tossed it over the coffee table.

I said, "Well, do you even think it works by sight?"

Amy shrugged. "If not, I wouldn't even know where to start, as far as precautions go."

Still, John put it in the closet, just to add one more layer of protection in the form of a flimsy wooden door.

Amy said, "All right, let's shift back into Sherlock mode. The thing wanted out of the pitcher and so turned itself into something that would make us want to free it. See? Even an alien bug thing operates on logic. So, what can we deduce from the other forms it's taken?"

John said, "Well, we know it plays on fear. Ted is a father and he saw a pedophile. I saw a Wall Street type because, as you know, I am concerned about issues of economic justice and class exploitation. Dave, what did you see? A clown? Your landlord? Fred Durst? Vegetarian meatloaf? Your own sexual inadequacy?"

"I saw myself. A cooler, healthier version."

John said, "Well, we'd be here all night unpacking that."

Amy said, "It couldn't fool the dog. It was trying to eat it, so its camouflage couldn't trick him. That's good, right? We've got a, uh, fudge roach detector. He tries to bite somebody, we know to be suspicious."

"Assuming," I said, "that there's more of these things."

"There are. John was dealing with Nymph at the same time I was dealing with the fake you. So yes, there's at least one more person's worth of these things out there."

John said, "There could be at least two more, if they're both midgets."

I could feel a headache coming on. I pressed my fingers to my temples and said, "Or a thousand. I mean, *how deep does this go?*"

Amy sat back on the sofa and ran her hand through her hair. "Well, what matters is we got the little girl back. As far as I'm concerned, that means we won today."

9. ANOTHER CHILD GOES MISSING

It was midafternoon when Amy and I got back home. The overflowing drainage ditches had brought burbling water just twenty feet from the foundation of the dildo store. For a moment, I was thankful we were on the second floor, but if the first floor flooded we couldn't just keep living up there and mocking the peasants drowning in the streets below us. I assumed the power would go out as wiring got submerged, plus the roads would be impassable. So, if the rain didn't stop and the floodwater kept coming, where would we go? I guess the first option would be to stay at John's place, but his neighborhood didn't seem to be on much higher ground than mine and about two days under the same roof would surely mean the end of our friendship.

Amy got out of her wet clothes and collapsed on the bed as soon as we got inside. She had to be back at work at eleven. You know, to keep food on my table. I lay there with her for a while, my arm around her shoulders, her facing away from me.

"Are you . . . okay?"

She muttered, "As okay as is reasonable to expect a person to be after this particular day."

She lay in silence for a bit, while I tried to think of how to phrase this next question.

I said, "The thing that was pretending to be me, my doppelganger . . . it didn't, uh, hurt you, did it? It didn't try to . . . assault you?"

"No. No."

"Okay."

Silence.

"But I know you're not telling me something."

"I swear to god, David, that I've told you every piece of useful information I can remember and if I remember more I'll tell you that, too. But no, I don't feel like reliving every single moment of what happened today. That shouldn't be this hard to understand."

"It's just . . . you don't keep things from me. Ever. That's not you."

"I keep things from you that you don't want to know."

"That's . . . no. Like what?"

"David, I need to sleep. When we fight, I cry, and I get this adrenaline rush and then instead of sleeping I lay here for six straight hours thinking about what we yelled at each other. Just . . . let me sleep."

"I don't want to fight. But, like, what do you keep from me? Just give me an example. What do you feel like you can't tell me? You told me how the painkillers make you constipated, if you were comfortable sharing that—"

"I can't tell you things that are going to send you spiraling into a depression. I mean, just what I'm saying now, I feel like that's enough to do it."

"I'm sorry if I give that impression. But come on, if I told you, 'Amy, there are really important things that I withhold from you,' you'd drive yourself crazy trying to find out what it was. There's nothing I could say that would be worse than what you'd guess. Give me an example, that's all."

She sighed, rubbed her eyes, and said, "We didn't have enough to make rent in February. I had to borrow it from John."

I felt a black ooze of shame bubble up from a drain in my skull.

Hey, she was right!

I tried to formulate the perfect response, one that would reassure her, one that would convince her that she was being silly, that I wasn't so fragile. Twenty minutes later, I was still trying to formulate that response and by then Amy was snoring softly, like she does. I quietly got up and closed the bedroom door.

I went to the bathroom, stood over the sink, just staring at myself in the mirror.

Then it hit me.

There is no drip.

It was still pouring outside, but the ceiling was dry. Wait, did the David doppelganger *actually fix the roof?*

I shuffled back through the kitchen. The breakfast plates in the sink, the syrup. I tried to picture Amy eating breakfast with a functioning copy of me, having a casual conversation with it. The junk had been cleared from the card table—the last round of crap I'd been mailed, the Rodman book and the demon marble, all of it was gone and I didn't see it on the floor. I went to the junk room and, sure enough, the stuff had been stashed away, presumably by my doppelganger. It was now arranged neatly on a shelf right next to the one-armed concrete snowman we always kept in there.

My phone rang. It was John.

I answered, "Fuck you and all the child slaves who manufactured your phone."

"Shit just got real. Turns out there are more."

"More what?"

"Maggie wasn't the only kid to go missing last night. There was at least one more."

"Oooooh, *fuck*."

"Kid belongs to a single mom, report didn't get taken seriously by police dispatch because she sounded out of her mind. Hers got taken around the same time, they think."

"What the hell, John?"

"I got in touch with her, name is Chastity Payton. She's willing to talk to us."

"Of course she is."

"She lives at Camelot Terrace."

"All right. You want to come pick me up?"

"I'm downstairs, in the parking lot."

"Of course you are. Give me a minute."

"One more thing."

"It can't wait thirty seconds until I come downstairs?"

"No. I was getting ready to leave, and I go to grab my keys, but I couldn't remember where I left them. Then I said to myself, 'Oh, I know where they are.' You want to guess where I thought they were?"

"I've totally lost track of the story."

"I was convinced my keys were in the closet, in the pitcher. I could vaguely remember sealing them in there for no reason whatsoever. It was the fuckroach, trying to get me to come let it out."

"Holy shit, that's weird. You can't keep that thing at the house, it's going to mess with your brain."

"What else can I do with it?"

"Yeah, one of these days we should establish some kind of procedure for that. For all of this."

"Anyway, I buried it in the backyard, we'll see if that helps."

I hung up and headed down. John urgently met me at the bottom stair, grabbing my arm and hustling me around the front of the building and through the entrance of the dildo store.

"What the—"

"Ted Knoll just pulled in."

I turned and saw the red Impala slide into a parking space. I assumed he wasn't here for a pair of edible panties. We pushed our way toward the back of the store and hid behind a shelf. Behind us was a huge wall of life-size silicone butts.

"Jesus Christ, John, he couldn't wait one day to go on a vigilante rampage? He should be home with his daughter."

"How long would *you* wait?"

I glanced back at the butts. "What are those for?"

"Dave, I can't emphasize enough how growing up in this town has stunted your worldview."

Ted stepped out of the car, striding through the rain and looking for an entrance to the upstairs apartment. No sign he'd seen us.

John said, "What are we going to do if he goes upstairs? Amy's up there."

"Yeah, we need a plan."

"How about we just go out there and tell him the truth?"

I said, "We don't even know what the truth is. There's another missing kid, so for all we know he has already come across somebody's cell phone video of me mutilating a small—"

A sales clerk walked by and John loudly said, "YES DAVID I AGREE WE SHOULD COVER OUR FLOOR IN RUBBER ASSES."

The front door dinged and in walked Ted. The store was tiny and hiding from him was a ridiculous notion. He made eye contact and strode up to us, saying, "Why don't y'all step outside with me."

I said, "I'm fine right here."

"Suit yourself."

"And you need to think hard about what you're about to do. About whether you really want to do it."

"You a mind reader, now? See, I been busy. Spent all afternoon catching up, reading about you. About this town."

"Ted, you want my advice? *Move.* There can't be anything tying you down here."

"You tellin' me how to live my life now?"

"Think. What's happening, Ted, is *exactly* what we told you to expect when this all started. Mind games. That's all it is. They're framing me for the crime because that's the sort of shit They do for fun."

"Uh-huh. You know, I started lookin' close at my alarm system, I couldn't get past the fact that nothing tripped it, that the cameras went dark at just the right time. I even called Littleton, the company I bought it from, they say everything looked just fine and dandy on their end. But then I talk to that detective, the one that was there this morning, and he tells me offhand that your girl works in the Littleton call center. Really interesting how you never brought that up."

Thanks, Detective.

I said, "You've got to be shitting me. You think, what, I had Amy shut off your alarm? She couldn't even do that if she wanted to." *As far as I know.* "She didn't even know about Maggie until I told her. But I'm not gonna convince you, am I? You're not here to find the truth, you're here to get revenge."

"I'm here because I wanted to look you in the eye. See, in a movie, the tough guy goes on the warpath, he's always got one thing you never get in real life— certainty. Batman stands on a roof and he sees a mugging happen down on the street, always right in front of him. Real convenient, doesn't have to wrestle with doubt, or findin' out he did harm to an innocent person by mistake. No, I'm not doing nothin' until I know for sure. But I *will* know for sure, one way or another. And soon."

"Then what? You kill me, you go to jail, and your little girl doesn't have a father in her life?" I pushed past him and went out the front door. He followed. "I'm telling you, Ted—walk away. Pack up and go, and I mean tonight. For your sake. And your little girl's. Loretta, too."

Ted grabbed my shoulder and spun me around. He stared at me and said, *"Is that a threat?"*

John

Lightning flashed across the sky and John saw the rage illuminated on both men's faces. In that moment, John was sure that one of the two—Dave or Ted—wasn't going home alive.

John said, "Ted, you need to just calm down."

"You keep your enormous cock out of this, John. This is between me and him."

Dave shrugged out of Ted's grip. His eyes narrowed in the way that they did when Dave was feeling that rage fire inside him. It was like he was trying to keep the blaze from flying out of his eye sockets and obliterating everything, Cyclops-style.

Dave gritted his teeth and said, "You've had a trauma, Mr. Knoll. You're not thinking clearly. Trust me, an additional trauma won't make it better. I don't want to fight you, but if you want a fight, I'll give you one." Dave pulled his shirt over his head, exposing the torso of a badly shaved bear. "Look. You see this scar on my chest? That's a bullet wound. You see this scar on my shoulder? That's a knife wound—I did that one myself. See the one on my cheek? I can't even explain that one in a way that you'd believe. I got a half dozen more I can't show you unless we go somewhere private. I've been cut, I've been burned, I've been chewed on, I've been Tasered. So yeah, you want to fight, I'll give you a fight. I won't win, you're a trained soldier and I'm a sack of guts designed to convert beer into piss and depression. But I'll say this—nobody who's ever fought me has ever come back for seconds."

Lightning flashed. Ted sneered and said, "Oh yeah? Well, maybe you don't survive this one."

John said, "Mr. Knoll, think about what you're accusing him of, and all you've seen today. You're not accusing him of stealing your child. You're accusing him of stealing your child *using dark magic.* You want to fight a kiddy diddler in a dildo store parking lot, I understand that completely, I've done that myself. But are you sure you want to fight a sexual deviant who is also *a wizard?* That's how you wind up with a cursed asshole."

Dave said, "Look. We just talked to the cops. Your Maggie wasn't the only kid to go missing last night. There was *at least* one more and John and I are the best chance at finding them and whoever's doing this. You want to think we're behind it, behind all of this, that's fine, you keep thinking it. Follow us around town if you want. But what's happening here, it's bigger than us. And if you think you're going to stand in our way, then I've just got one thing to say to you . . ."

Me

". . . I'm very sorry for everything you've been through, and all I can do is beg for your patience. Give us twenty-four hours to solve this. After that if you want to kill me, go right ahead. Not like the flags are going to fly at half-mast the next day."

Ted worked his jaw, grunted, then turned and headed back toward his Impala, shaking his head. He stabbed his finger back toward me and said, "I'll be watching. You can guaran-fucking-tee it."

As he pulled away, John stepped back under the awning of the Venus Flytrap to get out of the rain. He lit a cigarette and asked, "If it comes down to you and that guy, like if he forces the issue, what will you do? I know you don't want to kill anybody, but . . ."

"I don't know, man. You've killed him once already, how was it?"

"Let me ask you something else. When you walked in and saw what looked like me on the couch having committed suicide, did you believe it?"

"Well, yeah. It looked completely real."

"But in that moment, did you believe I had done it? That it was something I would do? Do you think I'm suicidal?"

"Well, no. I don't know . . ."

"Why didn't you assume that I was murdered, and it was just staged as a suicide?"

"I don't know, I only had a few minutes to think about it. I don't understand what you're asking."

"If Nymph creates these doppelgangers out of your own mind, if he picks through and pulls out the things you're most afraid of . . . why did you have that on the brain?"

"*I don't know.* I didn't."

"Because you know I would never do that, right? I would never leave the job unfinished. I would never leave you guys behind. It wouldn't even cross my mind. It wouldn't cross Amy's, either."

"Great, John, good to hear. Let's go."

"Aren't we waiting for Amy?"

"She's asleep. She has work."

"Did you ask her if she wanted to go?"

"No, she was asleep when you called."

"Go wake her up and ask her."

"I am not going to do that, because she's going to be pissed off that I woke her up to go do this bullshit when she has to work a night shift. You want to do it, go right up there. But let her know it was your idea when she tells you to fuck off."

Twenty minutes later, John, Amy, and I pulled into Camelot Terrace. Not the best trailer park in town, but not the shittiest, either. Maybe the fourth shittiest.

"The detective said she was nuts," said John. "But who knows what that even means, in this town. I asked her how to find the trailer and she said look for the one with the sandbags."

Amy said, "She's a single mom?"

"Yeah, don't know if there's a dad in the picture somewhere."

"That's interesting. The Knolls were separated. Could be a pattern."

John said, "I don't think that's a pattern in these crimes so much as it's just a pattern in America in general. Also got a similar-sounding name to the other kid—Mikey."

Amy said, "Up there."

Chastity's trailer was, in fact, the only one in the park with a waist-high wall of white sandbags around it. We climbed over the barrier and knocked. The door was opened by a black woman who was built like an NFL defensive lineman.

As a greeting, she said, "Oh, shit!"

John said, "Ms. Payton, my name is—"

"I know who you are, I got the Internet. Isn't there

supposed to be a third one? Little redheaded girl with glasses? Oh, there she is. Didn't see her standin' off to the side."

I said, "Yeah, uh, did John explain why we're here?"

"Come in, you look like a bunch of pissed-on toilet rats out there."

The furniture and floor of Chastity's living room were covered in clear plastic drop cloths, like she was expecting a bloodbath. There was a huge stuffed fish mounted on the wall.

I said, "If you don't mind me asking, how did you get sandbags?"

She shrugged. "I paid a couple of guys to put down sandbags. Did it two weeks ago, only took 'em one day. Couple of rednecks, worked like horses. Neighbors thought I was crazy. Now who's crazy? Got a gas generator, too. Enough to keep the fridge and lights on if the grid goes down. Got bighead carp in the Deepfreeze, caught with these two hands. Well, I used a pole, you know. If you can't do the basics for yourself, you're a slave to the system. You want something to drink? Got milk, juice, and water, that's it. No booze, no coffee, no soft drinks. Can't afford addictions in my life. You gonna ask me about Mikey?"

I said, "Uh, yeah, before he went missing, did a creepy guy come around? A stranger, I mean?"

"Not that I saw. Is he a ghost?"

John said, "Why do you ask that?"

"Whoever took Mikey, he was a ghost or a ninja, and I think I would've still heard a ninja. I was sleeping right there on that sofa at the time, guy would've had to go right past me. *Twice*. And I'm a light sleeper. And even if this freak's a master of stealth, even if he can float across the floor like a hummingbird, you'd think Mikey would have made a fuss all the way out the door. This is a boy who kicked a hole in the paneling by the bed because he was having a bad dream. You found that little blond girl out by the spooky old mine, right? You check around there real good to make sure no other kids were stashed nearby?"

We actually *hadn't* done that, but John said, "Yeah, the cops are swarming that whole area, but they haven't turned up anything. Not a lot of places to hide somebody, there's those few cabins and stuff but nobody lives around there."

"Nobody wants to. People think the devil lives down in that mine. Of course, that's just people tellin' stories. I always tell 'em, you want to see where the devil lives, you look in your own heart. He couldn't have put 'em inside the mine itself?"

I said, "Oh, no, there's tons and tons of rock sealing it off. Just making a path through it would be a major earth-moving project. Guy would need a backhoe or something. You didn't see anything unusual? I don't even mean that night, I mean anything at all leading up to it, even if it was months ago. Mikey never said anything strange to you, or had weird dreams?"

"No."

"Teachers at school never reported any odd behavior?"

"I homeschool. Don't need the government programming my boy to be a drone."

That fact seemed significant to John, judging by his face. Before I could ask why, Chastity said, "But of course, there is the Batmantis."

Amy said, "The what?"

"The flying monster that's been stalking this place for the last few months? You of all people should've heard of that one."

John said, "I probably have an e-mail buried in my inbox somewhere."

Chastity asked, "You wanna see it?"

I let out an exhausted sigh and said, "Sure, why not."

It turned out Chastity was just offering to show us a video of the monster, she didn't have the creature tied up in her closet or anything. She took us into her bedroom and pulled out a laptop that was at least four years old but didn't have so much as a fingerprint on it— she stored it in its original box when not in use, and it looked like she thoroughly cleaned it after each session.

She navigated to a YouTube video with only 165 views. It got off to a very slow start—it was a guy using his phone to record an attempt to train his Pomeranian to catch a Frisbee. After three attempts resulted in the plastic disc bouncing off the confused dog's face, suddenly someone in the background screamed and the cameraman panned up to the sky.

The creature that was flapping its wings up there was just low enough to make it abundantly clear that it was not a bird. From its silhouette, it appeared to be a pair of leathery bat wings connected by a body that looked something like a praying mantis that had been in a terrible accident.

A moment after it was spotted, it swept back its wings and dive-bombed the cameraman, the moron continuing to film as the winged horror swooped down. There was a blur and a yelp and now the creature was flying back up, the cameraman's little dog curled up in its hooked front legs. The title of the video:

BATMANTIS???

Chastity clicked back and paused the video near the middle, so we could get the clearest look at the thing as it skimmed the ground to snatch its prey. It was pure white. The wings didn't match the body. One of its hooked front legs was much smaller than the other. The midsection was wider than the rest, as if it had a beer belly. It had a pair of big, dark eyes but the shape of its brow gave it an expression like it was confused by the world it had been born into.

"Ever see one of them before?"

John said nothing, Amy looked pale. I said, "It's, uh, not in our database."

"Hold on, there's more here."

She hit play and the video cut away, picking up in another location—the scrapyard south of town. It was nighttime, a flashlight beam bouncing between the rows of rusting abandoned vehicles. The cameraman was no longer alone; he was flanked by two men with hunting rifles.

In a harsh whisper, the cameraman said, "There! Up there!"

The BATMANTIS??? was crouched atop a stack of six flattened cars—the top vehicle was an old convertible the monster was using as a nest. Muzzle flash and thunder filled the air, the men firing at the winged beast. It flinched and flew away, in seconds becoming a pale speck in the sky.

The men approached the "nest" and the cameraman climbed up the stacked cars to peer in, presumably holding out some faint hope that he'd find his dog alive in there. He shined his flashlight into the open interior . . .

The beam illuminated a bowl-shaped structure, like a huge bird's nest, filling the space where the front seats had once been. The "nest" was made of small bones, many still pink with blood and specks of remaining meat. Winding through the bones were colorful bits of rope and leather straps, speckled with shiny bits of metal here and there.

Dog collars and leashes. Dozens of them.

The cameraman screamed and the video ended. The only YouTube comment was simply:

FAKE

I heard rapid footsteps behind me and turned to see Amy was gone. From down the hallway in the direction of what was hopefully a bathroom, I could hear her retching.

Chastity said, "I guess I should have warned you guys about the content. I didn't react too well the first time I watched it, neither."

John said, "I know it's weird to say this, but for some reason it's worse when it's a dog."

"Not weird to say at all. A person, they can be good or bad depending on the day. A good dog, well, it just wants to make you happy, all the time. Is the little girl talking? Did she get a look at what took her?"

John started to answer, but I quickly jumped in. "She didn't see much, but she didn't describe getting swept up into the sky by a giant white mantis bat, either. That seems like the kind of detail even a child wouldn't leave out."

She said, "So, am I to understand that this here monster's appearance and Mikey's disappearance were totally unrelated?"

John said, "In this town? Very, very possible." He looked at me. "We'll need to give it a name."

"It has a name. As far as Mikey, we're not ruling anything out. The fact that we found Maggie safe and sound should give us optimism, if nothing else."

Amy returned and she and Chastity started simultaneously apologizing over one another, the way women do.

Chastity said, "You didn't tell me how much you charge."

Amy said, "Oh, we don't."

"Well, you do now. Either you're taking this job or you're not—I don't want some halfway bullshit where you act like you're doin' me a favor and congratulating yourselves for making half an effort. This is work I need done, if you take it on, I want you to treat it like work."

I thought for a moment and said, "Our fee is two hundred and seventy-five dollars. Payable if we find him."

Amy and John both looked at me, wondering how in the hell I'd come up with that exact number.

John said, "How much does Mikey weigh?"

"About sixty-five pounds."

He nodded. "Yeah, two seventy five."

Amy said, "Payable *after* we bring him back."

We all stood, told Chastity we'd be in touch and, once more, we were driving through the rain.

I asked Amy if she was feeling okay. She lied yes.

We drove in silence for a bit.

Then, out of the blue, Amy looked right at me and said, "We can fix all this. I know we can. We can beat Nymph and find this other kid and we'll be heroes. The cops will apologize and Ted will see he was wrong and everything will be okay." She nodded, as if agreeing with the words she just heard come out of her mouth. "Yes. Everything will be okay."

I said, "Amy, for all we know, there are already more kids missing as we speak. And just because you found Maggie in time . . . you know, this kind of situation doesn't usually play out like that. Usually by the time they get to where the bad guy is holed up they just find, well, a big pile of collars."

Amy stared out of the rain-streaked passenger window in the backseat, and then burst into tears.

I said, "*What?*"

10. A FLASHBACK TO AMY'S TRAUMATIC WAFFLE EXPERIENCE

Amy

About nine hours earlier, Shawn had dropped Amy off at the Venus Flytrap and she had gone upstairs to have that momentary weird sensation that David had frozen in place. But then he started talking and Amy didn't give it a second thought. That's because there was something far stranger going on:

David, for the first time in months, seemed *genuinely happy.*

She had asked, "Did you solve the thing with the little girl?"

"We did," David had answered, whisking his waffle batter. "She's back home safe and sound. Turned out there was nothing clown dick about it, it was just a local creep. We got the cops to track his phone and found his van. Whatever he was going to do, he never got a chance."

They had taken a moment to revel in the victory, Amy of course ignorant of the fact that at that moment,

John and the real David were still out trying to solve the case, and Maggie was still missing. Then Amy had noticed the roof leak was fixed and had been shocked to her core to hear that David had done it himself.

"I'm making you waffles. You hungry?"

She wasn't, but said, "Starving!"

He said, "Then have a seat. With what I've got planned, you'll need your energy."

"Oh, *really?*"

"You'll see. How was work?"

A question David hadn't asked her in probably a year.

"Boring. Had an old lady who kept calling saying her dead husband was trying to break into her house, but it turned out it was her alive son. She had Alzheimer's. No monster stuff. So . . . how're you feeling?"

"Great. I mean, we solved the case."

"You had a rough night last night . . ."

He shrugged. "Nothing some waffles can't fix."

She wandered over to the window. "Hey, where's the car?"

"Oh, it's in the shop. Brakes started making noise."

Of course the car was not in "the shop," the actual David was out driving it, heading toward the little church in search of John. But again, Amy had no way of knowing that.

"Can we, uh, afford that?"

"Don't wanna drive without brakes, Amy. What if the guy working the drive-through mistimes his throw? Have a seat."

She sat. The card table had been cleared and dishes had been set. Real ones, not the paper plates David had started buying when he decided he didn't have enough energy to wash dishes anymore.

"But that's what I want to talk about," David said. "John and I got paid for this one, parents had a lot of money and they wouldn't take no for an answer. And the father, he said something to me that really hit home, he said that all he could think about while his daughter was missing was how if he had known his last day with her had been the last, everything would have been different. He'd have taken time to read her a story before bed, he'd have told her he loved her in a way that showed he meant it. He said if he got her back, that he'd treat every day from now on like it could be the last, because it could. And, I thought, that's exactly what I haven't been doing. So then I thought, what would I do if I knew it was my last day on earth? The answer was easy. I'd go away with you somewhere, just the two of us. So, I figured, why not just do it? You're going to decline Saturday overtime tomorrow. Today, you and I are going on a little getaway. A place with no TV, no Internet."

"Uh . . . okay. You're not going to get bored?"

"Bored? The moment you walk in that door, I'm going to strip you naked, and by the time I'm done with you, you won't be able to move. If I ever get bored with *that*, maybe you should just put me out of my misery."

Amy folded her arms on the table. "Oh, *really?*"

"Only thing I ask—Shawn doesn't bring you home anymore. You don't go *anywhere* with Shawn anymore, not even in a group. Not that I blame him, he's acting how any man would act in proximity to one of the most beautiful women in the world. But if he threatens what we have, I'll lose control, you know I will. And I don't want to lose control. For my sake, or his."

"We can talk about that later."

"No. We can't. Waffle iron's hot, let's do this!"

And so they chatted, and ate their waffles, and Amy couldn't stop smiling.

She had suggested waiting for the rain to stop or at least slack off a bit before heading out, but as soon as they'd eaten, David insisted they go.

"It's just water. Your clothes will get wet, but you won't be needing them the rest of the weekend anyway."

She asked if they needed to call a cab, since the car was in the shop and all, but David said nothing, just walked out and headed down the stairs, toward the store's parking lot. She followed and found him unlocking a red sports car from the 1960s.

"What's this?"

"This is a 1967 Chevy Impala. Given to us by our grateful client. Title is in the glove box, it's ours free and clear. Get in."

She did. David twisted the key and the engine rumbled to life. He turned to her and smiled. "You hear that?"

Amy smiled back. "I feel like we should both have varsity jackets on, and at least one of us should be smoking."

"Then we'll go join a Vietnam demonstration. *In favor* of the war."

They both laughed. David threw it in gear and they took off, rain lashing the Impala's cherry-red hood, drops breaking and splattering against the layers of gleaming wax. A car that had been someone's baby.

Amy said, "The storm is getting scary."

David shrugged. "A whole bunch of noise and not

much else. Scary if you're in a plane or a small watercraft. If you're looking to go two miles in a kickass muscle car, not so much."

"Where are we going, again?"

"Part of our payment from the grateful family of the victim was one free weekend at their cabin at Mine's Eye. Got a screened-in deck overlooking the pond. We can listen to the rain and the local wildlife can listen to me screwing your brains out."

"Calm down there, cowboy."

"Ha! Sorry. This thing, with the missing girl . . . when I saw her parents, the look on their faces when we brought her back safe and sound . . . I don't know. It's like all at once, I realized that we do real good in the world. The detective on the case was there and he shook our hands and it's like, well, like we were *legit*. You know? Like we deserved to be there, that we had done what the cops couldn't."

"Well, yeah. You should feel great about that. I've told you, over and over."

"I know. But you know how I get, that cloud that forms in my brain, so that no sense can get through. Today, I just saw a break and a little bit of light came spilling in. And I can see the look on your face right now, you're trying not to get your hopes up because this is what I do, I get up for a while and then I crash. But that's the other thing. I called the doctor. I'm going to get a prescription, try to regulate these moods. Appointment is next Tuesday."

"Oh my god. David."

"It's just time, you know. All this bullshit in my past, this fucked-up childhood and those rough high school years, there's a point you've just got to let it go. Nobody is going to rewind and give me functioning parents. Nobody is going to flip a switch and make it so that I'm suddenly just like everybody else. I'm never going to fit in. But that's okay. All of this, it really can be okay."

She reached over and held his hand. He looked over at her. "Are you crying?"

She said, "No! Of course not." She laughed, through her tears. "How can you even see where you're driving? All I see is flying water. I can feel the wind pushing the car around. Are you sure you shouldn't pull over until this passes?"

"No need. We're here."

They sat in the car for a bit, waiting for at least a momentary break in the rain. The cabin standing in front of them was a modest but clean little place, perched over the mine pond. Then David put a hand on her thigh and leaned over and kissed her. She could feel him breathing, trembling. Barely containing himself. It was getting close to Green Stripes territory, she thought.

Amy had been known to read *Cosmo* from time to time, and in every single issue they'd do some variety of a BRING OUT THE ANIMAL IN YOUR MAN! headline. David had once pointed out that every woman can remember the first time she got legitimately frightened by pushing the wrong button—or the right one—and actually saw that "animal." Maybe it's heels in the bedroom, maybe it's a little bit of pain, maybe it's dressing up in a schoolgirl outfit and doing baby talk. Every man, said David, has something, and sometimes even the man doesn't know what it is until he sees it. Amy had stumbled across David's "animal button" when she showed him the Ulala costume she'd made for the game convention.

There was nothing particularly scandalous about it, a flared white vinyl skirt—maybe a little too short—with a hoop sewn into it to give it a retro futurism look. White boots, the dumb pink wig, the gloves. Part of the costume she had added without David's knowledge, though, was a modest pair of green-and-white-striped underpants. This was another inside joke, meant only for him. In the racier anime (Japanese animation, if you're too old or cool to know that word), half the time the girls are wearing these green striped panties—some kind of culture-specific fetish, apparently. David thought anime was ridiculous, and Japanese fetishes even more so. She figured he would get a good laugh from them.

David had been on his way out the door when she walked out of the bedroom to show him the finished outfit. He gave her a cursory compliment and, right before he would have closed the door, she had playfully lifted the skirt to show him the striped underwear. She laughed. David did not. He had gotten this look in his eye, then came back inside and closed the door behind him. What followed had been . . . frantic. The underwear actually wound up with a little rip in them. She had found one of his animal buttons.

That was the vibe she was getting from him now.

David pulled back, looked out at the rain, and said impatiently, "We're going to be waiting all weekend. Let's just make a run for it."

So, they ran through the rain and bumbled their way inside the cabin, giggling like teenagers. There were animal heads on the walls and the sound of the rain on the metal roof was deafening. Predictably, the moment they were inside, the winds died down and it was just rain again. Across town, John was investigating the trunk of Nymph's car, their pursuit having ended with it getting sandwiched between the Jeep and a utility pole.

Amy and David went through to the screened-in porch, the rain now falling straight down in a steady, peaceful rhythm. Across the pond there was a little chapel perched up on a grassy hill. David kissed her and pawed at her and she asked if they could slow down a bit.

She said, "We have all weekend, right?"

"I'll try to control myself, but I make no promises." He looked out toward the pond. "Do you like it?"

Today, there was no hint of the shimmering teal water that could look at times like a setting from a fairy tale—flood water runoff had turned it into a swollen, muddy puddle, waves of fizzy drop splashes rolling across the surface.

"It's beautiful."

David sat down on a wicker sofa and patted the seat next to him. "I would say that I wished it was a nicer day, but I know better. This is Amy weather."

"Yeah. Well, when I have a roof over me—I'm sure I wouldn't like it if I was standing out in it all day. And, you know, if the whole town wasn't under a flood warning. But yeah, this amount of rain right here—fat drops, falling straight down, just a cool breeze wafting in . . . makes me want to just curl up."

David put an arm around her. She leaned into him, felt his warmth.

She said, "I know this isn't your thing. The cabin, all

that. Aside from, you know, a private place to have just tons of sex. But this right here, just sitting here and melting into each other, us under a roof while the rain falls out there. This is Heaven, for me. These moments, like this."

"Do you believe in Heaven, Amy? Like a literal place?"

"I just meant it as a figure of speech."

"Still. Serious question."

"I don't know. But if it's real, maybe you get to pick what it's like. Maybe everybody gets their own. Some burly biker dude, he gets to ride his Harley forever with his gang, maybe the warriors go to Valhalla. But I just want this. Not the rain or the cabin but . . . just for all the distractions to go away. The money, the work, having to constantly stick food and pills into your body to keep it functioning. All that stuff that puts distance between us, all those boundaries, all those fears, it all goes away until it's just us, together. For as long as we want. Not even saying anything if we don't want to. Just . . . being together."

"What would Hell be like?"

She hesitated. "Well that took a dark turn."

"You've never thought about it?"

She considered, then said, "In Auschwitz, they used to have these little cells called stand-up cells. There would be a door about a foot tall on the floor, you had to crawl into it, and once you were inside you were in this little space about the size of a coffin but only about four feet tall—not enough room to sit, or lie down. You can't sleep or relax, you're just hunched over, in like this vertical, airless concrete box. Then they closed that little door at your feet and it was pitch black—no window. And you just stood like that, hunched over and cramped, alone, in pitch darkness, for months. So I guess it would be like that, only forever."

"*Jesus.*"

"You asked."

"But you don't believe in that, do you? Like any kind of Hell."

"I know you do."

"Yeah, because I say Heaven isn't Heaven if you've got Hitler and rapists hanging around, just soaking in Jesus's swimming pool and chatting up their former victims. And that wouldn't even be Heaven for them anyway—some people aren't happy unless they're victimizing somebody. Their only possible Heaven would be everyone else's Hell. So, do you believe in it? A place of eternal suffering?"

She said, "No."

"Why?"

"How did we get off on this subject?"

"Bear with me."

"I don't believe in Hell because it would make Heaven impossible."

"Because you couldn't enjoy Heaven if you knew those people were suffering."

"I think if you're capable of enjoying an eternal paradise while millions of other people are screaming in agony, forever, you're a sociopath."

David said, "That's my point. Right there. The assholes throw themselves into a fire, but then *your* happiness is ruined because *they* get burned. They use your sympathy against you. That's the final trick of Hell—its fire burns everyone."

Amy said nothing, because she wanted this tangent to end, already not liking where it was going. David thought for a moment, as if he was finally getting to what he really wanted to say, but having arrived there, wasn't sure how to say it.

Finally, he said, "Do you remember when we were first talking about getting married, uh, seven or so years ago, and I said I wouldn't do it until you had gotten your degree? Do you remember why I said that?"

"You wanted me to be self-sufficient. You didn't want me to be getting married because I was scared of trying to make it on my own. Because then I'd be stuck with you even if I was unhappy later."

"That's right. But I want you to know . . . it works the other way, too."

"I know."

"I don't think you do. I've done something awful, Amy."

"Uh-oh. What's her name?"

"Nothing like that. What I've done . . . I've let you believe that if you ever left, that I wouldn't make it. That either I'd hurt myself, or just crash and burn. I knew you believed that, and I let you keep believing it, on purpose. Because I wanted you to stay. Because I had come to believe that you were my little magical bubble of protection against all of the awfulness out there. All the awfulness inside me. But I want you to know I'd be okay. If you ever decided you weren't happy and bailed on this, I'd be upset for a while but I'd move on, because I'm a grown-up and that's what grown-ups do. They don't hold people hostage."

"I am happy, David. I love you."

"That's good. That's great. But if that changes. If *I* change . . . go. Just, go. I saved your life once and now you've saved mine every single day after that, day after day, month after month, year after year. You don't owe me anymore. In the grand scheme of things, I am an able-bodied white male with above average intelligence living in the richest civilization that will probably ever exist on this planet. I had every chance, and all of my problems are purely my own. But above all, I want you to be happy. Even if it's with somebody else."

"I know, you've said that before—"

"I never meant it. I mean it now."

Amy started to answer, but instead let silence take over. They lay there together, a dry island in the rain, Amy feeling David's chest lift and fall under her. She started to drift off to sleep.

He said, "There's something else I need to confess. But I need to show it to you. So that you understand."

"Oh. All right."

"We have to go outside. To see it."

"Can it wait?"

"It really can't."

David led her to the car again and drove them around the pond, to the church. Amy had a thought that he had arranged some corny marriage ceremony, but instead he parked and walked right past the church, to a winding gravel path that led down to the water.

Amy followed and near the bottom, David had said, "It's here."

"*What's* here?"

"You'll see."

"You're scaring me. Tell me what we're doing."

"Amy, I do things sometimes, and I don't remember them afterward. But it's still me. It has to be. It doesn't make sense to think of it any other way."

He took a deep breath and closed his eyes. Finally, he said, "John and I . . . we didn't find the girl, Maggie. Everyone is still out looking for her right now. But I know where she is."

Amy went cold. Without another word, David headed toward the water. He kept walking right into the pond, sloshing through until it was up to his knees.

Trembling, she followed him, her vision blurring as raindrops splattered off her glasses. David waded out toward the pile of loose rock that had been the mouth of the mine way back when. He approached a rusty NO SWIMMING sign that was now half-submerged.

She saw that tied to its post was a length of white plastic pipe, curved over at the top, as if to prevent rain from getting in. David stopped there and leaned his ear down toward the pipe, as if he was listening for something. Amy forced her feet to move, feeling like she was in a bad dream. The thought that swirled around her head was, *You knew it was going to end like this.* She waded out into the freezing water and arrived next to David, looked down, and screamed.

The pipe was connected to a hose and the hose was connected to a clear plastic bag about the size and shape of, well, the little blond girl that it clearly contained.

"She's alive," David said. "Sleeping. I gave her something."

"*You* gave her something?" Amy thought she was

going to throw up. But three seconds later, she swept that thought off the table and was up to her shoulders in freezing water, dragging up the bag, which had been weighed down with four cinder blocks. David was helping—knowing exactly how to disconnect the weights—and together they dragged the girl to shore.

David handed Amy his pocketknife and she sliced open the thick, watertight plastic. She cradled the little girl in the rain, Maggie's breath coming and going softly. Amy muttered incoherent reassurances to the girl, and to herself, and to nobody in particular. It was just a noise she was making.

David said, "Amy, look at me. I need you to listen carefully. Are you listening?"

She didn't answer, but met his eyes.

"I'm not David."

Amy said, "We can . . . look, she's unharmed, you didn't hurt her, on some level you must have come to your senses, you must have—"

"Hey. Amy. This is not a metaphor. I'm not David. I look like him, I sound like him. I'm not him. David is at John's house right now, still lost, still trying to solve this. You can call him. And in fact, I want you to do that, in a moment."

"What? What are you talking ab—"

"I need you to acknowledge that you heard what I said and comprehend it. I know you don't fully understand but I need to know you at least took in the words."

"You're not David. Then who are you?"

"I'm going to go now, I won't harm or pursue you, and you're going to make your phone call. Oh, and in all the excitement, you've forgotten to get your prescription refilled, you need to get David to pick it up today or else you won't be able to move tomorrow morning when your back seizes up."

"Uh . . . okay."

"And Amy . . . you deserve better."

"What? I—"

But he was gone. Vanished, like a popped bubble. The little girl moved in her arms. Maggie's eyes were half-open, looking but not seeing, in a drugged haze. Amy pulled out her phone, called David, and he sounded frantic.

"Amy! Is that you!?!"

11. THIS ISN'T WHAT IT LOOKS LIKE, I SWEAR

Me

Coming back from Chastity Payton's house, I was worried that when we pulled into the Venus Flytrap parking lot, we'd find Ted Knoll waiting for us again. He wasn't.

Instead, it was Detective Bowman.

He stepped out of his cop SUV and met us at the foot of the stairs. His young partner stayed in the car.

As I approached, I said, "Are you here to give us our reward? For finding the girl?"

"I think you can guess why I'm here."

I headed up the stairs and Bowman followed.

John said, "You don't have a warrant. That means you can't come in unless we invite you."

Bowman said, "You're thinking of vampires." He walked into the apartment after us, shaking rainwater off of his jacket.

I said, "So, I take it you've heard from Mr. Knoll."

"Actually, I had a long conversation with Maggie. Where were you last night, between the hours of two and three A.M.?"

"Asleep. In my apartment."

"Anybody that can verify that?"

Amy said, "I can."

I said, "No, she can't, she was at work."

"I came home at three. Night lunch. You were asleep."

"Anyway, then I woke up in the predawn hours because you needed me to do your job for you. Remember that? You gave me the finger and drove merrily into the night? Then we solved your case?"

"And now I have the victim pointing the finger at you, and an extremely convenient failure of the victim's Littleton alarm system, with your girl in position to sabotage it." That clearly startled Amy. I hadn't mentioned that part to her. Still, she said nothing. "And the father, he's made an ultimatum—either we haul you in, or he buries you himself."

"Then arrest *him*."

"He hasn't committed a crime yet. That would be for after he shoots your ass. And that's only if he refuses my offer to help him get rid of the evidence."

"Even if you think I did it, aren't I also the guy who brought her back? So what's the charge there, we took a little girl to visit Mine's Eye then brought her back home eight hours later? For what? We didn't even get paid for the work."

"And then we found out there was another victim. At least one."

I said, "You think I did both? At the same time, across town? And never got spotted? It's weird how you switch between having a really high opinion of me and a really low one."

He shrugged. "Well, *somebody* did it."

"Yeah, but it wasn't a person. Which you know damned well."

"Do I know that?"

John said, "So, now if we go and find the other kid, that just casts more suspicion on us? Well, guess what—we're going to go find him anyway. I'm sure you understand, at this point heroism is just a reflex for us."

I said, "And just to be clear, the only way to prove to you that we weren't behind this would be to successfully find the guy who did it, and for it to turn out to be an actual human being you can book and prosecute. Right?"

"Actually, Wong, if I see you anywhere near any of the victims' families again, or see you talking to witnesses, or otherwise doing amateur cop stuff, I will haul all three of you in for interfering with a police investigation. And I'm using the word 'haul' here to describe tying you to the rear bumper of a squad car and dragging you across town. You're going to stay home, you're not going to leave town, you're going to wait for me to tell you what to do. Understand?"

I said, "Of course. What you say goes. After all, you're *the police*."

He turned and opened the door and was aaaallllmost all the way out, when there was a thump from another room.

We all turned, including Detective Bowman.

Another thump, like someone kicking a door.

Coming from inside my junk room.

The detective said, "Who else is here?"

Simultaneously:

Amy said, "It was the wind."

John said, "It's the dog."

I said, "I don't hear anything."

The detective pulled his gun and said, "Get back. All three of you, go to the other side of the room."

We did.

Thump

I said, "I don't want you to take this as a threat, but the last cop to come into my house and yank open doors to investigate strange sounds, well, he kind of wound up with a monster in his face. And I don't mean it was near his face, I mean it was literally inside his face."

"Shut the fuck up."

Still, he approached the closed junk room door like he thought a velociraptor would come crashing through it at any moment. He positioned himself outside the door and, with his gun held close to his body where an assailant couldn't grab it, he reached out with his left hand and pushed the door open.

He jumped back from the door to create distance, then trained his gun on whatever horror was in the room. From where I was standing, I couldn't see inside but I mentally prepared myself to go running out the front door if he got yanked into the room by jaws, paws, tentacles, or a beak.

The detective looked inside, took in what he was seeing, then spun and aimed his gun right at me.

"Get down! Get on the floor! All three of you!"

"What is it?"

"GET DOWN!"

We obeyed, the three of us exchanging looks. I had

already pretty much guessed what he had found in there. Amy seemed quite sure she knew.

The detective grabbed his walkie-talkie and called in a squad car and an ambulance.

He had a young child, he said.

Alive, but unconscious.

We were handcuffed in the back of Detective Bowman's SUV—Amy's right hand cuffed to a belt loop—and had been sitting there long enough to see the sun go down. Red and blue lights flashed across the beads of water on the windshield. The employees of the Venus Flytrap had all gathered up front, muttering to each other, covering their mouths in shock. I watched as Chastity pulled up in an old but impeccably maintained Range Rover. She jumped out and ran toward the stairs, then was restrained by a pair of street cops, reassuring her that her little boy would be right down.

Then a paramedic carried Michael Payton's tiny body down the stairs, the boy wrapped in a blanket. Chastity easily shoved the two cops aside and flew up to snatch her baby from the paramedic and clutch him to her chest. A Channel 5 news team was there to get it all on camera, as were most of our neighbors—word travels fast anytime there are cop cars at the Wong residence. The child and Chastity were loaded into an ambulance and soon after, a crime scene team started filing up and down the stairs, all of them about to be very confused by the shit they would find in my apartment. Will somebody in the evidence room be in charge of figuring out what that clown painting is saying?

Detective Bowman's partner, the square-jawed dude with the fancy hair, climbed into the passenger seat of the SUV. Bowman was standing under the awning of the dildo store, talking to one of the crime scene techs, hopefully warning them about grabbing anything in the apartment with their bare hands.

To Bowman's partner, John said, "The only thing that bothers me about this bullshit is that I'm pretty sure the real bad guy is still out there. You know we didn't do this, and you know you need us. So what good does booking us do, other than let you cover your ass by closing the case?"

He said, "Shut your trap. I've got *no* patience for this bullshit."

Bowman slid into the driver's seat. As we pulled out of the parking lot, I said to him, "Will you just listen to us? You *know* this isn't going to trial. This stuff *never* goes to trial. The prosecutor probably looks these cases over, shakes her head, and pours herself a stiff drink while figuring out how to explain to the press why she dropped the charges. Every time."

Amy said, "Guys, he's not taking us to the police station."

Bowman glanced back at us and said, "She's right. Got a new procedure these days."

He drove us south, past some cornfields and around the scrap-yard, where we'd seen the guy hunting the BATMANTIS??? on Chastity's video. We turned into the lot of a large building that had been a farm supply store years ago, but had apparently been renovated and reopened under new management. The only marking was a nondescript sign at the entrance of the parking lot declaring it the IAEEAI LAB AND WELLNESS CENTER.

Sitting in the parking lot were several trucks, the kind of flat-black military vehicles that you see around Undisclosed now and again, and that you generally pretend you didn't see.

I'm not sure how many members of this shadowy organization John and I have killed over the years. This is partly because I'm not sure which of their employees were ever actually alive and partly because I'm never clear if it's the same organization from one time to the next. Do you have that one corner in your town that's a different restaurant every two years—a burrito shop, then a Chinese place, then a Pop-Tart buffet—because nobody can ever make it work but they keep trying anyway? Well, it's kind of like that, only instead of trying to squeeze a profit from a shitty location with no parking, they're trying to control vast, dark energies they barely understand. And, instead of skipping town once the lease runs out, they suffer screaming, spurting deaths that are but a warm-up for the unending frenzy of ravenous jaws that await them beyond the veil. But, hey, maybe it'll work next time, guys!

John and I had once dedicated ourselves to investigating the origins and power structure of this group, a task that we diligently pursued for more than twenty minutes while waiting for a pizza delivery to arrive. A Google search found sites full of animated GIFs tracing it all back to either an occult-obsessed nineteenth-century billionaire, a 1961 Soviet military teleportation experiment, the Illuminati, or "The International Jew" (the pizza arrived before we could find out his name).

Bowman's SUV rolled to a stop a short distance from

the vehicles. That is, the *completely dry* vehicles, standing on completely dry pavement, in the middle of a downpour, in a parking lot with no roof. I thought I could see raindrops splattering and bouncing off an invisible barrier overhead. I sighed. They apparently hadn't wanted to get wet.

Out of the trucks walked a dozen figures in hooded black cloaks, like the guys who had shown up at John's place a few weeks ago. Or, maybe it was the exact same guys, who knows? Under their robes they were wearing modern body armor and they were carrying bulky weapons with no obvious holes where bullets could come out. They all wore those droopy masks—at least, I think they were masks. They formed a circle in the parking lot and started chanting and drawing on the pavement with what looked like vials of blood.

Amy rolled her eyes and said, *"Really?"*

Detective Bowman took a drink from a flask he'd hidden under his seat and said to his partner, "You know, law enforcement has changed quite a bit since I was in the academy."

A ramp was extended from the back of one of the trucks, and a pair of normal-looking humans in business attire used a hand truck to roll down what looked like a huge, black, featureless casket. They wheeled it out to the middle of the circle of chanting cloaks and set it up on end, like a vampire was about to walk out of it (note: vampires aren't real).

One of the suits—a woman—gestured in our direction and Bowman said, "Will you willingly get out and walk over there, or do we have to march you over there at gunpoint? You know how I hate getting out in the rain."

I said, "This isn't right, Detective. You're supposed to uphold the law. Whatever's about to happen, you know damned well we don't deserve it."

"Hey, you know who else said that very thing to me? Literally every scumbag I've ever stuffed into that back seat."

John said, "You see those guys out there summoning the devil or some shit, right?"

"Is that what you think they're doing? Because I'm pretty sure all that witchcraft mumbo jumbo is supposed to protect them from *you*. And yeah, we're dropping you off here because nobody's sure a cell can even hold you. Now get the fuck out of my vehicle."

We all glanced at each other, but short of trying to overpower the cops and steal their SUV, there weren't a lot of options. His partner removed the handcuffs and we all stepped into the rain, took a few steps forward, and then were *out* of the rain.

Amy said, "Weird."

"Hello," said a stern-looking woman in a perfectly pressed navy pantsuit, striding toward us ahead of an even more stern-looking man with brown hair and a neatly trimmed beard. "My name is Agent Helen Tasker, my partner is Agent Albert Gibson."

Later, there would be some dispute between John, Amy, and me about what names the agent had given us. But Helen Tasker and Albert Gibson is what I heard.

John said, "And you're with . . . ?"

"Fish and Wildlife," said the male—Gibson—with a sneer.

I said, "So, are you the ones framing me on Nymph's behalf, or are you also pursuing Nymph? Or are you just altogether clueless about what's happening here? Honestly, from past experience with people like you, it could be any of the three."

The female agent—Tasker—said, "We are here to gather information, that's all you need to know. Now, to prevent you from coordinating, I am going to interview you separately, and simultaneously."

Gibson walked over and opened the casket (or whatever it was—it was just a seven-foot-tall featureless box, with a door). The woman looked at me and said, "Mr. Wong, please step through the door, I will be right behind you."

I said, "We won't both fit in there."

She didn't answer. I stepped toward the door and, when I got close enough, heard moaning and wailing from the other side. A stench of disease and death wafted out. I felt my guts clench. Stepping through that door wouldn't mean stepping inside the box. I would emerge . . . elsewhere.

At this point, things again get a bit mixed up in my memory.

John, Amy, and I all later agreed that each of us had stepped through the door of the black box and that each of us were questioned on the other side of it by the same female agent. But each of us remember being asked to go first, and none of us remember either of the other two being called. It's like in the moment Tasker asked to speak to us, we simultaneously split into three separate timelines. If you understand how this sort of thing could work, please write down your explanation with as much clarity and detail as you can, then throw it in the trash because who gives a shit.

I took a breath, steeled myself, and stepped through.

I emerged on the other side and was no longer in that parking lot, or in Undisclosed. A stench hit me so hard that I thought my brain had shit my sinuses. I tried to breathe through my mouth but I swore I could *taste* it.

I was standing over a dying man, lying on a filthy cot at my feet. Flies crawled over a row of yellowed teeth rotting behind cracked lips. His midsection was covered by a wadded-up sheet that was encrusted with dried diarrhea. Out from under the sheet were jutting pale white sticks that were his legs, the feet black as if from frostbite, and missing half their toes. On the ground around him was a scatter of discarded rags that were red with sprays of coughed-up blood.

The man had just enough energy to turn his head toward me slightly and hiss the word "Water."

Next to him was another man in a similar condition. Next to him, a skeletal woman, who appeared to be dead. I was, it turned out, standing in between two rows of fifty or so such cots, each containing an afflicted victim. Beyond each row was another row just like it. The grass beneath my feet was well-manicured and oddly artificial—Astroturf. There were rows of seats looming over us—a football stadium. Between the cots I could make out a faded New England Patriots logo in the turf.

I turned to find the door I'd stepped through but saw only agent Tasker. She said, "I'm sure this is a shock to you, but you understand we had to take precautions."

"Where are we, exactly? There's no plague in our Boston, right? This is the future or something? An alternate timeline?"

"What matters is that you cannot get back home until we reopen that door. To prevent your escape, we simply took you to a world into which you would presumably not wish to flee. You're going to answer a few questions for us."

"And then what?"

"That depends on your answers. But don't bother lying, or I'll know. In exchange, I will also not lie to you."

The dying man next to me hissed, ". . . *water* . . ."

I said, "I assume we're going someplace away from the, uh, pestilence? To conduct the interrogation? I'd prefer not to catch what these people have."

"In this world, you're never away from it. Your friend asked who we work for, and I am sure you're wondering the same."

I said, "Not really. People like you come to town, in your suits. You poke around, try to look smart, asking questions like you think you're even capable of understanding the answers. Sometimes you act like you're government, sometimes private, but I suspect none of you even know where your funding comes from. It doesn't matter, it's all the same. I'm guessing it always starts with some powerful people behind the scenes catching wind of what's going on here and they come rolling in to . . . I don't know. Try to take advantage of it, somehow? Try to harness the dark energies, to find a way to profit from them? Then it all falls apart and you pick up and leave, the rest of us go back to our weird little lives and try to muddle through. That cycle has probably been repeating itself since before this town was a town."

"Our organization is known as NON. Non-natural Organism Neutralization."

"Well, either way, one thing is always the same—you people never manage to improve the situation."

"Would you prefer we left it to amateurs like you? Your dossier says you were once seen punting a severed head across your yard, while naked."

"That was an isolated incident."

"You understand that scenarios like these cannot be left to play out on their own? Innocent children, taken in the night. The people are frightened. Understandably so. Panic is a self-sustaining chain reaction. Order must be restored."

"Hey, you want to fix this, go for it. I hereby defer to your judgment."

"Word around town is that you had something to do with it."

"The only word around this town is 'meth'."

"Why don't you tell me a little bit about your history."

"You just told me you have a dossier, you probably know more about me than I do. I was drunk for so much of it."

"I want *you* to tell it."

Another man came shambling by, in filthy rags that might once have been white. I realized to my horror that he was a doctor. He looked like he'd died of exhaustion a week ago and his body just hadn't gotten the message. He didn't even glance at us as he passed. The man on the cot rolled his eyes toward him and rasped, ". . . *water* . . ." but the doctor ignored him.

I said, "My history? Going back how far? To my birth?"

"To the start of your career, in this field."

"I, uh, lived a normal life until high school. Got into some trouble, maimed a kid in a fight. You know, the usual stuff. Went to a party, there was a drug going around there. Everybody who took it had weird shit happen to them. All of them died but me and John. Now we can see monsters and it's awful."

"And now you have gained some prominence, due to that. It is, as they say, your claim to fame. Now, eliminate that element—all of your supposed paranormal abilities and self-reported heroism—and just tell me about your life, as a man."

"Not much to tell."

"I know. Tell it anyway."

"Well . . . I worked in a video store for a while, out of college. Place went out of business, I've been in and out of work ever since."

"Amy supports you. Financially, I mean."

"We get by."

"Because Amy supports you."

"We help each other. What does this have to do with anything?"

"She has no family."

"Is that a question?"

"Her parents were killed in a car accident."

"Yes. When she was thirteen or fourteen, around there."

"You're certain."

"I wasn't there. Why would she lie?"

"Who's saying she is?"

The guy at my feet asked for water again. I turned away from him, and looked instead at the victim in the next row. He was moaning, and one hand was absently scratching at his belly. He had been at it for a while, it seemed, because he had scratched all the way through the skin, then through the fat, and then through the muscle, creating a ragged hole next to his navel. A loop of small intestine had flopped out, like a pale worm. Flies were swarming over it.

I quickly turned away, focusing my gaze into the empty bleachers. My stomach was roiling from the stench, I swore it was seeping into my pores.

Agent Tasker said, "That's the same car accident in which she lost her hand."

"Yep. Can we please leave?"

"Her older brother acted as her guardian after that." She paused, but I said nothing, because it wasn't a question. From somewhere a few cots away, a child started screeching. "And what became of him?"

"You *know* what."

"Do I?"

"He died under mysterious circumstances."

"But not mysterious to you. You were there."

"Oh, trust me. I'm just as confused as anyone. Is there a point to all this or are you just trying to piss me off?"

"My point is, now all Amy has is you. The man who she believes protects her from the monsters."

"I don't know what she believes, you'll have to ask her."

"I am, as we speak. If I were to go back and have her tell the whole tale from her perspective, would she speak of the same monsters? How much of it did she actually witness? How much of what she saw was seen in moments of panic in the darkness? How much were her memories augmented by the detailed stories written down by her beloved David, the only one she has in the world? The man she believes protects her from the very monsters he describes in such vivid detail?"

"Why are you obsessed with our relationship? How does that possibly matter, in this situation?"

"It all matters. The universe is a series of fulcrums, upon which fate tilts this way and that. A random application for an art school is rejected, and a young Adolf Hitler changes careers."

"Are you saying Amy is the new Hitler, or I am? If it's me, it just, you know, seems like a lot of work . . ."

"Would you say her life was better before she met you, or after?"

"Oh, fuck you."

"Look past your defensiveness and try to grasp the context in which I am asking this. Imagine you were looking at this case from the outside, observing how the situation in Undisclosed has degraded over the last decade. If you could go back and pick one single person to eliminate from the equation in order to alleviate the maximum amount of suffering, who would it be?"

"Are you going to kill me, Agent Tasker? Is that all this is, you did the math and decided that *I'm* the problem? Well, shit, who am I to argue?"

"Even if that was my intention, I do not have the authority to do that."

"Okay, do you need me to sign something or do you have to get your supervisor . . ."

"What I am saying is that the anomalous entity that exists in the Undisclosed coal mine is our concern, not yours. We will see to it that it is dealt with. If you want to slay the monster that stalks your town, well, there are numerous painless and quick methods. I have run the scenarios; I assure you that the outcomes are superior for virtually everyone involved. Especially Amy."

"*Jesus Christ*, lady. Did you just tell me to kill myself? It's like if the guardian angel in *It's a Wonderful Life* went up to George Bailey on that bridge and was like, 'Do it, you pussy.'"

"George Bailey is portrayed as the hero because he wanted to give cheap home loans to citizens who couldn't afford them—the very practice that just caused a worldwide financial crisis in real life. We'd have been better off if he and everyone like him were, in fact, drowned in a river."

"Well, I think you and your organization would be better off if you all drowned on *my balls*. Fuck you, you want me dead, man up and do it yourself."

She glanced at her watch. "All right, we're done here. Please step this way."

"We are? You didn't even ask me about the case. Hey!"

Amy

"Hello," said a stern-looking woman in a perfectly pressed navy pantsuit, striding across the parking lot next to an even more stern-looking man with brown hair and a neatly trimmed beard. "My name is Agent Emily Wyatt, my partner is Agent York Morgan. To prevent you from coordinating, we are going to interview you separately, and simultaneously."

The man opened the door to the device that to Amy looked like a big, black refrigerator from the future. The woman gestured to Amy and said, "Ms. Sullivan, please step through the door, I will be right behind you."

Amy did as asked and when she saw what lay beyond the door, she clapped her hand over her mouth and just stood there, in shock. Rows and rows of dying people, on stretchers, covered in rags.

"Where are we? What's wrong with these people?"

Agent Wyatt shrugged. "It's always an apocalypse somewhere. It's a world into which you do not want to escape, that's all you need to know."

"There's a plague, or something? Is it worldwide?"

"What you're seeing here is the work of a perfect bioweapon, one that quickly got out of control."

"Perfect, meaning it killed everyone?"

"Perfect, in the sense that it *didn't*. A corpse requires no further care or resources, so inflicting quick death is not the most efficient way to cripple an enemy. Instead, they developed a pathogen that would incapacitate a person within hours, rendering them unable to fight or work, requiring around-the-clock care and leaving them in that state indefinitely. And I mean decades. Wracked with pain, muscles seizing, unable to do anything but lie there and writhe as they rot from the outside in, all while leaving the brain and vital organs fully functional . . . until someone finally comes along and puts them out of their misery. Using the enemy's sympathy against them."

"That's awful."

"Ms. Sullivan, I need you to focus. Do you understand the gravity of the situation you and David have found yourselves in?"

"Are you seriously asking me that? Do you have any idea what we've been through?"

"Do *you*? What I'm asking, is David candid about what he does? About what he *is*?"

Amy started to answer, but the man at her feet said, "*Water*," and she turned to kneel down over him.

She said, "Find some water."

"Ms. Sullivan, we're not here to intervene in—"

Amy got up and scanned the area around her, trying to find a nurse, or someone who looked like an authority figure. "Hey! Somebody! This man needs water!"

"You're looking at the final stages of a worldwide pandemic. The system has collapsed, supplies have dried up. These people have been abandoned here, in twenty years this version of earth will be ruled by cockroaches—yet another world in which the bugs have won. That's not our concern today. Ms. Sullivan, I suspect that David has not been completely honest about—"

"I'm not saying another word until you get this man some water."

The agent had a look like she was entertaining a series of murderous fantasies, but ultimately decided it was easier just to comply. She reopened the doorway—which appeared right there on the turf, standing freely—and yelled for someone to get her a bottle of water. A moment later, she handed Amy a bottle of Fiji Water—a ridiculous brand drank by rich people—and Amy trickled a little into the mouth of the dying man. He sputtered and coughed, then closed his eyes and went back to sleep, or passed out. No "thank you," no expression of relief. Just some dim awareness from deep down in the dark caverns of his misery that one part of him felt a little better.

Amy looked up at Agent Wyatt and said, "Thank you."

She shrugged. "It hardly matters here."

"It all matters. You're not the cops, so you know that what happened with those kids is the work of something bigger than me or David or some random creeper around town. So are you here to help us stop it, or to get in our way?"

"You buy into David's mythology? Monsters and ghosts and demons? And that you're some kind of a select group of chosen ones who are humanity's last hope?"

"Ha, nobody has ever called us that. I just try to help whoever's in front of me. That's enough to keep me super busy."

"But you believe the kidnappings are the work of some kind of paranormal entity. A monster. One that only you can stop."

"You go read up on 'monsters' and you know what you find? Every culture has the same ones—even civilizations who never talked to each other. Every culture has demons and vampires and stories of people who turn into animals. They all just put their own little spin on it—in Europe it's werewolves, in Asia it's werebears, in Central America they're were-jaguars. But it's all the same because it's all for the same reason."

"Because they're real, you mean?"

"No, because it's all just an excuse for people to kill each other. Your kid gets attacked by wolves, there's no way to get revenge on the wolves, so you blame the village weirdo. 'I saw that guy turn into a wolf!' All the legends can be traced back to something like that—people needing a scapegoat. They've found old skeletons with stakes through their rib cages, where the villagers went crazy and stabbed some poor dude because they decided he was a vampire, when he was probably just an insomniac with anemia. Witches, they were just any elderly women in the village who never got married—the men decided they were old and ugly and worthless and so they blamed them for every disease and bad batch of crops. Just burned them alive, no family to come to their defense. They didn't have witch hunts because they believed in witches. They believed in witches so they could have witch hunts."

"You think that's why we're here? To carry out a witch hunt?"

"I think you're here for the same reason as the witch hunters. To lay blame for something you can't understand."

"So if you ran into what others called a monster, you would show it mercy? Protect it? Become its friend?"

"Yep, probably."

"Even if it put the world in danger? This is not a hypothetical. I need you to understand what I'm saying. There are entities out there who will use your pity to their advantage. Look around you."

Amy sighed and surveyed the rows of afflicted moaning around her. "Yes, Agent Wyatt, clearly the problem with the world is that we humans are just too darned merciful. Are you going to ask me questions about the actual case?"

"I already have. Step back through the door, please."

John

"Hello," purred the woman in the form-fitting suit and skirt, sauntering toward John along with a tanned Latino man with a beard and designer sunglasses. "My name is Agent Josaline Pussnado, my partner is Agent Sax Cocksman. To prevent you from coordinating, we are going to interview you separately, and simultaneously."

She stared into John's eyes and said, "You first. But I'm telling you now, if you so much as raise a threatening eyebrow in my direction, I'll replace it with a bullet hole the size of a golf ball. Am I understood?"

John said, "You might not find me so easy to kill. But I've got questions of my own, so let's get this shit over with."

John stepped through, saw the arena full of diseased humanity, and lit a cigarette. The place smelled like a stew made from cabbage and zombie scrotums.

"So in this dimension, this is their national sport? They line up all the sick people and fans buy tickets to come see which one dies first? Disgusting."

"Shut up," said Agent Pussnado. "Hold still."

She ran a wand up and down John's body, as if searching for hidden weapons. When it passed over his crotch, it let out a threatening buzz.

John said, "Your machine is broken. There's no metal in there. Not *yet*."

"It doesn't detect metal," she said, glancing at his groin. "It detects *danger*. Now, we know your friend is behind the disappearances of those kids. The only reason we haven't shackled him and thrown him into a deep, dark place is that we're also sure he's but one piece of the puzzle. Either he's working in conjunction with something, or on its behalf."

"And also, you're not sure if he can be shackled."

She didn't respond, but John knew it was true. John said, "You think what you think purely because *They* want you to think it. You're dancing right along to their tune, like those dancing cats they have in Japan."

"I've literally never heard of—"

"All these signs point to Dave only because the thing behind this wants you to go after him. Amy, too, all that stuff about the security cameras—they want us out of the picture, and are using you as a tool."

The man on the cot nearby whispered something. John leaned close enough to hear the man say, ". . . kill . . . me . . ."

The woman said, "Your loyalty to your friends is admirable. But the day is coming when you are going to have to make a terrible decision. Will you?"

The man on the cot started screaming. Something was writhing in his abdomen, thrashing under the skin, trying to tear its way out. There was a ripping sound, and out from the man's belly came a hideous creature, some horrific parasite having hatched inside him. It had teeth where its eyes should be and where its teeth should be, more teeth.

John looked around for a weapon and found a nearby flamethrower. He picked it up and unleashed a torrent of fire that consumed parasite and host alike, the man screaming out his gratitude for having been put out of his misery. Soon, other parasites were hatching all around them, one disease-ridden victim after another giving birth to their unholy offspring. John spun the flame thrower in an arc, setting everything in the vicinity ablaze.

The fuel quickly ran out. John tossed the flamethrower aside and picked up Agent Pussnado from where she was cowering on the turf.

"Will I do what has to be done?" he asked, sneering at her. "What do *you* think? Now let's get the hell out of here. I'm thinking the Patriots aren't making the playoffs this year."

John spotted where the portal had opened at the end of the row. He yanked the woman off her feet and hauled her toward the doorway, a horde of the skittering dog-sized parasites in pursuit. John tossed the agent through the open portal and spun to face the onslaught. He snatched his switchblade from its ankle scabbard and stabbed a thrashing parasite as it launched itself at his face. John's entire shirt was ripped from his body.

"Just come through and close the door!" screamed Pussnado, from the other side of the portal. "You can't kill them all! It doesn't matter!"

John slashed another of the parasites, then another. He glared at the woman over his shoulder and said, "It *all* matters."

Me

I found myself back in the parking lot, standing next to John and Amy, facing the two agents and unsure if anything had actually happened. It didn't feel like we'd moved. The dozen cloaked figures who encircled us each

193

had their strange weapons at the ready. I wondered if we ducked at the right moment if they would all just shoot each other.

John looked around as if confused and said, "Did we, uh, pass?"

The female agent I knew as Tasker said, "If we allow you to leave this place, what will you do?"

I said, "Nothing. Nothing whatsoever. Amy will go to work, I'll go home and masturbate, John will go to his place, feed his dog, and also masturbate probably. You'll never hear from us again."

"You are a practiced, yet unskilled, liar. I know that you will continue to pursue a resolution in this case. We cannot allow you to do that."

"But you already said you don't have permission to kill us."

The male agent, Gibson, said, "It's believed by our superiors that you are surrounded by a blowback sphere."

I said, "The last three syllables of that sentence were nonsense to me."

"They think any attempt to kill you will automatically recoil on us and our organization via some unnatural means. I say it's bullshit, but it's above our pay grade."

Actually, I thought, *the people who are nice to us also meet with horrific misfortune. I think it's a proximity thing.*

John said, "What, like we're protected somehow? Like we've got a guardian angel, or a force field?"

Tasker said, "I assure you, the forces shielding you are in no way angelic. If you are protected, it is only so that you can carry out Their will. Strings are pulled to clear the path wherever you go, surely you've sensed that."

I said, "Holy shit, I'd hate to see what my life would

look like if I wasn't getting help."

"Exactly," said Tasker. "But, while you cannot be harmed, there are alternatives available to us." She nodded at one of the cloaks. "Do you know what their weapons do?"

I said, "No, but I've always been curious to find out."

"On their current setting, they simply change your mind. I don't mean they convince you, I mean they change your mind completely. Forge new, somewhat random connections in your brain. They leave you perfectly healthy, but also completely unaware of who you are, how you got here, or what you're fighting for. You won't know your name, you won't recognize each other. You will be wiped clean, then each transported to separate locations with new identities. You will start your lives over as new people. You will no longer have any urge to interfere with the situation here, but will be otherwise physically and psychologically healthy, and thus should not trigger this supposed dark sphere of protection that surrounds you. The best of both worlds."

Amy said, "You can't do that."

Gibson said, "Hey, babe, it's better than a bullet."

"Put us together. Just do that. If you wipe us, put us in the same house, or the same town. Let us find each other again."

Tasker said, "We can't do that, for obvious reasons. The goal isn't to have you spend six months reverse engineering your lives to wind up right back here. The goal is for you to start anew, and never feel the compulsion. Don't worry, you won't miss David. You'll never know he was ever in your life. There'll be nothing to miss. It's like when they do surgery on an infant—they don't bother with anesthesia before they slice into its chest, as they know it will not remember the pain."

Amy turned to me and said, "I'll find you. Somehow."

Tasker said, "No, you will not."

John said, "This plan is idiotic. Supernatural shit is still going to show up at each of our doorsteps, and when it does we're going to get on the Internet and research it and you know what we're going to find? Stories about us. The past will all come rushing back."

"Those Internet searches will turn up nothing. Where you're going, those articles do not exist, because those events won't have happened."

"Oh," I said. "When you said we would be relocated, you didn't mean we'd be dumped off in Arkansas. You meant we're each going through the door."

"One at a time. Each to a different world."

John lit a cigarette and said, "No. You'll have to kill us."

"No, I won't. It'll be just like waking up from a deep sleep, you won't feel any desire for revenge or even a faint sadness about what you lost. You will be curious about your amnesia, of course, but when you go searching for your old identity, there will be nothing to discover."

Amy's arms were around me.

She said, "David, they can't do this. They can't."

She'll be happier.

John, now showing genuine alarm, said, "So, you take us out of the picture and the thing in the mine smashes its way out and starts impaling all of humanity on its million barbed penises. What then? Your people have to desperately track us down and beg for our help? Reprogram our brains back the way they were?"

Gibson said, "Getting you out of the picture is our only hope for keeping the entity in the mine contained, asshole."

I said, "Yeah, I can actually see that."

Tasker looked at John and said, "You're considering running, maybe trying to take me hostage. Just remember—we choose where that door goes. You make this hard for us, and you'll wake up in a world where the sky is black and worms crawl out of your rationed meat. Go easy, and I'll send you someplace that's pretty much like this."

John said, "Do you have one where Tupac is still alive?"

Amy said, "Give us a moment to say good-bye."

And time to think, I thought.

Tasker said, "Again, what's the point of a good-bye that won't be remembered?"

Amy said, "What's the point of all this explanation, if it won't be remembered? Why didn't you just shoot us with your brain rays right off the bat?"

"Isn't it obvious? This alleged invisible hand that protects you, I wanted to know that it wouldn't reach out to stop us at the moment of decision. It didn't. Now, I have a busy night ahead, so . . ."

Tasker nodded to the nearest cloak—his sagging face had a gray rubber mustache—and he pointed a thing at me that looked like a robotic elephant's detachable dick.

I recoiled. Amy threw herself in front of me and John said, "WAIT!"

There was a pop, sounding like a gunshot echoing in the distance. I didn't feel any different. Then the cloak with the elephant dick gun slumped to his knees, black blood running freely from what was supposed to be his forehead. As he went down, he fired his weapon wildly, an impossibly bright blue light blasting forth and hitting Agent Gibson right in his face.

Gibson got this weird look in his eyes. He blinked and took in what surrounded him, seeing first the three of us, who looked harmless enough, and then the circle of ominous black cloaks with their alien arsenal. One of them stepped forward and raised its weapon at us, looking to finish the project begun by his colleague.

Gibson's eyes went wide and instinct took over. He pulled a gun from a shoulder holster and in one reflexive motion put the cloaked thing down with a headshot.

Tasker screamed, "DROP IT!" and drew her own weapon on her rogue partner. But Agent Gibson, frantic over his inability to remember who the hell he was, had shifted into fight-or-flight mode. He spun, saw the gun pointed at him, and shot his fellow agent in the chest.

Eyeballs swollen with panic, he turned and ran, firing in front of him to clear a path through the cloaks. John, Amy, and I followed. I was about to yell for somebody to steal one of the NON trucks, but the moment we ran off the parking lot and hit the road, Gibson turned and saw the three of us in tow. Interpreting this as pursuit, he raised the gun toward me and pulled the trigger—

The man was blasted out of view by a Range Rover. It skidded to a stop in front of us, Chastity Payton at the wheel.

"Y'ALL GET THE FUCK IN HERE!"

We crammed ourselves into the back seat and she sped off into the night. There was a hunting rifle with a scope propped up on the front seat next to her.

Chastity craned her head around and said, "They following us?"

I said, "I don't see headlights, but I don't think they use them. You killed both of those dudes?"

"May they find peace in the next world, but their own choices took 'em there. If your people dress like that, you're on the wrong side."

Amy said, "Thank you."

"Don't thank me yet. The four of us, we're gonna have a talk. And I'll tell you right now, I'm just about sick of this shit."

John said, "They're coming!"

There was a black truck behind us, no headlights, coming fast. Chastity hunched forward and stepped on the gas. She had a determined look in her eyes that kind of scared me—a "They'll never take me alive" look.

We soon found our lane obstructed by a slow semi, barely managing the speed limit. Chastity swung to the left to pass and immediately was almost obliterated by an oncoming car that honked angrily as it flew by. The NON vehicle was growing in the rearview mirror.

We reached an overpass, and Chastity swung out to the left lane and once again found oncoming headlights—another semi. This time she didn't go back, she floored it, attempting to thread the needle. Everyone screamed.

She cleared the truck on the right and yanked the wheel over a split second before the honking juggernaut went whooshing past. I swore I heard it scrape paint off the side mirror.

The NON truck behind us had tried to follow.

199

It smashed directly into the eighteen-wheeler we'd just avoided.

Through the rear window I saw chaos, the truck's trailer jackknifing and rolling across the overpass, cargo spraying down onto the roadway below.

John said, "*Jesus.*"

"You see," said Chastity, "that's why you want the Range Rover. Jeep would have tipped over doing that shit. Always got to be prepared, that's what I say."

12. DIOGEE WASN'T A GOOD DOG

Chastity took a winding, random path back toward town, but we never saw any additional pursuit. I half-expected NON to roust a helicopter to track us beyond the blocked roadway, but we apparently didn't rate that kind of response, not yet.

We pulled over at a truck stop, parking in a spot where a row of trailers would hide us from the road. Chastity shifted into park, pulled out a revolver, and turned around in her seat so she could point it right at my face. I had lost count of how many guns had been pointed at me in the last hour. Was it five?

She said, "Tell me *exactly* what is going on here. Don't bullshit me, don't sugarcoat it. Tell me the whole truth. Right now. Because I'm tellin' you, I am on my last nerve here."

I said, "Are you going to believe me, if I do? Otherwise we're just wasting each other's time."

"I like to think I know the truth when I hear it."

"Good. I had never seen your son before they

found him in my apartment."

"I believe you."

"You do? Well, that's good, then. Someone stuck him in there, to frame us."

"No, that ain't right, neither."

"Okay. Well, why don't you tell me what—"

"There's somethin' wrong with him. With Mikey. He isn't right. None of this is right."

John said, "On that, we agree."

Amy asked, "Is he talking? Your son?"

"Oh, he talks."

"What does he say happened, that night? Does he remember?"

"Says your man here woke him up, standing in his bedroom. Says David snapped his fingers and suddenly they were someplace else, some kind of fucked-up Disneyland."

I said, "Joy Park?"

"How'd you know?"

"It came up in the Maggie Knoll case. It's not a real park."

"No shit it's not a real park. Mikey says when you walk in the front gate, everybody gets a pair of wings, lets everybody fly around from ride to ride. Try to look up Joy Park on the web, all you find are the biggest titties I've ever seen on an Asian girl. Then said you told him the last 'ride' would involve him living in the belly of a monster."

I said, "So, what do you want from us? And before you ask me to tell you what's going on, I'll just stop you there, because we don't have any fucking idea."

"I want you to see him. My boy. To talk to him. I

202

need someone else to understand, because I feel like my mind is splitting in half."

I said, "Fine, let us talk to him."

"Mikey won't talk to *you*. He thinks you're the one who snatched him."

Amy said, "What about me? He doesn't have any reason to be scared of me, does he? What is it you want us to find out?"

"I want you to find out if he's still my son."

I thought, *Oh*.

John said, "You think he's been . . . replaced? By a lookalike?"

She said, "The fact that you jumped right to that conclusion tells me you already know this is a possibility. Talk to him. You'll see."

I scratched my chin and watched the rain for a moment. If the child she had gotten back was in fact just a swarm of fuckroaches, then the implications were almost too much for me to grasp. The question of where the real Mikey was being held was just the first in a series of questions I'd need a spreadsheet to sort through.

John said, "All right, I want to get my dog in the room with him, then. He can sniff out weird stuff. It's hard to explain, but if he is what you're suggesting he is, the dog will go nuts at the sight of him."

Chastity said, "And then what?"

And then, I thought, *things will get awkward*.

NON wasn't staking out Chastity's trailer or John's place, and neither were the cops. Still, we decided it wasn't wise to linger at either location. We wound up following Chastity to a motel, the rear window of the Jeep open a few inches so Diogee could stick his face out into the wind. We had gotten a break from the rain, which had turned into the kind of delicate drizzle that feels like a ghost is silently sneezing in your face.

At 9 P.M. we were pulling in to what was without a doubt one of the five shadiest places in town—a sprawling, beat-up motel that never had any vacancies. This was the Roach Motel. It was owned by a local biker/cult leader named Lemmy Roach, and half of the rooms were meet-up spots for local prostitutes and drug dealers. The rest served as a headquarters/compound for Roach's motorcycle gang, Christ's Rebellion. In a town full of groups competing to see who could live the furthest off the grid, I'd say Christ's Rebellion probably did it with the most style.

The name wasn't intended to be ironic or sacrilegious—Roach was a true believer. Once, while recovering from a traumatic brain injury, he had received a revelation from God charging him with a singular mission: to do exactly what he would have done anyway, only more of it. Thus, his faction of Christianity was based around the concept that the only law was God's and that government prohibitions on victimless crimes were mere annoyances to be circumvented. Roach figured, if a person wanted to smoke methamphetamine or get a blowjob from a hooker, that was a choice that person was free to make. Harsh legal consequences were just adding suffering to sin, so humanity's duty was only to ensure that all was done under the umbrella of safety and consent. Otherwise, he said, each of us is responsible for our own soul.

I only know all of this because John bought shit from Roach and once had dragged me along to a big festival CR throws every November in which they gave out frozen turkeys and winter coats to needy families. Lemmy had spent an hour bending my ear with his whole convoluted Christian Libertarian worldview before I was able to escape clutching several typo-riddled pamphlets.

We waited in the parking lot while Chastity talked to a fat dude at the front desk. It seemed like not only did they know each other, but that he wasn't charging her for the room.

John said, "That's weird."

I said, "What?"

"Maggie's mom, I think she said Ted used to take Maggie to Sunday school here. That can't be coincidence, right? Maybe Ted's part of Lemmy's, uh, what's a more polite word for 'cult'? I think Lemmy's right over there."

There was a group of about six bikers across the parking lot standing around a fifty-five-gallon drum with a fire raging inside it. I spotted Lemmy among them, a gangly ginger guy. They were all shouting at a tearful woman, one of the men occasionally hugging her. It looked like an intervention of some kind. I noticed each of the men had a shotgun slung over his back. I'd recommend the same if anyone ever tried to spring an intervention on me.

Amy said, "We should talk to him."

I said, "Later. That whole situation looks super awkward."

Chastity came back out and got Mikey from the Range Rover—a perfectly normal-looking boy, about seven or eight years old—and led him to a room. The goal obviously was to figure out if Mikey was some kind of carnivorous doppelganger *without* traumatizing him for life if it turned out he wasn't. The plan was for me and John to stay out in the Jeep, while Chastity and Amy would go inside and talk with the kid (or "kid"). They'd chat a bit, explain to him what we were doing (or, you know, give him a version of the story that wouldn't terrify him) then bring in the dog.

Before going in, Amy spotted the local hot dog guy a block away, pushing his cart with the orange-and-yellow umbrella, the cart itself plastered with bumper stickers warning about the dangers of jihadists and Obamacare. A minute later, she walked into the room where Chastity was sitting on the bed with Mikey, armed with a hot dog and a soda. She closed the curtains, blocking our view from the parking lot while also blocking Mikey's ability to see that his alleged kidnapper was sitting creepily in a vehicle outside his room. We'd still be able to observe, thanks to the magic of technology; Amy set up a video call and propped up her phone on a dresser, so we'd be able to watch the conversation unfold from the Jeep via John's phone.

On the video feed, we watched as Amy held up the hot dog and soda to Mikey and said, "You hungry?"

Mikey looked at his mother, silently asking permission. She said, "Go ahead. You can trust her."

Mikey took the food and said, "Thank you" without having to be reminded to do it by his mother. He pulled the hot dog out of its wax paper wrapper and set it in front of him.

Chastity said, "This here is a friend of mine, her name

is Amy. She's not with the police, you can relax. She's not just a lot prettier than them, but I think you can tell just by lookin' at her that she's got a good heart. Just tell her what she wants to know. She wants to help us."

Mikey nodded but said nothing. He pulled the hot dog from its bun, then reached down with a pair of fingers and pinched off a piece of the hot dog's skin and ate it.

Amy said, "How are you feeling?"

"Okay."

In the car, John said, "Ask him if he's a walking pile of fuckroach." Amy couldn't hear him, fortunately. We were muted on our end.

Amy asked, "What do you like to do for fun?"

Shrug.

"Do you like to play video games?"

"Sometimes."

"What's your favorite game?"

"*Worst Day of Your Life.*"

"That's the name of the game? It doesn't sound very fun."

"I like the level where you make the old man poop his pants at the mall. I can make him cry every time. You have to make his grandkids laugh at him, that's how you do it."

He peeled another strip of skin off the hot dog, revealing innards that looked like pre-chewed meat.

"Your mom homeschools you, isn't that right? What's your favorite subject?"

He shrugged. "I like smellin' the bad memories. Mom says I'm the best at dream carving. We did metahistory this week. It's hard. Do you know why girls make more noise than men during sex?"

"I . . . what?"

I expected Chastity to be mortified, but instead she looked up at the camera as if to say, "See what I mean?"

"It was to attract other males in the tribe," said Mikey, sounding bored. "So that when one was finished, the next could jump right in. That's why a man's wiener has that mushroom shape at the end, it's to scoop out the cum from the last guy so his own can get in. I saw a video, where it was one woman and twenty men, one after another, she was tied down but you could tell she liked it. And that's how it was, for all of history, the whole tribe would share. That's what girls are built for. A guy shoots his wad and he's done, but a girl is good to go for the next guy, and the next, and the next—"

"Hey," said Amy. "Do you like dogs?"

Amy excused herself from the room, and came out to the Jeep to get Diogee.

I said, "If the dog goes nuts, you get out of there, right? Don't try to talk to Mikey, don't try to Taser him, just get out."

Amy didn't reply. She wrapped Diogee's leash around her hand and led him inside the room, ready to restrain him if he went wild. In the parking lot behind us, there was a commotion as the woman the bikers had been counseling went running off down the sidewalk. Lemmy gave chase, shouting, "You're making a mistake, Eva! *This* is your family! Right here!"

On the video feed, Diogee remained calm as Amy closed the door behind her. Mikey didn't take particular interest in the dog, just glanced at it as it came in. Diogee sniffed around, but it was clearly because he was trying to trace the origin of the hot dog scents.

Mikey looked away from the dog, shook his head, and said, "Pathetic. Packs of wolves used to own this land, all this. Thousands of years pass and we bred them down to *that* little yapping thing. Bred them to catch rats, gave them those tiny little legs. There's a place where the Nephilim did that to the people." Mikey had pulled the straw out of his soda, and was slowly screwing it into the end of his skinned hot dog, skewering it. "They took over, bred us so we'd have no teeth so they wouldn't get in the way when they wanted us to suck 'em off, gave us short little legs so we couldn't run. Only where we bred dogs so their brains would be addicted to our affection, the Nephilim bred us to be addicted to their semen."

Amy nervously said, "Diogee, why don't you go see Mikey over there?" She led the dog over, but it continued to show complete indifference.

I looked up from the phone and said to John, "I'm thinking your dog might be useless."

"You're assuming this is even the same deal here. That Mikey and Nymph are the same thing."

On the screen, Mikey said, "You don't think I'm the real Mikey, do you?"

Chastity shot an alarmed look at Amy, then at the phone, meaning us. She said, "Why would you say that, honey?"

"Maybe the real Mikey is still at Joy Park. Maybe you should check."

Amy said, "Where is Joy Park?"

"You know where. Unless you're talking about the girl with them titties."

Chastity said, "We'll be right back."

Chastity and Amy both stood up to excuse themselves, and it was here that Diogee first showed a reaction. Not to Mikey—he went nuts at the prospect of leaving the room. He barked and snarled at Amy, and even nipped at her when she tried to grab the leash. But when she backed off, he became perfectly calm. She wound up just leaving Diogee in the room. If Mikey tried to attack him or something, I guessed we'd have to go rushing in to the dog's rescue, even if it had turned out that he was shitty at his one job.

A moment later, Chastity and Amy slid into the Jeep and Chastity said, "See what I mean?"

I said, "Let's say it's an imposter. To me, the big news is that your son is still out there, and if he's really at Mine's Eye then I don't know where to . . ."

Chastity was shaking her head. "No."

"I know it's hard to wrap your mind around it, but we've seen—"

"No, it's deeper than that. All of this is."

I said, "If you've got a theory, please share."

Chastity stared out the windshield at the row of hotel doors, each painted a different primary color. It was probably supposed to be festive but the effect was more sad, abandoned circus.

She said, "One time, I read about this parasite, a tiny little roundworm. It spreads itself by getting inside birds, then the bird's droppings are full of its eggs. Well, the parasite's first problem is getting inside the bird in the first place, you see. So here's what it does. It infects *an ant*. Then it makes the ant swell up big and red, so that it looks just like a berry. Then it takes over the ant's brain and convinces it to go climb up a tree and stand there among the other berries. Bird comes along, eats the ant, thinking it's a berry."

I said, "I don't get it."

Chastity was staring hard at the hotel room window, nothing visible behind the closed curtain.

"When Mikey got taken, the first thing I thought of was two years ago, on Mikey's sixth birthday, I took him to Pizza Circus. And I remember he got scared by those fiberglass clowns they got on the wall and we had to leave early. Took him home and made him a grilled cheese instead. That's his favorite. We sat on the sofa and watched a movie, that cartoon where Chris Rock plays a zebra, and they're all zoo animals, tryin' to escape. I think I laughed more than he did."

She stopped talking, staring at that window. We waited for her to finish the story, but she just stared. I thought I saw the curtain twitch, like maybe Mikey was sneaking a peek out at us.

It was Amy who finally said, "Two years ago? That's not right, Pizza Circus got trashed during the last round of craziness, with the looting. Never opened back up."

Chastity just nodded.

"I don't have a son. I never did."

211

13. WAIT, WHAT THE FUCK?

I said, "That can't be . . . no. You absolutely thought you had a son as of like, an hour ago."

She nodded, absently. "And I got memories. Going back eight years. But they don't make sense, if you think about 'em hard enough. It's all bent and twisted. He don't got a room of his own at the trailer, supposedly on account of losing my last place in a fire. But he don't got clothes, or toys, neither."

"But . . . how would you not notice that? Like, instantly?"

She shook her head. "You seen them TV shows about the hoarders, people got garbage piled up so high that they can't even walk from one room to the next? Family tries to intervene, but those people literally can't see the garbage, can't be convinced anything's wrong. Your mind, it gets these blind spots to the most basic things. I got a cousin who weighs six hundred pounds, but all thought of that goes out the window next mealtime rolls around. And then I got to thinking about that parasite. All that little worm is doing is convincing the ant that it's always been there, inside it, and that walkin' up the tree to where the berries are is its favorite thing. Even though everything inside it should know it's suicide."

I said, "But humans *aren't ants*. You're saying this thing showed up, and convinced you that you had already had a son, complete with thousands of memories going back years. How would that even work?"

Amy said, "Your memories are physical structures in your brain. It would be the exact same process as the ant, just a little more complicated."

John said, "The fuckroach, we could all feel it trying to worm its way into our history. Not just looking like a cell phone, but making us remember that it was one. Making it just plausible enough."

Amy said, "What's worse, it looks like the dog can't detect these things after all. If we're now sure 'Mikey' in there is one of them . . ."

John said, "Eh, it's not the first time he's been wrong. He totally whiffed on that possessed stuffed bear I won at the Fall Festival. Just kept humping it."

Amy said, "*What are you talking about?*"

"You don't remember the thing with the bear? It was when I still lived in that apartment on—"

Amy clutched her hair with her one hand and said, "Oh my god. You think you've always owned that dog."

I said, "Uh . . . what?"

Amy threw herself back in the car seat. "I've never seen that dog before today. I thought John was just dog sitting or something."

I stared at the motel room door. "*No*. Just . . . no.

That's Diogee. He and Molly never got along? Chewed up one of your sandals one time?"

"I have never lost a shoe to a dog."

Behind the motel room window, the curtain twitched again.

John said to her, "No, this is . . . they're scrambling your brain here. This is you, not us. I remember *everything*. This used to be Marcy's dog, he stayed with me when we broke up, her roommate was allergic. Years ago, same year as we had that bad winter and . . . all the stuff happened."

I said, "Yeah, it has to be Amy who's wrong. *Again*." I said to her, "You remember the night all those guys burst in looking for the, uh, thing a few weeks ago? And you threw it in the river . . ."

She shook her head. "I remember that event, but there was no dog."

John said, "We took him to the vet! He ate the chocolate?"

"Do you have the receipt?"

"Sure, I . . . wait, no, she didn't charge us."

"We did not go to the vet that night, John."

Chastity said, "If you concentrate, if you focus hard on them memories, you can break them apart, find the real memories in there. Hiding. See, they picked the wrong target with me. You can make me doubt the world, but you won't make me doubt myself. My memory, my false memory, was tellin' me that Mikey's father was some guy I slept with, a guy I met at the lake and then left town after a one-night stand. But I ain't never done that in my life—the kind of man who does that, he don't make it to my bed. And if I had a kid, a real one, I'd be livin' in a better place. In a better *town*."

I said, "And your friends, your family, they wouldn't wonder why you're acting like you've got a child, out of the blue?"

"Don't talk to my family, what there is of it, and I'm not much for socializing. That thing, it knew it. Picked me for a reason, I'd say. But it didn't take."

John said, "Okay, okay. So, let's focus on the most immediate problem. Now they're both in there, in that room, the kid and the dog, neither of which are of this world. What the hell do we do? Leave?"

Amy said, "If we can get it to drop its disguise can we, I don't know, talk to it? Find out what it wants?"

I said, "How in the world do we get it to drop its disguise?"

John said, "We'd have to make it want to. Wait, while it's in dog mode, does it have to behave like a dog? Maybe I go in and say, 'Oh look, since you're just a dog, surely you wouldn't mind licking some peanut butter *off of my balls.*'"

"Maybe just knowing we can see through it will be enough," suggested Amy.

John said, "I wish we still had the Soy Sauce. It would know what to do."

Chastity said, "The what?"

I said, "What he's referring to is slang, for a, uh, substance. Think of it as a performance-enhancing drug for people with any kind of paranormal abilities. Or whatever. It's the reason we can do what we do."

John said, "I'm ninety-nine percent sure that on the Sauce we would be able to see through the thing's camouflage, through the whole illusion."

"Anyway," I said, "it's moot, because we tossed our only vial of the stuff into the river."

Chastity said, "Well, that conversation was a good use of our time."

I said, "All right, so we go in and we talk to it and try to find out what it wants. And if what it wants is to feed on us and, uh, breed on us, then what?"

We all just looked at Chastity. Only she could say this.

"We kill it. Only cure for a parasite." She looked at us. "Any idea how we do that?"

John said, "They don't like fire."

Amy said, "We're not going to start a fire in an occupied motel."

Chastity nodded. "So much crack in this place, fire would get the whole town high. No, we got to take him somewhere else, away from all the people. Mikey and your dog both."

John said, "I know a place."

All four of us cautiously approached the motel room door, the only one of us who was armed was Chastity, with her revolver. John asked her if she wanted him to take the gun.

"No. If this goes wrong and something has to be done, it'll be me who does it."

I said, "Just be ready—this thing is going to try to pull on your heartstrings. It's going to play up the little kid stuff, he's going to bat his eyes and say, 'You wouldn't shoot me, Mommy!' You sure you're ready for that?"

"Nope. But I'll do it anyway. If you're tellin' me you wouldn't have any problem pulling the trigger in that situation, well, that ain't nothin' to brag about."

She steeled herself, pushed open the door, and screamed.

From the neck down, the creature standing in the doorway was little Mikey Payton, just as we'd seen him, wearing a faded LeBron James T-shirt. From the neck up, he was Diogee. Specifically, the ass part. The dog's two rear legs were draped over Mikey's chest, its tail stuck straight up into the air where Mikey's forehead would have been.

The dog's anus opened and closed like a mouth and said, "Look, Mommy! I'm a butthead!"

Chastity slammed the door.

I said, "Okay, I was . . . not expecting that."

The huge, gun-toting, screaming black woman had drawn the attention of the bikers around the burn barrel. The fat guy from behind the counter leaned his head out of the office a few doors down, looking annoyed. It sounded like motel rules were being broken.

Lemmy Roach said, "Chastity? What's happening?"

I said, "Nothing to see here! It's fine!"

Then the curtains of our room were ripped aside and what appeared there wasn't Mikey, or the dog, or dog-butt Mikey. It was a naked young woman, visible from the hips up. She was splattered with blood and appeared to have one wrist shackled to a headboard with a pair of handcuffs. She pressed herself against the window and screamed, "HELP! THEY'RE GOING TO KILL ME!"

Two more guys ran out of a nearby room to join the bikers at the burn barrel. Roach yanked a pair of short shotguns into his hands and screamed, "THEY'VE GOT LACY!"

I was, in that instant, sure that no woman named Lacy had ever existed. I was also sure that every single person in the vicinity would instantly remember Lacy, have a head full of fond memories of her, and feel an overwhelming urge to protect her.

Roach led a pack of bikers toward the door, each of them drawing firearms. Chastity screamed at them to stay back and, when they refused, brandished the revolver.

"You go in there, you're gonna die! It's a trap!"

Of course, the bikers had no reason whatsoever to believe this was anything but the ravings of a lunatic who had kidnapped a female friend of theirs, and also they had shotguns. The sound of conflict had carried across the grounds and room doors were popping open all around us, disgorging biker dudes eager to join the fight. One woman in black leather quickly hustled away three young kids—some of these bikers had families.

The "woman" behind the glass continued to scream and beg for help. John, Amy, Chastity, and I faced a phalanx of shotguns and black leather.

Roach, brandishing a total of four shotgun barrels by himself, screamed, "CHASTITY, YOU'VE GOT THREE SECONDS TO PUT THAT DOWN AND GET OUT OF THE WAY!"

John said to him, "This may seem like a weird time to ask, but do you know Ted Kno—"

There was a commotion at the opposite end of the parking lot. Everyone spun around to see three black NON trucks come barreling in. There was no entrance to the lot over there, they just smashed through the motel's sign and flattened a row of shrubs, skidding to a stop. A dozen black cloaks flowed into the parking lot, bringing their weird-ass weapons to bear.

The naked woman in the window screamed and pulled on her restraints.

The downpour chose that moment to resume.

The nearest NON cloak was the same one that had led the charge into John's living room that night weeks ago—or at least, this one was wearing the same puffy-cheeked infant mask. It opened its baby mouth—it had tiny little rubber teeth—and said, "STEP AWAY FROM THE ORGANISM."

Thinking back, I'd say this was a mistake. These instructions made perfect sense to me, John, Amy, and maybe Chastity. That was it. No one else in that crowd knew what "organism" they were referencing, or where it was, or in what direction they should step in order to find themselves "away" from it.

Most of the bikers had now trained their guns on the NON cloaks, with a few seeming to remember that their most urgent task was to free their beloved Lacy. We all stood that way for a moment, getting drenched in the downpour. To me, it seemed like a perfect time to just slip away and let these people fight it out amongst themselves, but there was no way to communicate that to the other three in a way that wouldn't tip off everyone else.

At the window, "Lacy" screamed, "HE'S COMING! OH GOD, HE'S COMING!"

A muscular arm reached in, grabbed her hair, and yanked her back onto the bed, letting the curtains fall closed.

That did it.

Roach yelled, "Get off her, you sick son of a bitch!" and sprinted toward the door. He pushed past Chastity and blew the doorknob off with his shotgun. He yanked open the door and plunged inside.

Five seconds later, a spray of guts and black leather flew out of the door.

What walked out the door next, was a torso.

"Lacy" only existed down to her waist, which ended in rows of tiny fuckroach feet. She came scooting out of the doorway, the disembodied man's arm (which ended at the bicep) still clutching her hair.

Chastity said, "Oh, shit!" and shot at the Lacy thing with her revolver. It flinched and pulsed, the fuckroaches giving up their disguise for a split second each time a bullet struck home.

The NON cloaks screamed at Chastity to stop, in their weird pseudohuman voices. Then, Babyface fired a blue beam that was presumably intended to scramble her brain in some way that'd neutralize the threat. It missed, and instead hit a member of Christ's Rebellion. The man screamed, "VIOLENCE IS WRONG!" He then threw his gun aside and lay down on the soaked pavement, appearing to go to sleep.

The Lacy torso waddled its way toward the bikers, the spell having been thoroughly broken at this point. They opened up on it with their shotguns, blowing off fuckroaches with each blast. Babyface commanded them to stop shooting the specimen, and when the bikers didn't comply, another blue beam was fired at them. It hit a biker with a glancing blow that just brushed the back of his hair. He blinked, confused, then started firing his gun wildly into the sky screaming, "FUCK YOU, MOON!"

The rest of the bikers were now torn between the disembodied torso monster and the squad of spooky assholes shooting shafts of magic at them. Some turned their shotguns on NON, knocking down black cloaks and making a strategic retreat across the parking lot, toward where their bikes were parked.

Apparently frustrated at being ignored, "Lacy" dispersed completely into a swarm, the creatures whizzing around until they coalesced into a group of six severed heads, each of the same elderly woman, floating a few feet off the ground. The biker nearest to them had time to scream, "GRANDMA, NO!" before they launched themselves at him and started eating his face. The man tumbled to the ground at my feet . . .

. . . and onto the pavement rolled the brushed steel canister.

The vial Amy had chucked into the river three weeks ago.

The one that contained the Soy Sauce.

14. A BRIEF HISTORY OF INVASIVE FISH SPECIES IN THE MISSISSIPPI RIVER AND THEIR IMPACT ON INTERNATIONAL COMMERCE

After Amy pitched the metal vial into the river, it in fact did not float all the way to the Gulf of Mexico, as she had hoped. That would have required a series of remarkable coincidences, considering how many opportunities there are for a floating object to wash ashore or become ensnared in some obstacle along those hundreds of miles of heavily traveled waterway. The object did, however, make it to the Mississippi, where it was promptly swallowed by an eighty-pound Asian carp.

The carp boasted a proud, heroic lineage (though of course it was not aware of this, or anything else aside from a vague sense that being a fish was pretty sweet).

You see, it is well known that the best way to catch catfish in the Mississippi is with cruelty. You simply take a smaller, living fish, ram a hook through its back, and secure the line to a float or an anchor. The terrified, impaled bait will desperately try to swim away until its frantic struggle attracts a catfish that will swallow it whole. In the 1970s, fishermen started using Asian carp for their live bait operations, but the carp quickly turned the tables—they ripped themselves free from their rigs, found mates, started families and, having no natural predators, promptly spread down the Mississippi like a conquering horde.

It was only a few years ago that someone had the bright idea to catch and export Asian carp back to China, where they can still fetch a high price as a delicacy. Thus, the carp that swallowed the vial was caught the next day by a commercial fishing vessel owned by a man named Jon Minchin. The fish, with the vial lodged in its throat, was taken back to port and then crammed alive into a freshwater container along with a hundred other carp just like it. The container was then transferred by forklift into the belly of an airliner. As the carp swam in its cramped, dark prison, it had no idea it was being flown around the world and, in fact, did not even know it lived in a world that could be flown around. It should be noted that four minutes after offloading the fish, a crew member on Minchin's boat tossed a cigarette that ignited fumes from a leaking fuel line. The ensuing explosion killed two men.

The carp containing the metal vial arrived at a massive fish processing facility in Nantong, 7,370 miles away from where it had been caught. There, a machine designed to lop off the head of the carp smashed into the metal object in its gullet, causing the blade to shatter. This sent a shard flying into the neck of an unfortunate line worker who bled out in forty-three seconds flat. An hour later, the line repair tech, a twenty-three-year-old man named Mïn, replaced the ruined blade on the fish decapitator and, during cleanup, found the strange metal vial wedged in the works. Recognizing it as some kind of foreign object and not a loose part of any of the machine's components, Mĭn washed the metal cylinder and marveled at its properties. It felt cold, as if refrigerated from the inside, but was otherwise featureless—no seams where it could be opened, no inscriptions or decorations. It had mangled the teeth of the processor, yet had not a scratch on its surface.

Mĭn decided to take the object home. His young wife suffered from multiple sclerosis and was unable to work a day job. However, she had an artistic streak and had discovered that it was therapeutic for her to make sculptures out of found objects, welding the pieces together and selling the finished products on the Internet (if, that is, it was one of the few pieces she had not grown too attached to). Mĭn thus tried to bring home any items he thought she would find interesting (though regardless of what he brought her, she would always smile and make the same little sound every time, as if gasping with delight).

A week later, the metal vial had become the torso of a sculpture in the shape of a steampunk robot, its joints and limbs made up of springs and gears she had recovered from an old clock. The parts were held together with glue, as she had found the metal of the vial could not be welded or soldered. Still, she had finished the figurine and put it up for sale on the online craft marketplace Etsy. A week later, it sold to a teenager in Spain named Juan Jimenez. Unfortunately, he would never receive the item; the international FedEx flight carrying the parcel crashed into the

French countryside, killing everyone on board.

In the name of international cooperation and improving safety standards, the United States' National Transportation Safety Board (NTSB) frequently sends teams to assist in the investigation of crash sites around the world. The lead investigator, named John Mindelson, discovered the vial when he accidentally kicked it, his attention drawn to this lone unburnt object in a twisted pile of scorched metal that had been roasting in jet fuel for several hours. The vial was clean, the other parts of the sculpture having been blasted neatly off its surface. It seemed impossible that the item could be a factor in the crash, but he kept finding his curiosity drawn to it, particularly the way in which it seemed to always remain about thirty degrees below room temperature.

More out of blind curiosity than anything, Mindelson decided to ship the object to a private aviation forensics laboratory in Wichita, Kansas, for analysis. This time, the cargo landed safely in Newark and soon after, the vial was on a courier truck heading west. The route to Wichita would not have taken it through Undisclosed, as the interstate bypassed the town completely. However, the driver of the courier truck, Minnie Johnson, heard from dispatch that traffic was backed up on said interstate for miles due to a truck full of bees that had overturned, blocking both westbound lanes. Dispatch did not let her know that a young man in a passing vehicle had jumped out in order to rescue the driver of that semi, only to be attacked by bees and promptly die from anaphylaxis.

Minnie was forced to exit onto highway 131, toward the creepy small city she always tried to avoid whenever possible. Two minutes after entering Undisclosed city limits, the driver approached an overpass and saw some dumb fuck in a Range Rover trying to pass a semi in the eastbound lane, setting the SUV on a collision course with Minnie's own goddamned face. Minnie braked, but knew that it ultimately would have no effect on how this situation would play out—she had nowhere to go and at best could decrease the amount the Ranger Rover's cabin was compacted by 10 percent or so, to make it a little easier for the highway patrol to dig the body parts out of the wreckage. The life or death of the Range Rover driver was entirely in their own hands.

She felt only a split second of relief when the Range Rover jerked aside and threaded the needle between Minnie's rig and the one in the other lane. That's because right behind the suicidal Range Rover was a psychopath with an even more fervent death wish—the driver of the flat-black truck *had his goddamned headlights off.* Minnie uttered just one syllable of what was going to be an extraordinarily creative string of profanities before her rig slammed into the truck. Both vehicles went tumbling over the railing, the cab never detaching from the trailer, leaving it and the driver's shattered body dangling off the overpass just a few feet above the roadway that crossed below.

Passing under the overpass at that exact moment was a pack of six motorcycles driven by members of the Christ's Rebellion gang led by Lemmy Roach, with John "Beergut" Klosterman bringing up the rear. Beergut happened to glance up exactly at the moment that the horrific collision took place overhead, a semi-trailer rolling and flying to pieces, sending cargo raining down on the roadway around the bikes. Beergut was so busy dodging debris that he did not feel that a single, metal object had landed in the sweatshirt hood that was draped between his shoulder blades. The cylinder would remain there until he would tumble to the ground in the parking lot of the Roach Motel, being bitten by the flying heads of his own deceased grandmother.

15. SOY SAUCE

I reached for the vial, but Chastity yanked me back up to my feet. Damn, she was strong. She screamed, "LET'S GO!"

John saw what I was reaching for, and lunged for it. He accidentally kicked it away instead, sending it rolling across the pavement. A running biker stepped on it, causing him to trip and fly backward, breaking his neck when he landed awkwardly on a parking block. This caused the vial to roll forward again, right toward Amy, who picked it up in stride.

We all went stumbling away from the chaos. We were cut off from both of our vehicles, which were parked behind the bizarre three-way maelstrom behind us. We ran across a row of Harleys and without hesitation, Chastity jumped on one and kicked the engine to life.

John stopped, saw what she was doing, and straddled the next bike over. He started it, yelled at Amy to jump on behind him, and she did.

I do not know how to drive a motorcycle.

John peeled off down the street, and yelled back at me something that sounded like, "BEANIE WIENIE!"

Chastity turned back to me and said, "What are you waiting for? Get on!"

I did.

We dodged through the sparse nighttime traffic and I thought I was going to die. The raindrops were cold needles on my face. We followed John out to the industrial park, not too far from the ice factory where all this bullshit had begun. I knew where he was going. There were several vast buildings in the neighborhood that belonged to businesses that hadn't survived the economic downturn this town had gone through about seven economic downturns ago. One was a former beans-and-wienies cannery, a sprawling, gray structure with giant, rusting metal letters welded to the front that said,

BEANS
WIENIES

in a bombastic font that made it look like the slogan for a dystopian totalitarian dictatorship. John's band had played a concert here years ago; at the time the entire second floor of the abandoned cannery had been repurposed as a living space for a hippie artist commune. Back then, twenty or thirty people would drift in and out, living off the grid (though considering they were stealing power by splicing into nearby utility poles and getting city water from unmetered valves, they were actually very much on the grid—they just weren't paying for it).

Then, one day, a kid died of a heroin overdose and the company that still owned the land decided it was too much of a liability issue. They ran out the hippies and hired a security guard to drive around the place a couple of times a day to kick out homeless people who came in to drink and get out of the rain. Fortunately, said security guard was Tyler Schultz, a friend of John's. When we pulled up to the length of thin chain that served as a gate, Tyler dropped it and waved us past.

We pulled the motorcycles inside the building to shield them from view. The cavernous structure was a clammy, drippy space, and much of the artwork that had been left behind by the commune was ruined. There was a faded spray-painted mural on one wall depicting the Statue of Liberty covered in blood, underneath it were the words WAR KILLS. I passed a fiberglass Mickey Mouse with dollar signs for eyes and the word GREED spray-painted across his chest (I don't know what that was supposed to symbolize). There was a creepy concrete snowman with a misshapen face and a single arm made of rusty rebar.

John led us upstairs, toward the quadrant of the second floor that had been devoted to the living area—the roof didn't leak in that particular spot and four old sofas were positioned facing each other. There was still a pair of refrigerators in the corner, and a sink.

Chastity glanced around quickly, then went and stationed herself by a window.

John said, "As far as safe houses go, this is pretty much the last one in town that I've got access to."

I said, "I don't like it, the artwork out there is freaking out my worldview."

Chastity said, "It could be worse. Can see

approaching vehicles from right here, six ways out of the building if you've got to make a run for it." She pulled out a roll of cash wrapped in a rubber band.

She peeled off three hundred-dollar bills and said, "You got twenty-five in change?"

Amy said, "Keep your money. You didn't get Mikey back."

"Stop with that. This isn't about charity or having a good heart. I don't pay you, maybe next month one of my bosses assumes he don't need to pay me. Maybe that becomes the norm, everybody pressuring each other to turn down their paycheck in the name of courtesy. Then nothin' gets done, because people know they won't get paid and underneath all our generosity bullshit, it's incentives that make the world go 'round. You did the work, you took the risk. You got twenty-five in change or not?"

John did.

Chastity said, "I had a 'go bag' in the trailer, now I'm kickin' myself for not grabbing it when all this started. Too risky to go back there, assume the Range Rover is a loss, too . . ."

She was muttering all of this to herself, working through it. It was pretty clear she wasn't asking our advice.

I said, "You're leaving town?"

"You're not?"

Amy said, "We have to stay and see this through."

"And what does that entail, exactly? Seein' it through?"

"Well for one thing," said Amy. "We have to warn Ted."

I said, "About what?"

"About *Maggie*."

"Why would—oh, *fuck*. You think she's like Mikey? Like she never even existed?"

John scrunched up his brow. "Wait, no. They had a photo. Remember? Ted pulled it out of his wallet, looked like a picture you'd have taken at Sears."

"Do you still have it?"

"No . . . but, you know, just because Mikey was one doesn't mean Maggie is."

Chastity said, "If she is what Mikey was, then you've got to take it out. And I'm guessing the parents are still under the spell, thinkin' it's their kid. So good luck with that."

Amy said, "If they are still 'under its spell,' why did it work on them but not you?"

"I got a theory about that. See, I think it'd work on you, too, but it wouldn't work on your man there. John, I don't know him well enough. Could go either way. You, well, you seem like the kind of girl who'd wake a guy up at three in the morning just because you forgot to say goodnight."

"I guess I don't get it."

Chastity shrugged. "People can either feel unconditional love, or they can't. Depends on what you had growin' up, I think." To me she said, "I expect your parents weren't in the picture, right?" She didn't wait for me to answer. "Mine, neither. Grow up thinkin' love is somethin' you earn based on performance, and you dole it out just the same." She said to Amy, "I bet when you and your man fight, you get madder and madder, while he just gets quiet, and kind of dead inside. You get more and more upset because you've got that love for him that can't be undone, no matter what, and that strain pressing against it tears you up. David there, I bet he just gets *cold*. Same as me. Can't fake that shit. Well, with that unconditional love comes blind spots. That's what they depend on. So, Mikey started acting all crazy, my memories of him got all jumbled up, it didn't take too much to sever that connection. But a lot of moms, they'd die first. That love, that unquestioning love that pours out of some people, just wipes out all the wrongs. Make you overlook anything."

I said, "It's using it as a survival adaptation."

"You could say humans do the same. One thing we do know—they're real eager to get us to go to that mine. I assume something big and nasty is gonna jump outta there if somebody clears those rocks, right?"

John said, "That would probably be the *best*-case scenario."

"Well," said Chastity, "I do wish you luck. I'm gonna go someplace peaceful, and try to remember who I was before a monster rewrote the last eight years of my life."

Amy said, "You don't even feel the slightest urge to stay and help?"

"Sometimes the best 'help' you can offer is to get your own self to safety and not add to the pile of victims somebody else has got to clean up. Problem isn't that there's not enough heroes in the world, problem is too many dumb people assume they are one."

I said, "Wait, one last thing. What was your connection to the motel, back there? How did you know the Christ's Rebellion people?"

"Did some business with Lemmy, he owes me a favor

or three. And no, it wasn't drugs or whores, nothin' like that. I repair motorcycles, that's one of my several jobs. Why?"

Amy said, "The Knolls had connections there, too. Trying to figure out what it means."

"You could ask Lemmy, but I'm thinkin' he didn't survive getting splattered across the parking lot back there."

John was turning the Soy Sauce vial over in his hands.

Chastity said, "What's that?"

I said, "That there is the Soy Sauce. The container that Amy chucked into the river a few weeks ago. Found it on the ground in the parking lot of the Roach Motel, six inches from my feet."

"Well, that don't sound like luck."

I said, "In this town, it's not just good and evil. Behind the scenes, it's all these competing agendas. Those agents, the ones you rescued us from, they were convinced there's something that wants us to win."

Chastity scoffed and shook her head. "You people are cutting wires on the bomb and hoping you got the right ones. Promise me you'll give me a couple hours to get out of town before you blow it up."

John said, "That's why we have to take the Sauce. We need to understand what's happening."

"Uh-huh. And this isn't the kind of 'understanding' you get from peyote? Where you sit there and stare at the wallpaper and think it holds all the secrets of the universe, drool runnin' from your lower lip?"

I said, "Well . . . not usually." It's actually hard to succinctly describe the effects of Soy Sauce, in the sense that it's hard to succinctly describe the effect of a gorilla on a child's birthday party—it can go several ways. I said, "You ever play video games? Probably not. Anyway, one time, John and I were playing one of the *Grand Theft Auto* games, and our character glitched through the floor and wound up in some foggy netherworld full of floating random objects and distorted characters locked in these broken, looping animations. I think Soy Sauce is kind of like that—it reveals the nature of the game by breaking it."

"And you're going to try to convince me to take some?"

I said, "No, I'm pretty sure it would kill you immediately. Amy, too. With John and I, it, uh, isn't exactly pleasant, but once we come down we usually have a clearer idea of what needs done. Here's all I ask. Stay here with Amy while we take the Sauce, when we come back, we might just know something that will help you, too. Even if your plan is to run."

She watched the window. "One hour. If I see them coming before that, I'm gone. So what you're gonna do, do it now."

John was already twisting the cap off the Soy Sauce vial. You might have noticed that no one who examined the vial before now noted a cap, but that's how it works—it opens when it wants to be opened. Otherwise, I'm pretty sure that a group of guys with a diamond saw, a jackhammer, and that huge green laser from the Death Star wouldn't so much as smudge it.

John tilted the bottle toward his mouth. A single drop of pure black goo formed at the lip of the vial, dripped, then swerved as it fell. It completely avoided his face and splattered directly onto his crotch.

"Son of a—"

The Sauce ate a hole in John's pants. He slapped at it as Chastity looked on, bewildered. The Sauce vial tumbled out of his hand and landed on the tiled floor. John spasmed into a fetal position, clutching his groin. Then, a few seconds later, he stopped struggling.

The Soy Sauce took him.

John stood up, nodded thoughtfully, and said, "Okay, they are going to find out we're here in thirty-seven minutes, twenty-four seconds. Unless we take measures. Yes. Measures."

Then he sprinted across the room toward a window and dove through the glass.

We ran after him, arriving at the shattered window to see John running across the parking lot below.

Amy yelled after him, but I said, "Just let him go."

I walked back and kneeled down to grab the vial. A thin little stream of the Sauce ran out onto the tiles, inching toward me. No . . . *crawling* toward me. Like a little thread-thin worm. Acting with intent.

The tiny black worm writhed and then curled, as if sniffing the air. Then it flicked up toward my face, right at my left eye.

Pain exploded through the back of my skull.

And then, the world was gone.

My surroundings vanished from sight. This was not an uncommon experience on the Sauce. Instead of kneeling on the linoleum floor of the Beanie Wienie cannery, I found myself shambling aimlessly around a barren landscape in which it looked like everything had been eaten by locusts—all was dust and leafless trees and little sprigs of vegetation that had been gnawed down to the roots. The sky was an acrid, cancerous ruin.

As I wandered, I came upon what looked like a floating worm. It hovered about three feet off the ground; at its base was a pile of coiled loops that led up to a twitching bulb the size of a football, then a single segmented tube that extended upright until it ended in an opening. It turned toward me. At the top was a human mouth—the "worm" was a disembodied esophagus and digestive tract, ending in the bundle of small intestine. At the bottom it possessed an anus and, in the front, a six-inch-long erect penis.

The mouth opened. A guttural song emerged.

Soon, I saw another one—a digestive and reproductive tract, floating free of whatever body it had been attached to, this one with female genitalia at the base. Its mouth opened and out fluttered a high-pitched song, as if in response to the other. I backed away, but they were not pursuing me—they were pursuing each other. The two pulsing bundles of offal met, the mouths locked together in a kiss and soon the penis was pumping away, the wet tangle of intestines falling to the ground and thrashing against one another in ecstasy.

I soon encountered another such pair, and another, and another. Then I crested a hill and below me was a massive pink pile of the intestine monsters engaged in an orgy, the mass rippling and throbbing. All around the perimeter were tiny versions, little bundles that inched along the ground like knotted earthworms.

Then I blinked and it was gone. Or rather, *I* was gone.

I was now in a makeshift classroom, with small desks and a big sign on the wall bearing a Dr. Seuss quote ("Today you are you, that is truer than true. There is no one alive, who is youer than you"). The room was vacant except for a single rough-looking woman who was standing in the front, screaming and screaming into the empty room.

Then I blinked and I was standing in my apartment, in my bathroom. It was nighttime and I could hear the faint drum of the rain. In walked Amy, who closed the door, lowered the lid on the toilet, and sat on top of it. She stared straight ahead, in silence, covering her mouth with her hand. She was wearing her work clothes—a clean white button-up shirt and navy pants. The ceiling was dripping right into her hair but she didn't seem to notice.

And then, very quietly, she started crying.

I moved toward her, reaching out, but of course I wasn't there, and this wasn't happening, not right now, anyway. Soon she got up, dried her eyes, and left the room. I followed her, through the living room. She swung her red raincoat onto her arms and headed out of the apartment. I followed—drifting, like a movie camera on a rig—as she walked across the street to the convenience store, jogging through the rain with her umbrella. At the door she wiped her eyes again, then went in and bought the last blueberry muffin from the little case on the counter. And then I blinked and . . .

I had a body again. I was lying in a filthy room that looked like it had once been a hospital. I was on a gurney, and I was unable to move despite the fact that I could see no visible restraints.

I craned my head around, trying to get a sense of my surroundings. There was a huge cockroach crawling up my shirt, toward my face. That's what it most resembled, anyway; it was fully two inches long and had tiny pincers like a crab. I tried to kind of shake my chest, to knock it off, but I couldn't even move enough to do that.

I heard a voice say, "You're awake," and I saw Nymph step out of the shadows. It was that fit and well-to-do version of myself, only instead of a suit he was wearing the same clothes I had on (stained jeans and an old T-shirt that said CHICAGO BEARS, 1984 SUPER BOWL CHAMPS around a navy-and-orange-clad Dan Marino). As if to mock me.

I said, "Is that actually you? Or is this just more hallucination bullshit?"

He didn't answer. Just smiled.

I said, "Because if it's you, I have a bunch of questions. But I'm not going to bother if it's just some symbolic bullshit meant to teach me something about myself."

"Tell me," said Nymph, "if I asked you to eat that insect on your shirt, would you?" I didn't answer. What was the point? He continued, "What if I left and came back a week from now? Would your hunger be such that you would be willing to eat it then?"

The bug was scaling a wrinkle in my shirt just above my nipples. It had yellow eyes. It blinked.

"The answer is forty-six," Nymph said, before I could answer. "That's how many hours without food you could go before willingly eating a living insect. At any given moment you are less than two days from abandoning all dignity in the name of desire."

Next, he gestured to the corner and said, "What

about that corpse of a small child, lying over there?" There was in fact a little boy there, lying still in a fetal position. Dark skin, maybe Hispanic. "How long until you would eat him? I know the answer, but I'm curious to see how far off your own estimate is. I also know what that number would be if the boy was alive."

I said, "The thing in the old coal mine, your 'Master,' what is it? What does it want?"

He cocked his head with a look that said, *Are you seriously asking me that?*

I tried again, because why not? "Why is it trying to brainwash people with the idea of fake offspring? What's the point? Is it all just a game? Did the Master get bored?"

Nymph took a few strides my way and stopped next to a rusty metal tray attached to the gurney. "Look."

On the tray were three objects:

A surgeon's scalpel;

A hunk of black rock that had been chiseled into a crude blade, like something you'd find at an archaeological dig;

A hunk of black rock that was still in standard rock shape.

"Obsidian," said Nymph. "All three, I mean. Did you know that the sharpest blades in the world are made from obsidian? This scalpel has been sharpened to an edge just thirty angstroms wide—one hundred millionth of a centimeter. A razor's edge is twenty times thicker, by comparison. So, let me ask you—which of these three tools would you like me to use to remove your face?"

Since we both had my face I actually wasn't sure if he was talking about removing it from my skull or his.

Not that it mattered, since this was all some sort of vision and wasn't actually happening.

Are you absolutely sure of that?

The bug had reached the top of my shirt, standing on the elastic neck band. There was a soft hissing noise and I realized I could hear the thing breathing. Labored, like its tiny lungs had asthma.

"How about this," Nymph said. "I will ask you a question. If you answer correctly, we move on to the next round. If you answer incorrectly, I make a single circular incision beginning behind your right ear, looping around under your chin, behind your left ear, and across your forehead, meeting back at the right ear again. Then I simply peel off your face, like peeling an orange. Here is the question—which of those three is a naturally occurring object?"

I had trouble understanding how I was going to get any useful information this way, but it didn't seem like I had any choice but to play along. I looked over the three objects. Which is naturally occurring, he asks? Well, the scalpel was obviously man-made. Of the other two hunks of obsidian, one looked untouched by human hands, owing its shape to wind or erosion or whatever. The other had clearly been chipped into a blade, maybe by an ancient caveman. So, it was made of stone, which is naturally occurring, but the "blade" shape was man-made. Seemed like a semantic argument to me.

The man with my face said, "You have thirty seconds to answer, and then I start cutting."

"There is no right answer. You could make the argument that both the . . ."

And then it hit me.

"Okay," I said, "I get it. All three are naturally occurring."

"Please explain."

"Because humans shaped the stone blade and manufactured the scalpel, but humans are naturally occurring organisms. So anything we build or create is also naturally occurring."

"Correct! Erosion by flowing water and chiseling by human hands are both just atoms moving atoms. Molecules grow into cells and cells grow into brains and organs and limbs to shape the stone. A colony of fungi, an anthill, a human city—all are a convergence of particles and forces that alter the landscape. In fact, any substance or occurrence that is *not* naturally occurring must, therefore, be *supernatural* in nature. So, that leads us to the second question. Of the two cutting tools you see before you, which was made by choice?"

"I see where this is going."

"Do you? The crude blade there was made five hundred thousand years ago by a hooting, stinking creature you would in no way recognize as human. So, when that hairy primate fashioned this blade for the purpose of slicing meat from bone—the same purpose I intend to use it for—did it *choose* to do it? Or was it just following its animal instincts, the way an insect will scurry from the light?"

The wheezing bug on my chest had crawled off my shirt, and I could feel its feet tickling my neck.

He said, "Twenty seconds."

"I don't know, man, ask a scientist. Maybe it was just hungry and had a dead animal in front of him he couldn't bite into."

"So, you're saying that hunger was the inventor. Why, then, is that different from the scalpel? Otherwise, you would be suggesting that there is an energy that allows you, as a man, to defy the simple mechanism that causes the tree to grow toward sunlight or the insect to flee from it. An energy that lets you defy the physical chain reactions that govern the behavior of literally *everything else in the universe,* from subatomic particles to the grunting ancestor who made this blade. An energy that exists only in modern humans."

"Then none of them were made by choice. That's the answer you want, isn't it? So there you go, that's my answer. We're all just . . . fucking animals or whatever. How is that relevant to the situation at hand?"

"Final question. If you are correct and we are not able to make choices, and are just following the same impulses as the insect, then how do I have the choice to not peel your face? I would be driven along by impulse, as beholden to them as that insect."

The bug was scaling my chin now. It was breathing hard with the effort. I thought I heard it curse under its breath.

I said, "What you're saying is that you're going to peel off my face one way or the other. Which is irrelevant because this isn't actually happening. Right?"

"You tell me."

Nymph snatched the scalpel and climbed up on the gurney, straddling my chest. He grabbed my face, but then things got confused and suddenly I was the one on top, the struggling man's face in my own grip, the scalpel in my hand. It was John on the gurney, not me. The blade pierced skin and I pulled it across his jawline . . .

16. THE GREAT DILDO FLOOD

I snapped back into my own body and found I was in fact straddling John. In my hand, instead of a scalpel, was a pink dildo. I was pressing it against his chin, as if trying to slice it open. John meanwhile was cramming something into my face, something that was crumbling against my jaw. We were splashing around in an inch of dirty water.

John said, "EAT IT! EAT IT, YOU SON OF A BITCH!"

I said, "WAIT! STOP!"

We both blinked and froze in place, taking in our surroundings. We were in the Venus Flytrap, which had now succumbed to the encroaching flood. There were open empty sex toy packages scattered around the floor, as if the place had been ransacked by looters looking to spice up their marriages. The place smelled like farts.

I got up off of John. He groaned and dumped something out of his hand—a handful of Oreo cookies he'd been trying to shove into my mouth, for some reason. He stood up out of the water, then lit a cigarette.

I said, "What happened? How long was I out?"

"I . . . don't know. What's the last thing you remember?"

"Soy Sauce. At the Beanie Wienie cannery. I got some in my system, everything went weird. Then I woke up here. Just now."

John nodded. "Yeah, me, too."

"You took off running. You dove through a second-floor window."

"No memory of that. I'm really sore, though. Got scratches all over me."

I called out for Amy. No answer. A hint of sun was peeking through the windows, from the east. There were several shopping sacks from a local hardware store near the door. I briefly looked through them, and found several sealed plastic bags of a bright yellow powder. One had burst, spilling its contents—sulfur. So that's where the stink was coming from. Had we bought it? If so, why?

I checked to see if I had my phone, and did. I dialed Amy.

She answered with, "Is this you? Where are you?!?"

"Venus Flytrap. I woke up and John and I were having a dildo battle."

"Where have you been?"

"Don't know. How long have I been gone? All night?"

"All night? This is Monday morning. You've been gone for two days."

"Oh. Shit. Have you not heard from me at all?"

"You took the Soy Sauce, you looked at Chastity and yelled, 'It's dildos all the way down, baby,' and ran out of the building. You had told her to wait an hour but you never came back. That was Friday night. She actually stayed until the next morning but she's long gone now. I hear nothing all day Saturday, or Sunday. I've been worried sick. What were you doing for two days?"

"No idea. Maybe it'll come back to me. And nobody has come after you?"

She said, "Not so far. Maybe they don't work weekends."

"Okay. Okay . . . so, where are you staying?"

"I've been sleeping at the Beanie Wienie. Didn't know where else to go. Been sleeping in my clothes on the sofa, freezing at night. Got Nicky to bring me food. Nobody has bothered me here, though."

"Okay. Good. Well . . . shit. I'm sorry, Amy. But maybe John and I took care of it. While we were on the Sauce, maybe we fixed everything. Have there been, uh, any more developments while we were gone?"

"Yes. Ten more kids have gone missing."

"Did you say *ten*?"

"Went missing yesterday. All from the same place, the Roach Motel. They were the biker kids. They had a room there they were using as a day care. Yesterday most of the bikers were out at a memorial for Lemmy. They came back, the lady who was watching the kids was frantic. Says she turned her back for one second, and they were gone. Christ's Rebellion is on the warpath. They're tearing the town apart."

"Shit. Wait, now hold on—are these real kids or is this a situation like Mikey?"

"I've seen photos."

"Oh. You have?"

"Yeah, I'm talking to the parents now. I'm at the motel."

"What are you doing out there?"

"I just told you, *we're trying to help them find out what's going on.* What did you think I was doing all weekend? I'm working the case."

"All right, all right. We'll be right there."

"The world doesn't just grind to a halt when you're not around, David."

"I know, I'm sorry. Jesus."

"I love you."

"I love you, too."

I hung up and we sloshed out into the parking lot. John's Jeep was parked there, so we'd apparently gone back to get it at some point. A sign on the Venus Flytrap door announced they had closed until further notice, due to flood conditions. The entire neighborhood wasn't under water, not yet, but at this point it was a few islands of dry land where certain lots and patches of road were elevated. Everything else was swamped by a couple of inches of swirling brown water, the currents carrying sticks and garbage and clumps of dead grass.

We went upstairs to find the apartment pretty much as I'd left it, aside from the fact that there were now boxes piled everywhere. There were ten cases of Mountain Dew Code Red stacked by the door. There was a shipping invoice on the card table—apparently I had spent part of the Mikey Payton reward money having a bunch of soda overnighted to the apartment. Nearby were eight much larger boxes labeled VELVETSOFT EROTIC SILICONE BUTTOCKS. One of us, hopefully John using *his* credit card, had apparently bought every single rubber ass sex toy from the shop downstairs. I looked at John and started to ask if this was his doing, but he just shook his head, slowly.

"No memory either way."

I dug out a bottle of Mountain Dew and told him about the missing kids.

"Wait. Just . . . hold on. If they're decoys, could they just brainwash a whole group like that? A whole community?"

"That," I said, "is what we have to figure out first."

I went into the bathroom to take a piss and saw that scrawled on the mirror were three words, written backward in what was hopefully black Dry Erase marker:

ATTEROL OT KLAT

It was "Talk to Loretta" written in a mirror image, which made no sense because the text was written on the mirror itself, so it still read backward to me. If they'd written it on the wall behind the mirror, that would have worked. I recognized the handwriting as John's.

I said, "I think we're supposed to go talk to Ted's wife." I rubbed the ink on the mirror. It was not Dry Erase.

John looked it over and said, "Why didn't we just go talk to Loretta instead of leaving ourselves a note to do it later?"

"Maybe we . . . *no*. John . . ."

"What?"

"You didn't leave a bunch of cryptic clues behind because you wanted to do a *Dude, Where's My Car?* situation. You did not do that. Please tell me."

"Well if I did, I'm sure I had a good reason. You know what, I bet the butts are a clue, too."

"Oh my god."

"Look, what matters is that we go talk to Loretta. Like the note says. Maybe she'll have the next clue."

"Fuck you. We're going to the Roach Motel. That's where Amy is." I thought for a moment and said, "It just occurred to me that she said 'we' when she said she was at the motel. I wonder who's with her?"

"Maybe it's the cops? Or it's that dude from work she's having an affair with."

On the way to the motel, we came across several side streets that had been closed by the city for being under water—not enough to drown in, but definitely enough to ruin your traction if you weren't paying attention. I could only remember one really bad flood in my time living here, when I was ten. They had canceled school for three weeks and then everything smelled like fish for a month after the water went down. This looked worse.

The entrance to the Roach Motel parking lot was blocked by a pair of scary-looking biker dudes. We pulled up and the bigger of the two said, "We're closed."

Up from behind the men walked, not Amy, or Chastity, but that goddamned NON agent, Helen Tasker. She muttered something to the big biker and he stepped aside, giving us the stinkeye as we passed.

I said to John, "You didn't happen to bring a gun, did you?"

"Just let me do the talking."

We parked and as soon as John jumped out, he said to Tasker, "So you're not dead, then?"

"Why would I be?"

"You got shot right in the chest like two days ago."

"How high were you when you came to see me Friday night?"

"I came to see you?"

"So pretty high, then. I'm not repeating the conversation. My employers administered first aid and I was back on duty within an hour. There's not even a scar."

"Impressive. Is your partner around?"

"His brain was hit with a neuron scrambler and his entire upper body was crushed by an SUV. He won't be back on duty until later this afternoon."

John nodded. "Sure. So can you give me a brief summary of what we talked about Friday night?"

"You asked for my help."

"I did?"

"Yes. With a bunch of children who were *about* to go missing."

Amy approached from behind Tasker, wearing her red raincoat that made her look like the little girl from *Schindler's List*. She walked right up to Tasker and said, "I got him to talk to me, he says half of the CR thinks the kids were taken by a rival gang called the Flatlanders. Some think they were raptured by God and that this is the end of the world. The rest think it was the Batmantis, some say they even saw it that day." Amy glanced at me and John and said, "You guys look awful."

Tasker said, "What was that third thing?"

I said, "It's not relevant to the case. A YouTube video of a winged monster went viral around town, now people think they're seeing it everywhere. Typical Bigfoot shit. So, uh, you two are partners now?"

Exasperated, Amy looked at John and said, "*You told her to come find me!*"

I said, "All right, calm down." To Tasker I said, "The

bikers are talking to you, despite the fact that you staged a weird battle in their parking lot like two days ago?"

Amy said, "They think she's with the FBI. She has credentials from every agency."

I said, "Great, have you broached the subject with the agent here that there might not be any missing kids at all, that it's all just a series of false memories planted by a hive of mind-controlling shape-shifting bug monsters?"

The look on Agent Tasker's face confirmed that Amy had not in fact broached that subject.

John said, "Wait, were you withholding that from her for a reason? In that case, forget we said anything."

Amy hand-waved it away. "They've got documents, pictures. They're real kids."

John scrunched up his eyebrows in thought. "Can we see the pictures?"

We followed Tasker into the front office, which had apparently been commandeered by the "FBI." It stank of cigarettes and engine grime. Tasker had the documents in a folder she pulled from a flat-black briefcase that automatically unlocked when she spoke to it in Latin. She pulled out a handful of pages and handed them to John.

He flipped through them and said to Tasker, "And these all check out? They're not forgeries or anything?"

"No. Why would they be?"

He said to Amy, "You've looked at them, too? They look genuine?"

"They don't look like Photoshops or anything. I'm not an expert. Why?"

John handed me the pages.

Every single one of them was blank.

I sighed. "You explain it. My head hurts."

John took a breath, not sure where to start. Finally, he turned to Amy and said, "While I was on my Soy Sauce trip, I saw something. A memory, replayed from the third person. It was me showing up at the Knoll house, meeting with Detective Bowman. And we're talking and Bowman asks for a recent photo and Ted opens his wallet, and hands the detective an old membership card from Blockbuster video. The detective looks at it, and starts talking like he's looking at a photo—asking if the girl's hair is still that long, and so on. Then he hands it to me, and I showed it to Dave when he arrived. Always that plastic blue-and-yellow Blockbuster card, each time we see a little girl's face. Which makes sense, because if the fuckroaches can rewrite memories from a certain distance away, then they can make you 'remember' seeing what they want you to, a split second after you look. So the cops or somebody could devote a whole weekend to searching through government databases for these kids and they'd have a vivid memory of successfully finding page after page of records. But if Dave and I were watching them work—and I mean right now, while we're still under the effects of the Sauce—we'd see them staring at a blank computer screen. Or doing nothing at all."

Amy said, "That . . . no. It can't work like that."

"Why not?"

"Because then how could you trust anything you saw or heard?"

I thought, *Exactly*.

Agent Tasker said, "You're going to need to back up. What exactly are you suggesting?"

So, we told her. When we finished, she got an expression on her face like a short-order cook who just saw a huge group of hungry drunks walk in five minutes before closing time.

She said, "I have to take this to my superiors."

I said, "Sure. Let us know what they say."

"You wouldn't be capable of understanding what they say. Go home and wait there, don't talk to anyone. The news media will find out about the missing children eventually, but the longer we put that off the better chance we have at containment. Are you listening?"

I said, "Huh? Yes, thank you, I've been doing a lot of squats."

She turned and banged through the door, showing no reaction to the driving rain. As soon as she was gone, I said to Amy, "We found a clue pointing toward Loretta, Ted Knoll's wife. We need to go talk to her."

"A clue?"

John said, "I had written, 'Talk to Loretta' on your bathroom mirror. Any idea why, that you can think of?"

"It sounds like a *Dude, Where's My Car?* situation to me."

"No, I mean why we'd need to talk to Loretta specifically."

Amy said, "Well, I think Loretta has Maggie. Or"— Amy made one set of air quotes with her fingers—"she has 'Maggie.'"

John said, "Oh. Right."

I said, "So, we just have to go and, uh, explain the situation. She'll understand, right?"

John said, "You think twenty silicone sex butts would convince her?"

17. JOINING MAGGIE
FOR BREAKFAST

The three of us headed to Loretta's house, but had decided that we wouldn't stop if Ted's car was parked there, since we assumed he still was determined to shoot me on sight.

No Impala. Still, we took the minor precaution of parking at Taco Bill instead of in front of Loretta's house. The restaurant had a spray-painted sign in the window that said:

STILL OPEN
FUCK THE FLOOD

. . . though it looked like they had maybe forty-eight hours before the cooks would be standing in puddles while they grilled the flank steak. Cars were creeping down the street, swerving out across the painted lines to avoid the overflowing gutters.

To John, I said, "So, this meeting you had with the NON agent Friday night. You've no recollection of it?"

"Well, you know how it is on the Sauce. You see things. Seems like a dream, or the memories from when you're a little kid, the ones where you're not sure if they happened or if your brain just cobbled the memory together after you'd heard the story secondhand. So, I have this memory of running out of the Beanie Wienie building and I think, 'I need transportation.' Then this guy on a crotch rocket Suzuki motorcycle—just like the one I owned years ago—rides up and asks if I'm John, says he got a letter five years ago telling him to deliver a motorcycle to that specific place and time. So, I jump on and I ride and I run into the NON convoy. I somehow know which truck has Agent Pussnado in the back—"

Amy said, "Excuse me, who?"

"The agent we just talked to? Anyway, I jump off the motorcycle onto the hood of the truck—no, this is how I remember it—and they screech to a stop and I yell at the driver that I need to talk to her, that it's for everyone's safety. She lets me in the back of the truck and it's just me and her. I tell her I need five minutes, she says she needs eight inches."

Amy said, "Oh my god."

I said, "That is *not* what happened."

"That's how I remember it, I swear!"

"Do you remember anything else from when you were out? Anything that's not completely fucking stupid? Anything about Loretta, or Maggie, anything that would help prepare us for what we're about to walk into here?"

He shook his head. "I don't know. I don't think so. You?"

"No. I had a vision I ran into Nymph and he tried to

tell me the meaning of life, then I woke up."

Amy said, "*Anyway*. Obviously I have to go in again, because I assume Maggie and Loretta both still think you're the kidnapper."

"You're not going in there alone. Not after what happened last time. If we have to just barge in and do it by force, we will."

Amy said, "Do *what* by force?"

"Take out Maggie?"

"The sign said 'Talk to Loretta,' not 'Murder Loretta's child.'"

"It's not a child!"

"We don't know that yet. Look, you guys feel free to keep debating it, I'm going in. I'll stick my phone in my coat pocket and you can watch—"

I said, "But what if Maggie turns into—"

"Shh. Let me finish. The danger isn't Maggie turning into a big snake monster or something, the danger is she messes with my brain somehow. If she turns into a big monster I'll scream and run away. If she starts messing with my head, you guys will need to get me out of there and slap sense into me."

I said, "I don't like it either way."

"Sure, and you can sit out here and contemplate how much you don't like it while I go inside." She opened the door. "Love you."

"I love you, too."

We watched from afar as Amy's red coat bounced through the rain. She knocked on Loretta's door, then apparently got an okay to come in. I started watching on my phone, but didn't have a great view—the camera was just barely peeking up over the pocket of her coat. Amy pushed in through the door and appeared to be responding to a friendly greeting that I couldn't quite hear over the rustling of her coat against the microphone.

I said, "I don't like this."

John said, "Yeah, I think you said something about that. We'll give her one minute, then we bust in."

Amy entered the living room. We could faintly hear Loretta talking from the kitchen, saying, ". . . actually she's handling it better than the grown-ups. But you know, kids are tough. John was here yesterday, he explained everything. I know you're trying to help, despite what Ted thinks. And now all those other kids are missing . . . awful."

Amy said, "Oh, I didn't know John had come by. What, uh, did he explain, exactly?"

On Amy's camera, we watched Loretta step into view, holding a mug of coffee.

Half of her was missing.

She looked like she'd been torn apart by a great white. Most of her neck was gone, to the point that it should have been impossible for her to hold her head upright— just a white spinal column and a yellowish ligament surrounded by ragged meat and open air. About a third of her torso had been ripped away, from armpit to hip.

She continued talking like everything was fine. I could see her windpipe twitching, her exposed lung inflating and deflating with each breath.

That woman should not be alive.

John gave a start and I knew he could see it, too. But Amy replied politely to the conversation, oblivious.

Loretta said, "John told me the police had turned you loose, that the bad guy had the same build and hair color as your David but that they'd eliminated him as a suspect. Still, I'd prefer he not come in. Maggie is still in bed but I don't want to scare her. So, what do you need?" Through the video feed I watched as the woman's stomach twitched and quivered as it digested some bit of breakfast.

Amy said, "I'm not sure. You know, we're still just trying to help however we can . . ."

"Well, I know there's more to this," said Loretta, causing a little flap of skin to bounce around her throat. "Maggie wasn't acting right, before the abduction, I mean. I know this was something . . . unusual."

Amy said, "Has Maggie acted strangely since she's come back?"

"Not considering what she's been through, you know."

"Can I see her?"

Loretta invited Amy to follow her to Maggie's bedroom, and the camera tracked the mutilated woman down the hall. She opened a bedroom door a crack and said, "Mags? You awake?"

The answer that came from the bedroom was a terrifying guttural squeal. John glanced at me. Amy reacted like she heard an adorable child's voice and said, "Oh, you can just let her sleep. I didn't intend to—"

Loretta said into the bedroom, "I have someone who wants to see you, real quick. Won't be one minute."

"KREEEEE . . . KUKUKUKUKUK!"

"It's okay, she's helping the police."

"EEEEUUUUK. Eeeeeee . . ."

Loretta pushed the door open.

Lying on the bed was a maggot.

It was approximately the same size as a human child. Its skin was translucent and I could see its digestive system working, grinding up what looked like scraps of meat and leather.

John said, "Huh."

I said, "I'm going in—"

"Wait."

Amy said, "Maggie?" and moved gingerly into the room. The view from the phone leaned over the bed. "Are you feeling okay?"

"Maggie" screeched and clucked and made sucking noises.

Loretta sat down on the bed with "Maggie" and the creature squished its way over to her. The mother laid her hand across the maggot's back, the monster's face resting a circular row of teeth against Loretta's abdomen.

"I'm just so happy to have her back home. My heart breaks for the other parents missing their babies today but I have to admit, I'm selfish. I'm happy to have Maggie back and above all else, I want to make sure they never try to take her again. If you guys can help me with that, nothing else matters."

I knew that the lingering effects of the Soy Sauce were the difference between what John and I were seeing versus everyone else—if I concentrated, I found I could actually see the formation of fuckroaches swarming around the maggot, twitching and writhing in the vague shape of a girl. If I concentrated a bit more, I could see the little blond girl they were projecting to the rest of the world, the child Amy was seeing, the one that had been woven into all of Loretta Knoll's memories.

Then in a blink it was back to the larva. Hungry, pulsing.

"Maggie" opened her slimy mouth and took a bite out of Loretta's belly, ripping skin and fat and chewing noisily. Loretta didn't even flinch.

BOOK III

An Excerpt from *Fear: Hell's Parasite*
by Dr. Albert Marconi

*There used to be a famous thought experiment that went
something like this:*

*A child is born blind. She has in her possession two
wooden toys—a ball and a block. After years of playing
with both, she knows the contours of each object intimately by
touch—the sphere and the cube. Then, late in childhood, she
is given surgery to correct her eyesight. Now that she can see
for the first time, would this young lady be able to distinguish
the block from the ball on sight alone?*

*I say this "used" to be a thought experiment, because we
now know the answer: no. Real subjects who have had
their sight restored, upon seeing a cube for the first time,
cannot connect it with the eight pointy corners they remember
feeling in their hands. They fully expect it to feel like the
smooth sphere, until they hold it and learn otherwise.*

*The lesson? You do not see with your eyes. You see with
your brain.*

*The visual data that enters your optic nerve is meaningless
noise without the brain's ability to overlay meaning upon
it. This means, quite simply, that what you see (in a real,
not metaphorical, sense) is a result of what you have been*

built to see, and nothing more. If you would like a comparison, imagine the family dog lying in a room while its masters watch a film on television. Dogs cannot see television (their eyes are quite different from yours) so all they know is that the humans in the room are sitting motionless, staring listlessly at a noisy square object on the wall. The canine may note voices or other familiar sounds from that device, but because those sounds are not accompanied by smells, they do not represent anything of interest to it. Even if the dog could learn to converse with humans, it would be next to impossible to explain to the animal that the motionless, silent people in the room are interacting with other living beings located thousands of miles away, performing actions that actually occurred years earlier. Which is to say, the family and the dog are in the same room, but experiencing very different realities.

The very next day, the family takes that dog for a walk in the park. They are amused at how their pet frantically sniffs patches of grass, enthralled by seemingly nothing at all. They are mystified at its obsession with smelling the anuses of other dogs, yanking on its leash and discouraging it from indulging what they figure must be a curious fetish. How could the dog ever explain that its sense of smell is thousands of times more sensitive than theirs, that it can, in mere seconds, sniff out an entire life-or-death drama that played out in that very patch of empty grass weeks earlier? One whiff told the hound that an animal had recently urinated there, that said animal's metabolism was failing, and that it was extremely frightened. A sniff of another dog's posterior spells out its entire biography—its age, success as a hunter, its suitability as a mate and/or likelihood of winning a fight to the death.

Same park. Two different realities.

This is despite the fact that man and canine both evolved in the same environment, with extremely similar biology. Now imagine the difference between two beings who evolved in different worlds entirely.

Knowing my line of work, I suppose you have already guessed why this is relevant to my interests. If a being from another universe were to appear in ours, our ability to understand it would be exactly as limited as the formerly blind teenager trying to identify his or her beloved toys by sight alone. Our brains would paw around madly for some context to make sense of the entity but, finding none, would frantically try to construct a crude analog. Some of us would see demons, some would see aliens, some would see nothing at all.

When those conflicting impressions clash with one another, well, you need only to open a history book to see the result. We will live and die according to how we interpret the unfamiliar. All of human culture is nothing more than that very process, playing out again and again.

18. ONCE AGAIN, MARCONI SELFISHLY TRIES TO STEAL THE SPOTLIGHT

Amy slid back into the Jeep, took one look at our faces, and said, "What?"

I said, "I don't know how to put this, but while Maggie appears to you as an adorable eight-year-old child, she is in reality a huge carnivorous larva that is slowly eating her mother."

Amy said, "I guess I don't have to ask if that's just a metaphor. So during your drug trip, you left yourself a note to come here, so you could see that, right? So now what?"

"We have to kill it, Amy."

"You're going to kill Maggie in front of her mother? You'd have to kill Loretta, too."

"No. I guess we'd have to get her away from here . . ."

"Kidnap her, you mean. As in, the thing you were accused of doing in the first place. Will you listen to yourself?"

"Amy, it's a larva. That means it's going to grow into something, right? We can't let some monster hatch and go on a rampage through the city. Again."

"Okay, let me ask you this. You see one thing, me and Loretta see another. How do we know your version is right?"

"Is this like some kind of Socratic thought experiment? We already know it's a monster. I mean, you see a girl but it's actually a monster."

"But I talked to her."

"So?"

"She was able to think and express feelings. Fear, affection, all that. Why doesn't she qualify for all the same protections we'd afford to a human who can do the same thing?"

John said, "You didn't see what we saw. That thing is killing Loretta. Eating away at her. Like, taking literal bites from her flesh. I don't even know how she's still walking around."

"She looked fine to me. Looked exhausted, but relieved."

I said, "All right, this is exactly what you were afraid would happen. Do you need us to slap sense into you now? Just know that I intend to do the slapping on your butt. Slowly."

"If I'm not thinking clearly, show me where I'm wrong, I'll listen. In Loretta's mind, it absolutely is her daughter. Did you see the look on her face? That love, it was real. You kill Maggie, that loss she'll feel, that'll be real, too. Same as if you actually killed her kid."

I said, "Maybe after the thing dies, the spell will be broken, like it was with Mikey. Let's put it to a vote."

Amy said, "My vote is that I'm not going to let you do it no matter how you vote."

"That's not how democracy wo—"

John's phone chimed an e-mail notification.

"Oh, hey, it's Marconi. He says he got the specimen and wants to talk about it. Wants to know if we can do a Skype call."

"What specimen?"

John shrugged. "I guess we sent him something? While we were tripping?"

"That doesn't sound like something we'd do. And by that I mean it sounds like a really good idea."

Amy said, "That settles it. We go back to my laptop and talk to Dr. Marconi and we do that instead of murdering this child."

I said, "For now. But if in the interim Maggie hatches and eats an orphanage, it's on you."

Amy

They were several blocks from Loretta Knoll's modest rental house before Amy felt her guts start to loosen up just a little.

This whole thing was giving her flashbacks.

After the car accident that killed her parents and mangled her left hand, Amy had stayed with her Uncle Bill and Aunt Betty for three long, nightmarish years. The couple's marriage had always been a tire fire and Amy could feel the tension crackling in the air every time she walked in the door. The two of them *hated* each other. They devoted all of their energy to inventing reasons to be outraged, each desperate to be the wronged party at any given moment, as if they were both keeping track on a scoreboard they kept under the bed. Adding Amy to the mix had been the proverbial bottle rocket to the hornet's nest. The aunt was the blood relative, Amy's mother's sister, and it had been her decision to take Amy in. Aunt Betty then kept insinuating that Uncle Bill had sexual urges for their fourteen-year-old houseguest. Betty had known it wasn't true, it was just the worst thing she could think to accuse him of. That's how it worked.

Still, this meant that Amy couldn't just stay out of their vicious arguments, because she was now a party to them. She was also the only one of the three who didn't seem to thoroughly enjoy the conflict. The tension made her physically ill. She wasn't used to it. Her parents had been best friends, her father an enormous man with smiling eyes who had once spent six hours driving a young Amy from store to store trying to find a copy of *Final Fantasy II* for the SNES. His little princess.

But at Bill and Betty's, if there was ever to be peace for an evening, it would only be because Amy had devoted all of her energy to maintaining it, moment to moment. She would see signs of conflict on the horizon— say, noticing Aunt Betty had bought Wonder Bread instead of Bunny, Bill's preferred brand—and 100 percent of the burden for smoothing it over would fall on her. The bread-brand controversy had once resulted in Bill smashing a plate against a table and slicing his hand open on one of the shards. Amy remembered on one occasion throwing on her coat in the middle of winter and walking to a grocery store five blocks away, seeing they didn't have a loaf of Bunny Bread on the shelf, and bursting into tears right there in the aisle. The next morning she had stood there in the kitchen with a ball of heavy acid in her guts as she watched Uncle Bill go to make toast. He uttered a sarcastic grunt when he noticed the brand . . . and that was it, he just proceeded to make breakfast like normal.

On another day, that'd have been cause to punch the wall and scream the *c*-word over and over, to sneer to himself and tell Amy about the time he had sneaked into the bathroom at night and put his own bodily fluids in his wife's face cream. The uncertainty was what made it terrifying—if the outbursts had been constant, she could have started to brace herself in advance, to turn it into some kind of routine. Instead, the periods of peace would last just long enough that the explosions would be jarring again when they came.

To this day, she gets this little thrill of fear up her spine when she passes a bread aisle. Every. Single. Time.

Amy was getting that sick feeling today, the sense that she was going to have to play referee in a fight that was just around the corner. But even that wasn't right—a referee at least has rules to fall back on. This was more like throwing yourself between two speeding trucks in hopes your squishy organs will be enough to blunt the impact. They don't make movies or video games about that person, do they? The nervous, muttering thing tasked with convincing the knight and the dragon that there's more than just the one kind of courage?

She reached up between the front seats and squeezed David's hand.

Academic, man of the cloth, author, adventurer, and reality show host Dr. Albert Marconi's most recent book mentions me several times and each time makes me look like an asshole. So, he's good with research. He does specials for the Discovery Channel about strange phenomena and his production company has sent crews to Undisclosed at least half a dozen times. But Marconi himself has only shown up once in person and in general, he only returns our calls when our situation sounds like something he could parlay into another book. Kind of like a doctor who'll only take your appointment if your symptoms sound like some kind of horrific undiscovered tropical disease that he can name after himself.

We were back at Fort Beanie Wienie, and Amy was dicking around with Skype (if you're reading this in the future and Skype is no longer a thing, it was just a piece of video-calling software people used back then. Or back now. Whatever).

I said to John, "You stuck the fuckroach in the mail? There was no concern that the thing would brainwash every postal employee who came within a hundred feet of it between here and wherever the hell Marconi is?"

"The memory is still fuzzy, but when I was on the Sauce, I think I figured out a precaution. I don't remember what exactly it was, but I know it involved throwing a handful of sulfur inside the container, surrounding the interior with small mirrors, and then wrapping the whole thing in a dozen layers of aluminum foil. I also had thrown a couple of Oreos in with the creature but I can't remember if that was part of the precautions or if I just wanted to give it something to eat during the trip."

Marconi appeared on Amy's laptop screen. A man in his sixties with a neat white beard, wearing a cream-colored suit. He was sitting at a desk and, as I always did in situations like this, I wondered if he was pantless and only threw on the top part for the camera. It looked like he was in a cramped office, with various framed certificates on the wall behind him. I wondered how long he had spent framing up the shot to get those in there. Or, maybe he was just the type of guy where you could point the camera in any direction nearby and find a cluster of accolades.

"Gentlemen," he said. "And lady. It is a pleasure to see you again." *Now there's a fucking lie.* "I'm speaking to you from the road, we are en route. I have the specimen safely behind foil once more, and inside of a locked safe for which only I have the combination. Keeping it contained has been an adventure, to put it mildly. One assistant became convinced that we had locked her house cat inside the safe, and became so hysterical she had to be restrained and sedated. As camouflage goes, it is impressive, to say the least."

I said, "You say you're on the way, I take it you're bringing a camera crew?" I knew Agent Tasker would be very annoyed by that.

Instead of answering, he said, "Tell me of how you encountered the specimen, from the beginning."

We quickly told him all of the stuff that's in the story you've heard up to now, minus the parts about my depression, and John's implausible cock boasts. Marconi listened to our tale and said, "Fascinating."

John said, "Chastity—the second mother we dealt with—says there's a parasite that tricks ants into thinking they're fruit. They'll actually volunteer to be eaten. She thinks it's like that."

Marconi nodded. "A more appropriate example in this case may be a certain species of fruit fly, whose female has evolved to look exactly like an army ant grub. It will land itself right among a pile of the ant's larvae and the ants will unknowingly feed, clean, and protect it as one of their own. And, while I do want to be cautious about drawing too close a parallel—these organisms are not of our world, after all—what we have encountered here very much appears to be a hive, in that we have multiple organisms working in conjunction, each of which appears to be very specialized."

I said, "Okay. So whatever's in the mine, that's like the queen?" I was really just waiting for him to get around to the part where he tells us what magic is required to slay it, but Marconi likes to hear himself explain things.

"Let us for the moment speculate that the specimen you sent me is what in a hive we would call a worker. Let us further speculate that what is inside that coal mine is in fact a queen. So, the queen reaches the point in its life cycle when it lays its larvae. But, for some reason, its larvae need human hosts to survive—presumably for food, but that is just a presumption at this stage. So, the workers' only job is to obtain those human hosts, by any means necessary. It would appear to my eyes that these workers went into the world with the intention of duping humans into adopting larvae as their own."

273

"By imitating human children."

"By imitating human children *who are in need of rescue*. Note how far it went to present the supposed children's situation as dire."

I said, "Okay. So, Maggie went missing and then—"

"Maggie *did not* go missing. There was no Maggie. The queen laid a larva in that pond near the mine and the worker swarm went about convincing some humans to come retrieve it. Maggie never existed before that moment—the entire story, including memories of the kidnapping, was a brain imprint created after the fact."

I rubbed my temples. "Right. Okay. So 'Maggie' was found at Mine's Eye, but 'Mikey' just turned up in my apartment somehow."

"After you went to the mine."

"Yeah."

"You must have brought it back with you, unknowingly."

"What, like, stuck to my shoe or something? These things are huge."

"But invisible, if they choose to be. And that one was destroyed, you say?"

We all glanced at each other.

John said, "Uh . . . maybe? Last time we saw it, some guys at a motel were shooting it with shotguns. That should do it, right?"

Marconi said, "They were shooting at the larva, or the worker swarm that accompanied it?"

We didn't answer. Marconi read our faces.

"Let us assume, then, that that specimen is also still loose out in the world. But let's be clear—hive-based organisms reproduce by *volume*. It is in fact the single reason they are successful. In this case, the queen presumably needs to continue to draw people to the mine. So, now ten more 'children' have gone missing, in the minds of the townspeople. Do we need to guess where the clues are going to lead the manhunt?"

I said, "Holy shit, that's a convoluted reproduction process right there."

"Have you seen what the human reproduction process is like, Mr. Wong? Here's a hint—the automobile you drive was almost certainly designed with reproduction in mind."

Well not my car, but point taken.

Amy said, "So, we have to keep everyone away from the mine."

I said, "Hell, they're probably already out there. Everybody knows where Maggie was found, it was in the papers. You'll have the bikers out there, even the cops have to at least make a show of it."

John said, "Oh, and before we go any further, we need to name the creature in the mine, the queen. It's Amy's turn. I think she referred to it as the Creature with a Thousand Butts earlier, so is that what we're going with?"

I said, "She didn't, and that takes too long to say."

Amy said, "Millibutt."

John said, "Done. Also, where does Nymph fit into all this?"

Marconi shrugged. "There likely was never such a man, or being. Just a manifestation of the swarm."

I said, "But *why?*"

Amy said it before Marconi could. "To give us something to save the kids from. We each saw the villain we needed to overcome."

There was some sadness in Amy's statement that I didn't fully understand.

"So," John said, "we go into the mine and fight the main boss. What can we expect to find in there?"

I said, "And before you say it, yeah, we know to expect the unexpected or whatever. But let's make some educated guesses."

Marconi nodded. "Well, there are no uninitiated in this conversation, correct? Behind the veil of this world is a realm beyond the physical. The undying entities that dwell there do not have a shape or a size, but can only be measured in terms of their ability to exert will. I have reason to believe that the physical offspring we're encountering are one entity's way of inserting itself from that dimension into ours."

I said, "Sure, so it's an evil spirit or whatever. I guess that means it's not flammable?"

"Ask yourself how such entities would do battle with each other. The question is not merely academic within my school of thought—we believe we will find ourselves in just such a battle in the moment after death. Will versus will. Imagine a mortal body as an egg. When broken, what emerges might be a soaring bird or a runny yolk."

"And here I thought it was just a monster that wanted to eat us."

"In a sense, it is. Such a being would grow by subduing the will of others to its own ends. In our mythology, devils are always about possession and temptation—chewing up a human will until only a hollow puppet remains. You can decide for yourself at what point we can separate the symbolism from the reality."

John nodded, knowingly. "Exactly. It's just like those haunted puppets in your junk room, Dave."

Marconi said, "Not in the least. To give you just a hint of the complexity of the task at hand, you will note that I have carefully avoided uttering the true name of the entity. It wants to be spoken of. I would suggest you do the same if and when you repeat this story to others."

I was getting lost again. "But how do we kill what we can't even—"

I was abruptly cut off by the sound of shattering glass.

19. THE CREW ENCOUNTER SOME ADDITIONAL COMPLICATIONS

John

A nearby window exploded and a man came swinging in on a rope. John recognized the blond beard on sight. He was pretty sure that they'd left the front door of Fort Beanie Wienie unlocked, but Ted owned line and a grappling hook and by god, he was going to use them. He'd also brought reinforcements: a second window birthed a burly man in camouflage who had rappelled down from the opposite side.

"GET THE FUCK DOWN! ALL OF YOU!" suggested Ted.

John, Dave, and Amy all got the fuck down, hands over their heads. On the laptop, John could faintly hear Marconi say, "I suppose that concludes the call."

That night in the parking lot of the Flytrap, Ted had given Dave twenty-four hours to resolve the whole disappearing kids deal and John had to admit that not only had the deadline long passed, but that the situation was now actually quite a bit worse.

The two men unslung assault rifles and took up positions opposite their prone captives.

Ted screamed, "WHERE ARE THEY?"

Dave said, "Where are the what?"

"The kids! You've either got 'em here, or somewhere else."

"Okay, as implausible as it was to accuse us of simultaneously kidnapping the two kids before, this is just *weird*. We snatched *ten* children and made them vanish into thin air? What, did we show up with a panel truck and just load the little bastards in there while nobody was watching? In a building inhabited by heavily armed biker types?"

"No. See, I think you've got *capabilities*. And I think you use those capabilities for shit like this."

John said, "*We found Maggie. Why would we take kids just to release them again?*"

"Exactly so you can do that. In a couple days, you were gonna go to some locked room you've got 'em in, let them out in front of a bunch of TV cameras, and get called heroes. Probably think you'll be drowning in pussy."

Amy said, "I think you're a good person, but there is just . . . *so much* going on here that you don't understand."

"Well, by all means, miss, educate me."

"You don't want to hear it."

"*Try me.*"

Dave said, "Have you noticed anything weird about Maggie?"

"Don't turn this shit back on her. You want to guess

what alarm system the motel was using? You want to guess what happened the moment the kids were taken?"

John was about to say that was ridiculous, but stopped himself. That *was* weird. Both John and Dave looked at Amy, and she didn't look back.

Dave said, "We're being framed by whatever is behind this! That's just part of it!"

Amy said, "If you want to search this place for the kids, go right ahead. We'll wait right here on the floor. Okay?"

Dave said, "Just watch out, there's artwork out there that will reveal the modern world to be an edifice of lies."

Still, John was pretty sure that Dave had the same thought he did, which was, *But what if they* do *find the kids here?*

Before he could even finish the thought, there was a loud metallic *BANG* from below them, on the first floor.

Everyone froze, listening.

BANG.

Ted and his partner raced for the stairwell. John scrambled to his feet and ran after them. Behind him, Dave and Amy had a hushed argument he couldn't quite hear.

At the bottom, John was met gun-first by Ted's comrade, who'd been stationed there specifically to make sure the three of them didn't try to take out Ted from behind. The guy shouted something about how John wasn't to take another step if he didn't want to see his intestines go bouncing down the stairs like a Slinky.

From where John was standing, he could just see Ted edge toward a rolling metal door, on which was spray-

painted an Uncle Sam next to a word balloon that said, I
AM FULL OF LIES!

There was a *BANG* and the door shook.

Ted said, "HELLO? Can you hear me?"

If he got an answer from the other side of the door,
John couldn't hear it.

The door shook again.

"We're here to help you! Back away!"

The latch on the floor was held closed by a wad of
rusty brown chain and a heavy padlock—it looked like
no one had touched it in a decade. Ted switched to his
shotgun, blew the chain apart, then reached down and
yanked up the door. His companion turned to train his
gun on the opening, glancing back at John to make sure
he wasn't going to try to take advantage.

If John could have frozen time in that moment and
taken the rest of the day to think about it, he still wasn't
sure he'd ever have successfully guessed what was on the
other side of that door. Was it the supposedly missing
kids? Mikey? Diogee? Nymph? Some other kind of
imitation victim that would turn Ted against them, like
his wife? A doppelganger of Ted himself? A stray cat that
just got trapped inside the room somehow? Dennis
Rodman?

The door rolled up to reveal a dark room. Some old
cans of paint, a few dusty blue barrels of floor wax . . .

John had seen just the hint of a pale shape when
Ted's friend said, "Oh, SHIT!" and started firing.

Out from the shadows popped a pair of white leathery
wings stuck to a sinewy grasshopper body. The creature
the locals had dubbed BATMANTIS???

The monster launched itself forward and swiped a

claw at Ted. He jumped back and found he was now holding half of a shotgun—the rest was clattering to the floor, the creature having effortlessly snipped metal and plastic cleanly in two.

Gunfire and shouts. Both men were backpedaling quickly, but with purpose—creating distance, getting out of their enemy's attack range. The BATMANTIS??? absorbed a dozen rifle rounds and then leaped forward again, swiping with a crooked limb and sending Ted's partner crashing into a wall. It then quickly skittered away, clumsily, like its legs kept getting caught on one another.

Instead of running for the main exit, which was about twenty feet away, the thing crashed directly into the wall, mashing itself into it, like it didn't understand how walls worked. As Ted continued to shoot it in the back, the BATMANTIS??? kept pressing itself into the wall, misshapen feet scraping the floor . . .

And then it was gone. Right in front of them, the thing had dissolved through the wall like a handful of pudding slapped through a screen door. There was a muffled shriek from the other side, like the beast had injured itself in the process.

Ted flew toward the main exit. John followed. The moment they were outside, the BATMANTIS??? jumped into the sky, flapped its wings, and was airborne. Ted fired into the sky with his assault rifle. Not in a blind rage or confused panic—he was taking careful, aimed shots, intending to bring down his prey. Once more, Ted fell right into professional soldier mode—he could take time to be amazed by what he saw later, after the job was done.

John was pretty sure the shots were landing and fully

expected the creature to splash down onto the pavement, dead. But, the BATMANTIS??? just recoiled with the impacts and kept flying, vanishing behind the next building.

Ted sprinted after it. John followed, cold rain battering his cheeks.

They rounded the building and caught a pale glimpse of the beast. Ted unloaded on it, shooting until the magazine went dry. No effect. Then they were running again, Ted's boots slapping and splashing, the man frantically scanning the clouds as they pissed on his upturned face.

The creature was gone. Ted cursed the sky.

John, thinking quickly, stomped over and jabbed a finger at him.

"Hey. Listen. We tried to tell you. I get that you pride yourself on being hardheaded, but you see it now? You wanna know what's taking this town's kids, well now you know."

Ted said, "Why didn't you tell me that thing was in there? You hopin' it would rip my head off?"

"Because *we didn't know*. It was waiting in there to ambush us, probably because it knew we were getting close. How the fuck would we get that thing in there?"

This was of course bullshit, but chasing the BATMANTIS??? seemed like a perfect task to keep Ted out of the way. Still, the questions being asked were the right ones—why in the hell was the thing holed up in the Beanie Wienie warehouse? John assumed either he or Dave had in fact lured the thing in there over the course of their lost weekend. But how? And more importantly, why? Did it have something to do with the silicone butts?

"Look," John said, "here's the truth. We've been stalking this thing for *months*. Learning how to track it. That's why it tricked your little girl into thinking it was Dave there that night—it's using its tricks, trying to throw you off the scent."

"Wait, then who was Nymph?"

"*They're one and the same.* That's just another face it wears—a different type of predator, a human one. He transforms, like a werewolf. He's a were-Batmantis. A Batmantis-man. What matters is that underneath it all, it's just an animal. It can bleed and it can die. Find out where that bastard nests, you'll find the kids. Let's just hope you find 'em in better condition than they've been finding the dogs."

"The dogs?"

"It eats small animals. I say you sit down and map all the houses or farms where people have lost dogs and cats and chickens. Then you draw a big circle around all them houses and draw an X in the middle of that circle. That's where you'll find your monster and, god willing, that's where you'll find the kids. If you got a good relationship with the cops, you might be able to get them to help out. Unfortunately, that's not our situation right now. The cops want nothing to do with us and we've got an agency on our back on top of that. In fact, if you see black trucks prowling around somewhere, driven by spooky assholes in black robes? I bet you'll find they're hunting for the same thing."

Ted said, "If I find out this is bullshit—"

"The monster that just flew out here *was not made of papier-mâché and pipe cleaners*. I'm telling you now, Ted, that thing is going to try to scramble your brain. That's what it does. Don't let it. I don't give a shit if you believe me or not. But if you can't trust your own two eyes, what can you trust?"

John was proud that he was able to keep a straight face through that last part.

Me

Amy and I watched John trudge back toward us, soaked to the bone. Ted's partner had already vacated the premises, jogging off through the rain, clutching wounded ribs.

John nodded sideways and said, "They parked down the street. Hopefully they'll head off to spend the next month trying to find that thing's nest. God only knows what it was doing there. Unless one of you know?"

I said, "Did you see it phase through the wall? It can do that, but it still managed to get trapped in a supply room? I think it's just an idiot."

Amy said, "It started making noise when Ted pointed a gun at us. Maybe it was trying to protect us."

"I would love to spend just one day in your world. I know that came out like sarcasm, but it's not—I seriously would."

John said, "All right, we need a game plan."

I said, "Well, we have to figure this all out before Ted turns his attention back on us. And before the Maggie thing hatches. And before Tasker figures out how NON can murder us all without consequence. And before the manhunt for those missing kids draws the entire town to the mine. And before the biker gang blames us for all

this. And before the Batmantis comes back and eats us."
I raked back wet hair from my forehead and sighed.
"Anybody hungry? Didn't they say Waffle House wasn't
closing no matter what?"

John said, "We need to go to the mine, right? I mean
that's the root of the problem."

I said, "So, let's say we go there and find ten 'kids'
standing around. Then what? And don't say kill them
because Amy is going to start screaming."

"Whatever we do, it's better than letting the bikers
find them. We're seeing through their disguises, thanks
to the Sauce, but who knows how long that will last? I
say we go down there and, I don't know. We've got all
that sulfur. Maybe you throw it on them and it breaks
the spell or something? Plus we have all those butts."

"Would you drop the thing with the butts? You know
why you bought those? So that you could bring them up
every five minutes."

Amy said, "*What butts?*"

We piled into the Jeep. I was in the passenger seat
and had the sudden urge to pull down the sun visor,
even though the morning sun hadn't showed up for
work in a month and was clearly trying to get fired.

A note fell into my lap.

John's handwriting.

Amy asked, "What does it say?"

"It says, 'Don't let the Batmantis out.'"

20. THE ASS LETTER

John wanted to stop by his place to get gear for the mine mission and possible Millibutt showdown, but instead we wound up spending half an hour carrying electronics and furniture up to the second floor. John had some standing water in his yard and garage, but the house itself was up another few inches above the waterline. Still, it felt inevitable—Amy had pointed out that even if the rain stopped, runoff from higher ground would push the flood into his living room. It was going to be like that everywhere; there was just no place for the water to go.

I said, "What if it doesn't stop? What if the water just keeps coming, like those floods you see on the news where it goes over the rooftops?"

John said, "Then it's all up to the insurance, I guess . . ."

"No, I mean . . . like yeah, I'm worried about your stuff but in terms of the town, what happens? All these moldy waterlogged houses. Would people finally just leave? Just, abandon this place?"

"Dunno. I don't know why people stay here now."

"Why do *we* stay here?"

Amy said, "It sounds like you're rooting for the flood."

"I kind of am."

"You could put an end to the whole thing if you'd just buy some boots."

John said, "I'm going to dig around in my garage to see what I've got in the way of enchanted weapons. Look around for any more cryptic notes."

John left and I looked in the fridge; I didn't find any notes but did find a piece of leftover pizza. I took a bite of it and said to Amy, "Am I crazy or does it smell like perfume in here? You think John's back on the girlfriend wagon?"

Amy, as if resuming a conversation she was having in her head, said, "What would you do if it was your last day on earth?"

"Amy, I'm not worried about this thing killing me, I'm worried about it filling the world with weird monsters. Do you have any idea how many calls we'd get? Tell you what, I'm just canceling my phone altogether if that happens, live like it's 1995."

"I mean, just as a hypothetical. You've only got twenty-four hours left, how do you spend it? Like, say the doctor said you just had one day to live."

"I'd spend the last day trying to find another doctor. Or researching a cure. There has to be something left to try. I mean, why would I be putting so much stock in some doctor's opinion? You remember Dutch Vogless, from high school? He's a doctor now, in Indianapolis. He was a dipshit. Fuck that doctor."

"*It's just a thought experiment.* Like let's say you accepted the diagnosis and knew you only had one day."

"I'm not confused by the question. The answer is I would spend the last twenty-four hours refusing to accept that it was my last twenty-four hours. I'll tell you right now, if there's such a thing as fate, it can eat a bag of dicks."

This answer clearly annoyed Amy. I scrambled to think of a way to change the subject but before I could, she said, "I think you should see a doctor."

"What? You think I have a terminal illness? If so, that was a super weird way to bring it up."

"No. About medication. For your moods."

"This is totally not the time for that conversation."

"It's absolutely the time, because you're up. You're feeling energetic because you've got a project. When this is over you're going to get planted on the sofa again and when you're like that it's like talking to a grumpy log."

"Amy, I'm not depressed because of brain chemicals, I'm depressed because I don't have a job and don't have any skills or education. Because I've wasted my life. There's no drug that's going to make me okay with that. Other than alcohol, I guess. The point is, I don't need a doctor, I need work. I need a reason to get out of bed in the morning."

"That's what the drugs are for, they get you up off the sofa so you can go fix your life, find a job, get out of this cycle where you spend all day in bed because you're depressed, but the thing you're depressed about is the fact that you wasted all day in bed."

"We'll talk about this later."

"You know for a fact we wo—"

But I was already heading upstairs, to escape the conversation. I entered the master bedroom. John had a very expensive king-sized mattress and box spring, but kept both of them on the floor, insisting that he never understood what the rest of the bed was for (and I admittedly had no answer for that). There was a television mounted to the ceiling so that he could watch it from bed, the thing looked like it weighed a hundred pounds and would crush his skull if the screws came loose.

The bed was made. That was not typical.

A quick glance around confirmed that, yes, a woman was staying here. Girly clothes in the closet, makeup in the bathroom. This was hardly an unusual circumstance, but keeping it from me and Amy was *very* unusual, to the point that I don't think it had ever happened before. I would say that maybe he thought we wouldn't approve but, holy shit, when did that ever stop him? He's been hanging out with Nicky for more than a decade and I work so hard to avoid her that she hasn't even appeared in this story yet. She's got a PhD in some useless subject, and is one of those people who laughs at her own jokes and absolutely no one else's. Don't get me started.

I searched the room for notes from ourselves, found none.

I made it back downstairs at the same moment John was walking in from his garage, holding a medieval mace with three-inch spikes.

He said, "Okay, I've got Buddha's mace here. It's about twenty-five hundred years old but it should still work."

I said, "I was actually hoping it'd turn out we had built some kind of superweapon in your garage while we were on the Sauce. A big monster-killing bomb or something."

John said, "Well, we've got all that sulfur. And the—"

"The rubber asses, yes. Hey, uh, who's staying here?"

"Who's what?"

"If it's none of my business, just say so, it's fine. I just, you know, normally you're open about it."

"I don't know what you're referring to."

"There's plainly a woman living here. Her clothes and stuff are in your closet. Unless they're yours, which again, the only thing that would bug me is that you didn't feel like you could tell me."

John looked confused and more than a little alarmed. He stomped up the stairs past me, mace in hand. We followed him up and watched as he flipped through the skirts and tops in the closet, then examined the pile of makeup and face washes on his vanity.

"That stuff was *not* here before."

Amy said, "Well, is this some kind of monster-related thing or do you just have a squatter? Maybe one of your girlfriends got flooded out and came to stay?"

John said, "Not without letting me know. They'd have been incinerated."

"Well, maybe they did let you know, while you were tripping on the Sauce. And you just don't remember."

John gestured toward the clothes and said, "No, look."

Amy studied the clothes and said, "Hmm."

I said, "What?"

She said, "These don't belong to anyone we know."

"How do you know?"

"Because I've never seen these outfits before. I know what John's friends wear, David."

"You do?"

"This black skirt with the slit going halfway up the hip? Try to imagine any of the girls we know wearing that."

"Okay, give me a minute."

John said, "No, she's right. This is weird."

I said, "It certainly is. Crazy how your day can start off perfectly normal and then something like this happens."

"Yeah. All right, let me run to the bathroom, then we'll go." He was going to the bathroom with the owl jar above the toilet. John would smoke weed in front of me, but not meth. Weird the little boundaries people have.

The moment he was out of earshot, Amy said, "So let me get this straight, if you were confronted with a life-ending crisis you'd fight it to your last breath, but you're perfectly fine with slowly drowning in a warm pool of your own ennui?"

"My own what?"

"What if I told you that you were possessed by, like, a powerful sadness demon and that it was feeding off your life force? Would you fight it then? How about if I told you it was coming for me next?"

"What are you talking ab—"

We heard John burst out of the bathroom. He charged into the room, breathless, and said, "Dave, I need to see your ass."

I stared at him for forty silent seconds.

"Why."

"I found the next note. In advance, this time. It's written on my penis, in Magic Marker. It says, 'Check David's ass, there's an important message written on it that contains valuable information.'"

I said, "It clearly does not say all that."

"You want to see? You won't even need to get too close, because the font is—"

Amy said, "David, will you show him your butt?"

I gritted my teeth and glared at John. "You did this. You're the one who *Dude, Where's My Car'd* this shit."

"I have no memory of that."

"Yeah, *that's kind of the point.*"

"Why are you yelling at me instead of showing me your ass?"

"You stay here. I'll go check it in the mirror."

A minute later I stormed back to the kitchen. "It says, 'Don't let them' and then the letters *S, C, R* and a scrawl across to the other cheek. As if I woke up to find someone writing on my ass and then violently slapped their hand away."

John said, "Shit. Don't let them scr . . . Don't let them scream? Screw? Scrape?"

Amy said, "Guessing is pointless, since we don't know how much more there was to the message."

"Well it'd have to be enough to fit on one human ass. Screw the pooch? Script a sitcom pilot?"

"Scrawl things on your butt?" offered Amy.

I said, "Goddamnit, we've wasted like an hour and we have nothing to show for it."

Amy said, "And we had so much to show from the previous eighty thousand hours before that."

John got a notification on his phone and said, "Marconi's here. They're parking at the vacant Walmart, says it's on pretty high ground."

I said, "Good for him."

"He says he wants to meet."

I threw up my hands. "We might as well! Anybody have anything else they want to do before we go fight the monster? Anybody need to run to the DMV, get your license renewed?"

Amy said, "You want to swing by the doctor?"

21. WE ALL MUST LEARN FROM KURT RUSSELL'S TRAGIC MISTAKE

Marconi traveled in two huge RVs he used as tour buses, one for the man himself and another for his production crew. He was even less interested in anonymity than John—his enormous face was airbrushed on the side, though I noted it was on the production crew's bus, where Marconi's was a nondescript white and gold. Meaning, if a crazed fan tried to force their way onto the bus to murder Marconi, they'd likely get the wrong one. I wondered if he kept a bearded assassination double in there.

John, Amy, and I we were sitting pressed shoulder-to-shoulder in the cramped office in the rear of the bus, which it turned out was where he'd taken our Skype call earlier. The wall with the accolades was in fact the least interesting of the four—the rest of the room was stuffed with exotic artifacts. Whether these were genuine items collected from haunted houses and dig sites or cheap props created to look good in the background of his TV show, I didn't know. If it was the former, I was guessing it wasn't exactly legal to take some of them from their countries of origin. There was a crystal skull, a golden chalice, and an ancient-looking spear with a head of chiseled obsidian. Alongside these were seemingly random items—a Raggedy Ann doll, a clay bust of Lionel Richie, and in the corner, a one-armed concrete snowman covered in bird shit. On his desk, Marconi's pipe was leaning against an antique figurine that looked like some kind of Egyptian god, only it had an enormous, erect penis almost as big as its torso, the figure's left hand wrapped around the shaft.

Marconi asked everyone if we wanted a bottle of water, John and I declined, Amy said yes, as she always does. She must just like getting free stuff. When he returned and handed her the bottle, he nodded toward the penis figurine and said, "I thought you'd like that one. It's the Egyptian god Min, popular in the fourth century B.C., the god of fertility. It is believed that during the coronation of a new Pharaoh, he would be required to masturbate in front of the crowd, to demonstrate that he himself possessed the fertility powers of Min. If you have watched a State of the Union address, you will find that the ritual has not changed much."

He took a seat behind his desk.

He said, "It appears social media rumors have coalesced around the idea of a white winged creature, snatching the town's children and building a great nest of their bones in one of this region's many abandoned buildings."

I said, "Yeah, we may have accidentally started that rumor. You have to admit that's way more straightforward than the truth."

"There is no element of truth to it, as far as you know?"

"I . . . don't think so? Shit, I don't know. I have no idea what's happening anymore."

"Does such a creature exist? My team said if the YouTube video is a fake, it is an excellent one."

John said, "It exists, we've seen it up close. Very close. Don't think it eats children though."

I said, "Not much meat on them."

"Perhaps the subject of another episode, then. Is the situation the same as when we last spoke? Two larvae loose, ten set to arrive at any moment?"

I said, "As far as we know. And Amy objects to killing them because they look like children."

Amy stared down Marconi and said, "Could *you* shoot a child in the face because somebody else was insisting it was really a monster?"

Marconi put on a pair of wire frame reading glasses and said, "You are living in a cruel world, Ms. Sullivan. You see that oak tree, by the parking lot? That tree is a murderer, it would commit genocide if it could. Those leaves serve two purposes—to collect sunlight to nourish the tree, and *to block sunlight from anything below it*. Its height is a result of competition—growing taller than the plants next to it, getting between them and the sun. Starving them out. When you stroll through a tranquil forest, you are actually walking through a battlefield—it's just that the attacks and counterattacks occur too slowly and quietly for you to perceive their ruthlessness. Do you enjoy the smell of fresh cut grass? What you are smelling is a chemical panic signal, released by each blade in the moment its head was severed. That is the nature of the universe in which we live. Thus, if another species has designs on mankind, the choice has been made for us."

I said, "Exactly."

Marconi said, "However, it is very easy to fall into the fallacy held by every violent zealot and corrupt policeman in the world, the idea that we are always faced with only two options—fierce violence and cowardly inaction. Real life provides us with a vast array of nuanced choices. As for me, I try to hold to one central rule, in all circumstances—do not act out of ignorance."

I said, "Well, I'd never get out of bed."

"With that in mind," said Marconi, "we need a reliable method for seeing through the worker swarm's camouflage, one that does not require the observer to ingest any extraordinarily dangerous substances. I have a method I'd like to test, but I need a specimen."

I said, "Is it like that questionnaire they used on the humanoid robots in *Blade Runner?*"

Amy said, "The Voight-Kampff."

"I've got that whole Rutger Hauer speech memorized, if that will help. As far as a specimen, I guess you could try to bring in the Knoll girl, if the parents will cooperate."

Marconi shrugged, making a show of being casual. "Of course. But if you do not mind, I would like to test it now, just to get a general feel for the process. With those of us in the room. Get some control results down before diving in with an actual specimen. There will be no battery of confusing questions, just some cameras and an audience of some friends working off-site."

None of us moved. We all just looked at Marconi, in silence.

He said, "It won't take but a few minutes."

I turned to John and said, "Marconi thinks we're doppelgangers."

Amy, looking the most nervous of the three of us, said, "This is part of the test, by the way. Seeing if we're willing to do it."

Marconi said, "That should actually put you at ease. If you were not human, there would be a substantial risk of you becoming violent at the mere suggestion of a test. And, as you can see, I have taken no unusual precautions for such an eventuality."

Yet already, there has been too much hesitation.

John said, "All right, but if we do this, we do it right. I don't want some bullshit like Kurt Russell pulled in *The Thing* where we're all tied up in the same room with somebody when they monster out. We go in one at a time, lock the door, everybody else waits outside the room, ready to escape."

I said, "That is the exact sort of thing a hive of shape-shifting monsters would suggest."

"We'll see about that." John turned his eyes on Marconi and said, "I assume we'll need to be nude for this?"

We did not. John volunteered to go first. Marconi started setting up an array of various types of cameras on his desk, all pointing at his chair.

"In situations like this," he said, "I have had some success with layers of remote perception. You mentioned earlier that the Mikey Payton doppelganger was able to maintain his camouflage even through a live video feed, from outside the motel room. But every living entity has limitations. Here, I have four different devices—digital video, heat signature, ultraviolet, and a sensor pulled from a video game peripheral which creates a 3D map of the physical objects in the room using a method similar to sonar. The feeds from each are monitored by dozens of members of an Internet message board located in various parts of the world, who will each be able to observe the feeds and type up, via text, exactly what they are seeing. Members cannot see what the others are posting, and thus cannot be influenced as a group.

"My hypothesis is that we have here a sort of camouflage that works on the observer end, but as they say, you cannot fool all of the people all of the time. So, the concept is to simply give the organism too many observers, in too many places, viewing it through too many different wavelengths, for it to maintain its subterfuge. To mimic plausible feedback from hundreds of strangers, being read simultaneously by three of us, would simply be too much. That is the hope, anyway."

John sat at the desk and Marconi moved to the cramped lounge area outside his office where he had set up a laptop that would monitor the feedback in real time. He motioned for me to close the door to the office.

I made eye contact with John and said, "I just want you to know, if it turns out you're a fake person inserted into my memory, my whole life will make *so much more sense*."

"I was just thinking the same thing."

I locked him in—the door seemed fairly sturdy—and the remaining three of us huddled on an uncomfortable little fold-out sofa so we could all see Marconi's laptop.

The man smelled like cologne and fancy pipe tobacco. The feeds were switched on and

dried vomit cascading down the side of the sofa

I found myself holding my breath.

The laptop screen was split into quadrants, one for each camera feed. We didn't see what the cameras were capturing—we only saw the scrolling text from the collective feedback from each. That was the idea.

Digital video:
I see a dude sitting in a chair, got long hair, handsome but in a way that makes me want to punch him.

Ultraviolet:
Man sitting in a chair, looks like he's on heroin.

Sonar:
Either a male or a tall, flat-chested girl, nothin' weird unless there's not supposed to be anybody sitting there.

Heat signature:
Shape is like a tall thin male, check around the pelvis area he
OH GOD HE HAS AN ERECTION.

And so on. Nearly three hundred messages were posted, split across the four feeds, with little variation aside from people trying too hard to pick out curiosities in the background ("That doctorate doesn't appear to be from an accredited university"). Marconi, Amy, and I took turns reading the messages out loud, all of us agreeing we were seeing the same text.

We declared that round of testing over. I stuck my

head through the doorway and said, "All clear, but the machine does show you have herpes. Also Marconi wants to do a drug test after this is done."

Amy was next, and strangely, I wasn't as nervous for her. It honestly wouldn't matter what they said—they'd be wrong. They might as well tell me the universe doesn't exist. Amy is my constant, she is the only reason I continue to do any of this. If she's not real then my life isn't real and I'm not real and nothing matters anyway. If she's a monster then I'll take her home and hug her and we'll be monsters together.

We locked her in and John took her place on the narrow sofa. He watched the scrolling messages and said, "Marconi, your fans are kind of dicks." Still, that was as alarming as the revelations got:

Digital video:
Redheaded girl with glasses, pretty eyes but body is nothing special. Is she missing a hand?

Ultraviolet:
Looks like a girl with bad posture. Does she only have one hand?

Heat signature:
Heat pattern looks like a petite girl, nothing weird, one hand doesn't show up for some reason, did she have it dipped in ice water or something?

Sonar:
See a girl, sitting with her legs crossed, might be cute but I'd need to see the full-color vid.

And there were a few of the obligatory:
Wait, is that who I think it is?

I let out a breath.

It was my turn in the chair.

Four different electronic eyes stared me down. Marconi asked me if I wanted anything and I said no, which really is one of the biggest lies I've ever told. He made an adjustment to one of the cameras—viewers asked for a wider view of the background, he said—and then he and John left the room.

Amy, however, closed the door with her still on my side of it. She took a seat in front of the desk and looked right at me.

I said, "A bunch of Marconi fans want your phone number."

"I look like I slept in a warehouse. Good thing they couldn't smell me."

"Honestly, while this is a very clever setup and I can see what Marconi was going for, I don't see why it would—"

"OH, FUCK!"

From the next room. John, not Marconi.

Amy jumped to her feet, but didn't make an effort to leave.

I said, "What?"

From the other side of the door, Marconi said, "One moment, please."

I said, "I am not a monster larva."

John, sounding like he was pressed up against the door, said, "It doesn't show that. He changed the setup and it's, uh . . ."

"What does it show?"

Marconi said, "Please remain calm."

"*What does it show?*"

John said, "You have one in the room with you."

I was jumping to my feet now, knocking the chair over. "What? Where? Can you see it?"

I stared at Amy.

It can't be.

"They're saying it's that snowman thing."

I said, "The what?"

I turned and looked at the filthy, misshapen concrete monstrosity, MR. ICEE etched on its chest and

Have I seen it before?

shards of broken memories went spraying across my mind, a dozen contradictory origin stories of this stupid concrete snowman wearing a shawl of bird shit, none of the memories making a bit of sense.

The thing's misshapen, eroded mouth started moving and out from it came the sound of screams. Small voices, in abject panic—a roomful of children pleading for their mothers, begging for mercy, moaning in pain.

Its mouth grew and the noises grew louder, filling the room, vibrating my skull. Then the snowman exploded into a swirl of panicked and enraged fuckroaches. Amy screamed. The door lock clicked and the door opened—John coming in, completely defeating the purpose of the whole setup.

I batted at the creatures with my hands, and tried frantically to locate the larva itself. They kept getting in front of me, creating images, people.

The swarm formed a face—my face, the Nymph version. I swatted at them, grabbing one of the fuckroaches—it held the shape of my own laughing mouth—and crushed it in my hand. They couldn't fool me. Not now.

They scattered, then coalesced again. This time as my mother, a face I barely remembered. I smashed it with my fist. The whizzing insects were screeching and crying and laughing in voices from my past, the things sloppily sifting through my mind for something, anything. I heard Jim and Arnie and TJ and Hope and Jennifer and Krissy and Todd and Robert. I heard Molly's bark. I heard them imitate Amy, making her cry and beg, saying things that made it sound like I was her attacker.

I heard John, and I think it was the real John, say, "It's behind y—" at the exact moment the larva crashed into my back, knocking me to the floor, sending the fuckroaches scattering once more.

I rolled over just as the maggot raised up a mouth ringed by mandibles, at the center a gulping throat that made a sound like a drunken kiss in the back of a taxi. I tried to fight it off but it thrust is mouth down onto the side of my face, covering one ear. The mandibles bit down and . . .

There was an explosion of pain.

Then, all pain disappeared.

It was replaced by a vague warmth, and I don't mean the disgusting warmth like when you squeeze a bag of dog shit in your hand. It was warm like a hug, like a shared bed in winter.

And then, it was the weirdest thing.

The center of the universe just . . . *shifted*.

In that moment, I was no longer the main character in my story. This thing that was attached to me, it was

305

what mattered. It didn't hate me, it didn't hate anyone. It was hungry and cold and scared. In me, it found nourishment and warmth and safety. It not only didn't wish me harm, it desperately needed me to remain safe and whole, to be the provider. It wanted nothing more than for us to survive, together, in a universe that would just as readily see us die alone and forgotten. In that moment, the creature was no longer afraid, because I was there, I was the rock it could cling to. I think that was the first time in my life I was really proud of myself.

And then the creature recoiled, as if struck, or electrocuted. It unhooked itself, writhed and rolled off onto the floor next to me. I thought that John or Marconi had attacked it, but it had recoiled on its own. It had found that I was not its father, that I was poison, that I had nothing to offer.

It cried out in despair.

No, wait. That was me.

I reached out for it, but I was being dragged from the room. The fuckroaches were getting their act together now, landing on the larva, covering it, recombobulating themselves into some new form. Then I was pulled through the door and John slammed it shut, locking it. Amy was kneeling over me, asking if I was okay, examining my face.

From behind the door came the familiar screech of the maggot. Marconi got a look on his face that made me ask, "Who are you hearing?"

"A boy . . ."

Amy said, "It's being Mikey again. Begging us to let him out."

There was a moment when I could see doubt creep into Marconi's eyes, the fuckroaches' voodoo starting to take hold. We quickly ushered him out of the RV, slammed the door, and got some distance away from the vehicle. We stood there in the Walmart parking lot in silence, listening to the rain making army marching sounds on our skulls. We tried to catch our breath.

John said, "Well, it's Mikey's bus now. Does that mean he gets to host your show?"

Marconi said, "We gained some crucial information. Specifically, the fact that your 'Soy Sauce' does not give you perfect detection. And, more importantly, that the workers have the ability to imitate an inanimate object."

John said, "We actually already knew that. The first trick we saw one pull after we captured it was to mimic my cell phone. Sorry, I think I forgot to mention that."

"That would have been useful, yes. To know that not only any person or animal we encounter could in fact be these creatures in disguise, but literally anything in the environment itself. Any object in the universe. The implications of that are almost beyond my comprehension."

Amy said, "Hey, remember when this was just a missing person's case?"

I felt bumps on my face where the maggot had bitten me. Itchy, but not painful. That brief feeling of attachment . . . I felt dirty, just thinking about it. I wasn't sure why.

I said, "Just out of curiosity, Marconi, where did you think you had gotten a concrete snowman from?"

"It was a supposed haunted artifact from a quaint post-war ice cream parlor in Vermont. I remember the case well, the owner of the establishment was a feisty old Scottish woman named . . ." He trailed off. "Her face fades even as I try to bring it to mind. Fascinating."

I said, "That's one word for it. Well shit, now what?"

John glanced behind him and said, "NON's here."

The agents rolled into the parking lot of the abandoned Walmart in a black sedan. The female agent I knew as Tasker stepped out, looked over Marconi's TV production RVs, and said, "So when I told you to go home and avoid leaking anything about the case . . ."

She was accompanied by her recently deceased male partner, Gibson, who was walking with a cane and seemed to be having some difficulty.

John said, "I see you're up and around."

He grunted. "Fuck off."

There was a thump and Amy jumped—Mikey's face appeared in a window near the rear of the RV. He was crying and clawing at the glass. "Help! That old man lured me into his RV and he made me watch a puppet show he put on with his peepee!"

I said, "Hey, we captured a larva specimen. Need anything else?"

Tasker said, "We already have a vehicle on the way to retrieve it."

"You do? How did you—"

"You need to come with us. We're going to have a meeting."

Marconi said, "Am I invited?"

"No, this is not going to be part of your reality show, Doctor." She turned back to me. "We're going to come up with a plan of action, and you're going to be on board with it and you're going to stop impeding our every move. We have the exact same goal. There is no reason we can't work together."

John said, "Other than the fact that you would literally murder us right now if you could."

"Society is nothing more than people cooperating with other people they'd much rather murder. Listen to what we have to say, you'll find out we're not the bad guys here."

22. THE HEROES AGREE TO HELP MURDER A DOZEN CHILDREN

I was hoping we'd get to ride inside one of the NON vehicles—I was curious to see the interior—but apparently that wasn't allowed for non-NON employees, so we were simply told to follow them to the meeting location. I wasn't surprised to see that we were being led toward the converted farm supply store that was now calling itself the IAEEAI Lab and Wellness Center.

I wasn't quite sure what kind of occult temple shit to expect inside the building that NON was apparently using as a field HQ, but it was kind of disappointing. Inside was an open space that had been recently renovated for use as offices and could easily have passed for an insurance company's customer support call center. Past an unmanned reception desk were cubicles and glassed-in conference rooms. Against the wall to our right was a series of vending machines and that black coffin thing they'd rolled out in the parking lot a couple of days ago—the portable doorway to . . . wherever. A man in an orange jumpsuit walked over to it and opened the door. On the other side I got a glimpse of what appeared to be a green field on a sunny day. The guy took the last gulp from a Styrofoam coffee cup, tossed the cup through the door, then closed it.

The office area was only half of the building, however, and the insurance company illusion ended abruptly at a concrete wall with a thick sliding steel door in the center. So, probably not a supply closet. There was a row of red warning lights along the wall and below them, large painted letters said:

IF LIGHTS ARE FLASHING PERFORM RITES OF
BLACK VEIL
FAILURE = NERVE BURN CYCLE
THIS MEANS YOU!

I thought we'd be taken to the coffin door to hold our "meeting" in some nightmare dimension where the office furniture was alive and the bagels screamed when you bit them. But, no, we were just led to the largest conference room. Inside, one wall featured a single window granting us a view of the misty industrial park. Next to the window was an inspirational poster depicting a bunch of bees crawling over a honeycomb above the words, TEAMWORK KILLS THE WASP. At the center of the long conference table was a phone with speakers snaking out like the arms of a very spindly and fragile robot octopus.

Tasker directed us to sit on the opposite side of the table from her. Agent Gibson shuffled over and sat next to his partner with some difficulty, leaning his cane against the table next to him.

Tasker said, "Do you want a drink or any refreshments before we begin?"

John and I said no, Amy said, "Does your chip vending machine have those spicy Cheetos in it? I have change."

I shot her an annoyed look but, as usual, it just bounced off her. To my horror, Agent Tasker nodded to Gibson, who sighed and with a monumental effort climbed to his feet and shuffled out of the conference room, across the vast concrete floor, and over to the vending machine. He returned and tossed the Cheetos bag onto the table in front of Amy and began the laborious multistep process of sitting back down.

Amy noisily tore open the bag with her teeth and shook some Cheetos into her mouth.

Tasker said, "Now, you are to remain silent unless asked a direct question. You are not being invited onto this call to offer your opinion and this is not subject to a vote. You may or may not be asked for information. It will be explained to you what the next course of action will be, and we will seek reassurance that you will not interfere. Are we clear?"

Amy said, "I'm sorry, the crunching is really loud in my head. I think I got the gist of it though."

Tasker punched a button on the phone, then dialed, then entered a twelve-digit code. There was a tone, and she leaned forward.

"Sorry we're late, I'm going to do a roll call. Utah, are you on?"

The answer was muffled clicking noises.

"Utah, I'm not hearing you."

"We're here, is this better?"

"Yes, thank you."

"Las Vegas?"

"We're here."

"Chicago?"

"We're on, Josaline."

"Bangkok?"

An answer in a language I assumed was Thai.

"Effingham?"

Another answer in a language I didn't recognize.

"Bernard? I understand you're calling in from the road?"

The reply was the sound of an electronic voice announcing that Gate 34-B was boarding. A breathless male voice then came on and said, "Sorry, I'm here, I'm at the airport. Let me get to a quiet spot."

"And do we have HQ on the line?"

The answer was a series of deep rumbles, like the sound a mountain would make if it had gotten woken up in the middle of the night by the neighbor's loud music. I assumed it was the phone glitching again but Tasker nodded as if she could hear it clearly and said, "Yes, all three of them are here, my lord."

I exchanged a look with John. Amy stopped chewing. Agent Gibson sat up straighter, as if not completely sure the thing on the line couldn't see him.

Tasker, in her most professional voice, said, "You've all been briefed and I assume you reviewed the memo I sent out approximately twelve minutes ago. The issue as you know is that Undisclosed is in the middle of a Class G outbreak with at least one larva attached to a living host and a second now in containment, en route to this facility. Though there are no sightings as of yet, we now have reason to believe that ten more will manifest themselves, their origins already implanted in a group of human hosts. We've brought in the three locals discussed on yesterday's call to talk about options for containment. They are in the room with me now, you should see their dossiers on your screens, designated 919A, 919B, and John."

A male voice said, "Hey this is Tom in Houston, is this the budget call?"

"No, it is not, that was moved to Thursday at two. Now, as you know, the outbreak can be traced to the entity we have designated B3333B, which is attempting its second breech, via a reproduction cycle that has not previously been observed."

Amy said, "Excuse me, can you tell me what a Class G outbreak is?"

An annoyed voice on the phone said, "Who is that speaking?"

"Amy Sullivan, I'm one of the locals. Is a Class G, is that on a scale from A to Z? If so is A the worst or is Z?"

Tasker said, "Class G is potential extinction level. Please remain silent until asked a question. Now, the method for terminating the larva discussed in the memo was tested during Incident 404 twelve years ago and the results were very, very promising. We will proceed in two stages. First, we must track and collect the larvae and contain them in one location if possible, preferably here in the field office. Second, we must create a satisfactory cover story for the termination of same. There will then be a separate operation to disrupt the breeding cycle of B3333B itself."

Amy said, "Hi, it's me again, but just to clarify, we're discussing a plan for kidnapping and murdering a total of twelve children in a country where the entire news cycle catches fire over *one* missing kid? And the idea is to do that in such a way that nobody will care or even be slightly curious. Got it."

A deep rumble emerged from the speaker, the voice from "HQ." Everyone went quiet.

Tasker said, "It won't happen again, my lord. Now, the concerns raised by 919B are valid, the cover story will be paramount. The world will believe these children have perished."

Amy said, "Plus any parents or other concerned types who try to get in the way."

"We will try to minimize that."

An elderly female voice spoke up on the phone for the first time. "This is Martha, and I want to register my objection right now. I was told—assured—that first on the agenda for today would be the allocation of funds for the Miami project. We've been waiting on this since January, guys, this can't wait any longer."

Tasker said, "This isn't the budget call, Martha."

Amy said, "It's Thursday. At two."

Tasker grimaced, rubbed her temples, and said, "The cover story will involve an incident that would leave no recognizable bodies behind, for obvious reasons."

John said, "Right, like if they fell into the ocean and got eaten by sharks."

Amy said, "Why would they be in the ocean?"

John said, "We could have them win a contest or something? Oh! Make it a plane crash. Tell them they won a trip. Plane goes down in the ocean, in the part of the ocean where there are the most sharks."

"So these kids get to experience the terror of a plane plummeting to earth?"

I said, "They're not kids, and we have no indication that they can experience terror. And you don't need anything like that. You just need to do it in such a way that the public sees it as unavoidable."

Amy said, "How in the world do you do that?"

I said, "You say the kids are infected with some weaponized disease. Ebola, whatever. Say Nymph did it, and you've got to quarantine the kids to keep anybody else from getting sick. Say you're bringing them in for treatment. Then once you've got them in quarantine, just say they succumbed to the infection, that it was too late. Then tell them Nymph is dead and that there are no other victims. Tie up the whole story with a neat little bow."

There was silence in the room. The rumble from HQ sounded. Tasker looked very nervous.

Amy looked back and forth from me to Tasker and said to the latter, "That's your exact plan, isn't it? I don't know how to feel about that."

"Not Ebola," said Tasker. "That would be a recipe for panic. Polonium 210 poisoning. Slow-acting, fatal, but not contagious. Still, the corpse is mildly radioactive and we would explain that we will be unable to release the bodies of the children, for safety reasons."

John nodded. "Then you put the radioactive bodies on a plane, and arrange for the plane to crash right into the mine monster. The radioactive material in the kids' bodies triggers a nuclear explosion."

Tasker tried to pretend she hadn't heard that. Forcing calm into her voice, she said, "*Again*, all we need from you is your assurances that you are not going to interfere."

Amy said, "Wait, you're asking our permission?"

"We don't need your permission. There is no reason we can't all be in agreement."

"And if we're not in agreement, you'll have to find some other way?"

"We would discuss that."

"But you can't harm us. So you need our permission."

I said, "I don't think there's any disagreement here. You saw the larva attack me, that part of the debate is over." To Tasker, I said, "Then we should be good to go. Assuming, of course, the other ten children show up and you're able to corral them. If the bikers find them, good luck convincing them to turn their kids over to you shady fuckers."

"We have a plan for that contingency."

Amy sighed and crumpled up her Cheetos bag. "I'm sure you do."

To the phone, Tasker said, "Termination of the two existing specimens will proceed immediately. Mikey Payton is secure and will be here within fifteen minutes. A team will be dispatched to the Loretta Knoll residence momentarily."

Amy said, "I want to go with them."

"You are not going to interfere."

"I don't want to interfere. But I want to be there. If you don't let me, *then* I'll interfere."

Tasker said, "Any further questions?"

The rumbling mountain voice spoke up once again, and this time it continued speaking. It was a voice I could feel in my gut and in my shoes as it rattled the floor. Gibson and Tasker listened intently, the way you'd listen to a jury delivering a verdict at your murder trial. The sound of fates being decided.

It spoke for some time, maybe a full two minutes, and it was one of the longest two-minute spans of my life. I tried to detect emotion in that voice, to see if it was delivering good news or bad, if it was angry or pleased. But whatever sentiments were being expressed were beyond me, maybe beyond any human.

Finally the voice rumbled to a halt, the aftershocks subsiding. The sense of relief in the room was palpable.

Tasker nodded, swallowed, and said, "Yes, my lord. Thursday at two."

23. A PLAN WITH NO POSSIBLE FLAWS

Amy

They were in John's Jeep, parked outside Taco Bill on a street hidden under a sheet of rippling water in a neighborhood that looked like it had dressed up as Venice for a costume party and then woke up in a dumpster. Amy wasn't even sure why she had insisted on coming, maybe she wanted one last look at Maggie, to try to see the monster, to shake this feeling.

She had to admit, NON could certainly play subtle when they wanted to. Instead of rolling in with an army of scary-looking trucks and men in space suits (a sight all too familiar to the residents of this city), they had simply approached the Loretta Knoll home in the agents' nondescript sedan followed by an ambulance. (Had they stolen one?) Amy watched as they approached the door and explained the situation to an increasingly panicked Loretta, then tried in vain to calm her. The story would be that the other abductee had tested positive for this dangerous toxin, that they just needed to bring Maggie in for tests, that every minute counted, blah blah blah. They all went inside, Amy figuring that the odds of them deciding to take the child by violence increased with every passing second. She got that Bunny Bread knot in her guts.

But, finally, the NON people emerged with Maggie. And, right behind them, was her mother.

You'd have to kill Loretta, too.

David reached back, took Amy's hand in his and said, "You did everything right, babe. Everything you said, we need you to say those things, to be that person. You were basing it on what you knew. You can't let it tear you up inside—that's what They want. But once you land on the right thing, you don't look back, you don't apologize. I know this looks different from your end but you have to trust us here."

Amy said, "So now we're basically following NON's orders and you're fine with that."

"I'm not fine with anything, ever. But, as far as I can tell, what NON wants is to keep things on an even keel, to keep people from panicking. That's not always a terrible thing to want."

Amy said, "No. What they want—not just NON, but everyone like them—is for us not to panic, but to be just scared enough. You know that scene in *They Live* where he puts on the glasses and all the signs have all these propaganda messages hidden in them? In the real world if you put on those glasses all you'd see is one message, repeated everywhere: BE ANXIOUS. Buy this thing or your friends will laugh at you, eat this thing or you'll get fat and nobody will love you, watch the news to find out who's trying to kill you today."

"Yeah, but all that stuff is real! There's actual reasons to be scared!"

"The problem, David, is your cynicism only runs one direction. If somebody comes on TV and says everything is great and wonderful, you don't believe it, you say they're blowing smoke up your butt. You demand proof. But if one second later, some guy comes on and says everything is falling apart, you automatically believe it, no questions asked. If those people had told you that this mine monster situation was no big deal and that we should just go home, you wouldn't have believed them, not for a second. But the moment they said it was a Class G apocalypse, you were on board. As if nobody ever has motivation to tell you things are worse than they really are. And you know for a fact that's not true! Nothing controls people like fear."

John said, "We're moving."

They followed the sedan back toward the wellness center. On the way, a pair of the flat-black trucks silently moved in front and behind them, ready to do containment if "Maggie" should transform and get loose.

There were no incidents, however, and the three of them were allowed to follow the NON team back into the field HQ where they proceeded to haul Maggie past the office area and toward that rear concrete wall with its huge steel door. The bizarre painted warnings had been covered by a series of posters reminding staff to wash their hands and to please dispose of food waste properly, lest it attract ants.

The steel door slid open soundlessly and Maggie and her mother were hauled into the chamber beyond. The little girl was bawling her eyes out, and Loretta seemed on the verge of a breakdown. Amy, John, and David followed them back. The steel door, Amy noted, was a foot thick. Beyond it were a number of cells with clear walls that Amy suspected were forged from a substance much stronger than Plexiglas.

This facility clearly had not been built within the last two days.

Maggie was taken past the glass cells, into a room at the end of the hall labeled STAFF ONLY. This time, Loretta was made to stay outside, reassurances being muttered to her by a very competent-looking guy in doctor scrubs. Amy had the horrific thought that they were just going to euthanize Maggie right then, in that room, and that Amy would have to watch them break the news to Loretta.

But about ten minutes later, the STAFF ONLY door opened—it made a hissing sound—and a few kind-looking folks who looked like staff from a hospital pediatric unit led Maggie Knoll to one of the cells. Her hair was wet and she was wearing baggy hospital pajamas, as if they'd hosed her down. Amy wondered if those people were actual medical staff, or if they were just actors NON had hired for their false flag operation (the ominous black cloaks were nowhere to be found—today, the facility was playing the part of a laboratory and wellness center to a T).

Maggie Knoll went into the cell, crying but not resisting, and the glass door closed and sealed her in. Loretta, sobbing, was taken down the hall to answer some questions.

As soon as her mother was out of range, Maggie

instantly stopped crying. She stood perfectly still in the middle of her cell, made eye contact with Amy, and said, "Hi."

For some reason, this seemed to creep David out quite a bit, and he actually took a step back from the glass wall. Amy didn't answer. Loretta was now talking to the NON agent, who was entering information on a tablet. Amy noticed the agent glance her way the moment she heard "Maggie" speak.

Maggie said, "You seem nice."

Amy said, "What are you?"

Maggie shrugged.

"I know you're not a little girl. What are you really?"

"What are *you*? Really?"

"Or, maybe I should ask, what are you going to be, once you grow up?"

"I don't think I'm going to grow up."

Amy tried to read the expression on the little girl's face, but couldn't. Finally, she said, "What you are, what you really are, can't live here."

Maggie met her eyes. "When they brought me in, just now, they took off my clothes and scrubbed me. That man over there, in the lab coat? He watched, and he liked it. But he lies about it. About liking it. It's like that everywhere. Mommy thinks I'm weird but she won't say anything. When they said they were taking me away, she was mad but I could see that she was happy, too, way down inside. Like she wouldn't have to be scared anymore. But she will hide it. Everybody is hiding what they really are, way down inside."

"That is not the same thing. What you are, you're going to hurt us. If we don't do something."

"I said you seem nice. But you're going to kill me. Because of what *you* are inside."

Amy heard the agent rapidly walking their way.

"I'm not really talking to you. You can't even talk. You're not a little girl, you don't even have a mouth. This is all . . . it's all something you're doing to my brain."

"If a spider walks onto your bed, you squish it. If a butterfly lands on your bed, you take a picture. Is the butterfly 'doing something to your brain'? If I didn't make myself look like this, I would already be dead. You kill everything that doesn't have pretty wings."

"So you're not dangerous? You're not going to grow up and declare war on us?"

"Are you at war with the cows who give you milk?"

"We're not going to be your cows, Maggie. If that's what you're getting at. We can't let that happen."

Maggie shrugged. "It's already happened."

Me

Tasker's shoes clicked up the concrete and I sensed she was about to tell us to stop interacting with the specimen. Before she could say anything, I put a hand on Amy's shoulder. "Let's go."

I pulled her away from the glass, which was now smeared with the ooze that had trickled off the enormous maggot that was sucking on it, its mandibles clicking off the surface like it badly wanted to bite its way through. Amy had been talking with the thing and it bothered me that I couldn't hear both ends of the conversation. The effect of the Sauce was fading, but it was still next to impossible to hear "Maggie" unless I devoted every ounce of concentration to it.

As we walked away, one of the NON "doctors" escorted the half-eaten Loretta up to Maggie's cell. Loretta put her hands up to the glass, asking the creature if it was okay, if it was feeling all right, reassuring it that they'd be going home soon.

I put my hand on Amy's back and walked a little faster.

To Tasker I said, "Mikey's here? Or is he loose on the town, destroying everything we know and love?"

Tasker said, "He's here. Came along without incident."

John said, "Hmm. Just like Maggie. Didn't put up a fight, didn't blow the cover."

I said, "Okay, so can we trust you to actually kill these things? You're not going to change your mind and decide you want to keep them as biological weapons or something?"

Agent Tasker said, "Follow me."

"No, we don't need to see you do it. There's no reason to give Amy nightmares for the next twenty years."

Amy said, "I want to be there."

"*Why?*"

Tasker said, "There's actually another reason. Come."

She led us down the hall and then over to what turned out to be another cell block—how many were there?—which was uninhabited save for a single cell occupied by a pulsing larva that I had to be told was Mikey. I made myself focus and found I could sort of see the disguise. But what I saw was clumsy. Monstrous. A mannequin made by incompetent hands in the dark.

Ridiculous to think that it had ever fooled me.

Tasker said, "As we alluded to on the conference call earlier, our past experience has found that one substance seems to be fatal to the—"

"Is it sulfur?" said John.

Taken aback, Tasker said, "That's a key component, yes. Burning sulfur. It's embedded in a thermite compound, formed into pellets that will ignite in midair. They should continue burning once they've penetrated the hide of the larva, releasing the sulfur internally."

John said, "And if you combined that substance with a piece of silicone in the shape of a human ass?"

Tasker just stared.

I said, "So it's that simple? After all of this talk of interdimensional energies and entities and all that, we're just burning holes in them? So what are we waiting for?"

"It's actually *not* that simple. Sulfur doesn't work for its chemical properties. It works because it has, let's just say, symbolic power. There is an invisible mechanism at play."

"Sure, it's a vampire holy water situation. I get it."

"I don't think you do. From previous incidents with similar organisms, the effectiveness of the weapon has varied wildly according to who is wielding it, and their state of mind at the moment the fatal blow is struck."

I said, "Okay."

"We are requesting that you do it. At least for this specimen."

Agent Gibson shuffled over, holding a modified shotgun. "Don't get cute and shoot this at me, dirtbag."

Amy glanced at the gun and muttered, "*Wellness center.*"

John lit a cigarette.

Tasker said, "There's no smoking in here."

"If he gets to shoot a gun indoors, I'm thinking I can smoke a cigarette."

Amy said, "We're obviously not going through with this. Even I can see this trap coming." She nodded toward me and said, "They stick you in the cell, Mikey eats you. Since they didn't do it directly, they think they escape the supposed curse that's protecting us."

I said, "You two are staying outside the cell, right? I'm the only one that goes in, you guys stay out here and watch for shenanigans. I mean, we were just in the room with this thing earlier today, I don't think this is among the top ten scariest creatures that have tried to eat me. I've got to say, I'm fine with it."

Amy made an exasperated noise and said, "*Why* are you fine with it?"

"Because we were hired by Chastity to do a job and this is it. Didn't you just tell me I needed to see things through? Well, here's Mikey. It's not what we expected, but so what? For better or worse, this is the final resolution to the Payton case."

I took the shotgun from Agent Gibson. I pulled back the slide enough to confirm there were in fact shells in it, and that they weren't going to stick me in the cell with an empty gun. I sniffed it—the shells smelled like farts, all right.

I asked Tasker, "So how does this, uh, process work?"

"You'll go into the adjacent cell, here—the walls between cells slide open, that is done remotely, from the guard room. Exterior door closes, wall opens, there'll be nothing between you and the specimen. Fire at will."

Amy said, "David, this is stupid."

"That has literally never stopped us before, even once." I asked Tasker, "Loretta and Maggie aren't going to be concerned by the sound of gunfire?"

"We'll close the door between cell blocks, they're utterly soundproof. It'll be no louder to them than someone softly knocking on the wall."

I looked toward John and he shrugged. "I mean, if we're not here to do this, why are we here?"

To Amy I said, "You see the kid in there, right?"

"He's just staring at me. Accusingly."

"Do you need to go wait down the hall or something? You going to be able to handle this?"

"No, I won't be able to handle it and yes, I should be here anyway."

"Let's get it over with."

I stepped into the adjacent cell and the door slid closed behind me. The invisible hand of claustrophobia slowly but firmly squeezed my butthole. The wall that separated the cells was solid steel—I couldn't see what was happening in Mikey's cell.

Through the glass, I asked John, "If you concentrate, can you see and hear Mikey? Or is it just the larva the whole time?"

"Give me a second . . . yeah I can see Mikey pretty clearly. If I try."

"What's he doing?"

"Sitting on the bed, now. Crying. Asking why we're here, why his mother doesn't want him."

I made eye contact with Amy, who looked distraught. "Fresh-cut grass, that's all it is." To Tasker, I said, "There's not going to be any ceremony or ritual here. You open that wall, I'm pointing the gun and I'm pumping sulfur rounds into that thing until the gun goes click. Whatever data you're looking to collect, you'll have to collect it from *that*."

Tasker said, "You're ready?"

"Yeah."

The wall slid open. Sitting in the other cell, on the bed, was Mister Nymph.

24. AN EXPERIMENT YIELDS SOME INCONSISTENT DATA

He was wearing a clean black suit, coldly staring me down. I had the thought that it should have been like looking in a mirror—his was, in the basics anyway, my own face. I thought it seemed off somehow, then I remembered that it's because the image wasn't reversed—it put my scar on the wrong cheek.

He also just looked so much healthier. So much more *alive*.

I aimed the shotgun.

Nymph said, "Do it."

I didn't.

John said, "Dave? Do it, man."

Nymph said, "You heard him. Do it. I can see that you feel the doubts creeping in. The fear. Interesting to see if you can stand up to it."

I said, "Shut up."

"We keep arriving back to this point, do we not? So, are you a man, or are you a hollow vessel, echoing with mindless desire? Your fear says to take one step back and let them close up that wall again. So, which will act next—the man, or the fear? For it is in this moment—the moment in between feeling an impulse and succumbing to it—that *you* actually exist. Soon, the waves of impulse will crash in and your soul will be swept out to sea. When my Master consumes you, I doubt he will find you a terribly crunchy morsel."

"*You* don't exist. You're a manifestation of the swarm, built to play on our self-doubt. Break you down and you're just a bunch of mindless insects who've learned to push people's buttons."

"If I pull out a handful of *your* cells, would they add up to anything more? So, at what point do they become you?"

John shouted for me to shoot and this seemed like great advice. I raised the shotgun and in the time it took me to send the command to my trigger finger, Nymph managed to spring from the bed, fly across the room, and start ripping the gun from my hands.

The two of us both wound up on the floor and I had a moment to remember that John had done this exact thing with the Ted doppelganger, and that he had been tricked into "killing" "Ted" and then for the first time I realized that in that story, not even the gun had been real.

As if it *had wanted him to shoot*.

Why?

And, in that brief moment of doubt, the gun was torn from my grasp. Nymph stood and aimed it right at my face.

John said, "Shoot! David!"

"I don't have the gun!"

Confusion outside. I opened my mouth to say *what are you seeing* but at that moment Nymph opened his mouth and in my voice said, "John! What are you seeing?"

John said, to Nymph, "I'm seeing two of you."

Amy said, "Oh my god."

Agent Gibson said, "Well look at that. We got an evil twin situation here."

I said, "He's the one in the suit, guys."

John said, "You're both wearing the same thing!"

"Oh, goddamnit. John, concentrate, see past the disguise. The one without the gun, meaning me, is the real David. Look at me, look at him."

Nymph said, "He's lying! You know he's lying!"

John stared. First at Nymph, then at me.

He shook his head and said, "When I concentrate, you both look like, uh . . . I don't know, man. He's doing something."

Nymph somehow smirked without moving his face.

I sighed.

I said to Tasker, "You know what these things are vulnerable to and you knew what this facility would be used for. I'm going to take a wild guess and say that as an emergency measure, each of these cells are rigged to rain burning sulfur down on whoever's inside, despite being a massive violation of state and local building codes. Am I right?"

She didn't answer, because she didn't know if she was talking to a person or a monster larva. But her expression, plus previous experience with this organization, told the story. She—or somebody, probably in that guard room she mentioned—just needed to push a button. Probably.

I said, "Let's assume that's true. Here's what's going to happen. He's going to make a play to try to get you to open that door. He can do it one of two ways, either by trying to convince you he's me and to just let him out, or by doing what I think he's going to do, which is just shoot me and have me out of the way, at which point he'll have all the time in the world to convince you of whatever he wants. I'm going to try to stop him, but I probably won't be able to—he's stronger and faster. When that happens, when he kills me, I want you to push the button that fills this cell with fire. This cell, and the one with Maggie. Kill us all."

Amy said to Tasker, "Don't do it. That's what it wants."

I said, "You know this is me." I looked at John. "You, too. The monster just wants out. I want Amy to be safe. And by far the safest option is to just kill us both. Easy answer."

I stared down Nymph, who was grinning like an asshole.

I said, "I don't know who or what you really are and at this point, I really don't care. Whatever levers you think you can pull in people's minds, playing off their soft hearts, you're going to find all those circuits are dead in me. It's not pretty, but neither is that shit-encrusted plunger we keep next to the toilet. But in the moment that toilet starts to overflow, that shit-encrusted plunger is the most beautiful thing in the world. Well, that's what I've come to realize, over the years. I'm that plunger, that stinking, necessary thing. So, you're standing there with your gun and your plans, thinking you can reach into their heads out there and play their emotions like a tune. But it's not them in the cell with you, it's me, and your unholy hive mind forgot to account for one thing—I just *do not give a fuck*."

Nymph nodded, as if in admiration. Then he set the shotgun on the floor.

He said, "You know what? You're right."

He turned to the group in the hall and said, "Fry us both. It's the only way to be sure."

He turned to me and got a pensive look in his eyes. "I've seen things you wouldn't believe. I have seen a snail get eaten by a bird, survive its digestive tract, then get shit out two hundred miles away onto the roof of the World Trade Center, five minutes before the first plane hit. I have seen a man's body obliterated by a train because he was trying to retrieve a dropped slip of paper that a woman had written her phone number on, not realizing the number was fake. I have seen an entire species-changing genetic line wiped out when a single *Homo erectus* got his dick stuck while humping a knothole. All these moments forgotten, like piss in a swimming pool. Time to die."

I turned back toward the hall, feeling an odd sense of relief, trying to quickly put together my last words to Amy. It wouldn't need to be anything too profound (why start now?).

I met her eyes, and it took me a moment to realize there was no glass between us—she was standing in the *open* door to the cell.

She screamed, "COME ON!" at the exact moment Agent Gibson arrived to try to wrestle her away from the door.

Nymph flew toward the open door, trying to blow past me. I threw my body at him and slammed him onto the floor, and I couldn't tell if I was feeling the flesh-and-bone body of a dude in a business suit, or the squishy, pulsing mass of the fuckroaches. I think I was feeling them both, at the same time.

The shotgun skidded across the floor, bounced off the wall, and skipped back toward me. I crawled over Nymph, grabbed the gun, and shoved the barrel into the back of his head.

I yanked the trigger.

Click

I pumped it and pulled the trigger again and again, nothing.

Tasker had sabotaged it. Pulled out the firing pin, probably.

That bitch.

Nymph flung me aside and bowled past Amy into the hall. I followed.

Alarms were sounding. Black cloaks were flowing into the hall from wherever they'd been hiding. I yelled for John, but couldn't find him in the pandemonium. The cloaks aimed their strange weapons at both me and Nymph.

Tasker said, "Don't harm the specimen!"

I said, "You just said you were going to kill it!"

"That was a test!"

Nymph said, "Hold on, so now is it better for me to be the specimen or David?"

Amy pushed herself away from Gibson and pointed to me. "This is the human. Unfortunately."

The black cloaks moved in on Nymph, so I guess they

believed her? He raised his right hand. Everything from the elbow down disintegrated into a flock of about ten fuckroaches. They flew toward the nearest cloak, who was wearing a rubber mask that gave him the slack face of an elderly woman. The insects landed on various points of its body, then quickly burrowed through the cloak and body armor. The thing in the cloak screamed an inhuman scream, and then exploded, as if the fuckroaches had pulled it apart from the inside. Grayish-blue hunks of meat landed everywhere—it had the texture of a vegetarian recipe for imitation human tissue. The rest of the cloaks recoiled but again didn't fire—they were waiting for the order. Though at least they now knew which one was me.

Nymph gave me a smug look and said, "You cannot comprehend the suffering that is about to occur, Mr. Wong. You said you don't give a fuck, and I believe you. You think none of it matters, that it's all a big joke. But I assure you, Mr. Wong, right now, no one is laughing."

There was a commotion from behind Nymph and I heard John, screaming, "FART DILDOS, COMING THROUGH!"

There was a mechanical noise like air brakes. A projectile hit Nymph and filled the hall with sizzling sparks. Nymph went to the floor, a smoldering hole in his back, hunks of metal burning brightly in the wound. The smell of sulfur filled the hall.

John was holding a homemade weapon. The barrel was PVC pipe, leading to a complex mechanism like the cylinder on a revolver. Only instead of bullets, each chamber contained one sex toy. On his back was a tank of compressed gas.

John fired again. A pink projectile whizzed through the air, made impact with Nymph, and exploded in that shower of pungent fire.

The fuckroaches scattered. The black cloaks unleashed their strange weapons on the bugs, vaporizing them in midair, with orange beams that radiated ungodly amounts of heat. I wondered if they ever accidentally fired their weapons on the wrong setting.

Then, all that remained was the larva, writhing in pain on the floor, shed of its disguise. The burning chunks of thermite and sulfur were eating through its skin.

It seemed to be pulsing, swelling.

John cocked his dildo cannon and fired again. The maggot squealed and thrashed, but it was still not dead. The smoldering embers of sulfur ate through its husk . . . and still it seemed to get bigger.

I said, "Where the hell did you get that thing?"

"It was in the back of the Jeep! We must have built it while we were on the Sauce. The memory hit me all at once. Want me to shoot it again?"

Amy said, "Look!"

A split had formed in the maggot's thick outer skin, where the sulfur had finally burned through. The larva was now nearly twice its former size, it skin stretching and pulling like a bratwurst on a grill.

From within the wound, a sheer blackness seemed to leak out like steam. And from it, I sensed an infinite coldness that defied all reason.

We're too late.

John said, "Is it dying?"

Amy shook her head. "No. It's *hatching*."

25. WELL, THEY CERTAINLY FUCKED THAT UP, DIDN'T THEY?

I said, "How do we stop it?!?"

Tasker, thinking quickly, said, "Get it out of the cell block! To the front!"

I grabbed the maggot—it was unsettlingly warm—and tried to drag it. Its skin was slick but tough, hard to get a grasp on it. I twisted it in my fists and pulled. Like dragging a bag of wet cement.

I screamed for John. He tossed his dildo cannon aside and tried to grab on. We screamed for one of the cloaked guards to pitch in, but they didn't seem to recognize the command. The dark, foot-long fissure in the larva's hide grew wider. A dim rumble came from inside, low enough to shake the floor. Or maybe I was imagining that part. Agent Gibson came hobbling along and tried to help.

John said, "Roll it! Like a barrel!"

The three of us did just that, making slow progress up the hall, through the cell block door, and toward the open steel door to the office area. This would force us to roll it past Maggie's cell and I expected to hear

Loretta start screaming at the sight of us, but someone had apparently hustled her back into the STAFF ONLY area, getting her out of the way.

We made it past Maggie's cell—the larva inside shrieking and thrashing at the sight of us—and through the thick steel door. I was sweating with the effort—the thing seemed to gain mass with every step. We were leaving a trail of ooze behind us.

Tasker was waiting by the black coffin device to our left—the portal to other worlds. She waved us that way and we had to again do an awkward 90-degree turn with the pulsing grub.

Tasker pulled open the door and beyond was that vast green field I'd glimpsed earlier. Scattered around the other side was various trash—coffee cups, chip bags, at least one dirty diaper.

The maggot was too long to fit through the door now; all five of us—Amy included—had to wrestle it through lengthwise. It thudded on the other side of the door and Tasker yelled for us to push it farther in, to get it away from the portal so the offspring couldn't jump through if it hatched at exactly the wrong moment.

I said, "You go through first, sweetheart! We're not going through only to have you close the door behind us."

To her credit, she didn't hesitate. She jumped through and pulled as we pushed, shoving the larva across the field and down what turned out to be a grassy hill in some other time and place and universe.

The moment our hands were off of it, the husk of the maggot split along its body, its skin falling aside. For a moment, there was only a blotch of blackness there and all five of us stared at it, transfixed. Tasker held up her phone to get video, eyes wide in amazement. This was once-in-a-lifetime data. I noted she had a pistol in her other hand, until she glanced down at it and realized that what emerged from this thing would not even find her bullets particularly annoying.

The blackness grew.

Amy backed toward the portal and said, "This world, it's uninhabited, right? There's an empty universe for this thing to wreak havoc in?"

Tasker didn't answer. I turned to go back through the portal . . . and stopped.

There stood the door, and behind it was a well-dressed family of what looked like tourists, a father and two boys eating some kind of bulbous turquois dessert I'd never seen before. The father was staring at us in bafflement. He looked like a steampunk lawyer, in a waistcoat and high shiny boots, a gold chain draped over one shoulder. He had well-oiled black hair with a skunk stripe of white that ran back from his forehead. His two well-groomed boys seemed only mildly curious.

One of the boys looked at me and said something that sounded like "Away" but the accent and tone made me think it was a greeting in a foreign tongue. They had a little dog with them. It barked. The boy had been in the middle of feeding it a bit of his snack.

I started to say, "You should back way from this thing," but then my eyes registered what I was seeing and the words died. Behind the family was a scenic little town square—gift shops and fountains surrounding a large clock tower. Rolling down the narrow streets were cars of unusual design that seemed to all have three wheels, one in back, two in front. Beyond the square were neat little cottages as far as the eye could see.

Amy said, "Oh my god," and I turned back to where the larva had been, now a shriveled husk. Blackness poured out, up and up into the sky, like the plume from an oil well fire. The darkness coalesced into a shape like a giant headless man with goat legs at least a hundred feet tall. I knew I should run but when I tried, my feet stayed planted as if saying, *Are you seeing this shit?*

John grabbed my sleeve and pulled me toward the portal, but the moment I spun around, the shadow giant swept overhead, blotting out the sun.

It descended on the village. The tourist family didn't scream. They didn't have time, or a reason to. Neither did anyone in the village.

As the shadow swept over them, it did not destroy the village, it simply *changed* it. I knew the process from prior experience; it simply reached back in time— thousands of years, maybe millions—and tipped a series of events. As it passed overhead, striding on its goat legs, the village was replaced. And so were the people.

Where the tourist family had stood were now two eight-foot-tall humanoid beings, skin encrusted with ash-gray scales like the bark of a tree that had survived a forest fire. Their eyes were big and black and cold. They wore clothing that had the look of armor, polished and ornate, full of sinister sharp edges. One of the beings was holding a leash and at the end of it was a naked human child. Its arms and legs had been severed at the joints, the stumps covered in scars and callouses from where it had been walking on all fours all its life. It was starving, skin stretched over its ribs, a slit of white scar tissue where its genitals should have been. The child grunted—it was in the middle of defecating. It then turned and sniffed what it had made.

In the village beyond, I tried to take in the civilization that had replaced what had been there moments ago. The bark-skinned beings strode around stone buildings that all seemed to have been designed to withstand an invasion from the ground—high, windowless walls and heavy doors. The vehicles that prowled the streets all seemed to be military in nature—armored and on tank treads, rumbling slowly down streets made of some kind of black cobblestone. I saw two more human children, only I now realized they actually weren't children—that was just the size at which their growth was stunted. They were loping down an alley grunting after a rodent they'd seen. In the street nearest to us, there was a cloud of flies around a pale, twisted shape lying at the end of a brown smear. One of the humans had been run over and left to rot in the sun.

At the center of town, where before had been the tall clock tower, was a pile of human skulls. Maybe thirty feet wide and a hundred feet tall. It looked old and sacred, a memorial to some historic victory.

One of the bark-skinned things in front of us shouted a stern command in our direction. He pulled from his back a weapon that looked like a whip—a black handle that led to a bundle of lengths of thin chain. He clicked the handle and the end of each bit of chain glowed orange, as if the whip was designed to brand the flesh as it lashed it. He let go of the leash and the stunted man on all fours came bounding in our direction.

It made a noise at us, a wet, barking grunt. "AYE! AYE!" And then he spat something that sounded like, "SUBMIT!"

Amy screamed. I felt Tasker shove past me.

The man-dog ran, filthy shoulders and ass cheeks bouncing, eyes wild.

"AYE! SUBMIT! SUBMIT! AYESUBMITAYESUBMI-TAYESUBMIT!!!"

John was shouting and then I was being shoved through the portal and found myself back in the NON facility. Tasker had skidded to her knees, having stumbled in her rush to get through. Her suit jacket had flipped up, revealing the holster clipped to her waistband that contained her pistol.

"SUBMIT! AYE! SUBMIT!"

The man-dog was coming around, heading for the open portal. I could smell it, the stench of human body odor and fresh shit.

I snatched the pistol out of Tasker's holster, spun around, and shot the pathetic thing in its dumb, filthy face, an inch below a matted, filthy white streak of hair dangling over its brow. The thing flopped over and skidded to a stop inches from the door.

John quickly closed the coffin door and I tossed Tasker's gun to the floor next to her.

Breathing heavily, John looked at me and said, "That's the biggest night shart yet."

Tasker looked at Gibson and said, "Send a memo. This is now Class H."

I said, "There's a category *beyond* extinction level?"

John said, "Eighteen, apparently. Guys, the Maggie larva was, uh, birthed at the exact same time as Mikey,

343

right? So that means *she* could hatch at any second, if it's not happening right now."

We all stared at each other for a moment, then ran back through the open steel door, down the row of cells until we found Maggie's. Her mother was there now—whatever pretense had gotten her out of the way before hadn't held up for long. John, Amy, and I skidded to a stop in front of the half-eaten woman. Loretta's eyes went wide. Well, one of them did—the other had been chewed off, along with the left third of her skull—the harried woman wondering what the hell the commotion was about.

Agent Tasker, who'd been moving at a more dignified pace dictated by the constraints of her businesslike skirt, arrived behind us.

The Maggie larva looked unchanged, for the moment.

Tasker said to Loretta, "Why don't you come with me? We need to run some quick tests."

"You can run them with me here." Loretta, even with several bites having been taken out of her brain, was no dummy.

Tasker said, "This is a requirement, unfortunately. It would be dangerous for you—"

"I accept the danger. Give me a waiver, I'll sign it."

Agent Gibson was approaching as well, his cane a third footstep clicking on the floor with each stride. Reaching inside his suit jacket, ready to do this the hard way (or, let's be honest—the easy way).

He said, "Come on, Ms. Knoll. Don't make us—"

He flinched at the sound of exploding windows behind him.

26. GRAPPLING HOOKS AREN'T CHEAP, YOU GUYS

John

Everyone ran back out of the cell block, into the office area they'd just vacated. Ted Knoll and his comrade were disconnecting the ropes they'd used to swing through the conference room windows from the roof. They whipped assault rifles around to their shoulders and moved out among the cubicles.

A half dozen of the NON cloaks swarmed out to meet them. Ted and his partner fired exactly six shots. All six targets flopped onto the floor. Not a word had been uttered.

Ted pointed his assault rifle at Dave and said in a surprisingly calm voice, "Where is she?"

John said, "You don't want to do this, Ted. Because of the . . . radiation? It's just, everywhere. We're all radioactive."

"Drop the cover. She told me everything."

She? John wasn't sure who he was talking about

there. Was it Chastity? Maybe she'd come back to help.

Loretta appeared in the doorway to the cell block, yelling her husband's name, asking him what in the world was happening. Ted ran that direction, shouldered past her, and found Maggie's cell—the only glass wall that was smeared with the cloudy film from where the larva had been crawling over it. John, Dave, and Amy followed him in, Dave ineffectually telling him to wait, to listen.

Ted told Maggie to hang on, then to no one in particular said, "Open the cell door."

The agent Dave called Tasker but whose name was actually Pussnado sauntered up and said, "I will not be doing that, and I assure you, I have very good reasons."

"I wasn't talking to you." Ted touched an earpiece and said, "Are you reading me? I need that cell door opened, now."

The door slid open, the monstrous writhing maggot beyond it squealing and chittering in response. Ted reached down, clutched it to his chest, and shouted commands to his friend to cover their exit.

Dave said, "Mr. Knoll, you need to listen very, very carefully. You take her out that front door, everybody dies. Every*thing* dies. I can't even explain the degree to which shit will go wrong."

Now it was Ted's turn to look confused, which quickly turned to annoyance. He seemed to think the two of them were still playing a part, maybe for NON's benefit.

In a tone that was only somewhat convincing, he said, "Buddy, you can either stand aside and let me take my daughter outta here, or you can lay dead on the floor while I take my daughter outta here." Playing along, giving Dave an out.

Dave looked pleadingly at John. What could they do? Ted and his partner were armed to the teeth and apparently ex Special Forces. John had nothing but his car keys in his pocket—he doubted he could kill more than one of them before the other took him down.

Ted brushed past him and moved toward the front entrance of the wellness center, his partner covering the extraction, Loretta right behind them. John, Amy, and Dave watched as the larva passed out of the facility and back into the rain-lashed world.

From behind John, Amy said, "Guys, is this part of what you set up? Over the weekend, I mean?"

John said, "Maybe? Damn it, Dave, you should have let me finish explaining it on your ass."

But Dave was already moving, running after the dildo launcher John had discarded on the floor. John saw no good ending to Dave trying to fling flaming vibrators at this enraged soldier's little girl, but he didn't respond when John told him to forget it.

John turned and chased after Ted, pushing through the front door in time to see Ted's Impala skid to a stop, spraying rainwater from all four tires.

The passenger side window rolled down.

Korean adult website star Joy Park said, "Get her in! Move! Move!"

Dave ran up behind John with the dildo launcher, looked at Joy, then looked at John, bewildered. John just shook his head.

Ted gently handed the squirming larva to Loretta, who climbed into the back seat with it. Ted told them to get to the safe house, that he would meet them there.

Instead of raining dildo hellfire down upon Ted's family, Dave said, "Wait," and told them to pop the trunk. He threw the launcher in and told Ted they may need it. Which was true, but how in the hell they would figure it out in time—if it wasn't already too late—was anyone's guess. When Maggie hatched, John figured they'd have a brief moment to register the strange darkness . . . and then would know nothing at all.

Dave slammed the trunk and the car tore out of the parking lot. Ted—steadfastly ignoring John, Dave, and Amy—stormed back into the building with his soldier companion in tow.

Agents Pussnado and Cocksman were standing there, looking annoyed. John had expected a hundred of those black cloaks to come flying out from various doors to wipe out Ted's two-man crew, but the building seemed to have emptied. For a moment, John was amused by the thought of them just giving up on their field office at the first sign of trouble, then it occurred to him that NON may very well have given an evacuation order for all of their staff in the facility. Hell, maybe the entire planet. John imagined all of them fleeing to some other dimension, marking this one down as a loss.

Cocksman shifted his weight on his cane and said, "Mr. Knoll, I understand what you *think* you're doing, but you need to—"

Ted shot the man in the forehead, spraying blood and brain matter on his partner's blazer.

Amy gasped.

The man slumped to the ground and Ted said to the female agent, "Lie flat on the floor, put your hands behind your head. You and I are going to have a conversation."

She obeyed. Ted took her gun from under her jacket and kicked it across the floor. He then slung his assault rifle behind his back and pulled out a black, military-issue knife.

Dave said, "Ted, we should get outta here. Whatever you're about to do, it's not worth—"

Ted slapped Dave across the face with his dick, proverbially, via a stern facial expression. To the woman on the floor, he said, "Do you know what I did in Iraq?"

"I do."

"Say it."

"You were an interrogator. Among other things."

"Huh. Not many people got access to those records. How did I know you people would? Point is, I know how to spot a lie. And I got a short, short fuse for liars. You read about that, too, didn't you? Even though it was kept quiet, that whole incident."

"I am aware of your . . . issues."

Ted nodded. "Good. You know what it's like, being in a war zone?"

"Mr. Knoll, I can help y—"

"It's like wakin' up from a dream. I don't mean comin' back home is like that, I mean the war, being in the suck, it's like wakin' up. See, because that's when you figure out your old life—the barbecues and Monday Night Football and trips to Disneyland—*that* shit was the dream and this is real. Iraq was fucked and getting it unfucked meant killing a certain number of people and if it didn't get unfucked then they would kill a certain number of us and the future of the world would all depend on who killed who. Simple as that. Same as there's no woolly mammoths or saber-toothed tigers no more, same as how we're all fancy monkeys instead of smart dinosaurs. And aaaall that other bullshit, the steak dinners and Christmas mornings and beer commercials, it's all a dream we're havin', something to pass the time until somebody comes and wakes us up to the real world, where either you're gonna die, or you're gonna make somebody else die, so you can pass on your way of life to your kids. I'm sayin' all of this because I think part of what you're depending on here is me being unwilling to do what I need to do in order to find out what I need to know. So I'm letting you know, from one awake person to another, that the sight of your tears and the sound of your screams won't melt my heart."

She said, "Duly noted."

"Knowing that I can spot a liar, even one with her face pressed to the floor, I ask you—were you, or were you not, about to kill my daughter?"

"We were not about to kill your daughter."

This, John noted, was 100 percent true. Ted seemed to recognize that fact.

Amy said, "Mr. Knoll, we can actually explain—"

He ignored her, continuing his interrogation. "Do you, or do you not, know where to find the thing that's taking the children? The Batmantis?"

Pussnado hesitated, then chose her words carefully. "We *believe* we know where to find the creature that is behind all of this, yes. We *believe* we know how to kill it."

Also true.

"Why did you take Maggie?"

Again, she chose her words carefully. "You are aware,

Mr. Knoll, that the enemy is a shape-shifter—a being that has perfected camouflage. Examining Maggie was the only reasonable course of action, and there was no way to convey this without alarming her mother."

Ted stared, trying not to show any change in expression. He swallowed. "And?"

"We found that Maggie had not been replaced by a doppelganger."

Again, technically true.

Ted nodded. "See? That wasn't so hard. So, how do we kill it? The thing that's behind all this?"

"We just finished a device. It's in the back, in the armory. Take it to the creature's nest—those three know where it is—and set it off. And when I use the word 'nest,' I want you to understand that this nest contains larvae. That is, this creature is about to *multiply*. At any moment."

Ted said, "Outstanding. You're going to take us to the armory."

He handed John a heavy white plastic zip tie and said, "Bind her hands behind her back, and lift her to her feet."

John had no idea if the agent was planning an ambush here or if the device she spoke of was even real. He could read the same doubt on Dave's face. Amy, on the other hand, was just staring at the dead man on the floor. The look on her face said something different:

It's all falling apart.

Blood-splattered NON agent Josaline Pussnado led them past the cells, through the STAFF ONLY door and through another enormous steel door that she apparently opened with her mind. Inside, among five hundred objects that looked like spare parts for Satan's robot army, was a ribbed stainless steel box the size of a steamer trunk.

Pussnado said, "It's inside. Spherical casing, explosively formed penetrators all around the outer shell, at the moment of detonation it will throw waves of molten metal over a hundred yard radius—thermite and sulfur. No remote detonator, you've got three minutes on the fuse."

She nodded to John to open the case, making him wonder if it was booby-trapped. John considered making her open it, but he supposed that would mean untying her hands and for all they knew, the box was full of weird guns she'd whip out at them. John looked for a latch, but found none—there was just a hole at the front of the lid, about big enough to get two fingers into.

The agent said, "You need a special tool to open it. On the lid you'll see a hole about two inches wide. It leads to a shaft about eight inches deep. You need to insert a rigid object to depress the latch."

John said, "Don't worry, *I have just the thing . . .*

Me

"Here," I said, "we'll use this broomstick I found."

I unlatched the lid and inside was the bomb—a flat black sphere the size of a basketball, a thick foot-long fuse sticking out of the top. Along the front in white letters was stamped the word BOMB.

Ted yelled for his army buddy, who came and scooped up the device, then jogged off with it.

Ted pointed his gun at Tasker and said, "One last question. If I leave you here, can you guarantee that neither you or your people will come after Maggie?"

She paused, but not out of fear. Steeling her resolve.

"Mr. Knoll, I can guarantee that we *will* come after her. I'm sorry, but we don't have a cho—"

He shot her right in the heart.

27. THIS WOMB OF MINE

Outside the front door was waiting a camouflage pickup truck, Ted's army buddy at the wheel. Ted jogged toward it, making like he was going to leave without saying a word.

John said, "Wait! The woman who was driving your car—who is that? What's her deal? Or, just, what's the deal in general?"

"I hope you don't get offended, buddy, but communication within your chain of command is shit. Joy found me right after I left the cannery, said you sent her. Said Maggie was gonna get taken to this facility and that she had a way into the guard room. Acted like you people had been settin' it up for a while." He climbed into the pickup and nodded back toward the bed. "I've got the asses."

In the bed of the truck were the boxes of silicone butts that had been in my apartment.

I said, "Uh, good."

"Where's the nest?"

"The what?"

"The nest of the thing. The Batmantis."

"Oh. Right. Tell you what, I'll ride with you, I can show you. Speaking of which, where is, uh, Joy taking your daughter?"

"They're on the way to meet Marconi at the Walmart. Joy said she'd be safe with him."

"Oh. Yes. Right. Good."

I felt a pair of small moons roll off my shoulders.

Marconi will know what to do. And maybe we don't even need to be there to see it.

If, that is, Maggie doesn't hijack his brain.

Of course, we had no guarantee Joy was actually taking her there, or that she wasn't in cahoots with the thing in the mine. Or that Maggie wouldn't hatch on the way.

The pickup had a back seat; I climbed in and John and Amy ran off toward the Jeep. Ted nodded to the man in the passenger seat—the guy was holding the bomb in his lap like he was bringing home a watermelon from the supermarket—and said, "This here is Philip, everybody calls him Shitbeard."

"Good to meet you." He did not have a beard. "We're going to the pond at Mine's Eye. It's where we found Maggie. You're going to turn up here at the—"

"I know where Mine's Eye is. Been out there before."

"You have? When—"

My phone rang. It was Marconi.

I answered, "Yes, Doctor."

"Mr. Wong, I have received a very frightened little girl, her panicked mother, and a Korean woman who insisted I call you right away."

"Sure. The young girl and her mother are"—I glanced at Ted—"uh, in a similar situation to Mikey. The Korean woman is adult film star Joy Park, you're surely familiar with her work. Make sure Maggie gets, uh, treatment. Immediately."

"Treatment?"

"Yes, we were able to treat Mikey, he's all good now."

"He is? In what way?"

"Right, right, I'm in the car with Maggie's father right now. "

Hesitation.

"I see. Loretta Knoll is here in the room with me, in fact."

"Remember how Amy and I proposed two possible options? They went with my suggestion, not hers. It worked."

"I see. Our friends discovered a method, I take it?"

"Yes. You know what, call John, he can fill you in. There's something in the trunk of Joy's vehicle, it will require some explaining. Quite a bit, in fact."

"I see."

"Anyway, I just want to be clear that you definitely shouldn't keep her waiting. In a situation like this, every second counts."

"Are you and Mr. Knoll heading my way?"

"No. We're on our way to Mine's Eye. We're going to finish this."

Amy

Night had fallen by the time they arrived at Mine's Eye. The pond had turned into a popular gathering spot; motorcycles were parked along the hilltops and people were prowling around the cabins and the church, searching for the supposedly missing kids. Amy figured there were two ways to look at it: it was bad news that so many people were in contamination range of what the Millibutt was presumably about to do, but it was good news that they were still searching—it meant the kids hadn't been "found" yet. John parked a ways away from the church—its lot was full—and she wondered how they were going to deal with all the bystanders.

Ted, David, and Ted's friend jumped out of their truck and Ted pulled out a pair of futuristic binoculars—Amy figured they were night vision—to scope out the pond and the mouth of the collapsed mine, looking for a giant mantis bat monster.

David walked up, pulled her and John out of earshot and muttered, "You talk to Marconi?"

"Yeah."

"And just to be clear, that *is* Joy Park, right? We heard people call her that."

"It appears so?"

Amy said, "Remind me who Joy Park is, again?"

David said, "A porn star we saw on the Internet who we don't know and who doesn't live anywhere near here."

Amy said, "Is that who was living at John's place?"

John scrunched up his face in thought. "Maybe?"

David said, "I don't . . . I mean, is she real? If so, do we even know where she's from? Or how she could get here? Like, does she actually live in Korea? Does she work for the Millibutt? Is she going to—"

John nudged him to stop talking. Ted was approaching.

David said to him, "See anything down there?"

"No sign of the target, but there's a gaggle-fuck of bikers wanderin' around, in the way."

Amy said, "Do you see any of the missing kids?"

Ted shook his head.

John asked for the binoculars and studied the area below. He gave a start, as if he saw *something*, but quickly stifled his reaction.

He feigned disinterest and said, "I can't make out anything. Let's go down," in a way that made it clear to Amy that he had seen *something*, but for some reason couldn't let Ted in on it. She supposed she'd have to be surprised right alongside him.

So, they headed down the winding path, hunched over in their jackets while cold raindrops popped on their shoulders. Ted and his partner were going to pack up the bomb and bring it down after them—they had needed to get it inside something, as in its present state Amy agreed that it was fairly recognizable as a bomb. On the way down, they passed four guys in biker gear heading up the other way, looking like exhausted, tensed-up coils of rage. Near the bottom was a pair of leather-clad women comforting a third, who was convulsing with sobs.

An entire community, having lost their young. Or so they thought.

If it had been a clearer day and the pool had had time to settle to its usual dazzling shades of blue and green, Amy would have seen right away. But the rain and the gloom meant it wasn't until they were on the shore that she saw him.

A little boy, lying facedown in the water.

She knew what it was. Of course she knew.

And, still, she ran into the pond, after the drowned or drowning child. Stomping through the chilled water, tossing aside her raincoat. She couldn't swim. She didn't care.

David screamed and ran after her. He roughly put an arm around her chest and yanked her back.

"NO! AMY!"

He dragged her back out of the water, frantic, and she saw John looking terrified, keeping his distance on the bank. Not even risking putting a toe into the water, not even to help her and David. That's how scared he was of what he was seeing in there, what his eyes saw instead of the endangered boy.

John yelled to her, "What do you see?"

She tried to breathe. "A boy," she gasped. He had black hair, a dark complexion. "We have to get him out of there! We'll work out what's happening later but we have to get him out, he's face-down in the water. He can't breathe, David."

John said, "No. Amy. Trust us."

She said, "What do *you* see?"

David said, "A mouth."

"The boy looks like a mouth? How?"

"No. The whole pond. It's a mouth. The boy, what you're seeing as the boy, it's just a lure. Nothing more."

Amy watched as a few tiny bubbles floated up from the child's submerged face.

He's still alive.

Amy said, "What if I want to risk it? If I die trying to save a kid then maybe that's how I want to go. You see one thing, I see another."

David said, "Amy, I can't make this any clearer—*that is the point of the trap.* Of all this. You're being played."

"But it's my choi—"

At that moment, a man sprinted past them, apparently having run down the hill while they were arguing. It was, of course, Ted.

He flung aside his jacket, ripped off his shirt, and dove into the water.

John and David both yelled warnings at him, but even if he could hear them, he had no reason to listen. Even if they could convince Ted the boy was bait, that wouldn't justify letting him drown. Why couldn't they see that?

Then came the sound of more footsteps stomping toward them from behind—three of the bikers, shouting for everyone to follow, to call an ambulance.

Ted dragged the boy out of the water and started giving him mouth-to-mouth. David's eyes went wide, like he couldn't believe what he was seeing.

The boy sputtered and sucked in breath and came to life. Ted almost wept with joy. So did Amy.

John muttered to David, "Call Marconi."

Ten minutes later, the police had pushed most of the civilians back up the hill. The three of them were in front of the church. Nearby, a Hispanic man and woman were babbling and crying and hugging the rescued boy, who sat draped with a blanket on the back bumper of an ambulance. The father was wearing a soaked denim vest with biker patches on the back; he and a street cop were alternately comforting the child and peppering him with questions.

David kept dialing his phone, over and over—trying to get Dr. Marconi. He'd never gotten an answer and was growing more alarmed by the second.

John said, "Look, even if the Maggie situation has gone south, it hasn't gone *too* south or else we wouldn't still be sitting here, right? Maybe he's just, uh, busy with it."

From behind them came a voice, saying, "Looks like you geniuses are three for three on finding these kids. How about that."

It was Detective Bowman.

John said, "Got almost three hundred bucks to show for it. Is the kid talking?"

"He is."

David said, "Is he saying a bunch of weird, creepy nonsense?"

"No, that's Spanish he's speaking. It's a foreign language, you see."

"*What did he say?* Did he say how he wound up in the pond?"

"He said he swam out."

"Out . . . to the pond? From where?"

"From inside the mine, through a tunnel, full of water. He said he was taken inside a 'cave,' along with the others. He said all of them are in there, nine other kids. Said it was getting hard to breathe, that they're running out of air. Said he got desperate and dove down into a little pool on the floor of the mine and this is where he popped out."

David said, "That doesn't even sound possible."

The detective shrugged. "I'm not a geologist. I know most kids are lying sacks of shit. But we got a guy at the scene who says there could be a fissure in the earth or somethin', leads from the bottom of the pond to somewhere inside the mine. Be hard to see it under the water. But if they're gonna get the kids out, that's how. You try to pull out those rocks from the mouth of the mine, all that happens is more rocks fall in. They'd be at that for months."

Amy said, "So you're going in? For the rest of them?"

Me

Bowman looked back down at the "pond"—to me, a hundred-foot-wide gaping maw in the rock, wet flaps of pink flesh like tongues twitching and curling at the air, surrounding a two-foot-wide throat flexing and pulsing as if anticipating a meal.

"Yes ma'am," he said, and nodded toward a blue van that was making its way toward them. "In fact, dive team's here."

Over at the ambulance, the mother hoisted up the squirming maggot, carrying it like a child. Its mandibles latched onto her shoulder and blood poured down her shirt. Bowman trotted over to meet them.

John looked back and forth from the maggot to the orifice in the ground. He muttered, "Wait. I don't think that's its mouth."

In a low voice, I said, "We have to do this, and we have to do this fucking now. We have to get the bomb down there, jam it in, blow up the egg sac or birth canal or whatever the fuck part of that thing's anatomy that is. Before nine more goddamned maggots pop out of it."

Amy said, "You see these armed biker guys standing everywhere? They think their kids are still inside that hole, they'll shoot you to pieces if you blow it up with their children still in it. The police, too."

"Well, what we're hoping is that the moment the blast goes off, the spell will be broken. We sever the Millibutt's connection to this world, it'll break the mind control powers of the fuckroaches, everything will go back to the way it was. Memories of the kids will just go poof, there'll be some confusion but then everyone will agree we're heroes and give us all free pairs of leather chaps."

Amy said, "What evidence do we have that the roaches can't operate independently of their mother?"

I shook my head. "Doesn't matter. We have to risk it."

She said, "And that's even assuming the bomb works at all. Remember the shotgun that same lady gave you? Plus, we don't actually have the bomb, it's in Ted's truck."

I said, "You see the scuba guys getting ready to go down there? I'm going to give us exactly three minutes to come up with a plan to deal with all that stuff you just mentioned. Then we move."

28. A COMPLETELY SUCCESSFUL PLAN THAT ENDS THE STORY, THIS IS PROBABLY THE FINAL CHAPTER RIGHT HERE

Amy

Amy tried to be casual as she passed the camouflage pickup. The bomb was sitting in the passenger seat inside a camouflage backpack (though a completely different type of camouflage than the truck's pixel-style paint job—she wondered what the difference was). Ted's partner, who David had said had a profane nickname, was leaning casually against the passenger side door.

She kept walking and circled the little church. All of the cops and most of the bikers were down around the pond now, where the action was—she would have relative privacy for her end of the operation. David had actually suggested she use her Taser on Ted's friend—she had transferred it from her purse to her pocket the moment they arrived—but she knew for a fact that it hurt a whole lot and she also wasn't sure it even had a charge left. It was a last resort, at best.

Instead, once she was out of the man's sight, she

sucked in as much breath as she could and screamed her head off.

Splashy bootsteps stomped her direction. The grizzled ex-soldier arrived with his gun at the ready, eyes wide.

Amy was pointing at the sky.

"It's here! The bat thing! It's here!"

He pointed his gun up into the clouds.

"Where?"

She made a show of desperately trying to study the sky.

"I don't—I just saw it, I saw it plain as day, it went behind those trees. I think? Darn it. It knows we're messing with its nest." She turned to look the man in the eye. "It's going to come back. It wants its prey. Have you seen the video of this thing? When it swoops down, it can snatch a kid into the sky in three seconds. And that's who it's going to come for—the little ones. Go talk to whoever's got guns—tell them we need people watching the skies, and I mean every single minute."

Poopbeard nodded. "Affirmative."

Me

I casually walked past the camouflage truck and snatched the bomb bag from the seat. I shuffled quickly down the steep path and along the way texted John:

prepare the diversion

We were hoping the blast damage and shrapnel from the bomb would be largely contained in the orifice, but everyone involved in the project was largely unfamiliar with the anatomy at play here (it would be weird if we weren't). This meant that, on top of making sure nobody interfered with the operation, we needed to get the innocents as far away as possible, all within the next few minutes—that would be John's job. Someday, he will be remembered as the Michelangelo of loud, baffling distractions.

Shitbeard shouted for help with the BATMANTIS??? hunt and some of the bikers came trudging up the hill as I descended, but not all of them. I hustled down toward the pond, knowing I had to beat the rescue divers into the hole. I didn't want to blow the birth canal with a man inside it—that seemed like a super weird way to die—but still, if I couldn't get there first and it came down to one man versus the world . . .

I made it to the bank of what everyone else thought was a pond and waded out into the squishy mass surrounding the orifice, slipping and sliding on slime. The scuba divers were on the opposite shore messing with their gear, Ted was talking to a street cop nearby. No one was looking at me. I pressed on and found myself being resisted by an invisible force, then realized I was wading through a shallow pool of water that I couldn't actually see.

But if the water isn't real . . .

Someone shouted at me. Asking what I was doing.

I said, "Just got to check something! Just be a minute!"

I trudged forward. I patted John's lighter in my pocket, making sure it was there—it was Amy who had remembered that I needed one, bless her—and reminded myself to lift it out of the invisible water before attempting to light it, just in case it worked that way. We had three minutes on the fuse, according to Tasker, though it had occurred to me that may have been bullshit and the thing might just blow up in my hands the moment I touched it with the flame.

The orifice was just ahead, the "water" now up to my waist. I'd have to hold my breath to get the bomb into place. Maybe?

It might have been my imagination, but I thought I could sense something as I got closer, a heaviness in the air, kind of like when you walk into the room and can sense that you just missed a bitter argument, or some illicit porking.

Was it fear? No.

Power.

Menace.

Ravenous appetites and strange desires lurking just below, like I was bobbing on an inner tube in the middle of the ocean while below me swarmed the swift shadows of a vast school of Cthulhus. Despite Marconi's speech, I had still been thinking of the creature as being physically located inside the mine. But now I understood—this particular spot was just where it interacted with our universe, like the microscopic point where two perfect spheres contact one another. This was where our universe touched a sprawling, putrid nebula of dumb loathing and unfathomable, cruel strength. I thought that if it could be expressed as a physical size, the entity would be large enough to swallow our solar system whole. This thing, I thought, had far more than a thousand butts.

I found I had stopped walking, my own fear an invisible hand to my chest.

I shook it off, and pushed myself forward.

I squished toward the quivering orifice, now about twenty feet in front of me, and muttered, "I've got to get a real fucking job."

I pulled out my phone, typed out, "do it now" and just as I was about to hit the send button, I got slammed from behind, thrown face-first onto the squishy pink surface.

The bomb went rolling away, still in its backpack, the fuse still unlit. I felt water burn into my nostrils. Could I drown in the illusion? I had no idea. I held my breath anyway.

Ted Knoll stood over me, my shirt in his fists. He lifted me up and I felt myself break the surface of the "pond."

Ted said, *"What the hell are you doin'?"* He was shaking my torso with each word.

I sputtered, "Ending this! Killing the—closing off the nest."

"There's more kids in there, fuckstick! We got divers here, they're goin' in after 'em!"

I scrambled for a story. I briefly considered the truth. Over Ted's shoulder, I saw Amy up at the top of the path, looking down, hugging herself in the rain. I tried to think of a way to signal to her, but all that came to mind was screaming, "TELL JOHN TO START THE DIVERSION," which I figured would defeat the purpose of a diversion.

I said, "You say you can spot a liar? Well, watch my face real close—there are no children in there."

"What? Why would the kid lie?"

"It's a trick. It's an ambush. What comes out of there—ain't nobody gonna survive it, Ted. We've got to close it, and we've got to close it *now*."

Ted let me get to my feet. He then gathered up the bomb, slinging it over his shoulder.

"You look like you're lyin', all the time, no matter what you say. Maybe you're right about this, but if so, it'd be the first time since I ran into you. Dive team knows the risks, I've told 'em what's what. If somethin' hostile comes outta the water, we'll be ready. But you and your buddies are gonna stay the hell back, up there on the ridge. I see you approach before every one of those kids is free, I'll boot-stomp your ass into red waffles. Are we clear?"

I thought I could feel the Millibutt smirking at me, from some cold corner of the universe.

Ted turned, leaned forward, and "waded" his way out of the invisible pond. "Nine more kids in there. Once the last one is out, then we blow it. Not before."

But then, I thought, *it will be too late.*

Defeated, I met Amy at the top of the path. The two of us didn't speak as we made our way around to a spot behind the cabin nearest the church. There, John sat on a Harley-Davidson motorcycle he'd sneaked out of the church parking lot. He had strapped six silicone butts to various parts of his torso with bungee straps. He was holding Buddha's mace, which had six pink dildos taped to it.

I said, "Forget it, we don't need the diversion. I got intercepted by Ted."

John looked crestfallen.

There were faint cheers from below. We moved back to where we could see the pond just in time to watch a scuba diver crawl up from the twitching pink orifice, a squirming maggot in his hands. Three of them out in the world now, depending on what had happened with Maggie.

Speaking of which, I tried Marconi once again and felt my whole body seize up when he actually answered.

He said, "David?"

"Jesus, finally. Tell me you took care of Maggie."

"Not yet. There was a complication."

"Goddamnit, Marconi."

"Your friend, Joy, began acting strangely."

"Uh-oh."

"Yes. Not having met her, and knowing our situation, I had suggested she be vetted by our crowdsourced array, as you were."

Ah. Yeah, not a bad idea.

He continued, "As a response, she put a gun to my head. She is still doing it at this very moment." He sounded only mildly surprised by this turn of events. "You never told me how you know this person . . ."

"Let me guess. She doesn't want you to do away with Maggie."

"That would be correct. And, in fact, we are on the move. I am not sure to where, Joy is not forthcoming with answers."

I said, "I'm going to bet you're coming here, and that she intends to stop us from taking out the thing in the mine."

I heard Joy say, "Hang up," and the call disconnected.

I squeezed my eyes shut, pushed wet hair away from my forehead, and said, "Well, Marconi has fucked up his end. Now what?"

Amy said, "The good news is, we still know where every single one of the kids are, right? So, there's that. They're kind of contained, still."

"Yes, we can watch them all hatch right in front of us."

John said, "Well, I'll tell you one thing, I'm very disappointed in the Sauce-tripping weekend version of ourselves."

I shook my head and let out a long breath. I glanced at the church behind us, and for the first time noticed that on the door, in John's handwriting, had been scrawled, THIS IS A VAGINAPOND.

Amy

The rescue went quickly. There were two scuba divers, alternating trips into the fissure leading inside the old mine. At the moment, the last of the ten children was being hauled from the pond that David insisted was the pulsing birth canal of the Millibutt. The rain had slacked off into a light drizzle, which was as close to no rain as they got these days. Amy thought that soon she was going to wake up covered in mildew.

The kids were being loaded into a modified Christ's Rebellion school bus at the top of the hill. It was white and covered in red Bible slogans (WHERE THE SPIRIT OF THE LORD IS, THERE IS LIBERTY) and at least one image of a cartoon policeman getting run over by a motorcycle.

Amy could see the cops talking to the surviving leadership of the biker clan, clearly trying to convince them to bring the kids in to give statements and get checked out at the hospital. She could only hear muffled conversation, but Amy got the sense that the bikers weren't having it. No, these people were done with all that. They were, Amy assumed, done with Undisclosed. They just wanted to hit the road and feel the wind of the Lord's liberty on their rough cheeks until they arrived in a better place.

If I change . . . go. Just, go . . .

Amy watched as the kids boarded the bus, one by one, guided by biker moms. She had expected—or hoped—the kids would look like perfect *Children of the Damned* characters. You know—clones. Maggie had been a cute little blond girl and Mikey had looked like a big-cheeked black kid from an eighties sitcom. But these looked like, well, biker kids. Rough haircuts done at home—one boy had a shaved head, another had a mullet down to the middle of his back. Hand-me-down T-shirts, at least one ten-year-old girl wearing a tank top covered in cartoon cannabis leaves. One kid had a splint on his finger, like he'd broken it at some point, maybe trying to catch a baseball. Another had a red birthmark that covered half his face. A chubby little girl had a nasty rash crawling up her neck.

Every stitch of clothing, every Band-Aid, every blemish with its own backstory.

She tried not to look at them.

Me

I saw Amy staring at the bus and then making a determined effort to look elsewhere. The vehicle was now stuffed full of the larvae, they were squirming all over the windows. The female driver sat behind the wheel smoking a cigarette while a maggot munched on her scalp from behind. Blood ran down her face. She just blithely puffed away, waiting for the last of her cargo to board so she could head out.

If just one of them gets out into the world, we're fucked. Plain and simple.

The last of the "children" was now free from the "mine" and Ted didn't waste any time moving onto the bomb phase of the operation. He and Shitbeard approached the orifice, the former with the bomb backpack slung over his shoulder.

Ted had threatened to murder us, or at least me, if we got too close but we risked moving partway down the path to get a better vantage point. I was very confident the Millibutt wasn't just going to let Ted jam a bomb up in there, and I was 90 percent sure that whatever trick the creature pulled, it would require John and me to run down, rip the bomb from Ted's hands, and finish the job ourselves.

I was also curious to see how Ted and Shitbeard operated. I was specifically wondering how they would disperse the bystanders—Detective Bowman and his partner were standing right there on the pond's bank/meat flaps. But Ted just gave the cops a hand signal and both of them started directing people up and away from the blast site. So, he'd just discussed it with them and they had agreed it was a good idea. Why not, if the kids were safe? Must be weird to actually have authority figures on your side sometimes.

Motorcycles were rumbling to life above us, some of the gang already heading out, probably to go start packing up so they could all leave this god-forsaken place for good. I briefly wondered if John's meth supplier was going with them.

Shitbeard had the night-vision binoculars and positioned himself nearby to scan the sky for the BATMANTIS???, his assault rifle at the ready. Ted waded out toward the orifice with the bomb, doing a slow-motion walk, believing he was pushing through water up to his chest.

Even partway up the hill, I felt a tremor. But not in the ground—it was like the sky and the stars were trembling, a shudder in the cosmos.

John gave me a look and I knew he felt it, too.

Whether or not that bomb was actually going to work, I was pretty sure the Millibutt thought it would.

Yet, nothing emerged to stop Ted.

Why? I know you've got more tricks up your sleeve, you galactic piece of shit. I'm sure of it. Make your move.

Ted lit the fuse, took a deep breath, and disappeared into the pink hole. The phrase "muff diver" did not come to mind then or at any point after, and I'm not sure why you assumed it would.

John said, "There's no way it's going to be that eas—"

Amy said, "Look!"

There was a flash of headlights from above.

An RV pulled in, up by the church. Marconi's personal white-and-gold tour bus.

It skidded to a stop. Marconi spilled out of the side door, looking frantic. He was breathlessly yammering to us as he ran and tried to avoid tumbling down the steep path.

When he got within earshot, he said, "Thank goodness, you haven't planted the bomb yet."

I said, "*We* haven't. Ted has. He's, uh, inside the thing, right now. It's going to detonate in like two and a half minutes."

Marconi's eyes went wide. "No! We have to stop it!"

29. THE DANGER OF ACTING ON INCOMPLETE INFORMATION

"What? Why?"

"I am afraid it will take more than two minutes to explain."

Joy Park, who we had been told not very long ago was holding Marconi hostage, ran down the path behind him. She shouldered past him and kept running down toward the orifice, yelling, "We have to get it out!"

John, Amy, and I were all rapidly trying to figure out if this was, in fact, the right thing to do. But Marconi was already hustling after Joy, so it was either follow them or watch it happen.

Ted had just emerged from the orifice, covered in slime, yelling for everyone to clear out, saying there was fire in the hole. In response, Joy was waving her arms and screaming like a maniac at Ted, shouting at him to remove the fire from said hole.

Ted looked very, very skeptical. Rather than try to scream a rapid explanation to convince him, Amy had the ingenious thought to simply yell, "WE THINK

THERE'S ANOTHER KID IN THERE!"

Ted cursed and dove back in.

We all waited around the orifice, hearing faint squicking sounds from deep inside it. We were well within the blast radius of the device—how much time had passed?

I was just about to suggest we all flee, when Ted squishily emerged from the birth canal for the second time. He was cradling the mucus-covered bomb, which had about two inches of fuse left. He whipped out his combat knife and sawed off the fuse at the root. The next time somebody tried to light that thing, they'd only have seconds.

Marconi nodded and said, "Very good. Thank you. First things first—please call down the dive team, I'll explain everything. Also, your daughter is up in my tour bus, with her mother. Please go to her, she's distraught." He turned to Joy. "Go up and stall the Christ's Rebellion bus, tell them I need to have a word before they leave with the children. They will be skeptical. *Convince them.*"

Ted and Joy headed up the path. John said to Marconi, "Okay, what's the deal? You saying the bomb won't work? Will it work on the larva up there?"

"It will work. Just not how you think. The brimstone ritual—"

I said, "The what?"

"The burning sulfur, you're creating literal fire and brimstone. It will in fact pierce the larvae's skin, as you witnessed for yourself. And *that is precisely what it wants.* That's what allows it to hatch. It's the final stage in its life cycle."

I said, "Its life cycle depends on us happening to

invent a sulfur and thermite dildo gun at exactly the right time?"

"Not exactly that, but yes."

Amy said, "Oh god, why didn't I see it? The Mikey larva wasn't maturing or hatching or anything else until John shot it. It only hatched *because we tried to kill it*."

Marconi said, "Think of it like a rash. Have you ever been infected with ringworm? You scratch it, it spreads, the spores attaching to your fingernails. To prevent its spread, you cannot—"

"Scratch the itch," said John, nodding thoughtfully. He looked at me. "'Don't let them scratch the itch.' *That's* what I was trying to write on your asshole."

I said, "Wait, why would John and I have built that sulfur dildo cannon when we were on the Sauce if it was just going to make the situation worse? We should have been under the sway of profound cosmic insight or whatever."

John said, "I know exactly what happened. You built the dildo gun, I disagreed with that plan. That's what we were fighting about when the Sauce wore off. Looks like you owe *someone* an apology."

"What? *Who?*"

Marconi said, "We had assumed the larvae's camouflage was targeted only at the host parents, that it needed the parents only until it completed some life cycle over the course of time. However, I now believe that death—a violent death—is required for its final emergence. It's not as if the concept of transcendence to a higher plane of existence via death or martyrdom is unheard of in our mythology."

I said, "So, why not take some horrific form that

people couldn't resist killing? Why bother looking like adorable kids at all?"

"You have to think of a ritual like a chemical reaction—there are specific elements required in specific amounts at specific stages. The offspring feeds on human will, but requires a particular brew for nourishment. Not mere terror, but love and then betrayal, and the unique brand of fear and hatred that follows that sequence. It's like how we exploit a chili pepper—it develops harsh chemicals as a survival mechanism to deter insects, but we harvest them as a spice."

"All right, so what would the consequence be of setting off the bomb in the Millibutt's larva chute?"

"We have no way of knowing, but I think it is reasonable to say that the possible outcomes range from no effect at all, to an entire egg sac full of unseen larvae hatching simultaneously. What is important is that I have no reason to believe it would actually harm the entity itself."

"Well, we can't just let eleven of these bastards out into the world to keep chewing on their parents, so what do we do now?"

"Remember my creed—no action from ignorance. We need data and therefore we need time. So, we keep the larvae in a location in which we can control them and, above all, keep them saf—"

He was interrupted by an eruption of gunshots and screams from above.

Amy

Amy spun toward the chorus of bangs and screaming children from the hilltop. As it turned out, NON hadn't abandoned Undisclosed to its fate—they apparently just needed some time to regroup. This, Amy thought, would have been fantastic news thirty seconds ago.

The darkness above was illuminated by flashing threads of piercing light, like somebody had dropped a box of fireworks in a campfire. Amy took off up the steep path again and she had the thought that she needed to get her little noodle thighs onto a StairMaster if she was going to do this kind of work.

The creepy black cloaks had traded in their futuristic beam weapons for even more elaborate guns that fired handfuls of that hellish burning metal—she could smell the sulfur.

They had gone right after the school bus.

The remaining members of the biker gang, who were not big believers in passive resistance during the best of times, had responded with shotguns. With each shot that was fired, the children inside the bus shrieked in terror. At the moment Amy crested the hill, one of the bikers pounded on the side of the bus with his palm and screamed for the driver to go, just go.

NON had blocked the road with two of their trucks, but only in one direction—the bus went in reverse and backed up past the church, continuing on the looping road, going backward all the way while the cloaks peppered the front of the vehicle with brimstone. The bikers started hurling buckshot at the cloaks' backs and in the pitched battle that ensued, the bus slipped off into the night.

The boys came up behind her. Amy was about to say, "Thank god, they got away!" when David said, "SHIT! The larvae are loose!"

John said, "I do think it's time to admit that containment is not our strong suit."

The cloaks were retreating to their vehicles and, a moment later, a NON truck rumbled past, in pursuit of the school bus, soon followed by a second, and a third. There were shouts and the noise of Harley-Davidson exhaust coughing to life, then a chrome line of bikes went snaking down the road after the trucks. Detective Bowman's SUV was next, followed by a squad car, sirens blaring into the night. It was quite the parade.

Amy watched the herd of noisy lights disappear into the darkness, and in that moment the downpour chose to resume. She'd lost her raincoat at some point, and couldn't remember when. Cold water ran down her back.

David said, "Get to the Jeep! Let's go!" but no one was answering his call.

Amy looked to see where everyone had gone and found John, Marconi, and Joy all huddled together in the rain nearby, all muttering urgent commands to each other. Standing over something. Amy went over to them.

Ted Knoll was kneeling in the grass.

Lying there in front of him, was his daughter.

Maggie was trying to stifle a cry, taking rapid breaths, her little chest heaving. Ted, in a calm, controlled voice told her he was going to lift her shirt to get a look. The moment he did so, Maggie started wailing.

She had a cluster of smoldering dime-sized holes in her belly. The projectiles were still burning inside her, tendrils of smoke drifting out. Amy moved closer and could both hear and smell sizzling meat.

David walked up and said, "Oooooooh, *fuck*."

Loretta emerged from the RV, saw her daughter, and came apart. "Oh god. Oh god, no. Oh please god . . ."

Marconi said, "We have to move her. Get her in the RV! Now! I have medical equipment!"

David clearly seemed to think this was a horrible idea, but still helped haul the girl inside, through the RV's kitchenette, and into that cramped little lounge area near the back. They laid Maggie gently onto the narrow fold-out sofa. Her shirt was a crimson rag.

John said to Ted, "Don't worry, this guy's a doctor."

Ted said, "He looked right at her. Fucker had a mask like a little baby. Looked her right in the eyes and pulled the trigger."

"I know, man, they—"

"They'll keep coming," Ted said. "If I don't stop them, they'll keep coming. Keep her safe. You hear me? You keep her safe, or it's on you."

"What? What are you—"

Ted turned and ran out of the RV, John yelling after him.

Amy sprinted to the door of the RV just as the camouflage pickup pulled up, Ted's army buddy at the wheel. Ted leaped into the bed of the truck and they tore off after the convoy. Behind Amy, little Maggie was howling while her father became a shrinking pair of taillights that were quickly swallowed by the night.

Amy said, "We have to get her to a hosp—"

She was interrupted by a gunshot, the glass in the open door exploding right next to her face.

30. MOBILE SURGERY

John

A bang and the sound of shattered glass. Everyone hit the floor. Maggie screamed.

Dave yelled for Amy and ran to her, pulling her away from the door, telling her to get down.

John risked a look through a side window. NON agent Josaline Pussnado's black sedan was parked behind them, engine running, headlights illuminating twin horizontal shafts of glistening raindrops. She was standing behind the open driver's side door, wet shirt plastered against her bosom, aiming a pistol. She fired again, then moved toward the open door of the RV, shooting all the way like the goddamned Terminator, rain steaming off the gun. John ducked. Windows shattered along the length of the RV as her bullets whistled through.

From behind John, a female voice said, "HERE!" and there was Joy, running out from Marconi's office in the back. She had in her hand the obsidian spear that had been leaning in the corner. She tossed it to him.

John hefted it, felt its weight, then sprinted up toward the door. He leaped over Dave, who was still on the floor, shielding Amy with his enormous body. John was far from proficient when it came to spears, but you go to war with the weapons you have.

He leaned out of the door. Agent Pussnado hadn't so much as changed her clothes since Ted put an assault rifle round through her sternum—her white shirt looked like she'd had a mishap carrying a punchbowl. John found the scorched hole in her shirt, just off-center from the row of buttons between her perfect breasts. That would be his target.

He flung the spear with all his might, the shaft whizzing through the rain. The obsidian blade plunged itself into Pussnado's chest, right into what John was sure was her still-healing wound.

She stumbled back and stopped shooting, but did not die. The agent looked down, let out a groan of annoyance like she was having just the *worst* day, and tugged the spear out of her chest. She tossed it aside, reloaded her gun, and started walking toward the RV again.

John pulled the door closed and yelled, "Get us out of here!" to no one in particular.

Joy shoved past him. She threw herself into the driver's seat and started the engine. "Hold on!"

They rumbled out onto the main road, Pussnado's bullets clanking off the rear of the RV. When the shots stopped, John got a look in one of the side mirrors and saw the agent hobbling back into her sedan, intending to continue the pursuit. If nothing else, John hoped NON remembered her at bonus time.

Amy

The sound of Maggie wailing in the back was the worst thing Amy had ever heard. Pain and terror and helplessness, a plaintive wail that was absolutely raw and absolutely *real*. Amy and David clumsily climbed to their feet. David—who looked anxious but clearly was not hearing what Amy heard, glanced back that direction, then looked nervously at Joy, who was pushing the RV to its limits down dark, submerged streets.

Amy uttered a question that, considering the context, sounded ridiculously casual. "So, uh, where are you from?"

Joy, who was hunched over the steering wheel as if she could make the sluggish RV go faster with body language, smiled.

"You're sweet. Phrasing the question that way. I can tell you're cool."

John stepped toward them, with that look on his face like he was beginning to puzzle something out. Without a word, he held out his hand. Joy knew what he was doing; she took her right hand off the wheel and held it out to him. John examined it like he was admiring an engagement ring.

Four of Joy's fingers came off in his hand. While John held them, they transformed back into one of those worker bug things, which sat calmly on his palm.

David let out a long breath that carried with it the word, "Ooooookay."

Joy, trying to steer with her partial hand, said, "I do kind of need that back."

John handed the fudge roach back to Joy. It crawled

385

into place and became fingers again.

John said, "Well, that actually makes more sense than any of the other possibilities. At some point during the lost weekend, I learned how to control a flock of fuckroaches. That's all. Must have learned to train them or something."

I said, "Is there a, uh, larva in there . . ."

"No."

"Why can't we see through the disguise?"

Joy said, "Because you don't want to, dummy."

Amy said, "And you forced them to take the form of a Korean porn star. So you could do what with her, exactly?"

Joy said, "Ew, no. That would *not* be cool."

David said, "And we, uh, trust her to drive the bus?"

Joy said, "It's not that hard. *If* people aren't distracting you."

"That's actually not what I—"

Maggie howled again and Marconi shouted from the back that he needed their help.

They ran to the back, where Maggie's mother was trying to hold the little girl still while Marconi tended to her. Blood was everywhere—it covered the narrow sofa and had splattered onto the floor. Amy couldn't imagine that tiny body even having that much blood in it.

Amy yelled back toward Joy, "You're taking us to a hospital, right?"

Me

Marconi's tan suit looked like he'd just gotten home from a double shift in a butcher shop. Beads of sweat covered his forehead.

He said, "We can't keep her still."

The squealing maggot was thrashing around . . . and *growing*. The goddamned sulfur pellets were still burning through its flesh and I thought that if Hell was a real place, I now knew exactly what it smelled like.

Marconi said to the half-eaten Loretta, "All right. Run into my office, through that door there. On my desk is a large stone bowl. On the shelf to the right of it is a glass jar full of sand. Bring them both to me."

To John, he said, "Hold her still." Marconi had a long pair of forceps that he'd been using to try to fish out the sizzling pellets.

To me, he said, "I tried to cut the wound wider to grant us better access, but her skin snapped the blade off the scalpel. Utterly impenetrable. Then I tried to extract the projectiles . . ."

He shook his head and handed me the forceps.

I said, "What the hell are you doing? No. This is . . . no."

"Mr. Wong, *I cannot see the patient.* I'm seeing a little girl with an abdominal wound."

"*I am not a doctor!*"

"You believe a doctor would be more qualified to perform this operation? You're locating the projectiles and digging them out. They are not difficult to find— they are sizzling and glowing like miniature suns."

That part was even truer than he knew; the creature's

skin was translucent, it looked like a dirty plastic tarp wrapped tightly around twenty gallons of Vaseline. I could see four pellets, each the size of a pea, burning their way down to various depths. The worst was about two inches down.

Start with the deepest first.

John leaned over the monster with his forearms on either side of the surgical site, trying to at least keep the little patch I was working on stabilized.

Loretta came back with the bowl and the jar. Marconi poured the sand into the bowl and set it next to me—a place to set the burning projectiles where they would not ignite the interior of the RV and create a forty-sixth deadly problem for us to deal with.

I pushed the forceps in and the maggot howled, a noise like a screeching exotic bird being forced through a long section of pipe with a sharp stick. Loretta, watching over my shoulder, gasped and wept. I didn't want to imagine what *she* was hearing.

I had to try to force the wound wider to get the forceps around the sizzling projectile. Impossible—the skin was like thick leather, I could change the shape of the wound, but not make it bigger. Then, when I got the instrument deep enough, I found I couldn't really squeeze the burning ball because the grabby parts at the end of the forceps were the wrong shape to grip a sphere—it kept slipping every time I squeezed, and the maggot howled louder every time I missed.

Loretta was offering me panicked, unhelpful suggestions every step of the way. From up front, Joy was yelling something about having caught up to the convoy, and I thought I could hear sirens.

Finally, I got the first ball tenuously clamped in the forceps, gingerly drew it out, then promptly bumped my hand and dropped the glowing orb on the sofa. It burned right through the cushion, a little tongue of flame licking up from the spot. I quickly dug out the projectile and dropped it in the sand bowl, John rolling the larva out of the way of the burning cushion. Marconi slapped out the fire, whipping it with his suit jacket.

Three projectiles left. I was shaking. Sweat was stinging my eyes. The larva continued to swell and pulse.

I said, "What if it's already too—" and stopped myself. I wanted to ask what if it was already too late, meaning too late to stop the thing from hatching. But Loretta was standing right there and she would definitely interpret that the wrong way.

I leaned in to start working on the next deepest projectile, then almost toppled over when the RV swerved.

Joy shouted, "Hang on!"

The windshield in front of her was a kaleidoscope of flashing red-and-blue lights dancing across streaking beads of rainwater. I could hear sirens and shouts and Harley mufflers.

We'd driven right into the chaos.

Amy

They swerved again and Amy had to brace herself against the wall. She stumbled up to the cockpit. Joy had steered them around the scene of a multivehicle accident turned pitched battle.

Detective Bowman's SUV was on its side, blocking the right lane, exposing its mechanical underbelly. Its red lights were still swirling and flashing across the expanse of rain-splattered blacktop. The tailing squad car had then run into it, its snout crumpled between the SUV's tires. The squad car had on its hood a smoking motorcycle and its enraged rider, the guy having apparently gotten sandwiched between the two police vehicles. The rear tire of the Harley was still spinning, sending sprays of water whizzing across the police car's windshield.

Off in the standing water next to the highway was one of the NON trucks, having run off the road. It had a grappling hook and line tangled around one of the front tires. Cloaks were pouring out of it and shooting, pinning down several bikers who had skidded to a stop behind them.

The RV got clear of the wreck and Amy could hear muffled gunshots—the rest of the convoy was just ahead.

There were layers to the madness. Directly in front of them was Ted's camouflage pickup. The RV's headlights illuminated Ted, crouched in the bed with his assault rifle. His soaked blond hair was matted to his skull, his green jacket flapping in the wind. He was in the middle of reloading the gun and even in the darkness, in a moving vehicle in a howling rainstorm, the reloading process was smooth and fluid. Practiced hands. His fingers did not shake.

Ahead of him was an undulating swirl of taillights belonging to three Christ's Rebellion motorcycles that were still in pursuit, weaving back and forth, conducting a running battle with the two remaining NON trucks that were side by side, one of them driving with abandon in the oncoming lane. The bikers were shooting at the trucks, little fists of flame popping from their stubby shotguns. The rear windows of the trucks were scarred with white marks where the shots had landed, to no avail. These were military vehicles, made to withstand this sort of thing. Directly ahead of all *that* was the school bus, a vehicle that simply was not built for speed and thus couldn't get any kind of separation from its pursuers.

Also: it was clear that all of them were driving into the flood.

They were heading directly toward the river, which meant they were entering neighborhoods that had already been evacuated because their roads were impassable. There was an inch of water over the street and the next sudden movement could send them hydroplaning off in one direction or another, at which point the top-heavy RV would no doubt go tumbling over—wounded little girl and all.

Not that the vehicles involved in the pursuit ahead seemed to care. As Amy watched, the NON truck ahead and to the left picked up speed to overtake the bus. Once it was alongside, it swerved over and slammed into it, the black truck trying to drive it off the road, into the overflowing drainage ditch. The bus swerved, kicked up a rooster-tail spray of water with its rear tire, then swung back on the street. That driver, Amy thought, could pilot the heck out of a school bus.

Something caught Joy's attention in the side mirror and she cursed.

Headlights—the black sedan of the NON agent, racing up from behind.

The car sped up past the RV in the left lane, then passed Ted's truck before he had time to register it.

The three bikers, focused on trying to peel the NON trucks away from the bus full of their precious children, hadn't been expecting an assault from the rear. The sedan swept into their lane and slammed into the rear wheels of two bikes, sending both careening off the road, flipping and splashing into the standing water.

Ted tried to bring his assault rifle around to get a clear shot at the sedan. He fired into its side window. The sedan swerved over, smacking into the pickup and sending Ted tumbling over. The pickup slammed on its brakes, causing it to jerk into the third motorcycle, flipping the driver into the side of the truck and then onto the pavement.

Joy yanked the wheel and the RV swerved to avoid running over the tumbling body of the biker. When she swerved back, they ran over a pair of orange street signs now lying flat in the middle of the road, their stands knocked aside. They both said in all-caps:

BRIDGE OUT.

Me

The Maggie larva was now about 50 percent bigger than when we started. I could feel puffs of frozen dread pouring from the wound. It was a unique sensation; the best comparison I can offer is if you opened your fridge to realize something was rotten in there, then when you opened the cheese drawer, you found a photo of your mother fucking a Dalmatian.

This swelling effect did have the benefit of stretching the wounds slightly, though the pellets were getting deeper by the second. My plan to go for the deepest one first had been idiotic, the idea had been to extract them in order of threat level but in the time it took to dig it out, the other three had burrowed down just as far.

Still, I had the second burning pellet out and clinched in the forceps when the RV slammed to a halt. We all went lurching forward like the crew of the *Enterprise* when a torpedo hits. I came *this* close to dropping the pellet right back into the goddamned wound. People were shouting up in the cockpit.

John yelled, "What's happening?"

Joy said, "Bridge is out!"

Amy, sounding frantic, said, "They're in the water! They're getting swept away!"

"Who's in the water?"

"Everyone! The cloaks are going after them!"

I heard the RV door open. John turned and yelled, "Amy! Wait!"

Amy was gone, having run out into the storm to do god knows what.

John got up and ran after her. The larva started thrashing under me, John no longer there to restrain it. I screamed after both of them. Neither returned.

Two pellets continued to scorch their way into the husk of the larva. The creature squealed and sucked and chittered. Loretta ran over and tried to hold it still, putting her hands in all the wrong places, whispering to the thing that it would be okay, that everything would be okay.

From the darkness in the wounds, I thought I could hear voices, calling my name.

I blinked sweat out of my eyes and went back to work.

Amy

The bus was sinking. The children were screaming.

The bridge that was out was in fact the same bridge they had stood on a few weeks ago, when they were pursued to it from the other direction. This was the spot where she had chucked the Soy Sauce vial into a current that at the time had already been just feet below the rusty junk bridge that should have been replaced decades ago. Now, the river had overwhelmed the bridge and rolled it aside, rusty beams jutting out of the rushing whitewater rapids to Amy's right. Directly in front of her was the rear bumper and emergency door of the white and red bus, now tipped up toward the sky at a 45-degree angle, the front end submerged in the dark current. The rear wheels were still rolling helplessly in the air.

Amy had watched the Christ's Rebellion bus try to stop, but it was a lumbering, clumsy beast skidding through a few inches of standing water—it hadn't even been close. The bus had splashed face-first into the rushing current and Ted's pickup had soon followed. Ted's friend behind the wheel had tried to swerve around the bus wreck to the other lane, only to see the pavement vanish from under him.

So now there was Ted, upstream to Amy's left, standing on the bed of his sinking pickup and smashing at the rear window with the butt of his rifle so the driver could climb out. It wasn't working. Amy had the thought that the guy had probably already drowned. Meanwhile, tiny hands were slapping and clawing at the rear windows of the school bus, children and panicked biker moms screaming from within.

The hulking black NON trucks had in fact gotten stopped in time, and were now parked on either side of Amy. They were disgorging the black cloaks all around her, ready to finish the job. Behind her was the RV, headlights casting shadows across the chaos in the river. She could hear John shouting something from back there.

Then, two more headlights joined the party—the sedan of the unkillable female NON agent.

There was a scraping and a groaning noise from the bus, and it lurched to Amy's right. The current was grabbing at it, trying to yank it downstream, to swallow it up, to drown everyone on board.

Amy ran toward the rear of the bus, yelling, "Cover me!" in Ted's direction. No idea if he could hear her—all she could hear were screams and the thundering stampede of angry water. She would have to jump to climb up on the rear bumper . . .

The air exploded around her, and she tumbled down to the pavement.

She heard shouts—Ted yelling strategy commands that meant nothing to her. He was crouched on the bank of the river, water breaking and spraying around his legs, shooting in her direction. Not at her, but at the black cloaks that were now right on top of her. The cloaks fired back at Ted, leaving orange afterimages in Amy's vision like fiery claw marks.

She scrambled to her feet and ran toward the bus once more. It lurched and scraped again, getting pulled along the bank. She tried to jump up onto the bumper but at the last moment, a strong, bony hand seized her by the arm, yanked her back, and tossed her. She went face-first into the flooded area along the riverbank, nostrils burning as she inhaled water. She lost her glasses. She sputtered and tried to get to her feet. She heard screams and turned—a black cloak climbed up on the bus, ripping open the rear door.

John

The cloak was about to start pumping brimstone down onto the larvae and John knew he only had a window of about two seconds to do something about it.

He hadn't brought a weapon. Fortunately, the universe quickly granted him one: Ted, firing from the riverbank, nailed one of the cloaks between John and the bus, the thing's strange shotgun flipping into the air and right into John's hands.

John aimed and pulled the trigger. Yellow threads of fire laced through the air.

He hit the cloak right in the back. It stumbled forward, almost falling down into the bus, then turned to face him.

It was Babyface.

John reminded himself that, under the cloak, the thing was wearing body armor.

John aimed and pulled the trigger a second time, aiming right for that stupid puffy-cheeked face. There was only a dry click.

John tossed the gun aside, ran, and leaped up onto the back of the bus. He tried to wrestle the cloak's gun out of its hands, face-to-face with its ghoulish infant features and those tiny little rubber teeth.

They tussled and John felt something shoving his feet aside. Giant maggots were boiling out of the rear door of the bus, squirming out in every direction. The cloak took advantage of the distraction and smacked John in the jaw with the butt of his gun. John stumbled back, grabbed the cloak, and both went tumbling into the water.

Me

The larva was pulsing.

The two empty wounds from which I'd extracted the first pellets were now black holes, staring at me like shark eyes, a calculating, gleeful intelligence behind them. I could sense it talking to me, taunting me, making me promises about what awaited once it was free from its shell. Every time the forceps slipped off a projectile, it laughed. So ready to be free, gazing upon our world and seeing a new toy to play with, a helpless thing to torture.

I blinked and tried to concentrate. The two remaining pellets were deep—too deep for the forceps—and I couldn't get a firm grip on either one because the maggot kept thrashing around. Loretta had been joined by Marconi, both of them failing to keep my "patient" still.

I fumbled with the projectile, the larva howling under me.

I couldn't get it. I glanced at Loretta, who was watching

me, eyes wide. The life of her baby slipping out of my trembling, incompetent hands. She saw the apology in my eyes and I watched her die a little inside.

Desperate, I screamed, "Joy! Get back here!"

She appeared.

"Can you, uh, see what's going on here? Really see? Not just Maggie, but the . . ."

She nodded quickly.

"Help me hold her down."

"Why can't we roll her over?"

"What good would—"

Instead of explaining, Joy just pushed everyone back and rolled the swollen larva off the sofa and onto the floor, wound-side down.

She slapped the larva twice.

Then she rolled it back, and two smoking little balls were lying there on the floor, cooking the carpet. They had just fallen right out.

Amy

Amy saw John and the cloak tumble into the water. Kids were trying to crawl out of the rear door of the bus, climbing over each other, crying out for their parents.

The shooting had stopped from Ted's end and Amy could sense from his manner that he had run out of bullets. That infuriated Amy. How could he run out of bullets? Always having lots of bullets was his whole thing. That was like an Internet provider running out of snide indifference.

Ted pulled out a knife and splashed out of the water,

advancing on the one remaining cloak who was still on dry land and upright.

Amy moved toward the bus once more. It shifted again under the force of the current, tilting now, almost tossing the escaping children overboard. Could they drown?

She yelled for them to be calm, said she was coming, then there was a gunshot from behind her and Amy swore she felt the bullet whistle by her ear this time. She thought she might have peed her pants a little.

She turned and there was the female agent with the bloody shirt, Amy could no longer remember what name they were calling her.

Amy said, "You can't hurt me! Remember! It will blow back on you!"

The woman said, "Just step aside, it's been a long week."

Slung over her shoulder was the shotgun they'd given to David back at the wellness center, only Amy assumed it was now functional.

Amy said, "This may seem like a weird time to ask, but what's your name again?"

"Bella."

"Listen, Bella. Shooting them causes them to hatch. *That's what they want!*"

The agent sighed. "And who told you that?"

"I don't—we figured it out! You have to trust me!"

"So these creatures, whose entire process is based around deception, convinced you that they can't be harmed, and you don't see why I'm skeptical of this claim? What exactly is *your* plan? Long-term, I mean."

"I DON'T KNOW! I don't know, okay?"

The look of disdain on Agent Bella's face burned right through the downpour. The rain had spread her bloodstain down her shirt, fading to pink around the edges. Children were yelling. Nearby, Amy could hear what sounded like Ted stabbing a cloaked figure to death.

The agent brought the shotgun around and marched forward.

Me

We lifted the larva back onto the sofa. The four wounds were no longer smoking, but they also weren't going away, either. I held a hand over the holes and felt what I thought an astronaut would feel if he found a crack in the ship's hull while floating in the most desolate, frozen void at the edge of the cosmos. Not just coldness, but darkness and a sense of the vast, inhuman eternity that lay beyond. Was it too late? The larva was swollen, now in the shape of a football, tugging and straining on the gashes in the translucent leathery hide.

I said, "So . . . I'm not sure how to treat the wounds on this . . ." I almost said "thing" but Maggie's mother was right there, and already seemed pretty confused. ". . . uh, situation."

Marconi said, "Is there bleeding?"

"Not blood, no."

Loretta said, "*There's blood everywhere.*"

Joy said, "Then treat the wounds." She looked at Marconi. "Treat the little girl. Same as you would anybody."

He looked at me. I shrugged. The larva was no longer

thrashing around and howling with its piercing wounded bird noises. It just lay there and made a low, squishy moaning sound. In the sand bowl, all four pellets continued to crackle and burn, the stench of brimstone filling the RV.

Marconi dug out packages of gauze from his first-aid kit and went to work.

Outside, I heard gunshots and Amy yelling at someone. I left the larva and its three caretakers behind and ran for the door. When I grasped the handle to open it, I found my hand was sticky. I was surprised to find it was covered in blood.

Maggie's, I guess?

Whatever.

Just as I was about to step out, I noticed that leaning next to the door was Marconi's antique spear, wicked chiseled notches in its gleaming obsidian head. I grabbed it and shoved through the door, into the maelstrom.

John

If John and his attacker had fallen on the downstream side of the sinking school bus, he'd no doubt have been whisked down the river, on his way to the Gulf of Mexico. Instead they fell upstream, meaning the current was now crushing their bodies against the side of the bus. There was no ground under John's feet—the only thing keeping his head above the surface was the current pinning him to the white metal wall and the grip of his left hand, which was clutching a grating next to the bus's wheel well.

John had lost track of the cloak that had tumbled into the river with him and he had hoped maybe it'd gotten swept away. But then a hand erupted out of the water and clutched John around the throat. The fingers felt thin and sinewy, like the talons on a bird.

Up from the water came the baby-face mask, only blackness behind the blank eye holes.

In a voice that sounded like a colon tumor that had grown a mouth, the cloak said, "Even now, you do not believe you can die. Do you know what awaits you, once you have been plunged into the black swarm? A most profound penetration that will split you wide, a violation without end, your shock their narcotic, your despair their aphrodisiac. How can you not already hear their lustful howls, you who bear the mark of Min?"

The bony hand forced John's head under water. He struggled to grasp the side of the bus, to pull himself up, but his fingers peeled loose and he was drowning, the crush of the water an incomprehensible force, pushing the last air out of his lungs.

John clawed helplessly at the talons around his neck. Feeling his own numb fingers growing weaker.

Then there was a shape in the water above him, visible only as a shadow in the rippling reflection of the headlights from the shore. Something floating toward him, carried by the current.

Whatever it was, the cloak was distracted by it, turning away from his prey. John seized the opportunity and wrenched free of the claw, pulling himself up out of the water, sputtering and spitting. John wiped water out of his eyes and saw what was bobbing his way:

A pink silicone ass.

Ted's pickup was now fully submerged upstream and the truck's rubber ass cargo had spilled into the rushing water. The cloak stared in wonderment as one ass after another flowed its way, two dozen of them, bobbing along majestically.

The cloak screamed in despair, "The prophecy! It is true!" It turned its vacant eyes upward, rainwater filling the holes of the mask and dribbling out like tears. "You have summoned him!"

A pale blur whipped down from the sky. It snatched the cloak, whisking it from the water. It carried the struggling figure up, then flung it off into the distance, the cloaked thing landing soundlessly somewhere downstream.

John climbed up the side of the bus, shook wet hair from his face, and yelled, "HEY PUSSNADO, IT LOOKS LIKE YOUR SHIP JUST HIT AN *ASS*BERG! BECAUSE YOUR MAN JUST GOT ASS*ASS*INATED! HEY, DO YOU MIND IF I *ASS* YOU SOMETH—"

Amy

No one could hear what John was yelling from the water.

"You know what really gets me?" said the agent behind the gun. "The sheer arrogance of it all. You've convinced yourself you're taking some kind of moral stand, but you don't care that you're putting *the whole world at risk* for it. You're so sure you're right. I bet you win every argument with your boys. The little nerd girl? Bitch, your ego could blot out the sun."

Ted was shouting now, joining the chorus of shouts

from almost everyone in the vicinity. He was standing over the defeated black cloak, looking up at something, mouth agape.

He screamed, "GET DOWN!"

Amy didn't even have time to obey. She and the agent both looked up in time to see a pale blur whoosh down from the sky.

The BATMANTIS??? landed heavily on one of the NON trucks.

Gunshots rang out—the female agent was unloading on the beast with her brimstone shotgun. The monster leaped off the truck and pinned her to the street, water breaking and splattering around her shoulders.

The agent didn't drop the gun. She worked the barrel around and pressed it right to the BATMANTIS???'s face.

The creature made a quick swipe with one of its serrated claws and something went rolling away, splashing through the standing water at the side of the road.

It was the agent's severed head.

"AMY!"

It was David, running toward them, hands and shirt covered in blood, carrying some kind of pole. He frantically looked back and forth from Amy to the winged beast.

Amy screamed, "I think it's helping us! That's why it kept turning up! It's trying to help!"

But the BATMANTIS??? chose that moment to lunge at her, swiping a claw and missing only because it clumsily stumbled over its own misshapen feet.

David yelled, "No! It's an asshole! Get away!"

The beast lurched in her direction. Amy dove and rolled away. She sprinted toward David.

He brandished the object she now realized was a spear from Marconi's collection, putting himself between Amy and the monster.

The beast spun around to face them. Instead of teeth, it had a ragged kind of beak. Powerful jaws. It was no herbivore.

David yelled, "NO! We did not survive all this shit just to get eaten by your stupid ass. Just go away!"

Amy said to it, "We're the good guys! It's okay!"

The thing snatched at David. He thrust the spear at it, backing it off.

"NO!" he screamed at it. "No! Don't you see, you dumb son of a bitch? We don't want to kill you! Can you even hear me, you fucking animal? I will put this through your goddamned neck!"

The thing just looked confused. Not evil, Amy thought—just scared and hungry and lashing out blindly at a world it didn't understand.

The BATMANTIS??? lunged again—not at David, but past him. It was going for Amy.

David growled, "NO!"

He jabbed at it with the spear as it passed. He got it, right in the side.

It recoiled. Dark blood oozed. The thing screeched.

And then the monster . . . smiled.

Amy was sure of it. As if it finally had a fight, like this was what it had come for.

The BATMANTIS??? whipped a claw through the air with a pale blur, and David's spear went flying.

David, in a blind rage, did not back down.

"COME ON! Come over here and die, you fucking animal! I've fought shit that would keep you for a pet!"

He turned quickly toward Amy. "Run! I'll keep it busy!"

She didn't. The BATMANTIS??? swung a claw, bashing David to the ground. Effortless.

It jumped on him, pinning him just as it had done to the agent moments ago. Amy screamed.

David yelled again for her to go. She stayed.

He clawed at the thing's face, yelling, "LOOK AT YOU! YOU ARE A MISTAKE! A MALFUNCTION! YOU EAT ME, I WILL FUCK YOU FROM THE INSIDE!"

The thing raised a claw, meaning to lop off David's head.

Amy suddenly remembered the Taser. She yanked it out of her back pocket, ran up and pressed it against the monster's neck, the blue flashes of electricity popping against its skin.

It didn't paralyze it, but it did cause it to recoil again, to stagger backward.

Amy stabbed a finger at it. "Last chance! You have to *go*. You understand? We have been more than patient."

The monster snarled, then yelped and stumbled forward. Something had slammed into it from behind.

John

There were now six of the huge, squealing maggots clinging to the top of the bus and more were crawling out, crowding each other. John was thus having trouble finding purchase on the upturned rear and thought it would look bad to Amy if he just started shoving children off into the water to make room.

John heard someone from shore tell everyone to

get down, then the BATMANTIS??? swooped overhead, landing on a vehicle nearby. There were gunshots and then the shots abruptly ended.

Then it looked like the beast was confronting someone, its jumbled limbs and wings thrashing around in the silhouette of the RV's headlights. John heard enraged and panicked cries through the rain. Dave and Amy were confronting the monster, and from the sound of it, losing.

Frantic, John awkwardly climbed around to the rear bumper of the bus and tried to get his feet over the pavement—only a small corner of the bus still overhung solid land. He managed to drop onto the street. Two of the maggots were already there, having crawled off the bus.

John turned . . .

A man was running past him.

It was Ted.

Running with purpose and rage.

Running to confront the beast he believed had taken his child.

He was carrying the backpack containing the brimstone bomb.

Ted jumped onto the back of the BATMANTIS???, getting it in a chokehold, a muscled arm wrapped around what passed for the thing's neck. The creature thrashed and tried to reach back for him, its clumsy mismatched limbs badly failing at the task.

Frustrated, the winged beast jumped and took to the air, Ted still on its back, as if the BATMANTIS??? intended to get him up high and shake him off. Up the two of them went, up and up, a flash of lightning illuminating the pair for just a split second, revealing a glimpse of tiny flapping wings and a desperate, thrashing struggle in midair.

Then it was dark again. John lost sight of them in the starless sky.

He stared, squinting against the raindrops that were dive-bombing his face.

And then, a flash of light, like a new sun being born. Bright enough to blind.

The boom hit two seconds later.

Down came a spectacular rain of brilliant, sizzling particles, filling the sky, landing in the floodwaters around them with a soft hiss.

It only took John a moment to put together what had happened, that Ted had known the creature would try to take off with him attached, that flight was its only advantage. Ted was a soldier, a good one, and a hell of a lot smarter than the beast had been. He had just needed the BATMANTIS??? to get high enough, away from the innocents below.

The last of the falling embers burned themselves out and it was dark once more. No remains of either man or beast fell from the sky.

For a moment it was just silence, and the rain.

Then, the rain stopped.

Amy

The rescue effort was an awkward disaster at first. The combined efforts of the three of them managed to get a whole two additional kids off the bus—the children were terrified of the rushing water and didn't want to jump off onto the jagged ledge of partially submerged pavement for fear of slipping off and getting swept away. Amy couldn't blame them.

But soon there was a rumble of motorcycle mufflers and a flock of headlights, the rest of the biker gang showing up late to the party. They formed a human chain from the street up to the wobbling bus, handing the children down to safety one at a time. Rather than get in the way, Amy, John, and David trudged back toward the RV.

Amy had been so overwhelmed by events that it didn't occur to her until she stepped inside that she was bringing with her news that Loretta was now a widow and that Maggie was now fatherless. She made her way back to the lounge and sucked in a breath when she saw the blood. It covered mother and daughter, Marconi, the little sofa, and the floor. Loretta sat there, cradling Maggie's head in her lap, and Amy wasn't sure which one looked more exhausted.

Loretta said, "What blew up?"

Amy started to reply, but found she couldn't.

John said, "Ted blew up the monster. It's gone. But he died in the process. I'm, uh, sorry. He sacrificed himself, to save Maggie. And you, and all of us. Maybe the world. If anybody ever tries to say otherwise, you can tell them to come find me. Because I saw it myself."

Loretta closed her eyes and leaned back against the window behind her—the corner was shattered where a pair of bullets had punched through at some point. She pressed her lips together and swallowed. Amy sensed the woman was cutting off the grief, like crimping a hose.

Her daughter needed her, and there would be time to grieve for her husband later.

Amy said, "How is Maggie?"

From behind her, Marconi said, "From what I can ascertain, the four pellets perforated her small intestine. I have stopped the bleeding and given her something for the pain. But she needs a hospital."

David said, "She . . . does?"

Amy glanced out at the huddle of kids standing on the pavement outside, being tended to by their parents. The bus driver was among them. Amy had written her off for dead, and she now imagined her at the bottom of the bus, down where it was filling with water, lifting up the children one at a time so they could breathe. A hero.

With a tortured squeal of scraping metal, the empty school bus was wrenched free from the shore and went rolling down the river, colliding with the wreckage of the bridge. Several of the kids cheered.

Marconi fixed his gaze on David and in a lowered voice, said, "What I observe, with my five senses, is a child that has a very survivable wound, but that needs medical attention or else loss of blood or sepsis will finish the job. That is what I observe."

From the driver's seat, Joy said, "Hang on!" They were already moving before she finished the second syllable. Taking them to the hospital. How did she even know where it was?

David said, "Guys, *we can't just leave*. We have to . . . watch them, out there. Contain them. Figure out a way to, you know. Take care of them. The right way."

Marconi said, "What do you propose?"

David started to answer, but the words never came.

Me

I sat there and stared out of the bullet-riddled rear window, watching the RV shit a stream of wet highway, the biker kids shrinking in the distance. The farther away we got, the less I cared. I was so tired, and so cold, and so wet. Above all else, I just wanted to be dry again. Then maybe to sit down with a beer and hug Amy while she watched some terrible Japanese cartoon about magical girls learning the power of friendship.

No. I wouldn't do any of those things.

I would see this through. This, and whatever came after.

I turned my back on the window and watched the Maggie larva carefully. Then I blinked, and there was Maggie, the little girl. Bloody hair matted to her face, pale cheeks, a little gap in her front teeth. The Sauce was wearing off.

So small, so fragile, chest barely rising and falling as she clung to life.

Maggie opened her eyes with what seemed like a monumental effort. Looking right at me.

With all her strength, she raised one tiny hand, extended it toward me, and gave me the finger.

31. THE UNDISCLOSED HOSPITAL WAS RECENTLY RENOVATED AND IS NOW A PRETTY NICE FACILITY

After all that, we wound up spending the next few hours sitting quietly in a hospital waiting room, damp as dishrags, eating snacks and sodas out of their vending machine.

Why were we there? To see if "Maggie" recovered? To try to contain her if she erupted into a towering shadow of doom? Fuck if I knew. John eventually fell asleep, sprawled across five chairs and snoring loudly. Amy leaned on me and rested her wet head on my shoulder. Joy—who was completely dry—casually filed her nails. Marconi mostly stayed out on the sidewalk to smoke his pipe and talk on his cell—he apparently had people he could reach out to for advice in situations like this. That must be nice.

Eventually, Loretta came shuffling down the hall and I noted she looked whole again—no longer appearing to have been attacked by a great white. It wasn't because she *was* whole, necessarily, but that the Soy Sauce was wearing off and I was now starting to see what everyone else saw. I no doubt could have seen through the illusion with some concentration, but I had no concentration juice left in my brain. Besides, I knew the truth.

Loretta said, "The doctor says she's going to be okay."

John blinked sleep from his eyes and raised himself up on one elbow. "That's . . . good. She appears, uh, normal, and everything?"

"She's been through a lot."

Amy said, "I'm so sorry about Ted."

Loretta sighed and sat in one of the chairs across from us.

"This is going to sound awful, but Ted . . . he never really came back home. From Iraq, I mean. We were high school sweethearts and . . . well, you don't want to hear our life story. It just seemed like he never forgave himself for what happened over there. It's like he felt like he owed a life, somehow, like it was an overdue bill he'd shirked. He kept moving us, from place to place, paranoid about the government, about everything, sure that someone was going to come and make him pay what he owed. When Maggie got taken, it was strange, because I swear it's like that's what he had been waiting for, all that time. I don't want to say he wasn't upset, don't take it that way—but in those hours and days after, he was so *alive.* I hadn't seen him like that since right before he shipped out. He finally had another damned war to fight."

Loretta wiped her eyes.

Amy said, "I just hope that wherever he is, he's at peace."

Loretta said, "If he is, well, I guess that would make one of us. The son of a bitch got just what he wanted. A big, heroic sacrifice. Now the rest of us are left to clean up the mess. He probably thought he was being selfless or something. But look what he left behind. What he did, that's the most selfish thing you can do. I want to find the jerk who convinced males that martyrdom is cool and kick him in the teeth."

Loretta closed her eyes and pressed her lips together again. Reestablishing control. Then she quietly excused herself and went back to see her child.

Joy looked up from her nails and said, "I wonder if Waffle House is still open."

I said, "Do you even eat?"

"Don't be a dick."

Amy sat up, my hand sliding off of her shoulder. She was watching Loretta as she plodded her way back to her monster baby.

She said, "We were wrong, weren't we? We said the bug things dig up your worst fear to use against you, but it's not that. Ted got his war. John, well, he got his car chase, right? It's like . . ."

She trailed off, watching Loretta disappear around a corner.

From behind us, Marconi said, "I have found that our greatest fears and our greatest desires are, in fact, two sides of the same coin. I have known many who have died before their time, clutching that coin in their fist. Figuratively, of course." He had come up behind us at some point, now standing with his overcoat draped over a forearm.

I said, "Jesus, you don't just sneak up behind people and start spouting wisdom at them. Not at this hour." I turned back to Amy. "So according to him, your proverbial coin is . . . waffles, I guess?"

I went to put my hand on her shoulder again but she stood up, wandering away like she needed to stretch her legs.

Marconi said, "I'm afraid I must excuse myself, I've an early morning production meeting, then it's off to Minneapolis. Something is digging up graves, or so they tell me." He glanced at a pocket watch. "I'll assume any questions I have for you can be answered over e-mail."

I said, "Wait, what? This isn't over, Doctor. Do you know what's gonna happen with the larvae if we all just go back home?"

"No. Do you? The best I can say is that a chick that cannot break free from an egg eventually dies. Or, it doesn't get fertilized at all and someone scrambles it in a frying pan. All of this supposition is based on some very limited data."

John said, "And the Millibutt will continue to spit out new ones."

I said, "I'd have to consult my notes, but I'm pretty sure we didn't accomplish *anything*. We literally could have just stayed home and gotten the exact same outcome."

Marconi said, "I admit that this one will require some massaging at the editing stage."

"So what's the story gonna be?"

"Very straightforward, I should think. It's the cautionary tale of a town in the throes of a panic over a supposed winged creature that witnesses claimed could turn itself into a man. A creature that managed to snatch eleven small children. All of whom were, thank goodness, recovered unharmed, thanks to the noble sacrifice of a brave veteran. But was all of this the work of an unearthly creature of the night? Or a mere human with a deviant mind? Which kind of predator is more terrifying? That, dear viewer, is up to you to decide. Now enjoy this commercial for auto insurance."

Amy said, "Eleven children? There were twelve. You forgot Mikey."

"There is nothing to forget."

She stared into the middle distance and said, "Oh, right."

I stood up and stretched. "All right. We get a few hours of sleep, then we round up the biker kids and figure out what we need to do to contain this thing. Every minute counts, people."

32. FIVE DAYS LATER

We never saw the bikers or their kids again.

They apparently took the rain with them—we got nothing but sun in the days that followed. The water levels still continued to rise, as Amy had said they would—like all of life's bullshit, it keeps trickling downhill even after the storm is over—but otherwise all we could do was keep rooting for clear skies. I wondered how many people had bought rain boots just hours before it stopped. Suckers.

The neighborhood around the dildo store was all but impassable, but Amy and I had gotten our stuff and moved into Chastity Payton's sandbagged trailer. We had no idea where she was, but she was still alive and Amy had saved her number before she left. Chastity agreed to let us squat there in exchange for keeping looters away, as long as we didn't take the plastic off the furniture or "fart the place up." Still, she wouldn't have approved of how much red Mountain Dew I'd stashed in the fridge. I didn't even enjoy the flavor of it, I think drinking it just reminded me of my early twenties. Back when I enjoyed terrible things.

It was Saturday, the day before Amy's birthday, when we got a mysterious call telling us to go out to Mine's Eye and to bring John. We had actually been out there a couple of times since the night all the shit happened, waiting for the whole cycle to start up again. It hadn't, but the call hadn't been entirely unexpected—we surely weren't the only ones monitoring the situation.

We met John out there by the little church, which was surrounded by ladders and scaffolding. The owners were breaking local tradition by actually repairing the place, instead of just letting it rot—they'd already gotten the roof patched up. A black sedan pulled up and I was only mildly surprised when Agent Tasker stepped out, a bandage around her neck where her head had apparently been reattached. I wondered if it leaked when she drank coffee.

John said, "Is your partner coming?"

"No, he called in dead. I'm not here to harm or arrest you, and in fact I do not represent NON. That organization has been dissolved."

I said, "You mean they just renamed it again."

"There is a, let's say, housecleaning taking place. We have ascertained that your judgment on the B3333B breach was in fact correct. We do apologize for any actions taken against you by the previous regime—"

"Meaning you," interrupted Amy. "When you tried to personally kill all of us, over and over again."

"*But* I do want to point out that throughout the process, the information sharing between us was less than ideal, on both ends. That's something we should look to improve going forward. In terms of B3333B, we are actively monitoring all eleven offspring, and will continue to do so until an alternative course of action is found."

I said, "Well, problem solved. I'll just put this whole thing out of mind, then."

The sun was shining, and the pond below would have been shimmering turquoise . . . but there was no pond. The whole thing had been filled in with concrete. Crews had started filling it in the very next morning after the ten larvae had emerged. There were workers milling around the area now, dragging thick hoses that snaked down from several trucks that were perched on the hill above.

Tasker said, "As you can see, we've already gone to work on obstructing the breeding site."

I said, "I don't want to tell you your business, but I one hundred percent do not believe that a bunch of cement is going to keep the Milli—uh, the B3333B from doing its thing."

"Of course not. But we do have every reason to believe that physical proximity to the pond is a requirement for the process to work. The goal will be to simply keep people away. You wondered what connection there was between Mr. Knoll, Ms. Payton, and the Christ's Rebellion Motorcycle Club. Well, they all attended a barbecue right here, a month before the children turned up missing. That is, a month before the idea of the children were implanted in the adults, along with the trail of psychological bread crumbs that would lead them back here."

Amy said, "But people come here all the time. I guess

that was just when its breeding cycle started?"

"When we were interviewing members of the gang, we noted one man named Beau Lynch, who bore a striking resemblance to Ted Knoll's description of Mr. Nymph. This aroused some curiosity in the team, though the man appeared normal and was not otherwise suspicious. During questioning, it became clear that at one point during the cookout, Mr. Lynch and a young woman had sex in the pond."

This raised dozens of questions in my mind that I actually didn't want the answers to.

Tasker continued, "By tomorrow, there will be a twelve-foot fence around the hill up here. Those signs will be posted every twenty feet."

She nodded to where one of the signs was leaned against the church. In urgent red and white it said:

RAW SEWAGE
CONTAMINATION HAZARD
$1500 FINE FOR TRESPASSING
24-HOUR SURVEILLANCE

I shook my head. "It's not gonna work. People will figure out there's no sewage here. They're just going to get curious."

Below us, one of the crew members shouted a signal. Then there was a sputtering noise and a gush of raw sewage sprayed out of the hose. The stench reached us a moment later.

Amy wrinkled her nose and said, "That's . . . wow."

"Okay," John said, "just to get this straight, in the meantime, these parents have to spend the next however many days or months or years raising these fake monster children? How is that not going to end horribly for everybody?"

Tasker shrugged. "That is simply the way of the world. All they know is that they love their children very much. Love is not always a two-way street, sometimes you pour your energy into something that never gives back. Like people who keep lizards as pets. Is that worse than being alone, or without purpose?"

I said, "*Way* worse."

Tasker glanced at her watch and said, "Well, if you have any suggestions, you know where to find me."

I watched her duck into her car and pull away. I imagined her turning her neck too quickly the next time she went to back up and her head just toppling off her shoulders.

Amy said, "So, we need to resume the conversation we were having."

"Which one? About whether or not a plane could take off if it was sitting on a giant treadmill? We decided it would take right off, the wheels have nothing to do with it. Nothing to discuss."

"No, the one we were having at John's house. About your sadness demon? And you said that wasn't the time to have the discussion? Well, that time has arrived. I've got a number for you to call, I know for a fact they can get you in early next week."

"We can talk about it later."

"No. We can't."

She looked at John, like this was his cue to jump in. They'd planned this.

John, looking like he'd rather be chewed up in the

belly of a shark than standing here having this conversation, said, "She has a bag, at my house. Clothes and stuff. A little money. Friends ready to come and get her. She'd made the decision to go, is what I'm trying to say. I talked her out of it. Told her that if you knew, if you *really* knew what this was doing to her, you'd fight it."

That black pool of shame bubbled up in my head again. Then, a spark came along and set it alight. The choice between feeling the toxic ooze of self-loathing and the fire of mindless rage is no choice at all.

I turned on her. "You know what? If you want to go, why don't you—"

John stepped in front of me. "Can we just skip this part, Dave? The part where you have this knee-jerk anger reflex over being given an ultimatum? Because it's not an ultimatum and nobody is trying to push you around. I've been here a million times, you know I have, and that anger, it's the rage of a kid getting dragged out of a warm bed on a cold morning. That's all it is. Because that depression, it's the most comfy bed in the world and you will say whatever you have to say to stay in it for one more minute. But there's people out here who love you a lot, telling you that there's a truck heading for that bed. And if you can't work up any concern for your own life, then think of it like this. Somebody Amy and I care about a whole lot is about to get hit by that truck and only you can save them. The person we need you to save just happens to be you. Also, the truck is filled with shit, I don't know if I mentioned that."

"I just assumed."

I sighed and carefully studied the patch of nothing in front of my face. "I am ninety-nine percent sure this is just the way I am. Been like this as long as I can remember."

Amy looked at me like I was an idiot. "*Of course* it's the way you are. But having really hairy legs is the way I am, and I still shave them regularly. In our natural state, we're all smelly, sticky, angry creatures nobody would even pay to look at in a zoo. We're all at war with that awful, primitive version of ourselves, every day. You're scared. I get it. You're scared you're going to get cured and suddenly be this corny, boring person. Well, I have good news—there is no cure. You just wake up another day and fight it, day after day, until that's who you become. A fighter. Look, it's up to you. Only you can do this. But I'm not going to spend the rest of my life watching you slowly rot to pieces, stuck to the sofa like some kind of an airplane that is totally unable to take off from a treadmill, due to the laws of physics."

"If nothing else," said John, "remember that people depend on you. The next crisis is always right around the corner."

We stood there and watched the shit-flooding operation for a while.

I gestured toward the crews below us and said, "I don't like this."

Amy said, "Well, it's gross on like thirty-six levels."

"No, I mean, in general. We're basically being asked to turn a blind eye. Living our lives, knowing this is here. Like an—"

"An itch you can't scratch?"

John flicked a cigarette butt and turned to go. He put his hand on my back, as if to lead me away.

"Forget it, Dave. It's Vaginap—"

33. A COMPLETELY UNEVENTFUL DENOUEMENT. WE CAN PROBABLY CUT THIS PART, SERIOUSLY, STOP READING

Where the flood had receded, it had left behind a thin film of dried mud that turned lawns, sidewalks, and blacktop all the same grayish brown, like we had all been sucked into a sepia-toned photograph. But the town was still here.

We were doing Amy's belated birthday at John's place two weeks after the actual date, having agreed to at least hold off on the celebration until we were no longer at risk of trench foot. The stealth house had made it out of the flood needing only new carpet on the first floor (which had been badly overdue anyway, the old carpet having been assaulted by everything from coffee spills to fireworks burns).

We showed up at the door at eight that night, to hear John screaming at someone from inside. The last phrase I heard before we knocked was, "That shit isn't cute anymore."

He yanked the door open and let us in without a hello. He looked like shit, like he was five days into a bad flu.

John had been fighting with Joy. She was off in a corner, messing with her phone, as if she'd checked out of the argument long ago.

To John, I muttered, "So . . . she's still here."

John snapped, "She won't fucking go! This is fucking ridiculous."

Joy looked up from her phone and said, "I dumped his stash. He's not happy."

"You . . . what?"

"The meth, the Adderall, the weed, all of it. Down the toilet it went. Whoosh. Bye-bye."

John stabbed a finger at her. "*You* don't get to make *that* decision."

I said, "You're arguing with a swarm of shape-shifting bug monsters, John."

Joy said, "And losing!"

Amy said, "I'm going to go get the casserole out of the car," and went back out. There was no casserole, or anything else, out there.

I paused to contemplate the ridiculousness of inserting myself into this discussion, then said, "Seriously, uh, Joy, you can't make somebody stop being addicted that way. You get rid of the drugs, the addiction is still there."

She shrugged. "So? Doesn't mean I have to make it easy."

John looked at me. "See? This is fucking bullshit. I didn't ask her to live here. I didn't ask her to fucking watch my every move like she's a fucking parole officer. You know I sleep on the couch? In my own house!"

"You know you *made* her, right? I don't mean you made her stay here, I mean you made her, like that's the end of the sentence."

425

"That's what I keep saying. You see those clothes she's wearing? They're actual clothes! She bought them! With my credit card! She can make herself appear to be wearing anything!"

Joy, still staring intently at her phone, muttered, "I like to shop."

"My point," I said, in a lowered voice that Joy could probably still hear, "is that you can presumably make her just go away, right? I mean either go away as in leave, or go away as in, poof, she's just gone. Hell, John, there's a real Joy Park out there in the world. How would she feel knowing you've created a clone of her and that you live with it?"

Joy said, "It?"

John said, "Yes, Dave, if the actual porn star Joy Park somehow shows up here from Korea, we will have to deal with that."

Joy said, "Actual?"

He said, "You know what I mean!"

Joy looked up from her phone. "Do you really want me to go? If you want me to go, I'll go."

John took a deep anger-control breath, his hands balled into fists in front of him. He turned back to her and said, "I'm not saying you have to *go*. But you don't control my life. This can't be how it is."

Joy shrugged. "We'll just have to agree to disagree on that."

John started to explode again, but I put up a hand and said, "You're ruining Amy's birthday. Come on."

I went and stuck my head out the back door, and found Amy standing on the stoop, watching Nicky pull up in her Toyota Prius. John insists on inviting her to everything, just because she's been a dear friend for the last twelve years.

I said to Amy, "It's over, you can come in."

Nicky uncoiled herself from within the Prius, carrying a plastic box full of cupcakes. Her eyes were a pair of black portals into a soul that harbored only spite.

"David!"

"Hello, Nicky."

"I have two red velvet cupcakes in here, those are yours! If somebody tries to take them, smack 'em! Did you know red velvet is just chocolate with red food coloring added?"

"No."

Lying bitch.

We went inside and Joy's face lit up at the sight of Nicky. "Heeeey! There's my girl!"

They hugged. I assumed that no one had explained that she wasn't human; I'd have to take Joy aside later and let her know.

Amy pulled a birthday card envelope from her purse and said to John, "Why did you mail this instead of just handing it to me?"

John looked confused. "When did you get that?"

"It was in the mailbox when we went to check on the apartment yesterday."

"I have no memory of sending that."

I examined the card. "Postmark is three weeks ago."

John saw my expression and said, "Hey, I wonder if it's a clue. Open it."

Amy said, "I'm almost afraid to."

She opened it and inside was a card that said HAPPY FATHER'S DAY, DAD, in festive text that had been scribbled out with a ballpoint and replaced with BIRTHDAY, AMY SULLIVAN in John's handwriting.

There was something inside.

A scratch-off lottery ticket.

We all froze.

I said, "No. John . . . you bought that on the Soy Sauce?"

Amy looked alarmed. "That's like a form of cheating, right? We . . . we couldn't. Could we?"

I said, "Well, the whole thing is a scam. So, what, somebody buys a ticket with a one in a billion chance of winning, not knowing that in reality they had a zero in a billion chance? Seems like a pretty miniscule difference."

It said across the top in silver letters that the grand prize was ten million dollars.

Amy said, "We're giving half of it to charity."

I said, "Fine. We don't even know if it's a winner."

John said, "I'm actually pretty sure it is."

Amy fished a nickel from her pocket and scratched off three rows of boxes.

We had won.

$250.

John said, "Hey! You can buy Amy that book now! Almost. You can probably talk them down."

Amy said, "What book?" I had never told her about the signed copy of *Hitchhiker's* I'd shopped for. We had decided that my decision to follow through on treatment was my gift to her. Still seemed like she was getting cheated, but whatever.

I said to John, "You could have won us the freaking mega millions jackpot and you got us two hundred and fifty bucks instead?"

Amy said, "One hundred and twenty-five."

Out of nowhere, John started laughing. I didn't know what exactly he thought he was laughing at—I still didn't have a damn job. But then I was laughing, too. Then, so was Amy. Joy and Nicky asked us what was so funny.

Amy said we won the lottery and that this was the best birthday ever. Joy high-fived her and said she had two different homemade pizzas in the oven and I guess we were letting this thing make food for us now. Then Munch and Crystal showed up and it was like the whole previous month had never happened. Then there was a knock on the door and John went to answer it and standing there was the fancy-haired partner of Detective Herm Bowman.

He asked the three of us to come outside. I had assumed Herm would be waiting out here, but the young man had come alone. I closed the door behind me and said, "If you're here to tell me more kids are missing, I'll say right now, I don't think we're up for it."

"That's not it."

"And I don't see Detective Bowman . . ."

"Nah, he says case is closed. Won't even talk about it."

"But you're not ready to drop it. Right?"

"You see what your reality show friend said about all this? The whole bit about a flying monster, snatching kids?"

"Yeah. So? You were there, what did he get wrong?"

"One, I wasn't there, not really, and what he got wrong are all the parts that make you look guilty as shit."

"Ah, I see. Herm's putting ideas in your head. Well, believe what you want. We all live in the reality we choose."

"What kind of hippy bullshit is that? Look, the case is closed, like I said. So why not just tell me what really happened? From the start, for my own peace of mind. It won't leave this stoop and even if it did, who'd believe me?"

"The other cops will believe you, they just won't care. It's better that way. Ask Herm."

"So, like I said. What do you have to lose?"

I glanced back at John. "What do you think?"

John shrugged and said, "Fine. You want to hear a story? Well, buckle the fuck up."

So, we told him the story just as it's laid out in these pages. I finished with, "And then we all gathered here to celebrate Amy's birthday and then you showed up and here we are."

John said, "Uh, we may not have made it clear but Marconi had two spears on the RV."

I said, "Right, right. He had lots of them. They were all over the place."

The detective nodded, thoughtfully. "I was eating a donut, not a McMuffin."

"Yeah, but it seemed too cliché."

"You know what? I like Marconi's story better."

"Me, too, if I'm honest."

"Mainly because it actually lines up with the known facts in the case, where your impossibly convoluted version seems carefully crafted to be utterly impossible to verify at every goddamned step. What I know is there were twelve missing kids reported. No follow-up from any of the parents, all of whom are in the wind now, including Loretta Knoll. Sightings all over the place of this supposed bat monster . . ."

"Which," I said, "is now scattered in tiny chunks across miles of river. Problem solved."

"And two victims' statements identifying you as the perp."

"We've *been over that*."

"And one witness saying the bat monster is *you*."

This brought the conversation to a screeching halt for several brutal seconds. I thought I heard thunder rumble in the distance, but I think it was just a heavy truck passing by.

Amy said, "What? Who?"

"Philip 'Shitbeard' Hickenlooper."

"Ted's friend? The one who drowned?"

"Who said he drowned? He not only made it out, but says he watched your man here turn into the Batmantis on one occasion and suspects it in another."

That brought an even longer silence. Someone coughed.

I said, "Well, that's just ridiculous. Everything was chaos, who knows what he thinks he saw. That's probably why he has that nickname. He's so full of shit he, you know, wears it like a beard."

"Uh-huh. Did I mention he has you on video? Recorded it at the river, with his phone."

"When it was dark, and rainy. Plus, any asshole can download video editing software, they can add special effects and everything, make it look so real it'd fool an expert. Doesn't prove shit."

The detective just eyed me, silently.

I said, "What?"

"Instead of dismissing the idea that such a video could exist, you jumped right to calling it a well-made fake. Didn't even ask to see it first."

Amy said, "There is no video, is there?"

"Don't need one now, do we?"

I said, "Oh, fuck off. Don't play your cop mind games on me. Even if this ridiculous accusation was somehow true, and I'm not saying it is, but even if it was, then that still wouldn't implicate me. If anything, the Batmantis was trying to help. If it turned up where kids were being taken, it's because it was trying to stop it, and failing. If this ridiculous fantasy of yours were true and we took steps to hide its involvement, it would only be because we knew people would get the wrong idea, focus blame in the wrong place when it was clearly this other situation, with the mine and all that. But we didn't, because your story is rid—"

"Ridiculous, yes. Remember when I said I liked Marconi's version better? It's because I'm pretty sure you people made *everything* up, the larvae and the mine monster—one big convoluted parable about not judging monsters, just to cover for the fact that boy here started werewolfing out and snatching children."

I laughed. "Ha! Haha! Ha. No."

John said, "How about this—in our version, the Batmantis is dead and gone, nobody else gets hurt. In Shitbeard's version, it's still around—you know, because Dave is standing right here. Well, if the Batmantis strikes again, there you go, you'll have your answer. So, you see the bastard, feel free to blow it out of the sky. You have our blessing."

"I will do that. And I sure as hell don't need your blessing."

I said, "Again, you'll believe what you want. But what you believe, it says more about you than me. Is there anything else we can do for you?"

He walked away, saying, "I'll be seeing you. That's a promise."

He drove off into the night, his completely dry car rolling through the not-rain. I put my arm around Amy.

"I love you."

"Love you, too."

The door opened behind us. "Come in, guys!" spat Nicky. "Your pizza's getting cold!"

The nozzles of the anti-intruder flamethrowers whooshed to life. She was instantly burned to death.

Amy

That didn't happen.

An Excerpt from *Fear: Hell's Parasite*
by Dr. Albert Marconi

And now, a word about the Apocalypse.

The most fascinating aspect of our end-of-the-world obsession is our insistence that whatever cataclysm we have in mind would, in fact, be the end. The reality is that our history could actually be described as a series of apocalypses: a plague here, a famine there, a worldwide war that arrives with both in tow. What occurs in the aftermath of each is instructive.

Consider, for example, the ancient disaster known as the Toba event. It is theorized that approximately seventy-five thousand years ago, a volcanic eruption nearly wiped out Homo sapiens *altogether. It is believed that in the aftermath, the worldwide population of early humans may have withered to just a few thousand breeding pairs—enough to fit into a high school gymnasium. Just seventy-five thousand years later, we live in a civilization in which the population has rebounded a million times over and is on the cusp of landing a spacecraft on Mars.*

This is the legacy of humanity and I daresay that not enough of us take time to appreciate it. Our apocalyptic fiction depicts a world in which humans revert to the savagery of the jungle the moment our institutions fall, survivors tearing each other to pieces even as they are dying of plague or stalked by the undead. In our real history, we have been in that situation many times—left without government or law enforcement, none of the modern institutions we take for granted. From each of these scenarios what emerged was not savagery, but cooperation. When the pillars of our culture crumble, we rebuild them.

I once joked to a colleague that a true horror film would begin with a world overrun by the zombies, who find themselves having to fend off a sudden outbreak of the living. Imagine these poor groaning shufflers attempting to wage war against faster, healthier creatures capable of organization and strategy, able to build tools that would appear to be nothing short of magic to their simple, moldering brains (imagine their terror at the prospect of a rifle that can deliver invisible death from far over the horizon, let alone an atomic bomb!).

One almost begins to feel sorry for them. This is why, when asked why there is not greater evidence of creatures such as werewolves or vampires (not that I believe in either), I say the answer is obvious: they are too busy hiding from us!

My point is this: mankind is, and always has been, much greater than the sum of its parts. A lone human may appear to be nothing special if observed, say, blearily standing in line at a convenience store at two in the morning, or spitefully ripping a toy from the hands of a middle-aged woman in the chaos of a Black Friday sale. Yet, the combined efforts of these confused and volatile primates result in gleaming cities and majestic flying carriages. They have split the atom and peered across the universe.

In the blink of an eye, they have acquired the powers of gods.

This, I believe, is the fate of humanity: to colonize the stars over the next thousand years, to set down settlements in our solar system and others. Then, many centuries from now, one of our descendants will be strolling along some marvelous domed paradise on some distant planet and will see a drunken youth in offensive clothing, vomiting in an alley outside a pub. The man will look sidelong at the youth in that shameful state, shake his head, and mutter to himself that humanity is a ridiculous, doomed species, incapable of anything worthwhile.

He will believe it, because the true, wonderful, terrible, fearsome power of humanity is otherwise almost too much to comprehend. I recognize that not all of you share my faith, but you must admit that if gods are real and have observed humanity's evolution from afar, they must shudder at the possibilities.

AFTERWORD

Author here. Let me get serious for a moment.

Some of my fan mail is from readers who do not believe these books are entirely fictional, seeking advice because they themselves see or hear strange things that others cannot. To them, I want to make it clear that I have never encountered the supernatural and do not expect to in this lifetime. The creatures that roam these pages are either from my imagination or from the long tradition of horror tales humans have been telling each other over campfires since before the advent of the written word.

I believe that anyone can "see" a ghost, monster, or "shadow person" under the right circumstances—the brain is an imperfect organ and it misfires from time to time. If, however, you see unnatural things that frighten you or interfere with your life, I would urge you to see a doctor. We know as a matter of scientific fact that the entities that stalk you are almost certainly the result of a treatable condition. Your doctor will not mock you or demand you be restrained and banished to an island of misfits. You will not be their first such patient and, in fact, they've probably seen your situation enough that they don't even find it particularly interesting anymore (about one in twenty adults say they've had at least one hallucination, and that's just the ones who'll admit it). It's nothing to be ashamed of—often the greatest difficulty faced by people suffering from mental illness is society's inexcusable ignorance of the subject.

Other business:

Special thanks to Mack Leighty, my childhood friend who invented the character of John and who, by the way, has an audience of tens of millions of readers thanks to his day job at Cracked.com. You can find many of his hilarious and insightful posts here:

http://www.cracked.com/blog/author/John+Cheese/

This novel, if you didn't realize it, is actually the third in a series. The first was called *John Dies at the End* (which was made into a fabulous movie by horror legend Don Coscarelli) and the second was titled *This Book Is Full of Spiders: Seriously Dude, Don't Touch It*. That one was my first *New York Times* bestseller, a fact that I loudly share with every single stranger I encounter on the street.

Then, there is my most critically acclaimed, yet equally stupid novel *Futuristic Violence and Fancy Suits*. It is a cautionary tale of cybernetically enhanced morons and the smooth-talking team of suits who try to keep them from wrecking the world. I may have written a sequel to that book by the time you read this. I have no way of knowing, your present is my future and for all I know, I was shot to death trying to hold up a liquor store a week before this went to press.

Likewise, I have no idea if there will be another book in the "John and Dave" series. I would assume there will be and that it will presumably contain fewer butt references than this one (I mean, it's not like I can fit in more) but you'll just have to stay tuned. If you want to keep up with news of upcoming titles and other noteworthy things in my life, assuming the Internet still exists, I can be found at:

Johndiesattheend.com

or on Facebook at:
www.facebook.com/JohnDiesattheEnd.TheNovel

Or you can read my humorous nonfiction essays at Cracked.com, where I am the executive editor as of the writing of this Afterword:

http://www.cracked.com/members/David+Wong/

Even more special thanks go to my wife, who tolerates all of this. You can probably guess that the type of person who would write a book like this is not terribly easy to live with in person.

—David Wong aka Jason Pargin
January 2017

JOHN DIES AT THE END
by David Wong

My name is David Wong. My best friend is John. Those names are fake. You might want to change yours.
You may not want to know about the things you'll read on these pages, about the sauce, about Korrock, about the invasion, and the future. But it's too late. You touched the book. You're in the game. You're under the eye.
The only defence is knowledge. You need to read this book, to the end. Even the part about the bratwurst. Why? You'll just have to trust me.

Unfortunately for us, if you make the right choice, we'll have a much harder time explaining how to fight off the otherwordly invasion currently threatening to enslave humanity.

I'm sorry to have involved you in this, I really am. But as you read about these terrible events and the very dark epoch the world is about to enter as a result, it is crucial you keep one thing in mind:

NONE OF THIS IS MY FAULT.

THE ANNO DRACULA SERIES
by Kim Newman

Anno Dracula
It is 1888 and Queen Victoria has remarried, taking as her
new consort the Wallachian Prince infamously known as
Count Dracula.

Anno Dracula: The Bloody Red Baron
1918. Dracula is commander-in-chief of the armies of
Germany and Austria-Hungary. The war of the great powers
in Europe is also a war between the living and the dead.

Anno Dracula: Dracula Cha Cha Cha
Rome 1959 and journalist Kate Reed finds herself caught up
in the mystery of the Crimson Executioner, who is bloodily
dispatching vampire elders in the city.

Anno Dracula: Johnny Alucard
1980s America. Dracula has fallen from grace. A young
vampire outcast makes a new life for himself in America, but
it seems the past might not be dead after all...

Anno Dracula: One Thousand Monsters
Japan, 1899. Vampires exiled from Britain seek refuge in
Tokyo and are confined to a ghetto. But what secret lies
under the Temple of One Thousand Monsters?

THE UNNOTICEABLES
by Robert Brockway

The Unnoticeables

In 1970's New York City, all Carey's punk friends are being abducted by kids with unnoticeable faces. In present-day Hollywood, stuntwoman Kaitlyn's best friend goes missing and a former teen heartthrob tries to eat her. The survival of the human race is in Carey and Kaitlyn's hands. We're screwed.

The Empty Ones

1977 was a bad year for Carey. He needs a vacation. You know where there's a killer punk scene? London. Oh, and the cult that murdered his friends. 2013 was a bad year for Kaitlyn, too: she hooked up with a guy who turned out to be an immortal psychopath trying to eat her soul. Now she's out for revenge.

Kill All Angels (December 2017)

Carey is in early 80s LA. The punk scene is run by Empty Ones, but one named Zang has turned against them and may or may not be on Carey's side. In modern times, Kaitlyn and company have also returned to LA - her powers are growing, and she's been having visions telling her how to kill the angels. The downside being they have to find one, first.

For more fantastic fiction, author events, competitions,
limited editions and more

VISIT OUR WEBSITE
titanbooks.com

LIKE US ON FACEBOOK
facebook.com/titanbooks

FOLLOW US ON TWITTER
@TitanBooks

EMAIL US
readerfeedback@titanemail.com